Clive Cussler

SEA
OF
GREED

TITLES BY CLIVE CUSSLER

KURT AUSTIN ADVENTURES

NOVELS FROM THE NUMA® FILES

The Rising Sea (with Graham Brown)
Nighthawk (with Graham Brown)
The Pharaoh's Secret
  (with Graham Brown)
Ghost Ship (with Graham Brown)
Zero Hour (with Graham Brown)
The Storm (with Graham Brown)
Devil's Gate (with Graham Brown)
Medusa (with Paul Kemprecos)
The Navigator (with Paul Kemprecos)
Polar Shift (with Paul Kemprecos)
Lost City (with Paul Kemprecos)
White Death (with Paul Kemprecos)
Fire Ice (with Paul Kemprecos)
Blue Gold (with Paul Kemprecos)
Serpent (with Paul Kemprecos)

OREGON *FILES*

Shadow Tyrants (with Boyd Morrison)
Typhoon Fury (with Boyd Morrison)
The Emperor's Revenge
  (with Boyd Morrison)
Piranha (with Boyd Morrison)

Mirage (with Jack Du Brul)
The Jungle (with Jack Du Brul)
The Silent Sea (with Jack Du Brul)
Corsair (with Jack Du Brul)
Plague Ship (with Jack Du Brul)
Skeleton Coast (with Jack Du Brul)
Dark Watch (with Jack Du Brul)
Sacred Stone (with Craig Dirgo)
Golden Buddha (with Craig Dirgo)

NONFICTION

Built for Adventure: The Classic
  Automobiles of Clive Cussler
  and Dirk Pitt
Built to Thrill: More Classic
  Automobiles from Clive Cussler
  and Dirk Pitt
The Sea Hunters (with Craig Dirgo)
The Sea Hunters II (with Craig Dirgo)
Clive Cussler and Dirk Pitt Revealed
  (with Craig Dirgo)

CHILDREN'S BOOKS

The Adventures of Vin Fiz
The Adventures of Hotsy Totsy

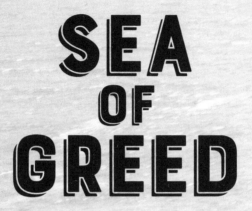

SEA OF GREED

A Novel from the NUMA® Files

CLIVE CUSSLER
AND GRAHAM BROWN

G. P. PUTNAM'S SONS | NEW YORK

PUTNAM

G. P. Putnam's Sons
Publishers Since 1838
An imprint of Penguin Random House LLC
375 Hudson Street
New York, New York 10014

Library of Congress Cataloging-in-Publication Data
Names: Cussler, Clive, author.
Title: Sea of greed : a novel from the Numa files / Clive Cussler and
Graham Brown.
Description: New York : G. P. Putnam's Sons, [2018] | Series: A novel from
the Numa files
Identifiers: LCCN 2018037962| ISBN 9780735219021 (hardcover) |
ISBN 9780735219038 (epub)
Subjects: | GSAFD: Adventure fiction. | Suspense fiction.
Classification: LCC PS3553.U75 S43 2019 | DDC 813/.54—dc23
LC record available at https://lccn.loc.gov/2018037962

International edition ISBN: 9780525542988

Printed in the United States of America
1   3   5   7   9   10   8   6   4   2

Book design by Amy Hill

CAST OF CHARACTERS

MEDITERRANEAN—1968

David Ben-Avi   Israeli genetics expert, stationed on Jaros.

André Cheval   French scientist and overall leader for Project Jericho.

Lukas   French commando and member of the SDECE, the French external intelligence.

Gideon   Executive officer on the Israeli submarine INS *Dakar*.

NATIONAL UNDERWATER AND MARINE AGENCY

Kurt Austin   Director of NUMA's Special Projects division, world-class diver and salvage expert.

Joe Zavala   Kurt's closest friend, mechanical genius responsible for constructing much of NUMA's exotic equipment.

Priya Kashmir   Lead member of NUMA's technology division, confined to a wheelchair due to an automobile accident but determined to get onto a field team.

Rudi Gunn   Assistant Director of NUMA, graduate of the Naval Academy.

Hiram Yaeger   NUMA's resident computer genius, owner of many patents relating to computer design.

St. Julien Perlmutter   NUMA historian and gourmet chef, owns thousands of rare books and artifacts.

Paul Trout   Member of the Special Projects division, has a Ph.D. in Ocean Sciences, married to Gamay.

Gamay Trout   NUMA's leading marine biologist, married to Paul, Gamay is a fitness aficionado and tends to say exactly what's on her mind.

Kevin Brooks   Captain of the NUMA vessel *Raleigh*.

CREW OF THE ALPHA STAR OIL PLATFORM

Rick L. Cox   Operations manager and drilling supervisor of the Alpha Star offshore rig.

Leon Nash   Roughneck and crewman on the Alpha Star.

NOVUM INDUSTRIA

Tessa Franco   Founder and CEO of Novum Industria, a high-tech alternative energy company, also the designer of the *Monarch*, a one-of-a-kind amphibious aircraft.

Arat Buran   Volatile leader of the Central Asian oil Consortium, Tessa's former lover and confidant, currently involved with Novum via a clandestine financial arrangement.

Pascal Millard   Censured French geneticist, now working for Novum.

Brian Yates   Engineer and architect of Novum's revolutionary fuel cells.

MERCENARIES

Volke   Submersible pilot and former mercenary, works for Tessa in various capacities.

Woodrich   Ecological fanatic, wants to see the end of the Oil Age at all costs, goes by the nickname "Woods."

Alexander Vastoga   Ex–Russian helicopter pilot and soldier of fortune, can be had for a high price.

FLORIDA

Misty Moon Littlefeather   Electronics expert and old friend of Joe's.

Redfish   Misty's father, always suspicious of Joe's intentions toward his daughter.

WASHINGTON POLITICIANS

Lance Alcott   Head of FEMA, jockeying for control of the Alpha Star cleanup.

Leonard Hallsman   Former geologist, now Undersecretary of National Resources and Energy Security.

James Sandecker   Vice President of the United States, founder and former Director of NUMA.

BERMUDA

Macklin Hatcher   Wealthy venture capitalist, false identity assumed by Kurt Austin.

Ronald Ruff   Hatcher's assistant, false identity assumed by Joe Zavala.

ISRAEL

Admiral Natal   Israeli Admiral, old friend of Rudi Gunn's, currently in charge of the Office of Naval Records in Haifa.

SHIPS AND AIRCRAFT

INS *Dakar*   Israeli submarine, purchased from the British, vanished on its way from the UK to Haifa in January 1968.

***Minerve* (S647)**   French submarine, vanished in 1968 roughly twenty-five miles from Toulon.

Monarch   Wide-body amphibious aircraft designed by Tessa Franco, built in Kazakhstan.

Gryphon   Well-armed NUMA hydrofoil, deployed in dangerous environments.

PART ONE

THE VANISHING

1

ISLAND OF JAROS, AEGEAN SEA
JANUARY 1968

DAVID BEN-AVI walked along a trail on the rocky, windswept island of Jaros. The barren clump of land was just three miles in length and no more than half a mile wide at its broadest point. It sat in an isolated spot of the Mediterranean, a hundred miles northwest of Crete. Though it was officially uninhabited, Ben-Avi and a dozen others had called it home for nearly two years.

With hands shoved in his pockets, Ben-Avi kept his face to the wind, walking briskly. The Mediterranean air had a bite to it in January. Fresh and pure in comparison to the stuffy laboratory and cramped barracks they lived in.

The solitude wasn't bad either . . . while it lasted.

"David," a voice called from behind him. "Where are you going?"

The words came in English with a distinct French accent.

Ben-Avi stopped in his tracks. *Mother Hen had found him.*

He turned to see André Cheval, rushing after him. Cheval was leader of the French contingent on the island but also acted as overall commander for the entire group. He was always after them about something. Trash in the correct receptacle, no outside lights after sundown, be careful near the cliffs.

He was dressed in outdoor gear and carrying a wool peacoat, which he handed to Ben-Avi. "Put this on. It's freezing out here."

Freezing was an exaggeration, but Ben-Avi took the coat without objection, he knew better than to argue.

"Where are you going?" Cheval asked.

"You know where I'm going," Ben-Avi said. "Out on the bluff, to watch the sunset and think."

"I'll walk with you," Cheval said.

"Can't I go anywhere without a chaperone?"

"Of course," Cheval said. "You're not a prisoner."

That was true. Ben-Avi and the others were here as part of a joint Franco–Israeli research project. They had all volunteered, but after so long on the barren island, with only the monthly arrival of a supply ship to break the monotony, it felt like they were marking time and waiting to be paroled.

"I have a feeling," Ben-Avi said, "that all who come to Jaros must be prisoners in one sense or another. The Greeks kept captured communist insurgents here after World War Two, the Turks used it five centuries before that and the Romans picked this desolate spot to exile a troublesome daughter of the Emperor Octavian."

"Really?" Cheval said.

Ben-Avi nodded. At the same time, he wondered how the Frenchman could live on the tiny island so long and not know a thing about it.

"At least the Romans put some thought into the place," Ben-Avi said. "All the Greeks did was put up those terrible rock huts we're living in. The Romans carved the harbor out of solid rock. They set up catchment basins, dug a series of tunnels and underground cisterns to hold the rainwater, even found a way of using limestone to purify it and keep it from becoming stagnant. You should really have a look at them, they're quite remarkable."

Cheval nodded but seemed unimpressed. "It seems Octavian's daughter commanded a nicer prison than communist rebels."

The two men continued walking, though because the path was narrow in places Cheval was half a step behind.

"So, what do you think about when you're out here?" Cheval asked. "Getting back to Israel?"

"That and the implications of our work," Ben-Avi said.

"Don't tell me you're having second thoughts? It's a little late now. The project is all but finished."

Ben-Avi stopped and glanced sideways at the Frenchman. The project, as he called it, was a giant step forward in an entirely new branch of science called genetics. It involved manipulation of cellular codes, tampering with the instructions of living things. The field had been talked about in theoretical terms for years, but like many scientific endeavors—everything from atomic energy to spaceflight—once the military became interested, progress had accelerated dramatically.

"We're changing living things," Ben-Avi said. "Distorting life, creating new life. That's an awesome responsibility."

"Yes," Cheval said. "Some of the others have suggested that we're tampering with the designs of God. Do you feel this way?"

"Which god?" Ben-Avi replied briskly.

"Any god," Cheval said. "Yours, mine . . . the universe at large. Take your pick. Is that what you're worried about? Divine retribution?"

Ben-Avi resumed his walk, continuing along the path, angry

now. "If God chose this moment to get into the retribution business, I would find that a very funny thing indeed. I would ask Him where He was when the Nazis came to power and *Kristallnacht* occurred. Ask Him where He was when the fires burned in the camps, incinerating the bodies of murdered Jews, day and night."

"So, the Holocaust shook your faith?"

"Not just the Holocaust," Ben-Avi said. "The entire war. I was an engineering student before it started. Because of my skills, the German Army dragged me into Russia with them. Whoever the Germans didn't kill on the way in, the Russians killed on the way out. After that, I was in Berlin when the Allies bombed it to rubble. Buildings shattered to bricks, bricks pounded to dust. Day and night the raids came until the air was black and we choked with every breath. And that was nothing compared to the firebombing of Dresden. It's a wonder that anyone survived."

Ben-Avi focused his attention back on the path, they'd come to the steepest section. When they reached the top, he would be able to see the ocean. "If there is a God, then either He doesn't care what we do or He's grown so disgusted with us that He's given up on His creation. And who could really blame Him?"

Cheval nodded. "You are troubled, my friend. If it's not God you're worried about, then what?"

"I'm concerned with the power we've unleashed," Ben-Avi said. "Every invention of man, every discovery ever made, has ultimately been used in war. This will be no different. Mark my words."

"Then why continue the work?" Cheval asked, suddenly sharper in his tone. "Why wait until we've finally succeeded to question our acts?"

Ben-Avi had asked himself that question a hundred times. He had a pat answer waiting. "Because the world is a harsh and unforgiving place and Israel must do what it needs to survive. With or without God's help."

"So, it's every country for itself," Cheval said. "Is that what you're telling me?"

"It has to be," Ben-Avi said.

Ben-Avi was breathing hard as he climbed the last section, too hard to keep pontificating. He made it to the top of the bluff and looked out over a sheltered bay. The sea was calm, the sunset glinting upon it, the long arm of the breakwater protecting the small harbor as it had since the Romans built it. But the harbor was not empty as it should have been. A long, thin, sinister-looking vessel lay at anchor inside the bay, a surfaced submarine. Its bow pointed to the heart of the island like a dagger.

Ben-Avi turned around and saw that Cheval was holding a pistol on him.

"I'm afraid you're right," Cheval explained. "It is every nation for itself. If we didn't act, your government would. And that we cannot allow."

The sound of muted gunfire reached them from farther back down the hill. A fight had broken out—not a battle-on war, but a burst here and a burst there.

Ben-Avi took a step toward the camp.

"Don't," Cheval warned. The Frenchman's face was grim as if performing a task he would have rather avoided. "I'm sorry. But if we had not acted, your country would have. The power you've unleashed with your *genetics* can reshape the world we live in more easily than a dozen armies. It's a weapon already. And it's a threat to France in particular. We cannot allow it to end up in foreign hands."

"No," Ben-Avi said. "It's a deterrent. No different from your atomic bombs. It would never be used."

"I'm afraid my country cannot take that chance," Cheval said.

The sound of additional gunfire reached them from the camp.

"So, you're killing us?" Ben-Avi said.

"No one was supposed to be hurt," Cheval replied. "Someone must have resisted."

Ben-Avi didn't doubt that. Though he suspected the French commandos might have hoped to encounter resistance. "And what about me?" he asked, his voice filled with disgust for his former friend. "Do I suddenly fall off the edge or are you going to shoot me first and then throw me in?"

"Don't be ridiculous," Cheval said. He nodded toward the submarine. "You'll be coming with us."

2

EIGHT DAYS after leaving the island of Jaros, the French submarine *Minerve* was nearing her home port of Toulon. It was operating forty feet below the surface, running at eight knots and using the diesel engines, which gulped air through a long metal tube known as a snorkel. They'd been running in this configuration almost continuously since leaving Jaros and André Cheval could not wait for them to surface.

The claustrophobia of being trapped underwater was bad enough. That the *Minerve* was carrying extra cargo, plus the equipment, supplies and samples from the laboratory, made it worse. That the submarine was overpopulated and carrying nearly twice the number of people it was supposed to house—thanks to the presence of Cheval, the other French scientists and the ten French commandos who'd conducted the raid—made the situation nearly unbearable.

The gnawing guilt that the commandos had killed all the Israelis except Ben-Avi did not help and Cheval had taken to drinking each night to put himself to sleep.

Still, they were in French waters now and almost home. By this time tomorrow, Cheval would be sitting in a café in Paris, forgetting his sorrows in the fresh air with a bottle of fine wine.

Until then, he stood in the submarine's cramped control room, watching everything that went on. Across from him, the *Minerve*'s captain leaned on the periscope handles with his face pressed into the viewer. Every few seconds he turned to scan a new section of the surface—*dancing with the gray lady*, as the sailors sometimes called it.

Finally, he flipped the handles closed and stepped back. "No vessels in sight," he said. "Periscope down."

As the periscope descended into its well, the captain turned to the radio officer. "Advise, Command. Weather deteriorating. Eight-foot swells and chop. We will remain at snorkel depth until we reach the channel."

This news was like a kick in the gut to Cheval.

And he wasn't the only one.

A man named Lukas stood nearby, hovering over the navigation charts. Lukas was the head of the commando team, a member of the SDECE, the French external intelligence apparatus. He was a harsh man in his mid-fifties.

"Must we crawl into port like this?" Lukas said. "We've achieved a great success. We should arrive with dignity, if not fanfare."

The *Minerve*'s captain was a lifelong sailor. Like many in the regular military, he distrusted secret operatives, with their hidden agendas and lack of oversight. His reply was blunt. "Do you really want to surface the boat and become a target at this point?"

Lukas pointed at the chart and a red line, approximately four hundred miles behind them, that indicated the nearest possible approach of Israeli ships. "There are no Israeli ships within twelve hours of our position. They cannot possibly catch us."

"They have aircraft, too, Monsieur Lukas."

"None with this range. And nothing our Mirage fighters could not handle."

"You might be right," the captain said. "Regardless, we shall remain submerged until the very last moment. And you shall remain silent while a guest on my boat."

Lukas fumed at the reprimand, turning his back on the captain and heading aft to join his men.

Cheval looked at his watch, fighting the claustrophobia. It was early morning on the twenty-seventh of January. They'd left the island on the evening of the nineteenth. They were almost home. Once they were back on land, he would report Lukas for what he considered war crimes.

Even though he could do nothing about those who'd already been killed, he told himself he'd would find a way to keep Ben-Avi from vanishing into an unmarked grave.

Three hours. He just needed to hold it together for three more hours.

"THE *Minerve* will reach port in three hours."

The words came from a grim-faced man, standing in a darkened control room very similar to the one on the *Minerve*. His name was Gideon. He was the executive officer of the INS *Dakar*, an Israeli submarine recently purchased from the British.

His face sported two weeks of patchy beard. Scars on his jawline cut across it like furrows in a field. He was tall for a submariner and spoke with his head ducked down to keep it beneath the pipes that ran overhead.

"The French have stolen something precious from Israel," he told them. "We're the only ones in position to prevent them from succeeding in this latest treachery."

The *Dakar* had been two days out of Southampton en route to Haifa when an ultra-coded signal from the Israeli high command had interrupted their shakedown cruise. They'd been ordered to proceed to the southern coast of France at top speed and lie in wait, while the high command entered false position reports into the record and prepared cover stories and obituaries should their high-risk mission fail.

For the better part of two days, Gideon and his men had been waiting and planning. After finally picking up a sonar contact, and confirming it was the *Minerve*, they'd allowed it to pass and had moved in behind it.

They'd quickly closed to within a hundred yards. So close that they could hear the *Minerve*'s screw turning without using their hydrophones.

The next task seemed impossible to accomplish. Gideon and his men were not commandos, most weren't even experienced sailors, but every single one of them was ready to fight and die for his country.

Gideon explained. "In the ancient times sea battles were not won by sailors but by soldiers. The Romans, the Phoenicians, the Greeks—they rammed their enemies and stormed on board, where the fighting and killing was done by hand."

The men looked on without blinking. Their smooth faces belied their desire to right a terrible wrong. They didn't know exactly what was at stake, but they knew the French had betrayed them yet again.

After enacting an arms embargo on Israel during the Six-Day

War. After keeping a squadron of Mirage aircraft and a small fleet of patrol boats that Israel had already paid for. After suddenly cozying up to Israel's Arab enemies. The French had now crossed a line that could not be tolerated. They'd killed Israeli citizens and taken something the Israeli high command was willing to risk war over.

"This will not be easy," Gideon insisted. "There hasn't been a ship boarded and captured in these waters for many centuries. One is damned well going to be boarded and captured today!"

The men cheered. They had only a few submachine guns and pistols as weapons, but they most certainly had surprise on their side. They were tucked in so close behind the *Minerve* that the French submarine could not possibly hear them over its own engine noise.

As the men readied themselves to go topside and storm the *Minerve*, a radioman several feet away sat with a hand pressing a headphone to his ear. "Intercepted transmission," he said glumly. "The *Minerve* is remaining submerged until they reach the channel."

This was unwelcome news.

"We can't board them in sight of the coast," one officer pointed out. "We'll have the French Air Force down on us before we can even find the materials."

"We could put a fish in their side and be done with it," the tactical officer suggested.

The captain shook his head. "Our orders are to get the stolen materials back *at all costs*. Those orders come directly from the Knesset and the Prime Minister. We're to sink the *Minerve* only if we're in danger of being destroyed ourselves."

"But we can't board a ship that's submerged," the tactical officer said.

Gideon took it from there. He'd been considering the problem for a while. "Then we'll have to force them to the surface."

ABOARD the *Minerve*, Cheval drummed his fingers on the chart table, remaining where he'd been during the argument with Lukas. Every few minutes he checked the clock and the boat's position. Both seemed to be crawling.

"How long until we reach the channel?" he asked.

The captain looked his way and then turned as the sound of wrenching metal ran through the boat.

What had to have been an impact was followed instantly by a suction wave that pulled air from the cabin, causing ears to pop and sinuses to ache. Yellow and red indicators lit up on a control panel and the suction grew worse.

"It's the snorkel," the dive officer said. "Valves are shut. Complete malfunction."

The snorkel was designed with an emergency cutoff that sealed the breathing tube if water overtopped the airway. With the snorkel closed off, the churning diesel engines were forced to suck air from the only place they could get it—the inner hull of the submarine.

"I ordered plus three meters on the surface," the captain said, referring to how high the snorkel was supposed to be riding above the waves.

"We're running at that depth," the dive officer insisted.

Either the weather had gotten suddenly worse and the waves larger or something in the snorkel had failed.

Every man in the control room looked upward, counting the seconds and hoping the snorkel would clear.

Cheval felt a wave of nausea, partly from fear, partly from the decrease in pressure. He looked at the clock, this time watching the second hand. Thirty seconds went by, then forty. The situation did not correct itself.

"Water in the periscope tunnel," one of the NCOs called out. "Upper seals must be cracked."

Cheval could think of nothing more fearful than water leaking into a submerged vessel. Even if it was just a trickle. He considered the sound of the wrenching metal, the shudder in the control room. "We must have hit something," he said. "We need to surface."

To Cheval's surprise, the captain agreed with him. "Floating debris perhaps," he said. "Take us up. Surface the boat."

The dive control officer blew the tanks and changed the angle on the planes. The *Minerve* began to rise, bow first. Cheval noticed water trickling down the periscope tube. He looked to the depth gauge, saw that they were rising and sighed with relief as he felt the submarine break the surface and level off.

A second loud bang sounded and the suction vanished, causing Cheval's ears to pop again. "Main vents open," one of the men said. "Engines breathing outside air."

"Ahead one quarter," the captain ordered. "I'm going up to see what kind of damage we've taken."

With the first officer at the helm, the captain led a damage control party up into the conning tower, opening the inner and then outer hatches.

Daylight poured in. Gray and monochrome but beautiful. As the last man's legs went up through the hatch, Cheval stared jealously at the opening. Without thinking or asking permission, he stepped to the ladder and began to climb.

He reached the top, poked his head out and paused in shock.

The periscope and the snorkel were bent to the side at a

thirty-degree angle. The steel was mangled and deformed from the impact. The antenna housing had been sheared off.

Stranger still, the captain and the damage control party were not studying the damage to make repairs, they were being held at gunpoint.

Black-clad men with submachine guns had forced them to their knees. Two motorized inflatable boats were peeling off behind them, heading toward the bow of another submarine.

Before he could process the scene and react, Cheval was yanked upward and thrown against the bulkhead of the conning tower. A large man with scruffy beard jammed the point of a machine gun into his chest. "Not a sound, if you want to live."

Cheval nodded his compliance. He knew instinctively who these men were, who they had to be. "You're Israeli."

"My name is Gideon," the bearded man said, nodding as he spoke. "Judging from the lack of uniform, you must be one of the French scientists. Which means you know what we're after."

Cheval hesitated, not out of defiance but from pure shock. "I know what you want," he then said.

"Good," Gideon replied. "Go down the ladder first. Do anything foolish and you'll die first as well."

Cheval led them back into the submarine, climbing down the ladder as calmly as possible. Halfway down, Gideon kicked him and sent him tumbling. The fall acted as a distraction and the crew in the command center were watching him when Gideon and another commando jumped down and landed on the deck.

With the machine guns drawn and the crew flatfooted, there was no way to resist.

"We have your captain," Gideon told them. "We're here to take back what you stole from us. No one will be harmed if you cooperate."

As the *Minerve* wallowed in the swells, additional commandos came down the ladder. Leaving two men to guard the control room, Gideon forced Cheval to lead them deeper into the submarine. They took more captives in each compartment, surprising most of the men in their cabins. The French commandos were rounded up as well. All except Lukas.

"Keep the others under guard," Gideon ordered. "Send two men to find this Lukas. Shoot him on sight."

As the men moved off, Cheval took Gideon to Ben-Avi's quarters and released him. "We've come to bring you back to Israel," Gideon told Ben-Avi. "But not without the materials."

"I don't know where they are," Ben-Avi said.

Gideon turned to Cheval. "Where are the bacterial cultures?"

"In the mess hall."

Cheval led them to the mess hall, with Gideon, Ben-Avi and another of the Israelis right behind him. They entered the hall, where several stainless steel cylinders with black bands around each end stood.

Gideon ordered Cheval to the side and sent Ben-Avi to check the equipment.

"This is the primary strain," Ben-Avi said, checking the first drum. "And this is—"

Before he finished his thought, the hammering of an automatic weapon rang out. Ben-Avi went down in a hail of bullets. Ricochets bounced around the mess hall and everyone dove for cover.

"Right corner, by the freezers," the other commando yelled.

Cheval was on the ground, scrambling for cover, as Gideon

opened up with his weapon. By the time Cheval looked up, Lukas was dead, lying prone on the deck in a pool of his own blood. A few feet away, Ben-Avi was faring little better.

Cheval rushed to him and tried to check or stop the flow of the bleeding. "I'm sorry," he said. "This is all my fault. Please forgive me."

Ben-Avi looked past Cheval as if he wasn't there. He moved his mouth to say something but never spoke a word.

WITH THE SUBMARINE under control and the first batch of materials and a few prisoners on their way to the *Dakar*, Gideon contacted the captain. He received bad news.

"French aircraft on radar, heading this way. Unsure of intentions. Our escape may prove to be more difficult than expected. We're submerging and departing immediately. You and your men are to remain on the *Minerve* and sail her to Israel."

Gideon seemed surprised. "We're commandeering her?"

"I'm not going to send her to the bottom with her crew on board, nor can I put them in lifeboats or let them sail into port and tell the world about us. We must take the ship. We'll send the sailors home once we reach Haifa."

"Without a wreck to find, the French will be suspicious," Gideon insisted. "They'll come looking that much faster."

"Do your best to deceive them," the *Dakar*'s captain said. "Dump some oil and toss some life jackets and other materials overboard, then submerge and head south. Hopefully, they'll think the *Minerve* went down."

"And if they do come looking?"

"They'll be looking for us," the captain replied. "Either way, two boats gives us a better chance to get the materials back to Israel than one. But if at least one of us gets through, then Israel will be safer than she is today."

Gideon would have preferred sinking the *Minerve*, with or without the crew on board. He had no desire to lead the French crew at gunpoint. There were too many ways to sabotage the ship, too many things that could go wrong. Still, he did as ordered, dumping four hundred gallons of diesel oil and tossing out anything that might float and look like wreckage.

The attempt to make the French think their submarine had gone down took only a few minutes. When it was completed, they were ready to move off.

As the submarines turned away from each other, the *Dakar* signaled *Good luck* with a flashing light and then submerged.

The *Minerve* dove less than two minutes later. Neither ship would ever surface again.

PART TWO

INFERNO

3

RICK L. COX stood in the operations room of the Alpha Star oil platform, ten stories above the water.

Cox was a *tool push,* which meant he oversaw the whole drilling operation. It was a job he loved and after thirty years in the oil business he had a sixth sense about things. He didn't need it today. One look at the panel told him a bad day was getting worse.

The flow rates and pressure levels in the pipelines were off. And they were off in the wrong direction. Low and dropping lower, even though the Alpha Star platform and two of her sisters were pumping massive amounts of filtered water into the seabed to pressurize the oil field and force the black gold and natural gas upward.

"This can't be right," Cox said to one of the crew. "How much water are we pumping?"

"We're maxed out on capacity," one of the techs yelled back. "All pumps are running at full power."

Even so, they were registering only a weak stream of natural gas and no oil at all.

Cox tilted the OSHA-mandated hard hat back to scratch his head and then grabbed a radio. Alpha Star was working in concert with two other platforms to save a dying offshore field. Maybe the other two rigs were holding back on him.

"Alpha Two, pick up," Cox said into the radio.

"Alpha Two here," a voice with a healthy Southern accent replied. *"Reading you loud and clear."*

"What's your injection pressure?"

"We're right up against the redline."

Cox pressed the talk switch again. "Alpha Three, can you give us any more pressure?"

The foreman from the third platform replied without hesitation. *"We're maxed out here as well, boss. If that oil doesn't break loose soon, we're gonna have to back off."*

"I'll be the judge of that." Cox looked over the gauges once more. "Keep the pressure up. The geologists insist there's an ocean of oil down there. If so, we're going to force it out. I'm drilling down another hundred feet. That'll tap it for sure."

As Cox finished speaking, he glanced over at Leon Nash, one of the roughnecks on his crew. "Take the bit down another hundred."

Nash hesitated. "The guys are a little worried, Chief. No one wants a blowout."

Cox brushed off the comment. "We've got measures in place. Just check the drill angle and punch it down another hundred feet."

Nash didn't argue further. With great care he double-checked the setup and reactivated the bit. In the center of the huge oil rig, a thick pipe began to turn. Six thousand feet below, a carbide drill bit started burrowing deeper into the earth, churning through the mud, salt and layers of porous rock. Slurry came rushing up the pipe, but nothing more.

"Fifty feet," Nash said. "Seventy feet."

"Anything?"

"No increase in flow," Nash said.

Cox was puzzled, they should have been well into the active oil by now. "Careful, now," he urged. If the oil was there, it was being held under great pressure, then more pressure from the water being pumped down beneath it. Tapping it too cleanly could result in a sudden release, also known as a blowout. Like opening a soda bottle after you've vigorously shaken it up.

"Thirty feet to go," Nash said. "Twenty . . ."

The needles on the panel flickered. The pressure in the collection grid began to rise.

"Stop it there," Cox said.

"We have liquids and gas in the pipeline," Nash said, pumping his fist. "Pressure coming up."

The roughnecks behind them cheered.

Before Cox could join them, a series of indicators on his screen went from green to yellow.

At the same instant, the radio came to life. *"Pressure buildup in the collection grid,"* the foreman at Alpha 2 said. *"We're getting some awfully high numbers here."*

Cox could see that. He turned back to Nash. "Are you still drilling?"

"Negative."

The radio chatter increased. Soon, Alpha 2 and Alpha 3 were talking over each other.

"Ten thousand psi and rising."

"Heat buildup in the main line."

"Shut off the injectors," Cox said.

Levers were thrown from open to closed and the sound of the whining pumps in a distant part of the rig died. With no more water being pumped into the underlying rock, the pressure should have stabilized. It didn't.

"Twelve thousand psi," Alpha 2 reported. *"Thirteen . . ."*

Cox didn't need the running commentary. He could see it right in front of him. The yellow indicators started blinking and then turned to angry, flashing red.

"Shutoff valve failure," Nash said from the other side of the room. "Pressure in the main line at fifteen thousand. Vent the pipes or the whole line is going to blow."

Cox had no choice. He palmed the button for the emergency pressure release and pressed it.

Down below the rig, a network of crisscrossing pipes connected the oil platforms to one another and the collection grid. At critical points along the network, large valves opened to vent the gas pressure into the sea.

It should have caused a massive but harmless release of bubbles as vented natural gas funneled upward, spreading and thinning while it rose to the surface. Instead, a rumbling sound traveled through the platform.

"We got fire on the water," Alpha 2 called.

In the gap between the two rigs, a towering blaze erupted from the sea. It spread across the surface in a snaking motion, joining other waves of fire and soon engulfing all three platforms.

"Seal the rig," Cox ordered.

Doors to all compartments were slammed shut against the smoke and flames, but as they buttoned up the platform, a shudder ran through it from deeper down. It shook the floor and buckled knees.

"Pressure spike in the well," Nash called out. "Blowout failure."

This was the worst news yet. It meant a surge of gas had burst past the bit and was traveling up through the hole they'd drilled.

The pressure gauge went off the scale. The bubble of gas exploded through the blowout preventer and surged upward into the heart of the platform. It ignited the instant it hit the air, detonating in the heart of the rig like a thousand-pound bomb.

4

THE SAPPHIRE WATERS of the Gulf of Mexico surrounded Kurt Austin, buoying him as he kicked rhythmically. He wore a wetsuit and fins, but no diving gear, as he swam toward a submersible that bobbed on the surface a few yards away.

A dark-haired figure sat on the nose of the small submarine. "About time you got here," Joe Zavala said. "I was about to call Triple A."

Kurt reached the small craft and grabbed onto a handhold, floating beside it in warm water. "You couldn't afford their rates."

Fact was, the submersible was sitting no more than a hundred yards from its mother ship, the NUMA vessel *Raleigh*, a two-hundred-foot ship packed with scientific instruments, operated by Kurt and Joe's mutual employer, the National Underwater and Marine Agency.

"What happened?" Kurt asked. "You were supposed to be on a two-hour dive. By my count, you've only been down thirty minutes."

"Hit something," Joe said. "Or, I should say, something hit me. On the underside of the hull."

"Any damage?"

"Not sure."

Kurt knew Joe needed to stay on the submersible to help the *Raleigh* hook on. "Throw me a mask," he said. "I'll take a look."

Joe pulled a diver's mask from his kit and tossed it to Kurt. After adjusting the straps, Kurt took a deep breath and dived under the small craft. The bow of the submarine looked fine. A few feet back, he found a mark on the hull. Running his hand over it, Kurt decided it was organic. Some large fish or marine mammal had rammed the sub. It happened from time to time.

Still holding his breath, Kurt continued aft, checking for more damage. He was just about to surface when he felt a strange sensation, like someone had thumped him in the chest. At the same moment, a pressure wave boxed his ears as it swept by.

He surfaced, grabbed the handhold and flipped up the mask. "Did you feel that?"

Joe was standing now, looking out toward the horizon. "No, but I saw it," he said. "Shock wave running on the surface. Are you all right?"

"Felt like a mule kick, but I'm fine." Kurt pulled himself onto the submersible next to Joe. "Might have been seismic."

"I don't think so," Joe said. He pointed to the horizon. A trail of smoke was rising into the sky due east of their position.

Sound and shock waves traveled four times faster and four times farther in water than they did in the air. Nearly a minute after Kurt had felt the pressure wave below, an echoing boom rolled over them from the distance.

"That's a long way off for us to hear and feel it," Joe said.

Kurt did some rough calculations. "Twelve miles," he suggested, "give or take. Who's out there?"

"Only the oil platforms," Joe said.

A grim look settled on both of their faces. Joe dropped back into the submersible, sat in the command chair and powered the sub up.

Kurt climbed up and dropped in beside him, grabbing the radio.

"*Raleigh*, this is Austin," he said. "Prepare for pickup. And contact the Coast Guard. I have a feeling our assistance is going to be needed."

TWENTY MINUTES LATER, Kurt and Joe stood on the bridge of the *Raleigh* with the ship's microphone in Kurt's hand. The *Raleigh* was already traveling at flank speed, heading in a direct line for the inferno in the distance.

Kurt's estimate of twelve miles had been almost dead-on. The Alpha Star oil rig was burning 11.7 miles away. Holding the microphone near his mouth, Kurt adjusted the frequency and pressed the transmit switch. "Alpha Star, this is *Raleigh*. We're coming to render aid. Please advise status."

Kurt stood six feet tall, with a rugged build, a square jaw and a thick tangle of prematurely silver hair on his head. Tanned from days on the water and weathered from years in the elements, he looked older than his age, though he was squarely in his mid-thirties.

He was the head of Special Projects at NUMA, a branch of the federal government known for taking action when the calls came in, especially in situations like the present one.

He changed frequencies and sent out the same message. There

was no response. "Nothing on any of the regular or emergency channels."

Across from him the *Raleigh*'s captain, Kevin Brooks, took the information stoically. "Coast Guard reports three rigs on fire," he said. "Two of them are evacuating. But the Alpha Star is in the thick of the inferno."

"There has to be help on the way," Joe suggested.

"Plenty of it," Brooks said. "But we're the closest ship. That oil rig will be a melted pile of slag by the time anyone else arrives."

Kurt expected that to be the case. "Let's see how bad it is."

Putting the microphone in its cradle, he switched on a monitor and tapped a few keys. The screen was linked to a pair of high-powered cameras at the top of the *Raleigh*'s antenna mast. The cameras had long-range lenses and high-powered optic sensors that allowed them to see in many wavelengths simultaneously. They could make out a license plate from a mile offshore and were stabilized on gyroscopic mounts that enabled continuous, crystal clear video, even as the ship pitched and rolled.

As Kurt focused the cameras, the inferno came into view. The Alpha Star platform was half shrouded in dark smoke and burning everywhere they could see. Only the upper rigging remained in the clear.

"Worse than I thought," Brooks said. "It's no wonder they can't respond."

"There's an odd angle to the rigging," Joe pointed out. "The platform is listing. It has to be taking on water down below. We need to get there before that rig turns turtle on us."

Kurt adjusted the camera, pulling back. In the wider shot, they could see fires raging all across the sea, surrounding the Alpha Star and both of the other rigs. "We're going to have to sail through the fire to do that," Kurt said.

The captain glanced at the screen. "You know they're probably all dead."

"They might be," Kurt said. "But if there are survivors, they won't be getting out of there without our help."

Captain Brooks had his own crew to think about, but he didn't hesitate. He grabbed the microphone and switched the selector to the shipwide intercom. "All hands, this is the captain," he said. "We're taking this ship into the fire. I want it buttoned up like we're entering a force ten typhoon. Prepare to take on casualties and render assistance."

Kurt nodded at the captain and took another look at the screen. The fires were immense. The smoke already two miles high and drifting toward Florida.

"I can get you in there," Brooks said. "But what on earth are you going to do after that?"

"Nothing on earth," Kurt said. "We're men of the sea."

With that, he turned and left. Whatever Kurt had in mind, Captain Brooks knew better than to try to stop him. Kurt's reputation was too well known for that. Some called him brave, others hardheaded, reckless and foolhardy, but no one doubted him. If anyone could get through that fire and pluck a few survivors from the inferno, it was Kurt Austin.

5

ALPHA STAR PLATFORM
CONTROL ROOM

RICK L. COX regained consciousness in stages. First he realized he was awake, then he realized he was alive, then he realized he was in a great deal of pain.

He lay on his side, with a tremendous amount of pressure on his body. Something was crushing him, though he couldn't tell what it was. Looking around didn't help, the control room was dark except for a pinprick of light coming from one of the battery-powered emergency lights on the wall.

Finding something to push on, Cox forced himself forward, squirming out from under a pile of equipment that had fallen on him. Free of the weight, he took another look around him and tried to stand. Getting up was one thing, remaining vertical was something else. He took one step and found himself falling and grabbed the wall.

At first, he assumed his balance was off, but once he steadied himself he realized the entire room was tilted over.

That's a bad list, he thought, trying to remember how far the Alpha Star could roll before capsizing.

With a pronounced limp, he struggled forward, grabbing the emergency light and pulling it from the wall. Pointing it this way and that, he spotted several crew members. Three of the crewmen were dead. Nash was huddled with a crewman named Haney and two others who were so new to the team that Cox could not remember their names.

Neither of the rookies looked able to walk.

"Anyone else?" Cox asked.

Nash shook his head.

Cox searched desperately for a working radio. The main system was obviously out, but a handheld was found. He dialed in the emergency channel and began broadcasting.

"Mayday! Mayday! Mayday! This is Alpha Star Control. We've had a blowout. Rig is on fire. Five men trapped in the control room. Believe the rig is sinking fast. Send all possible help."

As Cox waited for a response, sweat poured off his face. They were standing inside an oven and the heat was rising.

"It's a short-range radio," Nash said. "No one's gonna hear it. Unless they're within a few miles of us."

Cox knew that, but he had no other cards to play. He tried one more time and then grabbed onto the wall as the rig lurched to the side. The list worsened, but to Cox's amazement the rig didn't tip over.

"We've got to get out of here," Cox said. "The platform is gonna roll before too long."

"They can't walk," Nash replied.

"Then we'll carry them."

Clipping the radio to his belt, Cox lifted one of the men to a standing position and shouldered the load as they walked.

As the man leaned on him, Cox felt his injured leg cry out in pain. It almost buckled, but there was no way he was going to allow himself to fall. He'd pushed too hard and drilled too deep. And he'd probably gotten half the crew killed in the process. If at all possible, he would lead the survivors out of this misery.

Nash and Haney helped the second man up and the five of them moved across the tilted floor. They arrived at a buckled door. Putting all his weight into it, Cox managed to wedge it open. The gap was just wide enough for each man to slip through. Cox began to step through but stopped.

The corridor ahead of them angled downward. Water swirled at the far end. That was bad enough, but when Cox shined the light toward it, he noticed gas bubbles popping as they reached the surface. "Go back," he shouted. "Everybody back."

He pushed his way through the door as the water burst into flame and a line of fire surged through the corridor toward him. The rush of flames singed Cox's neck as he dove through the gap.

Turning around, he saw Nash slam the door shut. It was supposed to be watertight, but the bent frame meant it no longer sealed tightly and water soon began to trickle in under the sill.

"We're sinking and listing," Cox said. "That's why we haven't capsized."

"And that corridor is the only way out of here," Nash said.

"Not true," Cox replied. "We can go out through the window in my office."

As the tool push, Cox got an office connected to the control room. He didn't do much in there, except sip scotch at the end of the day, but the room had a large window that looked out onto the Gulf. Normally, it would be a sixty-foot drop to the water, but considering the list and the flood coming down the corridor, the window couldn't be more than a few feet above the water now.

Working together, the men crossed the room, thankful that they were heading toward the high side. They pushed into the office and found that all the furniture had slid down against the near wall.

The window was on the far side. It was scorched in places and covered in a spider's web of cracks. They could see no daylight through it, only thick, dark smoke and the occasional tongue of orange flame.

"So, we either drown or burn," one of the injured men said bitterly.

Cox doubted they would do either, the fumes were growing toxic. They would pass out and die from smoke inhalation long before anything else.

Hoping to avoid all three of those fates, Cox went to the jumble of furniture and looked for something to attack the window with. He would have preferred a fire axe, but all he could find was the old 9 iron he kept by the desk, which he used to hit golf balls off the top deck from time to time.

He moved back toward the window and swung with all his might. The steel head of the club hit and rebounded, causing little more than a chip in the window. Summoning all his strength, Cox swung again and again and again. He swung until he dropped, but the window, made from multiple layers of high-strength plexiglass, was still intact.

"It's no good," he said. "That window is designed to take a direct hit from a sixty-foot wave."

He sat down, coughing and exhausted. Across the tilted floor, water began seeping under the office door.

Nash tried to stand and take the golf club from his boss, but he could hardly move. The fumes had begun to choke them and the fire in the corridor was consuming all the oxygen.

He made only one swing and then dropped to the ground, his chest heaving. "There's . . . no . . . air . . ."

The rig suddenly settled further and the view through the window changed. Half was smoke and fire, while the lower portion was now a blue-green shimmer like that of a dimly lit pool. They would be underwater soon. The only reason the room hadn't flooded was the bubble of air trapped in there with them.

Cox knew it was over. "I'm sorry, boys . . . I shouldn't have . . ."

His eyelids drooped but he kept them open. He thought he'd seen movement on the other side of the splintered and frayed window. It looked like a reflection, but it continued growing brighter, coming closer and moving faster.

Just as the light got blindingly bright, something slammed against the window from the outside. This time, the plexiglass shattered and green water began pouring in over the sill. The yellow nose of a strange-looking vessel remained lodged there for a moment and then pulled out of the way.

Cox recognized it as a submersible, much like the ROVs they used to inspect the pipelines and wellheads.

The submersible pulled back, the main hatch popped open and a figure in advanced firefighting gear climbed out. By now, Cox thought he was hallucinating, but the man jumped into the water, swam up to the shattered window and allowed himself to be washed inside.

Once he'd escaped the torrent, the man came over to Cox. He wore a full-face helmet, but, as he spoke, his words came through a small speaker on the outside of the helmet. "How many men in here?"

"Five," Cox stammered. "Five of us. Who are you?" he added. "Where did you come from?"

"We're with NUMA. Our ship is about five hundred yards away. That was as close as we could get. We heard your radio call. Sorry it took us so long to find the control room, but it's not where it's supposed to be."

"NUMA? I know a few guys in NUMA. What's your name, son?"

"Kurt Austin," the man said. "Now, let's move."

Cox didn't know if he was dreaming, seeing reality or already dead, but the room was half filled with water and the fire was burning outside the door. Whether this was real or not, Cox didn't want to miss the ride.

He grabbed one of the injured men and helped him through the window into the water. Nash and Haney followed with the other injured crewman and Austin followed behind, helping them paddle to the side of the submarine, where they crawled aboard and up toward the hatch.

Cox helped pull the last man up before squeezing into the submersible himself. There was almost no room to breathe. The small submarine, designed for two men, now held six people, the five who'd been rescued and the pilot, an athletic-looking man with close-cut dark hair and the name *Zavala* stitched to his jumpsuit pocket.

"This will be a short trip," Zavala said. "So, I'm afraid we won't be serving drinks."

Austin's helmeted face appeared over the hatch above. "Looks like this bus is full," he said. "You guys get out of here, I'll catch the next one."

"You can't be serious," Cox said.

"We got another call," Austin replied. "One of your lifeboats is hung up, I'm going to knock them free."

Cox was glad to hear that at least some of the men were alive, but he doubted Austin's chances to reach them.

With that, Austin grabbed the hatch and shouted to Zavala, "I'll be on the south side. Don't forget to come back and get me."

"And lose all that poker money you owe me?" Zavala said. "Not a chance."

The hatch slammed shut, the wheel spun and locked tight and the submersible backed away from the edge of the oil rig, turning as it went and then submerging beneath a wall of fire.

To Cox's surprise, the water itself was lit up all around with multiple columns of fire. The flames didn't start at the surface, they were burning all the way down as far as the eye could see.

"It makes no sense," Cox said. "Fire shouldn't be down in the water. It just shouldn't be down here."

Cox couldn't know it but Joe Zavala was thinking the exact same thing.

6

NUMA VESSEL *RALEIGH*

CAPTAIN BROOKS stood on the *Raleigh*'s bridge as the windows slowly blackened from soot and the paint began to blister on the outer edge of the hull. They'd sailed in through the first waves of fire, cutting a path like an icebreaker in the Arctic, but as they neared the Alpha Star platform the flames became impenetrable, forty feet high, half hidden in the black smoke.

They'd stopped two hundred yards from the shattered rig, deployed the submarine and spent twenty intense minutes waiting and blasting at the water around them with the ship's firefighting hoses. When the heat became too much for the men on the deck, the nozzles were locked in place and left on full blast. The result was a bubble of safety in the middle of the firestorm with an outside temperature approaching two hundred degrees.

Brooks looked on as the ship's executive officer used the mast cameras to search for Kurt and Joe.

"They're ten minutes late already," the executive officer said.

Brooks didn't respond. Instead, he turned the windscreen wipers on to scrape away the grime that was slowly blocking their view. It wasn't much help, smearing everything. "Any sign of them on the cameras?"

"Nothing on either wavelength."

"They're probably keeping below the surface," Brooks said. "Use the sonar array. Angle it directly to port."

The executive officer switched to a second control panel and powered up the bow-mounted sonar emitter, which was contained in a bulbous housing beneath the front of the ship. At the touch of a button, it began sending pulsed sonar signals in a wide band, sweeping the turbulent waters between the *Raleigh* and the imperiled drilling platform.

"There must be something wrong with the sonar," the XO said. "The readout is distorted."

Brooks looked over at the sonar display. He saw a pixelated image with areas of gray and black, other sections of the image were clean, including an area showing wreckage on the bottom. "It's not the sonar unit, it's the water. Or more accurately the bubbles in the water, those are walls of gas coming up from below."

The radio squawked before the XO could reply. "*Raleigh*, this is Zavala," a cheery voice announced. "We're on the surface fifty feet from your stern. Ready to unload survivors."

Brooks grabbed the microphone. "Great job," he said. "How many did you find?"

"Five," Joe replied. "But we're not done yet."

The hell you aren't, Brooks thought. "I'm putting a stop to the risks being taken. Sit tight, we'll haul you aboard."

"Negative," Joe said. "I have to go back."

"The safety of the ship and crew takes priority at this point."

Joe did not relent. "If we leave now, you'll be leaving one of the crew behind. Kurt went for the lifeboat. He'll be waiting for a pickup."

Brooks turned his eyes to the wreckage of the oil rig. The part of the rig housing the control center had broken off slowly and sunk. The rest stood tall, engulfed in flames, like a proud tree in a forest fire. Equipment and pieces of the structure were falling from up high, weaker materials bending and melting in the heat, dropping from the structure like meteors.

Austin's reputation may have preceded him, but Brooks now thought Kurt had to be certifiably crazy. "If Kurt lives through this, I'm ordering him to have a full psych eval," he grunted. "Get the survivors on board and go look for him. We're pulling the ship back at least half a mile."

"We'll meet you out there," Joe promised. "I'm approaching the lower cargo hatch. Send some of the crew to open it and get these people inside. As soon as they're off the sub, I'm going back."

7

ALPHA STAR PLATFORM, LOWER LEVELS

KURT HAD TAKEN plenty of firefighting courses during his years in the Navy and NUMA. He knew the basics, advanced techniques and everything in between. He'd helped blow out oil rig fires on land several times. All his training told him one thing. *Fire was a living thing that needed to breathe. Take away the oxygen and you cut off the fire's life.*

The problem was this fire seemed to be supernatural. Not only was it an unearthly mix of orange and blue, it burned in sealed compartments where there couldn't possibly be any free oxygen. It burned in and under the water. He couldn't swim beneath it, only around it.

As he made his way from the sinking part of the rig to the surviving section, he was forced to circumnavigate one column of flames after another.

Reaching the main section of the rig, he climbed out of the water and onto a stairway, moving through a tangled mess of burnt and twisted metal.

So far, the platform's auto leveling system was keeping it from tipping over, even if that required taking on so much ballast that the lower decks were now underwater and the remaining section of the platform was slowly settling.

Making his way around the side, he reached the outer stairwell. Kurt found himself free of fire for the moment but surrounded by smoke and toxic vapors. A monitor strapped to his arm was reading four different kinds of poisonous gas, along with a lethal level of smoke. If Kurt weren't suited up like an astronaut, he wouldn't have lasted thirty seconds.

The heat was another problem. Though the heat-resistant suit and the coolant still running through it were keeping his body temperature from rising too much, it wouldn't last for much longer.

He checked the oversized chronometer strapped to his other arm. It showed eleven minutes of oxygen and five minutes of coolant left. He would have to work quickly.

Continuing upward, he climbed three flights, fought his way past a set of loose pipes and spotted his destination, an orange-colored pod, roughly fifty feet long, with a pointed nose and rounded tail.

The escape boat resembled an oversized torpedo and was designed for its own type of launching. The vessel wasn't lowered into the sea like a ship's lifeboat. Instead, it sat on rails that were angled downward. Once the restraining clamps were released, it dropped nose-first, sliding forward and then free-falling from the high decks of the oil rig.

Kurt had endured a test ride in a similar escape boat. It hit the water at fifty miles an hour and, despite the pointed nose designed to break the surface tension, it felt like they were smashing into a brick wall. Because of that, the occupants sat backward, wearing harnesses and head restraints that kept them from suffering from whiplash. This wouldn't do them any good unless the boat could get free of its cage.

Kurt saw the problem as soon as he got close. One of the launch rails that directed the pod as it slid forward had been bent inward by the explosion. It was now acting like a gate, preventing the boat from releasing.

"That's not going to be an easy fix," Kurt said to himself. He wondered why the men hadn't come out to free themselves or look for a second boat.

Picking up a length of pipe, Kurt climbed onto the rails and then banged on the hull to get the occupants' attention. With his gloved hand, he rubbed away the soot and oxidation that had covered the porthole.

Putting his face up to the glass, he counted ten people inside. They were strapped in and waiting. Even from his limited view, Kurt could see that several were injured and burned. Another man was at the controls, desperately working a radio that he'd used to call for help.

Kurt banged on the hull again and the man finally noticed him. He staggered over to the porthole. "You're caught up," Kurt shouted.

The man pressed a button and his voice came over a speaker. *"We tried to shake the boat loose by rocking it back and forth. But no luck."*

"And you're not going to have any," Kurt said. "If you come with me, I can lead you to another boat. Or we can get to the water. I have a small submersible coming back to pick us up."

The man shook his head. *"I got injured men and women in here, five with burns, two with broken legs, three more unconscious. None of us has fire gear. It took us forever to climb down two decks just to get in the pod. We'll never make it."*

Kurt realized instantly that the man was right, it was either escape in the boat or die inside it. "Strap yourself back in," Kurt said. "I'll try to cut you free."

"With what?"

"Swiss Army knife, if that's what it takes."

Kurt looked around for something to slice through the metal rail or bend it out of the way. Nothing obvious jumped out at him. But he had an idea. "Get ready for the drop. It's going to come suddenly."

"Hurry," the man said. *"We're cooking in here."*

Kurt had no intention of wasting time. He backtracked to the bundle of loose pipes that he'd climbed over earlier, found a long, thin one made of a lightweight alloy. It had threaded ends where additional pipes could be attached by screwing them together.

He grabbed three matching pipes, compared the ends and then went back to the stranded escape boat.

His first thought was to use the pipes as a long lever, bending the misaligned launch rail back and freeing the boat, but that proved impossible.

"Give me a lever and a firm place to stand," Kurt said to himself. "But if there's no firm place to stand—"

Something detonated in the lower levels. The catwalk shook and debris tumbled toward him from above. Kurt ducked out of the way. The water was the key.

He quickly screwed the pipes together, twisting them tight. With all three sections linked, he now held an unwieldy forty-foot tube of metal, which he lowered into the water below, deliberately submerging the pipe into a dense area of flame.

Balancing the pipe against the catwalk, he removed his secondary regulator, split the hose and directed a jet of oxygen across the open top of the pipe. This created a low-pressure area that drew the volatile gas into the pipe and gave the fire pure oxygen to breathe.

It took a few seconds for the gas to rise up the pipe, but when it reached the top, a jet of fire burst out the end.

Kurt held it up against the launch rail, stretching dangerously over the gap to direct the fire against the actual bend in the rail where the metal was already the weakest.

The pipe warmed in his hands, with the heat soaking through his fireproof gloves. "Come on," he whispered.

The jet of flame was continuous and intense. It quickly blackened the launch rail and then reddened it like the embers of a fire.

With the rail glowing red, it softened quickly. The escape boat inched forward.

"Just a little more . . ." Kurt grunted, his hands beginning to burn.

All at once, gravity took over. The boat slid forward, breaking off the weakened rail and knocking the makeshift torch out of Kurt's hand.

Everything fell in tandem. The pipe clanging into various things and the orange pod hitting the sea like a small bomb.

The impact forced so much water aside, it created a temporary void in the flames down below.

"No time like the present." With two steps, Kurt jumped over the edge. He dropped feetfirst, with both arms holding the helmet in place. He plunged twenty feet below the surface and then kicked upward with all the strength he had left.

Kurt broke the surface and swam for the tail end of the escape boat, which was already motoring away.

A desperate grab for a trailing rope failed and Kurt was on his own. He began swimming, following the wake made by the orange boat. It kept the fire off him, but he was rapidly being left behind. Eventually, the boat pulled far enough ahead that a wall of fire closed between them.

Kurt stopped swimming and began treading water. He turned from side to side, looking for a gap in the wall of flames. There wasn't one. He looked below the surface, but the fire extended downward as far as he could see. He couldn't swim through, couldn't swim under and couldn't swim around.

"Definitely need a Plan B," he said to himself.

Slowly, the ring of fire closed in on him, the safe space in the middle shrinking until Kurt was treading water in a circle no more than fifteen feet across. Just as he was about to pick a direction and swim for it, something hit his feet, lifted him up and left him sprawled out flat.

Joe had surfaced the submersible directly beneath him.

Kurt grabbed on and steadied himself.

The hatch opened and the smiling face of Joe Zavala popped out. "The weather's a lot nicer on the inside."

Kurt was already moving toward the hatch. "You don't have to ask twice."

He swung his feet over, dropped down inside and sealed the hatch tight while Joe vented the tanks and took the small craft downward.

With an oxygen alarm beeping and a coolant warning flashing, Kurt pulled off his helmet for the first time in what seemed like hours. "Took your own sweet time getting here," he said to Joe.

"I was giving you a chance to get out of there on your own," Joe said. "Thought it might help build up your self-esteem."

"That's thoughtful of you," Kurt said, pretending to be appreciative, "except that I almost ended up like a baked potato."

"More like pasta," Joe said. "Actually, it was hard to find you. And hard to navigate through all this fire, even in a submarine. It was only when the escape boat hit the water that I got a clear bead on where you were."

Looking through the forward glass, Kurt could see the columns of fire clearly now. Joe navigated around them but also had to avoid sections of the half-submerged rig, tangles of wreckage and floating debris.

"This isn't oil or natural gas," he mused.

"I don't think so either," Joe said. "But, then, what is it?"

"No idea," Kurt said. "Something tells me we'd better find out."

8

NUMA VESSEL *RALEIGH*,
ON STATION OUTSIDE THE FIRE ZONE

KURT HAD SHED the firefighting gear, showered and thrown on some jeans and a NUMA T-shirt. Never had normal clothes felt more comfortable.

He made his way to the sick bay, where the ship's doctor checked his hands and found them to be burned—something Kurt could have told him without all the poking and prodding.

"Nothing too bad," the doctor said. "Just first-degree. Don't high-five anyone for a few days and you'll be fine."

After applying some Silvadene cream, the doc released him and Kurt met up with Joe, Captain Brooks and Rick Cox at the command and control center for the *Raleigh*'s dive teams—a compartment the crew referred to as OSLO.

The acronym stood for *off ship and land operations.* The crew pronounced it like the name of the Norwegian capital and referred to it that way, too. *Meet you in OSLO for the briefing. Where have you been all day, stuck in OSLO?*

From here, a project leader could monitor the status of crew members and submersibles conducting dives or landside operations. Screens around the room could display images beamed in from helmet-mounted cameras, ROVs and anything else NUMA used.

Sonar images, including those relayed from other ships, buoys and sleds, could be combined into one coherent picture and presented on the centerpiece of the room, a 3-D virtual display that its designers called a holographic presentation chamber.

The crew of the *Raleigh* called it the fish tank because it was the size of a billiard table and, when turned off, appeared to be nothing more than a huge block of frosted glass.

Once turned on and supplied with sonar data, it created a miniature, three-dimensional view of whatever area was under observation, including accurate positions and scales of any divers, submersibles, reefs, wrecks, obstructions and surface ships in the sonar area. All in incredible detail.

Looking into the tank from above provided a top-down view. Moving around to any of the sides gave the observer a side-on view and allowed the project manager to gain a big-picture understanding of any operation that was being conducted.

He walked in to find Joe, Brooks and Cox studying several wall-mounted screens at the far end of the compartment. The first screen was displaying the ongoing fire as viewed from the masthead cameras. Another showed them a satellite view of the Gulf, with the pall of smoke that was drifting eastward.

A third screen displayed a map of the Gulf, showing the positions of every active drilling rig, capped wellhead and pipeline in the area. The arrangement looked like a mess of tangled string.

A fourth screen showed the grim faces of two men in Washington. Rudi Gunn, who was NUMA's Assistant Director and second-in-command, and Lance Alcott, the head of FEMA, the Federal Emergency Management Agency.

Alcott was talking as Kurt walked in. ". . . and the Coast Guard is sending five ships to help fight the blaze, but until they arrive, the President has put NUMA in charge. A decision that makes no sense to me, but there you have it."

Alcott shot Rudi a sour look. Rudi ignored him completely and took over the conversation. "First order of business is to assess the damage."

Captain Brooks had already done that. "We've circled the fire zone, studying the surviving rigs and scanning the waters below with sonar. We have a full picture of the destruction. The pipeline network is damaged and venting gas. The Alpha Star is a total loss—she won't be on the surface much longer. The other two rigs are in better shape, the crews are safe, but the platforms are in danger. They remain surrounded by fire, though not directly ablaze at the moment."

Rudi looked toward Cox. "Your company was hoping we could save the other platforms."

"They cost almost a billion dollars each," Cox replied.

Rudi nodded. "So I've heard. We're sending a pair of oceangoing tugs to drag them out of danger. But looking at the video, I don't see any hope of getting a line on either one unless the fires dampen down."

"That's unlikely," Cox said.

Alcott had a suggestion. "We're sending tankers to latch onto the outer wellheads. They'll draw some oil and gas off to decrease what's venting. That might reduce the flames."

"Might as well turn the tankers around," Kurt said. "They'll only get in the way."

The head of FEMA bristled at that suggestion. "We found them useful in the *Deepwater Horizon* incident. Kept two million barrels of oil from hitting the Gulf waters."

Kurt looked toward Cox. "Maybe you should tell them."

Cox stood and cleared his throat. "There isn't any oil coming to the surface."

Alcott looked shocked. Even Rudi tilted his head as if he hadn't heard correctly.

"No oil?"

"Just flammable gas," Cox said.

"They can still snap onto the outlying wellheads and draw some of that gas up, even if they simply flare it off."

"It's not natural gas," Kurt said. "Nor is it methane or any other type of hydrocarbon that I've ever seen. It's reacting with the water. Burning on its way up. Dousing it spreads and thins it but does nothing to extinguish it."

Alcott sat back, looking flummoxed. "That makes no sense. I've never heard of a gas that burns while submerged in water."

"Neither have we," Kurt replied. "So, I spoke with Paul Trout, our chief geologist. He suggested two possibilities. Either the ruptures are venting oxygen vapor along with the hydrocarbons or we're dealing with a previously undiscovered compound. All we can be sure of is that the gas is hydrophoric, meaning the fumes ignite spontaneously when they make contact with the water."

"Makes it even harder to imagine towing the rigs to safety," Rudi said.

Kurt nodded. "We'll work on it and let you know."

Rudi and Alcott signed off and Kurt glanced at Brooks. "Let's see what we're up against."

He walked over to the fish tank and turned it on. The lights in the room dimmed as the hologram came to life. The seabed appeared first—depicted in olive green—then orange lines crisscrossing revealed the locations of the submerged pipelines. Finally, vertical red lines appeared, representing thousand-foot lengths of pipe string, which led up from the seafloor toward icons representing the oil platforms at the surface.

"Let me add the fires," Kurt said.

He tapped a few more keys and soon columns of purple and white could been seen traveling vertically from breaks in the orange pipes. They spread out as they rose upward and bloomed on the surface like giant, deadly flowers.

"Each fire is coming from a different pipeline," he said, looking at Cox. "The main fire is here, venting upward through the wellhead you and your crew drilled. It's hitting the surface directly under what's left of the Alpha Star."

The three-dimensional image showed the Alpha Star engulfed in purple.

Kurt turned the image slightly and it was easy to see that the other platforms were ringed with fire and getting toasted from the outside but not sitting directly over the flames.

Cox moved closer and squinted into the projection chamber. His bloodshot eyes were wide. "We use a lot of high-tech junk when we're looking for oil, but I've never seen anything like this."

He scratched his head and studied what he was looking at. No one knew what lay below the rigs better than him. "Those other fires are coming from the field collection lines," he said, pointing to small sections of the orange pipe. "There's no way to shut them off, they lead directly to the main well."

Joe leaned closer. He was an engineer. He'd built submersibles and subsurface aquatic habitats and had even worked on an oil rig in his youth. He pointed to an area where the orange pipes merged. "If we closed the transfer valves here, that would block the flow of gas to the fires near the other rigs."

"In theory," Cox said. "But the controls to operate those valves were on the Alpha Star."

"Can we do it in person?" Joe asked.

Cox shook his head and all four men went back to studying the fish tank. Finally, Kurt had an idea. "We can't put the fires out and we can't move the rigs, but what if we move the fires?"

Cox looked Kurt's way. "How, exactly, does one move a fire?"

Kurt pointed out the largest pipe that was still intact. It led back to a spot directly beneath the burning wreckage of the Alpha Star. "If we cut the pipe here, the gas that's venting near the other rigs will escape here instead of at the other ruptures. What's left of the Alpha Star will take the full brunt of the fire, but the rest of the inferno should die on the vine. With the other two platforms free of the flames, you can tow them out and they should end up no worse than blackened Cajun chicken."

Cox leaned closer, studying the arrangement, and then walked around to the far side so he could see it from the reverse angle. There, he dropped down and gazed into the fish tank like he was staring at lost treasure.

"Sacrifice the ruined platform to save the others?" he said. "I could sign off on that. But if this gas does what you say it does—if it detonates the instant it contacts the water—then you're going to get an enormous blast when you cut into that pipe. Knowing what it did to our rig, I wouldn't want to be anywhere near that line when it goes."

Kurt nodded. "Then we'll use explosives and blow it remotely."

9

THE SUN was dropping toward the horizon by the time Kurt and Joe climbed back onto the *Raleigh*'s main submersible. To the east, the sea continued burning, a nautical vision of Hades, obscured by smoke and blurred by waves of heat.

With Joe already at the controls, Kurt climbed in and sealed the hatch.

Kurt took the briefest glimpse of the inferno and then gave a thumbs-up to the crane operator. The submersible was lifted off the deck, swung out over the side and lowered into the water.

"Once more unto the breach," he said, settling in beside Joe.

"We're going to cause our own breach," Joe said. "So technically . . ."

"Right," Kurt said. "Let's go."

Joe opened the valves and the sound of air rushing out of the tanks roared in their ears until it was replaced by a soothing quiet as the submersible dived beneath the waves. A mile from the nearest fire, the sea appeared serene—at least until a flickering glow became obvious in the distance.

"Coming up on the outer fires," Joe said.

Their progress was being monitored by Brooks, Cox and others back in OSLO. Brooks replied to Joe's comment over the radio. *"Outer fires confirmed. Steer five degrees to port and you should have smooth sailing through to the next danger zone."*

"Strange that they have a better view of things up there than we do down here," Joe said. "I imagine the tiny icon of our sub looking like the miniature sub in *Fantastic Voyage*."

Kurt laughed. "And yet I'm stuck in here with you instead of Jessica Chastain."

As Joe made the course correction, Kurt slid a control panel with a lighted keyboard in front of him. From it, he could control the submersible's robotic arms.

"Leveling off," Joe said. "Continuing east."

"We see you," Brooks replied. *"In a quarter mile, you'll be closing in on what's left of the vertical shaft that blew out under the Alpha Star. All you'll see is a column of fire, but sonar confirms there is still metal debris in there, so watch yourselves."*

Kurt could sense a backseat driver situation forming, one drawback to having the OSLO system in full swing.

"Campfire dead ahead," Joe said. "Hope you brought the marshmallows."

"Fresh out," Kurt said. "How about fifty pounds of C-4?"

"That ought to liven things up."

The radio came to life again. This time, it was Cox. *"You boys are approaching the main transfer line now."*

"I'm not seeing anything," Joe replied.

"The line is buried, but you'll see a distinctive bulge running perpendicular to your position. Follow that and it'll lead you back beneath the Alpha Star."

Kurt spotted the bulge in the sediment and pointed.

"I see it," Joe said. "Commencing turn."

They followed the raised line of sediment toward their destination, passing between two fiery eruptions along the way. Kurt noticed the columns of flame beginning life in narrow, concentrated jets and then widening as they went upward.

"Whatever this hydrophoric gas is, it's blasting out of the pipes at high pressure."

As they neared the fires, a rumbling sound reverberated through the steel hull of the sub.

"Sounds like a freight train," Joe said.

Kurt would have agreed but the racket became so intense that it blocked out all conversation. Up close, the fountain of flame became too bright to look at and Kurt averted his eyes, looking beneath the point of ignition. He saw a crater in the seafloor and a broken pipe, bent and splayed outward.

With the fire behind them, the sound levels returned to normal and the seafloor ahead was lit up like a sandy beach on a sunny day.

"Next thing you should see is a group of exposed pipes. A three-into-one connector and then the valve assembly sticking out of the silt like a tree trunk. Fifty feet beyond that is the best spot to place the explosives."

Joe brought them over the valve assembly and down onto the raised section of sediment. "This looks like the spot."

"Hold her steady," Kurt said.

Using the keyboard, he activated one of the submersible's robotic arms, powering up a water jet contained in the arm and blasting away the sediment. A swirling cloud engulfed, drifting away only after Kurt shut off the water jet and focused on the newly exposed pipe, which was as thick as a telephone pole.

What had once been gray-painted steel was now covered in barnacles and flakes of rust.

"Pipe exposed," Kurt said. He retracted the first robotic arm and extended a second. Gripped in the claw at the end of this arm was a large block of C-4 connected to a detonator and a circular band that would allow them to clip the explosives to the pipe. The band was open at one end and would slip over the pipe with a slight shove, clipping on like a bracelet.

"Don't bump it too hard," Joe said. "The pressure in that line is nearly ten thousand psi and there's no telling if the other explosions damaged it."

"I'll be gentle," Kurt insisted.

With a deft hand, Kurt forced the clip onto the pipe and it locked into place. "Easy peasy," he said. "Now back us off."

Joe engaged the propellers once more and the sub pulled away from the pipe. As they moved back, a thin wire spooled out. A hundred feet out, Joe slowed to a halt and held station.

"Setting the countdown for fifteen minutes," Kurt said. "That ought to give us time to get back on the *Raleigh*, crack open a beer and settle in to watch the fireworks."

With a nod from Joe, Kurt started the timer. A digital readout on the control panel flashed *15:00* and then began clicking down.

With the timer operating, Kurt disconnected the control wire and Joe spun the sub around to take them out.

. . .

UP IN the OSLO compartment, Captain Brooks watched on the remote screen as the timer started clicking down. Cox stood over the fish tank, watching the tiny electronic version of the submersible navigate back along the orange pipeline trail. He marveled at the detail. "I feel like Zeus, looking down on the world from Mount Olympus."

"More like Poseidon," the captain replied. "But I know what you're saying. I've almost gotten used to it now, but I remember feeling the same way the first time we used it on a salvage operation."

Circling around the display, Cox studied the shattered arrangement of pipes, the bits of wreckage that had come off the Alpha Star that now littered the seafloor, and the miniature version of the slow-moving sub that Kurt and Joe were piloting. To his surprise, it wasn't the only thing moving in the tank. "What's this?"

Brooks looked his way. "What's *what*?"

"There's another guppy in your tank."

Captain Brooks crouched down beside Cox, took a long, hard look and then shook his head. Reaching for the control panel, he tapped the key to zoom in. He tapped it once, twice and then a third time.

After the third increase in magnification, he could clearly make out a disk-shaped object, moving to the south. It flickered, reappeared and then vanished again.

"Is that a glitch?" Cox asked.

"I don't think so," the captain said grimly. "The tank can only show us what the sonar is picking up. The fires, venting gas and wreckage are blocking the signal in places, causing it to cut out. But there was something there all right."

Brooks picked up the phone and contacted the bridge. "Helm, give us five knots and pull us around to the northeast. Have the sonar team max out the pulse, if they haven't already."

Brooks continued scanning the display as the ship began to move. For several moments, there was nothing to see. And then the red disk reappeared.

"Looks like a Frisbee," Cox said. "Or a flying saucer."

"Which seems appropriate," Brooks said, "since it's completely unidentifiable."

Brooks pressed the intercom button again, this time reaching out to the sonar operations room. "Sonar, this is the captain. I'm down in OSLO, we're seeing a contact bearing zero-four-five, depth eight hundred and fifty feet, heading directly for the danger zone. Any chance this is an artifact or a biological reading?"

"Negative," the sonar operator said. "Speed and sound profile indicate electrically powered water jets."

"What does that mean?" Cox asked.

"It means Kurt and Joe have company."

10

"WHAT DO YOU mean *another* contact?"

Kurt was responding to the news from Captain Brooks. He wasn't sure that he'd heard correctly.

"Just what I said," the captain replied. *"Another submersible, heading across what's left of the collection grid down there. We lost it as it went behind the largest of the fires, but it was definitely there."*

"Are you sure it's not just drifting wreckage?" Joe asked.

"Not unless the wreckage is powered by an impeller."

"Any idea who it is?"

"Not a clue."

"If this was sabotage," Joe said, "whoever did it would need a vessel to plant the explosives. And if they realized the other two platforms are salvageable, they might be coming back to finish the job."

"Our thoughts exactly," Brooks said.

Kurt pressed the talk switch once more. "We'll go have a look. No point trying to save the other rigs if we're going to let someone come in and blow them up."

"We've already plotted an intercept course," Brooks said. *"Head zero-seven-seven, assuming they haven't changed course or depth, which should bring you right in behind them and fifty feet above."*

Joe made the adjustments to the controls and the sub turned and picked up speed. They crossed the tangled arrangement of pipes at an angle, navigating away from the main fire. "You know," he said, "we could just leave them down here and let them get a monster headache when our explosives go off."

"The thought crossed my mind," Kurt said. "But there's a chance it's not a hostile vessel. A lot of wealthy people have their own submarines these days. And I wouldn't put it past one of the news networks, or an independent reporter, to charter a submersible and send it out to get the first video of the disaster. The pictures would be worth millions."

"We should be so lucky," Joe said. "But on the chance it's not a wayward reporter, what do you propose we do about them? Unless you've forgotten, we're not armed."

"When has that ever been a problem?" Kurt said.

"At least eighty percent of the time."

Kurt had to smile. "You're not wrong," he said. "Let's find out what we're dealing with first. Then we'll come up with something."

Joe kept them moving at the submarine's maximum speed. He diverted slightly to avoid one of the smaller fires and in doing so came upon something new. Something he or Kurt couldn't have possibly expected to find.

Down on the seafloor, lined up side by side as if they were in a parking lot, sat four full-sized tanker trucks without the tractors attached. The tires had been stripped and the steel wheel hubs were buried in the sediment up to the axles.

An intricate series of pipes connected the cylindrical bodies of the tankers to a thick pipe that ran horizontally and then downward into the seabed.

"What in the world . . ." Joe whispered.

"*Raleigh*, are you seeing this?" Kurt said.

"*We're looking at it.*"

"What kind of setup are you guys running here?" Kurt asked.

The question was for Cox. "*I have no earthly idea what those trucks are doing there. They're not ours, that's for sure.*"

"They're connected to the pipeline," Joe said. "Could they be responsible for the flammable gas we've been dealing with?"

"Even four tanker trucks couldn't hold enough gas for what we've seen," Kurt replied.

"*Those aren't the collection pipes,*" Cox said. "*Those are the injection lines. We use them to pump pressurized water into the rock layers beneath the oil field. That's how we force the oil to the surface in these old wells.*"

Joe circled the arrangement. A little farther off, he spotted four more tankers connected to another line in the distance.

Before he could move to investigate, Captain Brooks spoke. "*Target reacquired,*" he said.

Kurt and Joe glanced around. "We can't see anything."

"*It's a quarter mile to the east. It's heading right for you.*"

Joe slowed the sub and turned to the east, but still they saw nothing.

"*Three hundred yards,*" the captain warned. "*Two hundred . . .*"

Normally, in the depths of the ocean there was zero light to see by. Even powerful lights would be absorbed in a few hundred feet of water. But with the columns of fire burning all around them, the seafloor was a patchwork of light and shadows.

Through that kaleidoscope, Kurt spotted an object headed toward them. It was thin and flat. And then it seemed to expand as it changed depth, raced above them and dropped three items that looked suspiciously like the charge he and Joe had just placed.

"Get us out of here," Kurt said.

Joe shoved the throttle to full and the submersible began to move away from the parked tankers. It seemed to move very slowly.

"Is this all we've got?" Kurt asked.

"This thing wasn't built for speed," Joe replied.

The objects dropped slowly behind them, landing in the nest of submerged tanker trucks.

Kurt knew it wouldn't be long. "Take us up."

Joe vented the ballast tanks, raised the bow and held on tight as three flashes went off in rapid succession.

The shock waves hit simultaneously, slamming the submersible and sending it tumbling.

Fortunately, what the NUMA submersible lacked in speed it made up for in strength. Designed to operate at depths below ten thousand feet, the hull was incredibly strong and stiff. It neither bent nor flexed, absorbing the punishment and righting itself as the shock wave passed.

Kurt and Joe were shaken around inside but remained in their seats, held tight by shoulder harnesses.

With Joe righting the submersible, Kurt looked around for their attacker.

"I can't see him," Kurt said, grabbing his headset off the floor and putting it back on. "*Raleigh*, do you have the target?"

"*Negative,*" the captain said. "*The explosion scrambled our sonar picture. It's going to be a moment before it settles down.*"

"He blew up one set of those tankers," Joe replied. "I'll bet you a month's pay he's going for the other set before he departs."

Kurt nodded. "Let's get him before he gets there. Kill the lights and bring us around. He gave us a shot, now it's our turn to surprise him."

Joe switched off the external lights and brought them in a half circle toward the second group of submerged trucks.

Kurt pointed. "I see him. He's coming in on the port side. Looks like he's setting up for another bombing run. If you can get above him, I can grab on with the robotic arms."

"I think I can arrange that," Joe said.

He took the sub upward, turned onto a new course and then began to descend in a curving, intercepting line, dropping toward the other sub like a hawk moving in for the kill.

The flat, disk-shaped submersible was slowing as it approached the tankers. Its lights came on, illuminating the group of trucks.

Joe closed the gap, dropping faster. "I'm willing to pounce on him, but if little green men come out, all bets are off."

Kurt got the robot arm ready to grab anything he could and kept his eyes locked onto the target beneath them. "Hit him hard."

Joe shoved the stick forward and the heavier NUMA sub nosed over, delivering a shuddering blow to the alien-looking craft. Extending the robot arm, Kurt grabbed at a set of conduits on the outer shell of the other sub, clamping down on the metal tubes and pulling back.

Instead of speeding up or slowing down, the other sub spun like it was on a turntable and extended an arm of its own toward them.

Kurt ripped the conduits from the back of the other vessel, hoping to deny it power. But the vessel continued to operate. It pulled free of Kurt's grasp and moved upward. As it passed the front view port, its own claw opened, releasing a block of explosives, which hit and stuck to the bow of the NUMA craft.

Joe threw the sub into reverse and pulled away, but the explosives had already attached to the hull. "Magnetic."

The other vessel spun once again, powered up its water jets and sped off, blasting the silt as it went and creating a swirling cloud that obscured its departure.

"Neat trick," Kurt said.

"I'd follow him," Joe said. "But we've got bigger problems to deal with."

Kurt pulled the robotic arm back, noticed that the conduit he'd grabbed and some attached components from the other submarine were now dangling from its grasp. He locked the grip.

"Might want to look at those later," he said, switching to the second arm.

"Assuming we're not obliterated," Joe said. "Can you get that bomb off our hull?"

Switching to the other robot arm, Kurt stretched it out and grabbed at the explosives. But because of where they'd attached themselves, there was no way to grasp them. The best he could do was knock them with the side of the arm.

"He's heading back for the other trucks," Joe said. "If this bomb is linked to go off simultaneously with those . . ."

Kurt knew they didn't have much time. He swung the robotic arm sideways, slamming it into the charge. A direct hit. The charge slid several inches, but the magnetic base simply reattached itself to the hull and in a position now completely out of reach.

"This is another fine mess you've gotten us into," Joe said.

"True," Kurt said. "Assuming we survive, I'll take the blame. Any ideas? Scraping it off doesn't seem to be working."

"Heat," Joe blurted out. "Heat will demagnetize the material. We've got to take the sub into the fire."

"Do it."

Joe had already turned toward the nearest fire and was heading right for it. Approaching the swirling column was tricky because of the turbulence created by the burning gas, but he managed to ease the nose of the sub into the fire zone and fought to keep it there.

The temperature rose quickly.

"No time for a slow burn," Kurt urged. "Melt that thing."

Joe pushed the sub farther in. It became caught in the rising vortex of flame, gas and water. The temperature spiked, the magnet weakened and the explosives slid off the hull.

"Get us out of here," Kurt said.

Joe turned the sub and guided them free of the fire, but they'd only gone a short distance when twin explosions rocked the depths where the other tanker trucks had been.

Kurt braced himself for the inevitable, but the charge that had been attached to their hull—wherever it had fallen—never exploded.

Kurt looked over at Joe. "Fire must have melted the detonator."

"Obviously," Joe said. "I knew that would happen. I wondered what you were so worried about."

Kurt looked at Joe and then burst into laughter. Both of them had expected to be blown to bits even as they pulled away from the fire.

Kurt pressed the transmit switch on the panel. "*Raleigh*, do you read us?"

"*You're coming in very faint,*" Captain Brooks said, "*but as long as you're not calling from the afterlife, that's a good thing.*"

"Any sign of our sparring partner?"

"Sorry, Kurt. We lost them again. Whoever it was, they were running to the east the last time we spotted them."

Joe pointed to the timer on the panel in front of them. "We've overstayed our welcome as it is."

Kurt agreed. *"Raleigh,* we're heading your way. Be ready to pick us up."

They reached the surface with a minute to spare, hooked on and were hoisted out of the water. Kurt had just stepped onto the *Raleigh*'s deck when the show began.

First came the white flash of a shock wave, which vanished like a fleeing ghost. It was followed by a narrow column of water erupting at the surface. As the column fell back in a windblown spray, a ring of light grew beneath the surface. It brightened considerably in the seconds before it hit the surface and then erupted in an expanding ball of flame.

A new wave of heat radiated across the deck of the *Raleigh*, more than half a mile away, and what was left of the Alpha Star vanished in the flame.

Farther off, the other fires began to wane, dwindling to almost nothing and then flickering out one by one, leaving only a rising cloud of steam. The other two oil rigs, blackened and burned, now stood in the clear.

A cheer went up on the deck of the *Raleigh* and Cox walked over to congratulate Kurt and Joe.

"Heck of a job," he said. "Someone ought to write a book about you two. In the meantime, the least I could do is buy you men a drink."

"I'll take you up on that drink," Kurt said. "First, I want to figure out who those guys were and why they decided to take out your drilling operation."

"How do you intend to do that?"

Kurt made his way around to the front of the submersible, stopping beside one of the robotic arms. Dangling in its claw were the remnants of the equipment he'd torn off the other submarine. "This came from the other submersible, which had a unique design. It wasn't Navy surplus. It wasn't off the shelf and it didn't look like anything built by any of the manufacturers I know of. In fact, it was unlike anything I've ever seen. That means someone built it to spec. I intend to find out who."

11

THE IMMENSE AIRCRAFT sat on the water, sheltered by a barrier island only twenty-five miles from the Mississippi shoreline. Though it was at rest for the moment, the plane seemed poised for flight, its nose aimed seaward, its outstretched wings reaching for the wind like a great mechanical albatross yearning to fly.

The aircraft was called the *Monarch*. It was nearly the size of a 747, though shorter from front to back and wider in cross section. It had a squat, flat-bottomed fuselage that fanned out like the hull of a boat, its wings attached at the top, drooping slightly and supported at the tips by torpedo-shaped floats.

Six turbofan engines were nestled in the top of the wings instead of hanging beneath, a design that prevented them from taking in the spray generated by the body of the plane as it landed and took off from the water. The twin tails soared higher than they might have needed to, but the extra height made it easier to control the aircraft both on the water and in the air.

The *Monarch* was a triumph of engineering, the only plane of its kind, the creation of Tessa Franco, a wealthy and brilliant designer who'd been called a modern-day Howard Hughes. The comparison was meant as both compliment and put-down, hinting at creativity, recklessness and possible madness.

Tessa—who with her dark hair, smoky eyes and continental beauty seemed more likely to be found on the red carpet at Cannes than in an engineering lab—responded to the comparison by pointing out that she was neither male, nor mad, nor generally reclusive, though she was otherwise quite content to be compared to the adventurous and innovative billionaire.

Sitting in her plush office in the forward part of the aircraft's upper deck, she divided her attention between the light of dusk that came through the window and the flat-screen monitor in front of her.

Staring back at her from the screen was the square face of a powerfully built man with a dark mustache. His name was Arat Buran. Buran was a shadowy but important player in the oil business with extensive holdings in Kazakhstan and other areas of Central Asia. He and Tessa had a long and complicated relationship. Business and pleasure might not have been a good mix, but lust, greed and the desire for power were aphrodisiacs both of them enjoyed. Their latest collaboration was the riskiest of all and, as such, the most enticing.

"*My dear Tessa,*" Buran said. "*You look ravishing as always. I trust you're feeling well.*"

"I'll feel better when I've been paid," Tessa said. "I've done my part. I promised you and your Consortium rising oil prices and I've delivered. Now I expect the Consortium to transfer the funds we've agreed upon."

"*Oil prices have been rising,*" Buran admitted, "*though at a very slow pace.*"

"That will change by morning," she replied.

He tilted his head. "*Surely you're not claiming the disaster in the Gulf as evidence of your success?*"

It wasn't exactly success, but she had every right to claim it.

She felt it necessary to explain. "The U.S. government has been keeping oil prices artificially depressed, even as I've succeeded in sabotaging production around the world. With this incident playing on TV and soon appearing on the cover of every magazine in the world, they won't be able to keep prices down much longer. You'll have your windfall. And I will take what was promised me."

Aggression was her nature. Some men responded to it. Others were put off by it. Buran was a man who preferred control, but he also savored a challenge. It had made their romantic relationship fiery, combative and exhilarating.

On the screen, Buran paused before responding to her demands. He shifted in his chair, gently stroking his mustache, smoothing out the bristly surface. "*You and I have known each other a long time now, Tessa. It was I who helped you complete that great aircraft of yours and I who convinced the Consortium that you could do the impossible and change the world's oil market once and for all. But such a claim must be proven before it can be paid.*"

More equivocating, she thought. More delays. Delays that were driving her toward bankruptcy.

Buran continued. "*The requirement is for a long-term, sustained rise in prices. One that would make the Consortium the most powerful oil cartel in the world. And simultaneously allow your company to become the largest alternative energy firm in the world.*"

Divide and conquer, you said. You get your half of the planet and we get ours. Isn't that how you sold it to me?"

"It was," she said. "And that's exactly how it will be. But I can't finish the job without more working capital."

Buran sighed. *"Tessa, you spend money faster than anyone I know. In hopes that this is your last request for an advance, I'm willing to extend to you an additional installment. But you'll have to agree to reduce your final payment . . . by a third."*

The condescension left her seething. But all that really mattered were the numbers. "Trade billions for a few million? I think not."

He shrugged. *"I told the others you wouldn't accept it, but I was obliged to make the offer. Unfortunately, that means we have nothing further to talk about, at least until it's clear that the price of oil will continue to get higher and remain so indefinitely into the future."*

"You're weakening your own position by weakening me," she said.

"You're anything but weak," Buran said with a smile. *"I suspect you'll have the world wrapped around your finger soon enough. Contact me when the conditions are irrefutably changed and I shall trumpet your achievements to the Consortium."*

The screen went dark. Tessa looked out the window at the smoke marring the dusky horizon. She felt certain that the market conditions were turning in her favor. Soon enough, Buran and his Consortium would be throwing money at her. And not only them—other investors, other companies, even powerful world governments. They'd be climbing all over one another to throw money at her. The hardest part would be deciding just how much to accept and from whom.

Tessa turned her attention to a second flat screen. It displayed the view outside the plane. A commotion in the water had frightened away a pair of the gulls that gave the island its name. As the birds flapped madly and propelled themselves into flight, a disk-shaped craft surfaced behind the plane.

"About time," she said to herself.

Without delay, Tessa got up and left the office. Striding through the aircraft, she traveled down a hall, passing her master suite and a control room behind the cockpit. A ladder took her to the middle deck, which held space for entertaining, including a marvelous lounge and a workout center where Tessa spent much of her time.

Another ladder took her to the lowest deck, with its unadorned metal decks and gray-painted walls. She walked aft along this deck, passing multiple vehicles, including a black Mercedes SUV and a silver Ferrari. Behind them were several ATVs, a pair of Jet Skis and two powerboats with large outboard engines.

Beyond the boats lay the tail end of the plane, which was comprised of a large door that lowered and doubled as a ramp. It was locked in the down position and two men wearing waders were standing halfway down the ramp up to their knees in water as they attached cables to the craft she'd seen on camera.

As it was pulled on board, the sleek disk revealed itself in detail. It had no conning tower or control fins to speak of, just various vents and panels that opened and closed to direct water across and through its hull, allowing it to pitch, roll and even rotate in any direction. It was powered by water jets instead of propellers, and a pair of bubble canopies on the top that resembled eyes covered the occupants.

All was not well, however, as Tessa noticed mechanical damage on the aft end of the hull and scrape marks near the nose.

As the craft was secured, one of the canopies opened and a man with peroxide-blond hair popped out. He was fit and muscular and looked to be in his mid-thirties. His face was angry and drawn.

"What happened?"

"There were problems," he said.

"I can see that," she replied. "Did you manage to get rid of the incubators?"

"The first set of the tankers were destroyed in the initial explosion," Volke said. "The other tankers were still in place. I used the explosives to destroy them. There's nothing but scrap metal on the bottom now. The tanks, the incubators, the injection systems—all of it has been obliterated."

"And what happened to the *Discus*?" she said, pointing to the damage on the submarine's hull.

Volke glanced at the scrapes. "I ran into some resistance down there. Another submersible."

"From the oil company?"

Volke shook his head. "No. It had a NUMA logo plastered on the side."

Tessa paused at that. She'd spent much of the last few years studying the design of submersibles, the methods used to build and recover things from the bottom of the sea. NUMA was very well known to her. Their presence concerned her. "What were they doing there?"

"I couldn't tell you," Volke said, "but you needn't worry. I dropped one of the magnetized charges on their hull. Whoever was operating that sub is now waiting in line at the Pearly Gates."

Done explaining himself, Volke jumped down and supervised the loading and storing of the *Discus*.

As he worked, another of her crewmen walked up the ramp. He was a burly man with a scruffy red beard. His name was Woodrich.

They called him Woods. He differed in appearance from Volke, big, lumbering, earthy, nothing polished about him. But he was a fanatical environmentalist and his devotion to the eradication of fossil fuels had been very useful to her so far.

"That fire is spewing poison all across the Gulf," Woods said. "That's not what we came here to do."

"Consider it creative destruction," she replied. "Sometimes you need to burn down the old world before you build a new one."

Woods could be as aggressive as Volke, but he tended to simmer quietly for a long time before blowing. For now, he held his tongue. That was enough for her.

"Get everything secured down here," she said, forcing them to work together. "And make it quick. We're leaving."

As Volke and Woods went to work securing the submarine, Tess made her way to the cockpit. The pilots were there, ready and waiting. "Time to go," she said.

Ten minutes later, the engines were roaring and the *Monarch* was accelerating along the smooth water behind Gull Island. As it picked up speed, the aircraft rode higher in the water, until only the very bottom of the keel was skimming the surface. All at once, it pulled free, soaring into the sky and shedding a trail of mist behind it.

12

RUDI GUNN was at the Capitol Building, briefing the congressional delegation from Louisiana on the latest developments in the Gulf, when Lance Alcott arrived.

Rudi acknowledged him silently and continued his explanation. When a short break was called, Alcott leaned over and whispered in Rudi's ear. "Just came from the White House," he said with glee. "Sorry to tell you, Rudi, NUMA's off the project and FEMA is taking over. We're going to be directing the Coast Guard on this."

Rudi was used to this kind of jockeying in Washington. Early on, when disaster was a distinct possibility, there was plenty of hand-wringing about who should take charge. Once the fires had been put out and the disaster avoided, everyone wanted to be seen as a hero of the cleanup. As the saying went, *Failure is an orphan, but success has a thousand fathers*. And it sounded like Alcott had just become a father. "By *project*, I assume you mean the Alpha Star disaster."

"I mean the whole thing," Alcott said. "The disaster, the cleanup, the investigation. Let's be honest, NUMA isn't really equipped to handle something like this. Your ships can go back to surveying wrecks or studying fish migrations or whatever it is you do most of the time."

Rudi stood. He was neither angry nor surprised. In all honesty, he was pleased. "What we do is whatever needs to be done." He slid a bulging file in front of Alcott. It was so full of papers it couldn't be closed. "Have fun with the senators. None of them are really happy right now."

Leaving Alcott behind, Rudi packed his briefcase and walked toward the door. On his way out, he passed the junior senator from Louisiana, who was coming back in.

"Where are you going?" the senator asked.

"Vacation," Rudi said with a grin.

And while Rudi hadn't taken a vacation in years, the idea suddenly appealed to him. At least until his phone buzzed with a call from the White House.

"Rudi Gunn," he said, holding the phone to his ear and making his way down the hall.

"*Rudi, this is Sandecker,*" a voice said over the phone.

James Sandecker was the founder of NUMA and its leader for several decades before he'd accepted a position as the Vice President. He and Rudi had worked side by side for years and had a friendship that trumped politics and policy. A rare find in Washington these days.

"Mr. Vice President," Rudi said cordially. "What can I do for you today?"

"*For starters, you can stop calling me Mr. Vice President,*" Sandecker said. "*Admiral will do just fine.*"

Rudi almost laughed. Old habits die hard and Sandecker had been an admiral far longer than he'd been the VP. "Yes, Admiral."

"*And when you're done snickering at that, you can make your way over to the White House. The President wants to talk to you about this Alpha Star catastrophe.*"

Rudi stopped in the hall. "Afraid I was just relieved from that post."

"*I know you were,*" Sandecker said. "*It was my idea. Need to free you and NUMA up for something else. Something more important.*"

Rudi didn't like it when Sandecker played things close to the vest. It usually meant things were worse than they seemed. "I'm almost to the door now. I'll walk down Pennsylvania Ave and see you in a few minutes."

"*Turn around,*" Sandecker said. "*Head downstairs to the mailroom. Need you to take the train. We don't want anyone to see you arrive or leave today.*"

"I'm sneaking into the White House?"

"*Yes, you are,*" Sandecker said.

Rudi put the phone away and backtracked into the heart of the Capitol Building, eventually making his way into the underground mailroom as Sandecker had requested. There, he flashed his ID and was escorted by a member of the Secret Service to another, deeper level, where he hopped on a small train.

To call it a *train* was an overstatement. There was only one car, about a third the size of a standard subway or Metro car. It sat on a narrow-gauge set of rails only three feet apart. Once he and the Secret Service agent were seated, the train began to move, accelerating briskly and silently into a lighted tunnel.

The ride was incredibly smooth and quiet. The tracks were polished and gleaming in the light.

As the track curved to the left, Rudi noticed a siding and a small platform. Doors leading from the platform were sealed and locked, but Rudi knew Washington's layout as if he had a map printed in his head. Considering the speed, direction and time, they'd just passed the National Archives Building. Interesting place for a secret subway stop, he thought.

A minute later, the car slowed, coming to a halt in front of a formidable steel door.

Reaching out of the tram, the Secret Service agent typed in a code and then placed his hand on a scanner.

Rudi recognized the device. It not only checked the agent's fingerprints, it measured his heart rate and skin temperature. The theory was, if he were being coerced into betraying the President, his heart would be beating faster than normal and his skin would be registering a higher temperature. In which case, entry would be denied.

The same held true if he'd been drugged or, even worse, if his hand had been forcibly removed from his body. No heartbeat, low temperature, anything out of the ordinary, and the steel doors— thick enough to keep Superman out—would remain closed.

"What happens if you get nervous?" Rudi asked.

The agent looked at him without smiling. "Reassignment to other duties."

Fortunately, the agent wasn't the nervous type and his heart rate checked out. The doors opened and seconds later they were pulling into the White House subterranean station.

After passing through two more layers of security, Rudi found himself in an elevator, which let him out in the Emergency Operations Room. This was not the normal Situation Room but a bunker-like facility two levels below the main building.

The President was there, along with Vice President Sandecker. A third man, with narrow features and gray hair, sat beside them. His ID badge had the Energy Department logo on it.

Introductions were made and Rudi learned that the man's name was Leonard Hallsman. He carried the cumbersome title of Undersecretary of National Resources and Energy Security. "I use it to impress and confuse people," Hallsman insisted. "I'm a scientist, actually. A geologist specializing in oil reserve estimates."

Rudi shook Hallsman's hand and sat down. "We seem to be awash in oil these days. Does that make your job easier or harder?"

"Both," Hallsman said. "But it doesn't raise my pay."

A round of soft laughter circled the table and Rudi got to the point. "I assume this has something to do with the Alpha Star incident. Am I being taken out behind the woodshed or given a gold star?"

The President leaned forward. "Gold star wouldn't cover it," he said. "What your people managed to do in such a short period of time was incredible. I'd give them an award, but Jim says they'd never accept it."

"The Admiral's right," Rudi said. "But send over a case of Don Julio Silver tequila and you'll have their eternal gratitude."

"I'll see what I can arrange," the President said. "You know, when I picked Jim to be my VP, I did it mostly for political reasons. I also knew enough about what he'd been able to do with NUMA to know it was top-notch from stem to stern. I've only had that idea reinforced during my term as President. Your actions during the *Nighthawk* incident prevented a worldwide calamity and your operatives' quick thinking and tenacity in Japan last year not only prevented a second calamity, it saved an alliance that's crucial to world stability. As I understand it, some of the same people involved in those incidents are the ones out in the Gulf right now."

"That's correct," Rudi said. "Kurt Austin and Joe Zavala."

"Can they keep their mouths shut?"

Rudi wondered where this was going. "I'm sure you've already asked your Vice President about that. He hired them. He brought them up through the ranks. I'll defer to him on that question."

The President sat back and then glanced at his VP. "You really know how to pick them, Jim."

"I got lucky," the Vice President said. "Should we cut to the chase?"

"By all means," the President said. He looked across the table to the geologist from the Energy Department. "Hallsman, the show is yours."

The first thing Hallsman did was slide a file across the desk to Rudi. It was far thinner than the one Rudi had left with Alcott.

Rudi slid his hand under the band and broke the seal, opening it. The first page showed a map of the world, with pie charts on each continent showing the total oil reserves. There were sections for proven reserves, unproven but estimated reserves and, finally, theoretical recover scenarios.

The second page was a chart depicting total world oil supply over the years and dividing it into used-up and remaining amounts. The numbers went up continuously, with the estimated recoverable supply climbing each decade, even though nearly a trillion barrels of oil had been extracted from the earth since the 1850s.

Rudi looked through the numbers. "As I said, awash in oil."

"Yes and no," Hallsman said.

"I'm not sure where you get the *no* part," Rudi said. "The amount of recoverable oil has gone up by thirty billion barrels in the last decade alone."

"Most of that is a result of the fracking revolution," Hallsman said. "But, at any rate, these numbers are estimates. At this point, they can only be described as deliberately fudged estimates."

Rudi put the papers down. "What are you telling me?"

"About eighteen months ago, we noticed an odd pattern," Hallsman said. "Fields around the world that had been producing successfully for years suddenly began to run dry. At first, it seemed irrelevant. There was so much oil around, the big companies just shuttered the dying wells and opened the spigots on other projects. Supply remained abundant. The price remained low."

"*At first,*" Rudi said, repeating Hallsman's words. "Am I to assume we're no longer in that *first* phase?"

Hallsman continued without answering the question. "Initially, we thought it might be caused by bad drilling techniques or wasteful, inefficient recovery systems, but the occurrences were too widespread. Over the next year, we began getting reports of dying fields in Africa, the Middle East and Malaysia, as well as similar tales coming from Venezuela and Russia—"

The President broke in. "Central Intelligence confirmed that the Russians were having a horrible time keeping up production, drilling two wells for every one that went dry and still losing ground."

"It's the same in every country," Hallsman said. "Fields that had been producing for years and were expected to have decades of life were slowing to a trickle or drying up completely in a matter of months. Even newly discovered fields are being affected."

"Could it be a supplier's trick?" Rudi asked. "A way to rattle the market and drive up the price? They've done that before. I recall hearing as a kid that there wouldn't be any oil left by the year 2000. That didn't turn out to be true."

"Not by a long shot," Sandecker said. "And a few years back, it was peak oil and a downhill slope for reserves that would never be reversed. That wasn't true either."

Rudi looked at Hallsman "But you think this is different."

"For two reasons," Hallsman said. "First, if someone is trying to convince the world that the oil is running out, they're doing a lousy job of advertising it. Every nation dealing with these changes has gone to great lengths to pretend it's business as usual and the oil is still flowing freely. The false numbers I gave you came directly from nations that have been hit hardest by this sudden change."

"Can't tell the world that the oil is running out when you're too busy telling them you have plenty," Sandecker added.

"Agreed," Rudi said and then turned back to Hallsman. "You mentioned two reasons. What's the second one?"

"Because the effects are now hitting home," Hallsman said. "Six months ago, a large North Slope oil field in Alaska went into a rapid decline. From half a million barrels a day to a quarter of that in six weeks. It has continued dropping to less than a tenth of the normal production and is still falling. Randomly scattered fields in Texas, Oklahoma and California have gone through the same thing. And the offshore field that Alpha Star and the other platforms were attempting to revive crashed even more dramatically. In eight weeks it went from full production to nothing."

Rudi nodded. He could see the connection.

"Taken individually, these things don't add up to much," Sandecker said. "But when you step back, you can see a different picture emerging. Oil fields going dormant all around the world, the corporations and companies who own them powerless to revive them and desperate to cover up the losses. And now a human element connected to the events. This is an act of war. A worldwide act. But by who and for what purpose, we don't know."

Rudi looked at the chart again. "What are the real numbers?"

Hallsman slid another paper toward him. It showed recoverable reserves down nearly fifty percent in the last eighteen months.

"Aside from those of us in this room," the President said, "very few others know the full scope of what's happening. And we'd like to keep it that way. That's why we're not launching a big public investigation and why you'll need to be discreet in everything NUMA does. I don't want other agencies involved. That leads to leaks, which leads to us losing control of the message, which leads to panic."

"I understand that," Rudi said, "but how is the price of oil not skyrocketing already?"

Hallsman explained. "A glut of oil that had been built up in tankers and storage facilities around the world has cushioned the blow. That supply has largely been used up. To fill the void, we've been releasing oil from the strategic reserve. We think the Chinese are doing the same from their own reserves. But those actions will only keep the lid on for so long. Once the public gets wind of this, people will panic. Traders will bid the prices through the roof and everyone will scramble to grab what's left on the table."

"How bad is it going to get?"

"Two hundred dollars a barrel by the fall," Hallsman suggested. "And if current trends are not reversed, seven to eight hundred dollars a barrel a year from now is not out of the question. I don't have to tell you what happens if we get there."

"We'll never get to seven hundred dollars a barrel," Sandecker said. "World economic collapse, multiple wars and global depression will hit before then."

Rudi nodded. "Scarcity has been a precursor to war since the caveman walked the earth. What is it you want NUMA to do, Mr. President?"

"Based on what your people discovered in the Gulf, we have our first direct evidence that there's a man-made cause to this," the President said. "I want NUMA to figure out who it is, what they're doing and why. And if possible, find a way to stop it. We know there's oil down in those fields, but it's no use to anyone if we can't get at it without blowing ourselves up."

Rudi sat back. "That's a tall order. Wouldn't the CIA and FBI be better used to investigate this?"

The President shook his head. "Those two organizations have their own areas of proficiency, but there are factors here that go beyond what they do. To begin with, we have no idea how many offshore fields have been compromised. But when the final tally comes in, we expect it to be extensive. I have no doubt we'll need NUMA's aquatic expertise to both establish and deal with that issue. More importantly, you people in NUMA get things done. Those other agencies spend a lot of time talking about getting things done. We don't have time for that."

Rudi nodded. He would leave no stone unturned as he attempted to fulfill the President's request. "I appreciate your faith in us. I'll do everything I can to get to the bottom of this."

The President stood and everyone around the table did likewise. "Good," he said. "The sooner, the better. Otherwise, my limo will be a horse and buggy by the year's end."

13

ELEVEN COFFINS lay on the deck of the *Raleigh* the morning after the disaster. Inside the coffins rested the bodies of ten men and one woman, all crew members from the oil platforms.

Some had died in the explosion, others were burned to death, still others had few obvious injuries but had been overcome by the toxic fumes or drowned trying to swim to safety.

A dozen additional roughnecks remained missing.

Standing by them, Kurt wondered briefly about each life that had ended prematurely. What had they left behind? What dreams had they never been given a chance to fulfill?

Captain Brooks came up and remained respectfully silent for a moment before speaking. "Sad day," he said. "You did all you could. More than anyone could expect."

Kurt nodded. He wasn't thinking about the past but the future. He shifted his eyes from the coffins to the horizon.

"Somewhere out there, the people who did this are reading the headlines and celebrating," he said. "They might even be laughing with glee. Whoever they are, they're not going to be so happy when I find them."

"Three of our own crewmen are in the sick bay with smoke in-halation and lung damage. Another crewman has chemical burns on him from pulling one of these bodies out of the water. So, when you find whoever did this . . . you give them my regards."

Kurt nodded. "With pleasure."

Brooks changed the subject. "Paul and Gamay Trout are on their way in. Joe's waiting for you inside. He's been taking apart whatever device you pulled off that submersible. Asked me to send you his way if I saw you."

"Thanks," Kurt said.

Kurt stepped inside and found Joe in one of the *Raleigh*'s recovery holds, where artifacts and salvaged items were stored during a mission.

There, Joe had taken apart what they'd assumed was a battery pack and was examining it under a small microscope.

"Making progress?" Kurt asked.

"Depends on your definition of the term," Joe said. "I called everyone I know in the submersible business, no one has even heard of a disk-shaped submersible, not even a design concept for one."

"Must have been built in-house somewhere," Kurt said. "That might help us narrow down the list of suspects. What about this battery pack?"

"It's not a battery pack," Joe said. "It's a fuel cell. But its design and materials are like nothing I've ever seen. Very advanced stuff."

"Must be, if you can't figure it out," Kurt said. "Know anyone who can?"

Joe nodded. "I have a friend in Florida who might be able to help. Her name is Misty."

"As long as she's discreet and trustworthy, I'm game."

"Misty's a lot of things," Joe said with an odd look on his face. "I can't exactly explain her to you. But she fits your requirements and she's an electronics genius."

"Perfect," Kurt said. "Pack this up. We'll leave on the helicopter that's bringing in Paul and Gamay."

14

GAMAY TROUT peered through the bubble canopy of the Hughes 500 helicopter as it traveled across the Gulf at an altitude of five thousand feet. She had her seat pulled so far forward that the curved acrylic of the windshield ran up above her head. She could see sky and horizon above and around her. She could see past the rudder pedals at her feet to the shimmering sea below.

"When I lean forward, it feels like I'm flying an invisible jet, like Wonder Woman."

"Glad you're enjoying this," a voice said from behind her. "When I lean forward, I hit my chin on the back of your chair."

"So, lean back."

"Then I hit my head on the ceiling."

Gamay twisted around to see her husband, Paul, having folded himself into an area that was far too small for an individual only a few inches shy of seven feet.

Gamay turned to the pilot, who was a member of the NUMA aviation division. "How long before we arrive?"

He pointed across his body to a column of smoke in the distance. "We had to swing wide," he said, "so we could come in upwind and stay out of the smoke. But we'll be landing in five minutes."

The pilot's estimation proved spot-on as he set the egg-shaped helicopter down directly on top of the *H* precisely five minutes later.

Gamay unlatched her seat belt and waited for the rotors to stop before popping open the side door. She climbed out, pulled a helmet off and shook out her red-wine-colored hair. She couldn't see the fire in the distance, but from the sheer volume of smoke being produced, it was obvious that the fires were still raging.

Paul climbed from the helicopter behind her, arched his back and stretched. Several audible cracks accompanied his realignment. "Ahhh . . ." he said. "That's better."

"About time you two got here," a voice said from the hatchway beyond the helipad.

Both Gamay and Paul turned to see Kurt standing there. His silver hair was tucked under a NUMA ball cap.

"Where's the Alpha Star platform?" Gamay asked. "We couldn't see it from the air."

"It went down late last night," Kurt said.

He walked up, gave Gamay a hug and then shook Paul's hand.

Stepping up beside her once again, Kurt offered to shoulder one of their bags. Gamay noticed the raw color of Kurt's palm. It looked like a bad sunburn. She assumed it came from the fire.

She pulled her backpack up onto her shoulder. "That's okay," she said. "We packed light. Now, what exactly is it you need us for?"

Kurt waved them toward the hatch. "Your job is to collect samples of the gas that's venting down below, figure out what it is and where it's coming from. All we know about it at the moment is that it's toxic, explosive, and it burns hot enough to melt steel. And the unsavory fact that it reacts with water, igniting upon contact."

"So you said," Paul replied. "That's rare. Especially for a gas. Are you sure it's not another liquid or a solid dissolved in the flow of liquids?"

"We're not sure of anything," Kurt said. "That's why you're here and why Joe and I are leaving it in your capable hands."

"You're not sticking around?" Paul asked.

"We have something else to take care of," Kurt said.

At that point, Joe appeared in the passageway carrying a pack and some large items that had been hastily boxed up in cardboard and wrapped in an overabundance of duct tape.

"Souvenir," Joe said, heading to the helicopter.

Kurt took Paul and Gamay inside, showing them to their quarters. "One other thing," he said. "You need to pretend that all you're doing is studying the environmental impact of the fires. FEMA and the Coast Guard are technically in charge of everything else."

"Why not let them handle this as well?"

"Because someone very high up wants us to do it and they want it done in secret."

Gamay stared at Kurt as he explained what Rudi had told him. "They'll never keep this quiet for long," she said.

"We'll let them worry about that," Kurt said. "Just find out what you can."

"And what will you be doing in the meantime?" Paul asked.

"Meeting one of Joe's ex-girlfriends," Kurt said.

Kurt's sly grin did nothing to ease Gamay's sense that she and Paul were getting the short end of the stick, but she also knew Kurt would never take the easy road out. "Good luck with that."

"You, too," Kurt said. "Keep me posted. And watch your backs."

15

EIGHT SHIPS from different sources clustered in the sea west of the fires. Two Coast Guard ships, two tugs, NUMA's *Raleigh*, one tender operated by the Navy and two other ships chartered by FEMA.

To make the mixed fleet work together, the head of FEMA had put representatives with satellite phones on each boat to coordinate with the captains and crews. Derrick Reynolds had come aboard NUMA's boat.

He was nearly forty, had grown up around Louisiana and had worked two dozen oil spills in the last decade. He knew how hard it was to get the oil companies or the government agencies to admit they'd done anything wrong. There would be hearings, committee meetings, maybe even fines—which the oil companies would pass on to their customers—but things never changed.

He hoped this time would prove different. He hoped this time there would be action, that the regulations would change or a total ban on offshore oil would be put into place. He hoped for these things, but he doubted any of it would happen.

After *Deepwater Horizon*, he'd given up on government action and began acting on his own. He'd met others who thought like him and they'd brought him into a loose underground network. Knowing he was on the scene, someone from that network had reached out to him. And Reynolds intended to answer.

Watching through a pair of binoculars, he studied the Hughes 500 as it took off and headed northeast. After reading the tail number, he made a call on his satellite phone. But it wasn't being placed to FEMA.

"This is Reynolds," he said, identifying himself. "I have the information you requested."

There was a brief pause before the party on the far end of the line responded. *"Please continue,"* an electronically filtered voice said.

"Two new arrivals," he said. "Both named Trout. A biologist and a geologist, based on their listed profiles. From what I've learned, they're here to look at the eco impact."

His contact didn't seem too concerned. *"Anything else?"*

"Two of the other NUMA personnel left on the helicopter. They were carrying some oddly shaped equipment. I couldn't get close enough to see what it was, but the rumor is, they brought something up from the failed blowout preventer."

"Interesting," the voice said. *"Where are they going?"*

"The helicopter took on a lot of fuel. One of them said something about New Orleans."

"Give me the tail number."

"N541NM," he said. "It was a NUMA helicopter."

A brief delay followed. *"They lied about the destination. That helicopter is traveling to Pensacola, not New Orleans. They're already beginning to manipulate the truth. Be careful. Contact us if you see anything else out of the ordinary.*"

As he broke the link, Reynolds considered the lies. It meant NUMA was part of the cover-up. That was too bad—he'd heard good things about the organization, indications that they'd done their fair share to care for the environment. Apparently, that was only window dressing and they were just part of the big-government machine like everyone else.

16

KURT AND JOE borrowed a car from the Navy motor pool after landing at the Pensacola Naval Air Station. Driving west, they cruised along the coast for a while, before cutting inland over marshes and wetland areas.

"So, who is this mysterious Misty Moon Littlefeather?" Kurt asked. "Old fiancée? Love of your life?"

"She's a friend," Joe said. "Her dad wouldn't have her dating a Navy man."

"Ah-ha," Kurt said, grinning. "The one that got away."

"Trust me," Joe said. "I did more of the getting away. And you're having too much fun with this."

Kurt laughed. "I can't wait to meet her."

The drive from Pensacola took them back along the beaches and across a portion of the wetlands. They didn't notice anyone following them because there wasn't anyone following them, but neither of them noticed a drone tracking them from high above.

Thirty minutes later, they pulled onto a dirt road and then onto a private stretch of land complete with a pristine beach. At the end of the road lay a group of trailers, one of which was attached to a wooden barn. Nearby were several pens with animals grazing and, beyond that, piles of electronic junk stacked up in mounds ten feet high.

A dock made from weathered gray planks stuck out into the water. An old man, tanned as a baseball glove, stood on the dock, fishing. He didn't react as they pulled up.

Joe got out of the car. "Better let me do the talking."

Kurt opened the trunk. "I'll get your effects."

Joe walked on ahead, making his way past a pen with baby goats and a second that corralled a small pack of stray-looking dogs. Finally, he made it onto the dock. The old man was reeling in his line when Joe approached.

"This is Seminole land," the man said. "You government people have no right to be here."

"What makes you think we're government people?" Joe replied.

"Your license plates are government issue," the man said, before casting his line again. "And I know you, Joe Zavala."

Joe was amazed. Misty's father hadn't seen him in ten years and had only glanced at him for a few seconds as he walked from the car. "Redfish, you have a mind like a steel trap."

The man looked at him and turned his attention back to the water. "I do. And I haven't forgotten how I caught you messing around with Misty all those years ago."

Joe offered his hand and then retracted it when it became obvious Redfish wasn't going to shake it. "I tried to explain," Joe said, "but you were chasing me with a baseball bat at the time. Hard to talk sense when you're running for your life."

Redfish smiled. "You could have made the Olympic team that day."

Joe laughed at that. "I probably could have."

"Okay, Joe," Redfish said, "I forgive you. Misty's inside, if you want to see her."

"I want to show her something." Joe paused when he realized that sounded a little like how the incident began years ago. "Electronics," he clarified. "I need her to look at some electronics for me."

Redfish shook his head and laughed and then cast the line out with an easy flick of the wrist. It made a peaceful sound as the reel unspooled. "I still have that bat," he said as Joe walked away. "And you're probably a lot slower these days."

Joe made his way up a wooden ramp to the trailer that was connected to the barn. He knocked on the door and then opened it, ringing the old-fashioned bell that was attached to it with a string.

The sound of wheels on the floor came next and a figure in overalls slid backward into the room on a rolling mechanic's seat.

Joe smiled. "Hello, Misty."

Misty had an oval face, long, dark hair that was woven together in a French braid and several piercings through her right eyebrow that made it look like she was permanently squinting.

Spying Joe, she shook her head. "Just look what the tide brought in," she said in a boisterous voice.

Laughing, she rolled back to her workbench, put down the tools she was holding and came over to greet Joe properly, wrapping her arms around him in a bear hug and kissing him on the lips.

With Redfish's warning still fresh in his mind, Joe did nothing to reciprocate.

Pulling back, she fixed her gaze on him suspiciously. "You owe me money," she said as if suddenly remembering. "Eight dollars. I loaned it to you for lunch the last time I saw you."

Kurt walked in just then. "Never borrow money from someone with a photographic memory," he told Joe and then turned to Misty. "Kurt Austin," he said, extending a hand. "I suggest you make him pay penalties and interest, compounded daily."

Joe raised a hand as if he was about to mount a defense and then thought better of it. "What is all this?" he asked, looking around.

"My repair shop, salvage facility and gold mining operation," Misty said.

"Gold mine?"

"Did you see all the computers and phones outside?" she asked.

Both of them nodded.

"That's where the gold is," she said. "And platinum and other valuable items that can be extracted. People throw everything out nowadays. Computers and TVs and phones. They get tossed because the cost of parts to repair the old one is more expensive than getting a brand-new one. I help people recycle, repair and repurpose instead of replacing. But most people just want a way to get rid of their junk. I take it off their hands, extract the precious metals and recycle what's left."

She spoke with giddy enthusiasm, explaining the rest of her operation, stopping only to take sips from an extra-large soft drink, twirl her braid or wrap her arms around Joe's shoulder. She squeezed him tight in the middle of one explanation and punched him in the arm when he seemed a little slow on the uptake.

When she left for a moment, Kurt leaned in and whispered, "I'm getting the bigger picture now. I think her father may have used the bat on the wrong party."

"I tried to tell him," Joe said, "but that just made it worse."

Kurt laughed, and Misty soon reappeared with another soft drink in her hand.

"So, what have you brought me?"

Kurt placed the package on the bench and removed the conduit and power pack from the box.

Misty looked at it, then put on a pair of magnifying glasses, like surgeons sometimes wore. "Weird stuff, Joe. Most guys just bring roses."

"I know you'd prefer electronics to flowers."

"You got me there," she said. "This is unique. We're going to need a closer look. May I?"

With a nod from Joe, she picked up the conduit and power pack and took them to another bench. There, she pulled the cover off an expensive piece of lab equipment. "Scanning microscope, very expensive. The university sold it to me for a song . . . Not a literal song," she corrected. "I had to pay, but only a fraction of what it was worth. They were getting a new one anyway."

Placing the strangely dense power pack underneath the scanning beam, Misty changed the magnification. At a power of 100, the battery pack looked like a collection of silica dust. At a power of 1,000, they began to see a structure to the arrangement. At a power of 2,500, they could see individual cells in a honeycomb formation and a thin barrier in the center of each tube.

"It's a combo unit," Misty said. "Part battery, part fuel cell."

"Fuel cell?"

"Takes hydrogen, mixes it with oxygen and creates electricity and freshwater. Although this may use other chemicals as well."

"I know what a fuel cell is," Joe said. "But there is a stored electrical charge in there."

"That's unusual for sure," Misty said.

She ran a couple of additional tests, checking the load-generating and electrical charge capacity of the unit. "Based on how tightly this design is packed and depending on the fuel source, I'd say this small unit would produce a lot more power than your average cell. In fact, the battery portion alone would be enough to power a car for several hundred miles."

"Car battery packs weigh hundreds of pounds," Joe pointed out.

"This one wouldn't," she said. "Then again, it might cost more than a Rolls-Royce to build this thing. I've never seen anything like it, even on the NASA probes."

Kurt asked the important question. "Any idea who might be working on something like this?"

"My first thought would be government, NASA or DoD," she replied. "But if that was the case, you guys would know about it, wouldn't you?" She turned to Joe. "Did you liberate this from somewhere overseas?"

"Under the sea," Joe corrected. "We tore it off a submersible that attacked us."

"That's the Joe I know," she said. "Always in one scrape or another. Apparently, not much has changed."

Joe couldn't deny that. "We want to find out who built this power pack and, if possible, who built the sub that attacked us. And, we're hoping you can point us in the right direction."

"It'll cost you dinner and a movie," she said. "Plus, flowers—I'm still a girl."

"He'll pick you up in a limo," Kurt said, accepting on Joe's behalf.

She grinned and looked at the design again, studying different parts of the fuel cell itself and then the connectors and even the type of wiring. "These connectors are pure gold, the type used in high-end electric cars. This type of wiring is often used in high-performance aircraft. The fuel cell itself would probably be a prototype. I can't tell you who built it, but I can tell you where you might look next."

"All ears," Joe said.

"And Redfish thinks you're all hands."

"That was you," Joe said. "And you should have told him the truth before he attacked me."

"And ruin the fun of watching him chase you?"

Kurt coughed loudly. "Hate to break up this love connection, but you were going to suggest a place we might look for answers."

Misty grinned. "Sorry. There's a big conference going on in Bermuda. It starts tomorrow. It's called the R3 Conference, Renewables, Redesign and Reward. It's an engineering conference where cutting-edge designers take their ideas, prototypes and finished products to get venture capital. You'll find hundreds of brilliant nerds there, most of them looking for handouts from millionaires and billionaires looking to put their excess cash to work. Someone there will recognize this design, I can almost guarantee it."

"R3," Joe said.

"Sounds like the place to start," Kurt said.

Before another word was spoken, the dogs started barking outside. All of them at once. Several gunshots followed and the barking turned to the sound of yelping dogs running from danger.

Misty got up and sprinted for the front of the building, Joe chased her down, tackling her to the ground just as a shotgun blast exploded through the thin front door.

17

JOE AND MISTY hit the ground as the front door swung in from the impact of the buckshot. It slammed against the wall and rebounded to a closed position. The barking and yelping continued outside, accompanied by the sound of heavy boots charging up the wooden ramp to the front door.

"Let me go," Misty shouted. "I have to get to Dad."

"Redfish can take care of himself," Joe said, pulling her to her feet. "We need to get out of here."

As Joe dragged a reluctant Misty back toward the workroom, the door was kicked open. A large-framed man pushed into the doorway with a pump-action shotgun in his hand. He spotted Joe and Misty and turned toward them, but before he could level the shotgun, the wheeled mechanic's stool came flying down the concrete floor and slammed into his shins, courtesy of a mighty shove from Kurt.

The impact buckled his legs and he stumbled forward, discharging the shotgun into the floor at point-blank range. The barrel of the shotgun blew apart, spraying shrapnel everywhere.

Bleeding, stunned and grasping his numb right arm, the intruder crawled backward and out through the door.

Joe gave Misty a gentle shove in Kurt's direction and then sprinted forward to grab the damaged shotgun.

With the shotgun in hand, he ran back to join Kurt and Misty. "This thing is useless," he said, examining the barrel. "Might be good for a warning shot or last line of defense."

Kurt turned to Misty. "Do you have any weapons out here?"

"In the main house," she said. "My dad has a thirty-aught-six and I have two revolvers."

"Can we get there from here?" Joe asked.

"It's about a hundred yards," Misty said. "Back through the brush. But I'm worried about Dad. We can't just leave him out there."

"If they had him, they'd be using him as leverage by now," Kurt said. "Telling us to come out or else. He's probably hightailing it to your house, too. Either that or he's hiding."

"Probably looking for his bat," Joe added.

Misty smiled nervously.

"Let's go," Kurt said.

They doused the lights, went to the back door and paused. Peering through the screen door at the back of the trailer, they saw a problem.

"We've been surrounded," Joe said.

There were three men out back. One taking cover behind a tree, a second hiding by a corrugated steel shed, a third crouching and inching forward through the brush. As the men waited to ambush them, a drone buzzed over the top of them.

"I have an ATV," Misty said, pointing up. "We could speed past them on it."

Joe looked up. On a metal ramp above them sat a small four-wheeler. He gave Kurt a knowing look. "Beats running."

THE GROUP OF MEN who'd attacked the house had been getting information from the drone flying overhead. The unofficial leader of the group, a man named Bricks, did most of the talking and listening. He held his hand against an earpiece and listened for more information.

He'd been told by the drone operator that an old man was on the dock, fishing, and the others were in the main trailer, blissfully unaware that they were being watched.

But when Bricks and his men arrived, the old man was gone. All they found was a lonely fishing rod resting on the planks of the dock, the line jumping just a bit, his having gotten a bite.

As they looked around for him, a pack of dogs appeared out of nowhere, charging and swarming around them like wolves. A few shots scattered the dogs, but the element of surprise was gone.

Bricks had sent his largest man into the building only to see him come stumbling back out, bleeding and without his weapon. "Careful," he shouted to his men. "We got bad intel on this. These targets are more dangerous than we've been told."

As the men took cover, Bricks argued with the drone operator. "I'm telling you they're armed," he said into the radio. "One of my men is already down."

"You're not living up to my expectations," the voice on the radio told him. *"You have six men against four and one of those four is an elderly man. Eliminate them quickly and get yourselves out of there."*

Bricks gripped his 9mm pistol and looked at the damaged front door. He had three men out back. His injured point man and another shooter, plus himself, out front. "What's the view from the drone?" he asked. "Where's the old man?"

"Forget about the old man," the voice told him. *"Get in there and do what I'm paying you for."*

Bricks knew the truth—fail this job and the next hitman would be looking for him. He charged forward, firing into the door as he went. Reaching the flimsy door, he kicked it open, ducked to the side and then dove through the gap, firing blindly in all directions as he hit the floor.

He hit no one, but not for lack of trying. There was no one inside.

The sound of a two-stroke engine roared from the barn side of the structure.

Bricks got off the floor and ran toward the sound, reaching the back door just in time to see an ATV racing out of the building and charging across the grass. Right between his men.

They reacted too slowly, turning and firing at the four-wheeler, but the vehicle sped on and the men charged after it.

Bricks paused. There was something odd about the ATV. It had a blanket trailing from it, something wrapped up inside, but . . .

A thud sounded behind him. Bricks froze as something jabbed him in the back. "This shotgun might not work that well anymore," a male voice said, "but it'll blow your guts out if I pull the trigger."

Bricks raised his hands instinctively. The dark-haired man they'd labeled *Target 1* took the pistol from his hand and gave it to the woman who lived there. Relieved of his weapon, Bricks was forced to the ground.

In a minute, he was tied up and gagged. The two men who'd come inside with him were in the same condition. The other three hadn't stopped chasing the ATV. He knew at that moment, it was a job he should never have taken.

18

WITH THREE of the attackers subdued and their weapons now in friendly hands, Kurt sensed they'd improved their position greatly. "We've evened the odds," he said, "but we're not in the clear yet."

As if to prove his point, the drone buzzed back, turned and made a strafing run, unleashing a quick hail of bullets as it passed.

Kurt glanced down at the leader of the group. "You don't look like the type to own an armed, high-performance drone. Who are you working for? Who hired you?"

The man shook his head and Kurt noticed the tiny bud stuffed into the man's ear. He yanked it free. "This is highly unsanitary, but . . ."

Putting the earbud in his own ear, Kurt picked up the chatter from whoever was directing the operation.

"You idiots, they're still in the main building," an electronically distorted voice said. *"The four-wheeler was just a diversion."*

Another voice chimed in. *"Any sign of the old man? He's not in the main house."*

"They haven't found your dad," Kurt whispered to Misty.

"I told Bricks to forget about him. Get back to the main building and burn it down."

"They're going to burn us out," Kurt said. "We need to hide. Woods or the water?"

"Can't burn water," Joe said.

"We can hide in the reeds, near the estuary," Misty said. "That's where Dad fishes when he's not on the dock."

Kurt glanced out the door, waited for the drone to make another pass and then took off running.

They'd passed the animal pens and the piles of computer hardware before they were spotted.

"Targets running to the northwest. Away from the buildings."

Kurt listened to every word. He couldn't even tell if it was a man or a woman, but there was a pattern to the words, short sentences, clipped delivery. He would remember that pattern for the future.

"We'll cut them off," an unmodified voice replied.

The sound of the ATV was growing louder as they ran.

"They have the ATV," Kurt said. "How far do we have to go?"

"Just over the hill," Misty said.

By now, the drone was turning toward them and setting up for another attack run. It locked in and accelerated, the propeller buzzing feverishly as it approached.

Kurt, Joe and Misty sprinted down the hill toward a shallow, reed-filled glade. But even as they ran, the drone bore down on them, opening fire.

Kurt dove to the side as the dirt kicked up at his feet. Joe and Misty darted in the other direction and the trail of bullets passed between them.

The drone raced by, leveled off at ten feet and then flew out over the water. Just as it tilted upward to climb and turn, a figure appeared out of the marsh and fired several shots with a rifle.

The drone jerked to one side with the first hit, lost part of a wing with the second and then burst into flames with the third. It fell in a corkscrew motion, spinning out of control and slamming into the placid water with a large splash.

"Dad," Misty shouted.

Redfish stood in the reeds, soaking wet and holding the thirty-aught-six. He hugged Misty with one arm as she ran up to him.

"Be glad he chased you with a bat," Kurt said.

"Believe me," Joe said, "I am."

The ATV and the men on foot were the next danger.

"Over here," Redfish said. "They'll never see us."

Kurt and Joe dropped into the shallow water with Misty and her father. Crouching and waiting, they watched as the ATV came over the ridge.

At first, it traveled on a diagonal, coming down toward the water but not directly for them. The rider slowed and looked around as he drove.

The other men came over the ridge behind it. They'd rescued their leader and were now back to full strength. One of them held a scope to his eyes.

Kurt and the others were crouched down in the water and hidden behind a layer of reeds. They would be difficult to see, but they were not invisible.

"If they spot us," Kurt said, "open fire."

He gripped the pistol firmly, in both hands, set the hammer and rested his finger on the trigger.

When the man with the scope turned toward them, Kurt pulled the trigger. The spotter went down in a heap and at the same instant Redfish fired and knocked the rider off the ATV.

The other men scattered. Instead of pressing their attack, they grabbed their injured comrades and took off, heading for the cars they'd come in.

With two vehicles racing away, Kurt and Joe emerged from the water.

"Do you think they'll come back?" Misty asked.

"Unlikely," Kurt said. "These men had nothing personal against you. They were hired to stop us. Still, you might want to put in a call to the sheriff and find another place to stay for a while."

"The sheriff is Dad's fishing buddy," Misty said. "I'm sure he wouldn't mind staying over for a few days."

Knowing that Misty and Redfish would be safe, Kurt and Joe said their good-byes. Misty gave Joe one more bone-crunching hug and then let him get into the car.

"You come back, if you want to," Redfish said. "But no funny business."

Joe promised and then climbed into the car. "Home, James," he said to Kurt.

"Only if home is Hamilton, Bermuda."

19

PAUL TROUT found himself thankful that the *Raleigh* carried several ROVs. He'd been underwater in plenty of NUMA's submersibles. Not one of them had enough head- or legroom for him. He was much more comfortable sitting in the air-conditioned confines of OSLO.

Gamay sat beside him. "Take a sediment sample outside the impact zone for a baseline. We can take a few more as we get closer to ground zero."

Paul did as requested, directing the ROV to hover over the bottom, where it extended a tube into the silt and vacuumed up a small quantity.

"Sample one secured," he said.

Sitting behind Paul and Gamay, the FEMA observer yawned. "What's the point of all this?"

To make you believe we're doing something other than what we're doing, Paul thought.

Gamay offered a better answer. "Sediment samples will allow us to test the damage to the aquatic ecosystem more accurately than water samples." She spoke in her most cheery scientific voice. "For example, certain types of microbes that are abundant in the water might be settling down into the sediment with significantly affected genetic structures. You could see DNA intersplicing errors, mutations. And, of course, any contamination in the aquatic microbe community affects the fish and then the larger predators, including humans. Best way to search for a problem is starting at the bottom of the food chain."

Reynolds looked at them blankly. "But there's nothing living down there," he said. "It's all inert mud."

"That's exactly why we have to check it," Gamay insisted.

"How many samples do you think we'll need?" Paul asked.

"At least a hundred, spread out over various parts of the disaster zone," Gamay said.

"That could take hours," Reynolds said.

"Five or six at least," Gamay added, laying it on as thick as she could.

That was enough for Reynolds. He stood up. "Well, I have to report in anyway. I'll check back with you in a few hours. When you're halfway done . . . Good luck with all this."

He gathered up a few belongings and left.

With the door shut tight, Paul looked over at Gamay. "Think he'll be back?"

"Not unless someone forces him," Gamay said. "Looked like he might physically die of boredom if he had to watch us for six hours."

"I would, too," Paul said, "if we really had to get a hundred samples of barren sediment. Let's get the fun part done first in case he does come back."

Gamay turned the 3-D system on and began directing Paul based on the sonar readings. "Head due east. You should find the smallest of the fires about half a mile out."

Paul guided the ROV on a heading of 090. It took a few minutes to cover the distance, but soon the glow of the nearest fire began to appear on the ROV's cameras.

"That's smaller and less intense than it was this morning," Paul said. "Whatever gas is causing this must be dwindling."

"That's good and bad," Gamay said. "Let's get our samples before the candle burns out."

Paul maneuvered the ROV into position.

"If you get the probe into the broken pipe, you can capture the gas before it ignites," Gamay suggested.

"That's the plan," Paul said. He directed the ROV right down onto the pipe itself. The fire burned only sixteen inches from the camera.

"Be careful," Gamay said. "That fire is over a thousand degrees."

Paul nodded, held the ROV steady and extended the probe. The interior of the probe was lined with tempered glass, the exterior was made of titanium. The chamber they would suck the gas into was currently vacuum-sealed, containing no air, water or other contaminants that the gas might react with.

Once Paul had the probe in place, he would break the seal and the volatile, hydrophoric gas would be sucked into the chamber and held in its inert form.

"Let's hope this works," Paul said. The probe inched forward, banging against both sides of the broken pipe.

"Careful," Gamay said.

"I'm being careful," he replied.

Finally, the probe was in the pipeline.

"Here goes nothing," Paul said. He pressed a button and broke the vacuum seal. A liter of gas was sucked in through the probe and stored, with the system automatically resealing itself once the container pressure rose to a certain level.

"We have it," Paul said. "And without blowing ourselves up."

"All right, now get out of there."

Paul retracted the probe, pulled the ROV back and turned it away from the fire. He'd come through one hundred and eighty degrees and was moving the ROV away when the door to the OSLO opened and Reynolds popped his head back in.

Gamay acted quickly, flicking off the holographic display.

Paul sat tall and rigidly. He realized the fire was plainly visible in the ROV's aft camera. Switching it off would be too obvious, but Reynolds might not be able to see past him if he sat up straight.

"I forgot to ask," Reynolds said, paying no attention to the screens. "Can you forward me a copy of your report when you're done examining the sediment samples? I just want to send it up to Washington with everything else."

As Reynolds spoke, Paul brought the ROV down to the sediment layer once more, turning it so that the fires weren't visible on camera.

"Sure thing," Gamay said. "It'll take a while, but I'll send you a copy as soon as it's done."

"Thanks," he said. "How many samples have you collected?"

Paul knew better than to blurt out an answer—in case Gamay was about to voice a different lie. He looked down at a paper with scribbled notes on it as if he'd been keeping track. "This is, umm . . ."

"We're up to sixteen," Gamay said.

To maintain the illusion, Paul vacuumed up another sample of sediment, which would be stored in a separate container. "Sixteen going on seventeen," he said.

Reynolds sighed. "I admire your dedication. See you later." With that, he backed out and shut the door once again.

"That was close," Paul said. "At least the hard part is over."

"For you," Gamay said. "I have to write up a fake report detailing a hundred sediment samples. None of which will have anything in them because all of this takes place below the photic zone."

Paul had to laugh. He knew Gamay would want his help, but, thankfully, he'd be too busy studying the gas.

He glanced at the instruments, checking on the sample. The gas was steady and holding stable at forty degrees. The sediment samples were . . .

"There's a slight pressure build in the sediment tank," he said.

Gamay leaned closer. "Only in the sediment sample you just collected. Did you suck in some of the gas?"

"No," Paul said. "There was no cross-contamination."

"The pressure is rising ever so slightly in the sealed chamber," Gamay said, fine-tuning the instrument. "If I didn't know better, I'd tell you there was bacteria in that barren soil."

A system check told them the instruments were working perfectly. "It's not a false reading," Gamay said.

Paul grinned at her. "Looks like you're going to have something to put in your report after all."

20

THE ISLAND OF BERMUDA runs diagonally from the airport in the northeast, down to a fishhook curve in the southwest. Situated within that curve is one of the finest natural harbors in the world, home for centuries to ships of the Royal Navy and now a favored port of call for cruise ships and the yachting crowd.

With a mild climate, British traditions and excellence in banking, Bermuda had become one of the wealthiest countries in the world. Its banks and financial institutions were filled with cash, bearer bonds, jewels and precious metals. Its hills were dotted with multimillion-dollar villas, many of which were bought just for investment purposes and often sat empty for months, or even years, at a time.

The arrival of the R3 Conference had changed that. This week the villas were full, the five-star hotels overflowing and the harbor crowded with yachts—each one larger and more ostentatious than the last. But none of them compared to the presence of the *Monarch*.

The hulking amphibious aircraft was the center of attention in Bermuda, making front-page news upon its return, even knocking the cricket championship to a spot below the fold.

Its majestic landing in the Great Sound had been attended like the arrival of a king or queen. The fact that the aircraft was based on the island was of little consequence. For one thing, it was rarely here. For another, there were thousands of tourists present who'd never seen the aircraft. They lined the docks as it taxied across the water toward a small island called Baker's Rock, which sat in a sheltered section of the Great Sound.

Tessa Franco owned Baker's Rock and had built a large estate on the high ground. To protect the aircraft, a stone wall had been added to the naturally curved bay, which acted as a berth for the great plane.

Pleasure boats passed by during the day, onlookers snapping photos. Cruise ships saluted the aircraft with blasts from their horns usually reserved for other ships, while a constant security presence was posted to keep the curious from getting too close or setting foot on the island.

For the most part, Tessa enjoyed the attention. It was publicity. Publicity meant money. And money was becoming a critical factor at this point in her operation. With Buran and the Consortium withholding her payments, Tessa was in desperate need of cash.

For a year, she'd been talking about an initial public offering, but for reasons she kept to herself she hadn't moved forward with it yet. R3 gave a different opportunity, private money, the kind that came without attention and often without many strings attached.

But before she could go looking for cash, she had a more pressing problem to deal with.

"What do you mean they escaped?" she said, glaring at Woods from behind her desk.

"They got away from the men I hired," Woods said.

"It was a simple task," she said. "Find out what they knew and eliminate them. You said they were heading out into the middle of nowhere. That it would be an easy job."

Standing behind Woods, Volke grinned, obviously glad he hadn't had any part in this particular operation.

"You gave me an hour to find someone who could take them down," Woods stammered. "I went to the only people we could reach that quickly."

"They were obviously incompetent."

"It was the best we could do on short notice."

That much was probably true. "Did they get our equipment back?"

"They retrieved the power pack and the other items the NUMA agents were carrying," Woods said. "All traces of it have been destroyed."

"I suppose that's something," she said. "All right, we have work to do. The freighter is going to be here tonight. Millard and his people keep complaining about the danger they're in. You two go talk to him and make sure he understands that now is not the time to panic."

Volke nodded. Woods did the same and the two men walked out. Tessa checked the time. The opening ceremonies for R3 were already beginning. It was time to switch from growling at people to charming them.

21

THE *Lucid Dream* was a fifty-meter steel-hulled yacht with three decks and a gleaming white and blue paint job. Classic luxury materials filled the interior spaces, while modern touches gave the vessel an edgy look.

A sound system that could shake up an entire harbor and a pool that could be covered over by glass and turned into a dance floor made it a great party boat for those who were young, rich and nocturnal.

A small hangar on the upper deck held three drones that could be used for fun and entertainment or for surveillance. Personal watercraft and a high-speed boat for towing water-skiers and wakeboarders were stored in an enclosed compartment just in front of the engine room.

As impressive as it was, the *Lucid Dream* was just one of many yachts to arrive in time for the R3 Conference.

There were at least fifty vessels of equal or larger size visiting the island at the same time. Not to mention hundreds of smaller craft and two of the five largest yachts in the world. Tech money tended to get spent on toys and many of the dot-com billionaires had taken turns outdoing each other on the water.

In that environment, the *Lucid Dream* drew only passing glances— and a parking spot out in the sound a half mile from dry land. All of which suited Kurt Austin just fine.

He stood at the stern of the yacht. He watched a small boat motoring toward them, while enjoying the sunset, the eighty-degree weather and the soft, humid breeze.

He was dressed to impress, wearing expensive slacks and an Armani jacket with the sleeves rolled to display the cuffs of his limited-edition Robert Graham shirt. Handmade Italian sunglasses covered his eyes and his hair had been professionally dyed from its silver color to a dark blend of black and gray.

Standing on the deck, Kurt looked like a movie star, which seemed logical since he was essentially playing a role.

Thanks to some friends of Hiram Yaeger—NUMA's resident computer genius—Kurt was arriving in Bermuda billed as a reclusive venture capitalist who'd helped fund a dozen start-ups. The expensive wardrobe was required to look the part and Kurt certainly wore it well. The only thing he found odd were the bespoke, nineteen-hundred-dollar high-top sneakers he'd been told he had to wear.

The footwear made no sense to Kurt, but Yaeger assured him that many of the VCs in the tech world chose to dress in unique and counterculture styles. Being unique was almost as important as being rich. Some wore berets or fedoras as a calling card. Others never wore anything but white T-shirts, jeans and boat shoes. Steve Jobs had been famous for his black turtlenecks. Zuckerberg for his hoodies.

The man Kurt was pretending to be had a sneaker obsession and wearing wingtips or boots or even expensive Italian loafers would have been a sure giveaway. If nothing else, the sneakers were comfortable.

"Water taxi approaching," he called out to Joe. "It's showtime."

Joe came out onto the aft deck dressed in more traditional tech guru clothing. He had his hair slicked back, his shirt buttoned to the neck and a pocket protector firmly in place and filled with a half dozen pens. His khakis were rolled at the ankles and he also wore sneakers, though his were a checkerboard pair of low-sided Vans. He carried two computer satchels, one for himself and one for Kurt.

"So glad to have an assistant with me on this trip," Kurt said.

"Don't even think I'm hauling our luggage around all weekend," Joe warned.

"First rule of undercover work," Kurt said. "Never break character."

"I wasn't," Joe insisted. "My character doesn't do suitcases . . . no upper-body strength."

Kurt laughed. "As long as your character tips well, we should be okay."

As Joe checked his cash supply, a woman with short, dark hair, dazzling mahogany eyes and Indian facial features came out onto the deck, maneuvering the compact wheelchair she was confined to with surprising ease.

Priya Kashmir was one member of Hiram Yaeger's team, a computer genius who'd studied at both Oxford and MIT before joining NUMA. She'd been hired on to a field position when a car crash had left her paralyzed from the waist down. After healing from her injuries, she'd accepted a new position in the tech department, though she continued hoping she'd get back in the field. This was her first opportunity.

She held out a pair of laminated badges with computer chips in them. "Your passes, gentlemen. As long as you have these, you won't need any additional ID. They've been coded to your profiles and embedded with your facial recognition data. All of which has been falsified to match your cover stories, of course."

"That was fast," Kurt said, taking his badge and handing the other to Joe. "And I thought we'd have to pretend we lost them."

"Just trying to earn my keep," Priya said. "Thanks for having enough faith to bring me along."

"I have a feeling we're going to need all the assistance you can provide," Kurt said. "For now, you're in charge of the boat. No wild parties while we're gone."

"No promises," she said, "but I'll try to keep it down. You both look great, by the way. Good luck."

"Thanks," Kurt said.

With the water taxi finally pulling up to the stern, he took one of the computer bags, slid it onto his shoulder. He stepped onto the boat as it bumped against the yacht.

"Mr. Hatcher," the pilot said in a Bermudian British accent.

Kurt nodded and introduced Joe. "This is my assistant, Ronald Ruff. We call him Numbers. You might as well, too."

Another nod. The pilot nudged the throttle, moving away from the yacht and back toward the shore. "Let me welcome you both to Bermuda. I'll tell you a little about our history. To begin with, like Mr. Numbers, this island goes by other names as well. Some people call it Somers Island."

"I've heard that," Kurt replied. "And some call it Devil's Isle."

"True," the pilot said. "It was the shipwrecked sailors who

named it that. The island is surrounded by treacherous reefs. And those men found they could neither navigate them to get safely on shore nor escape them once they were stranded here. But even those survivors found pleasure and happiness here. You will, too."

That, Kurt thought, would depend on what happened at the R3 Conference.

22

PAUL TROUT found himself both intrigued and frustrated by the work he was doing. Sitting in the *Raleigh*'s medical center—using it as a makeshift lab—he'd been doing his best to determine exactly what kind of gas they'd pulled from the ruptured pipe.

So far, his efforts had been hampered by the properties of the gas itself. Air caused it to burn, so did water. It corroded various metals, including stainless steel, and its slightest touch on the skin burned like acid.

The only way to contain it was to keep it in a vacuum-sealed container with a glass lining or to drown it in nitrogen. Studying it that way stopped the explosions but presented other problems.

Paul removed a tiny probe from the gas-filled test tube and found the end of the probe smoldering like a burned-out match.

"How's it going?" Gamay asked. She was across the room, running her own series of tests on the sediment they'd recovered.

"My latest experiment melted the sensor," he said dejectedly.

"Rudi will dock your pay for that," she joked.

"Not if no one tells him about it," Paul said.

"Lucky for you, I can be bribed."

Paul laughed. "This gas is corrosive like an acid and explosive like a petrochemical vapor. When I put a few drops of seawater in with the gas, it split the water into hydrogen and oxygen and then reacted with the oxygen and caught fire. That's why it ignites while it's still underwater."

"I thought I heard a small explosion."

"Good thing I only used a few drops," he said. "Look."

He held up the tempered-glass beaker he'd used to perform the test. It was blackened on the inside and hairline cracks could be seen running through the curved glass.

"You'd better have your safety goggles on," she said.

"You, too," Paul said.

"I'm only working with marine clay," she said.

"You don't want mud in your eye?" Paul said. "Especially considering that the sediment is mostly—"

"I know what it is," she snapped. "And you're right . . . I don't want it in my eye."

Reluctantly, Gamay put her safety goggles on and then proceeded to conduct her next experiment. She was trying to figure out what was causing the increased pressure in the sealed beaker containing one of the samples.

She scraped a portion of the mud onto a slide and put it under a microscope. Increasing the magnification, she finally saw what she was looking for. Tiny bubbles were forming in the watery clay. They appeared, popped and vanished, only to be replaced by new bubbles. Raising the magnification to full, she saw the cause of those bubbles.

"Biofilm," she said.

"Is that a new movie?" Paul asked, still looking for a sensor to replace the melted one.

"Biofilm is a telltale sign of bacteria forming a colony," she explained "It's one of the things that makes some strains of bacteria hard to treat with antibiotics. The film is a kind of slime that acts as a barrier. It prevents the antibiotics from reaching the bacteria themselves."

"Meaning . . . what?"

She looked up. "It means there's a large amount of bacteria in the sediment near the pipeline. But not in any of the other locations we tested."

Gamay was the biologist of the family, but Paul knew a thing or two. "Isn't it supposed to be barren sediment down there? Too deep and dark for life to exist?"

"It should be," she replied. "Maybe the heat from the pipelines or some leaking chemicals has become a food source. Or maybe the bacteria is feeding on the volatile gas."

She went back to the microscope and raised the magnification. "They're oddly shaped," she said, studying individual members of the bacteria colony.

"How so?"

"Bacteria are usually oval-shaped blobs. These are more like red blood cells. They have a donut-like form."

Paul was suddenly more interested in what she was studying than in his own work. "Maybe we should expose some of the bacteria to a sample of the gas. If their growth rate increases, we'll know that's what the little beasties are feeding on."

"Great idea," Gamay said.

She put a sample of the bacteria into a clean test tube, injected some water and sealed it. As she brought it over to Paul, there was a loud pop. The sound startled her and she dropped the vial, diving to catch it before it hit the ground.

Paul raced around the table and found her lying on the floor with the test tube in one hand and her safety glasses askew. She was staring at the vial. The glass had been blackened on the inside, exactly like the beaker Paul had almost destroyed in his earlier experiment.

He and Gamay came to the same conclusion at the same time.

"The bacteria aren't feeding off the gas," Paul said.

"No," she agreed. "They're generating it."

23

POLARIS BALLROOM, CONSTELLATION HOTEL AND CONFERENCE CENTER, BERMUDA

KURT HAD BEEN to more trade shows and conferences than he cared to remember, but he'd never seen anything quite like the R3 Blackout Conference. It was less a trade show and more like an electronic version of Mardi Gras.

In large rooms, lit by black light, electronic music thumped away while glow-in-the-dark drinks were poured and passed around.

Men and women wore "active clothing" equipped with LEDs and fiber-optic lights that changed with their body temperature. The colors supposedly corresponded with their state of mind. Fear, aggression, arousal and contentedness were all represented by different hues.

And everyone in the hall wore clear glasses with little computer displays projected on the lenses.

"Feel like I've died and gone to electronic hell," Kurt said.

"You should embrace this," Joe replied. "Remember that whole 'remain in character' thing. Besides, when in Rome, and all that."

"But if this is Rome," Kurt said, "then the barbarians have already conquered."

A woman in a neon-green rain slicker with lighted piping around the collar came up to them and scanned their ID badges. "Welcome to the Blackout," she said. "Here are your complimentary sentience goggles."

She handed them each a pair of not-so-stylish glasses with lenses tinted a pale pink color. Kurt put them on and was instantly presented with a wave of information. The words *Amanda: Host* appeared above the woman in the green outfit.

"Your name is Amanda?" Kurt asked.

"It is," she said. "I'm a guest facilitator, sometimes called a host. If you tap the side of your glasses, you'll get more information about me or anyone you're speaking to."

Kurt tapped a spot on the right arm of the glasses. Immediately, more information appeared about Amanda.

Sex: Female

Status: Single

Home: Palo Alto, California

Employer: Sentience Industries

Education: B.S. in Technology, M.S. in Network Science, Stanford University

Quote: "If you think you can keep up with me, go ahead and try . . ."

Standing next to Kurt, Joe was reading the same thing. He grinned. "That's something I might be interested in attempting," he said.

"Easy there, Numbers," Kurt said. "We're here on business."

As Joe flirted, Kurt scanned the room and read the names of other people nearby.

"You can also get directions via voice activation," Amanda said. "Press the other arm and speak."

"Elevator," Kurt said, testing the system.

A faint line appeared on the glass. It led across the room, appearing like a shadow on the crowd before brightening against the far wall and turning.

Their host beamed. "All you have to do is follow that line and you'll be taken right to the elevator."

"Personal GPS," Kurt replied. "I like it."

"Let me try," Joe said. He pressed the sensor on the left arm of his own glasses and spoke. "Directions to winning Amanda's heart."

A line pointed directly toward Amanda, but nothing more appeared.

"Unfortunately, it doesn't give emotional directions," she joked. "But if you're good at foot rubs, you're halfway there."

She tapped a sensor on the arm of the glasses for Joe and a little heart appeared beside her name. Joe raised his eyebrows and smiled.

"Thank you," Kurt said, "we won't take up any more of your time."

Amanda left to speak with other guests and Kurt and Joe began wandering around the main convention hall, talking to other attendees and getting used to the idea of knowing who one was speaking with before even asking a single question.

Kurt found it stilted the interactions. "One thing's for sure, you don't have to make small talk with these things on. It's just right to the chase."

"I'm saving all the single women in my list of favorites," Joe said. "Unfortunately, that leaves no room for you."

"I'm heartbroken," Kurt feigned. "Time to get down to business." He pressed the sensor on the arm of his glasses and spoke. "Fuel cell displays."

A list of several companies hawking their most advanced fuel cells appeared. Kurt pressed the sensor again and spoke the name of the first company. A line directing him across the room led to an impressive booth with promotional video running on multiple screens. Each mini-movie showed different uses of the fuel cell system, but the technical information suggested there was nothing revolutionary about this company's products.

He and Joe moved to a second booth and then a third. The results were the same.

"Nothing special about these designs," Joe said. "Just a little more efficient than your garden-variety fuel cells."

"Don't bother saving them to your favorites," Kurt said. He tapped the button on the arm of the glasses and spoke the name of the last company on the list. "Novum Industria."

"Don't you mean Industrial with an *l*?" Joe asked.

"That's not what it says here," Kurt replied.

The line on the glasses led Kurt through a swirling crowd and past a wall covered with falling water. Like everything else in the Blackout Conference, the water appeared to glow in the black light.

As he passed the end of the wall, he arrived at another display. Here, he saw samples of magnetic material and information about batteries and storage systems.

As he watched through the glasses, words appeared from a background that seemed to be made of solid rock. *Novum Industria.* This time, the glasses offered a translation. Latin for *New Energy.*

In a small lounge behind all the technical stuff, a woman with wavy dark hair, full lips and a formfitting suit was holding court. Kurt noticed her eyes, partly because she wasn't wearing the sentience goggles and partly because they were instantly alluring, almond-shaped and canted slightly, which gave her an almost feline appearance.

As Kurt scanned the group around her, the glasses told him her subjects were all potential investors. He moved in with the others, focused on the woman and was rewarded with information about her.

Tessa Franco: Founder, President and CEO of Novum Industria, Inc.

Kurt didn't bother getting the rest of the information. He took off the glasses, stood and waited for her to finish her pitch about where her company was going and why.

". . . The events in the Gulf of Mexico are only the latest indication of our need to end this mad reliance on fossil fuels," she said. "We're burning our way to a new kind of hell on earth—global warming, climate change, record hurricanes, not to mention bleached reefs and drastically affected fish populations. The effects are obvious. But people are kidding themselves if they think any government or UN program will end this reliance, that's a liberal pipe dream and a foolish waste of money. The only thing that will end the suicidal use of fossil fuels is the development of something better. Novum Industria has come up with that something."

She stepped aside and a holographic video vaguely described their newly integrated fuel cell and battery system. It gave away no proprietary details, but Kurt could tell it was different than anything at the other booths.

He noticed the men around her hanging on every word.

"Is it money or love they're after?" Joe whispered.

"A little bit of both," Kurt said. "The question is, what does she need?"

"A little of both," Joe said.

"My thoughts exactly."

Each of the potential investors took a moment to address Tessa. They all spoke with confidence, but it was obvious that Tessa had the high ground. She commanded the room well, talking to one man, then the next, turning to avoid follow-up questions and keeping each of them wanting more.

Kurt wasn't interested in joining a crowd of fawning onlookers. He needed to stand out in the crowd.

Instead of waiting his turn, he stepped forward, pushed through the line and offered a hand, interrupting her midsentence. "I know it's old-fashioned, but a handshake tells you a great deal about a person. Far more than any pair of smart glasses can reveal."

Tessa stopped in the middle of an explanation, eyeing Kurt for a moment. Since she wasn't wearing the sentience goggles, Kurt had her at a disadvantage.

"Macklin Hatcher," he said. "Firelight Investing."

She paused for another moment and then shook his hand. "Tessa Franco," she replied. "Pleased to meet you, though it's odd for a technology investor to choose gut instinct over hardware."

"I don't invest in hardware," Kurt said with the confidence only a billionaire could have. "I invest in people. Whatever you've built here, someone else will copy it soon enough. Maybe even one of these men, if you don't take their money. Even worse, someone will build off your design and surpass it. But if you're who I think you are, you'll be on to something new by then. As they say, the driven soul will always succeed."

At this, Tessa brightened and Kurt didn't need any interactive clothing to know he'd gotten her exactly right.

"Excuse me," one of the potential investors said. "We were in the middle of—"

"Yes, you were," Kurt said. "My apologies to everyone. Enjoy your evening—especially you, Ms. Franco."

With that, Kurt offered the slightest bow and took his leave of the group.

Joe rejoined him as he walked off. "I never realized that annoying someone was your best way of introducing yourself."

"All that matters is making an impression," Kurt said.

Joe nodded. "Think she's storing your name in her favorites?"

"That or deleting me altogether," Kurt said.

"I'm sure we'll find out," Joe said. "In the meantime, I looked at their display. The design elements are very similar to what we pulled off that submersible. Though without a microscopic examination, there's not much I can prove."

"It's our only lead for now," Kurt said. "If we promise enough money, she might give us a sample to test."

They'd gone halfway across the room when Kurt felt a buzzing sensation in his pocket. He pulled out the glasses, found them vibrating and put them on.

"A message has been delivered," he said.

Joe shook his head. "If she's asking for a date, I'm going to have to rethink my entire existence."

At the tap of a button, Kurt opened the message. It displayed out in front of him as if the words were floating in midair.

You're right, Mr. Hatcher, I am a driven soul. So perhaps there's something to this handshake business of yours. Would you care to join me for dinner tomorrow night and explore the possibilities of additional skin-to-skin contact?

—Tessa F.

"I haven't been deleted after all," Kurt said. "Now, let's see if I can figure out how to reply."

After scrolling through a menu and finding the message app, Kurt spoke softly. "Tomorrow's no good, it'll have to be tonight."

The words appeared in his vision and then vanished as he hit send. The response was disheartening.

I'm afraid I'm meeting with Oliver Warren tonight. Perhaps some other time if fate allows.

—Tessa F.

Kurt didn't respond.

Joe shook his head. "The mighty Casey . . ."

"So it seems," Kurt said. "Let's wander around and see what else we can find."

24

BERMUDA

BACK ABOARD the *Lucid Dream*, Kurt took off the expensive jacket, poured himself a drink and made his way to the media room, where Priya had already linked up to the NUMA computer systems using the yacht's satellite dish.

"What can you tell me about Tessa Franco?"

Priya began typing, giving Kurt information as she found it. "Thirty-one years old, born in Italy to American parents. She now has dual citizenship. Her father was a big success in the first computing wave. She had a privileged upbringing but lost her mother when she was ten and her father while she was in grad school. At that point, she inherited a small fortune and immediately plunged vast amounts of funding into all manner of high-tech businesses and start-ups, trying to turn millions into billions."

Priya stopped, scanned down and found more pertinent information. "Three years later, she was almost broke. Shortly before being forced into bankruptcy, she sold a design for a new type of lithium battery. It's been used in half the world's computers and most of the phones ever since."

"Act 1," Kurt said. "Soar and fail. Act 2, Rebuild your fortune. It's a classic story."

"According to another article," Priya continued, "she then began spending money on even more varied pursuits. She bought a Formula 1 racing team, funded a historical preservation society that salvaged several wrecks. And then built a one-of-a-kind amphibious aircraft as large as a 747."

Joe sat up. "I saw a photo of that in the paper. The *Monarch*. It's here now."

"Should be," Priya said. "She lives here. Not sure if it's for the weather or tax reasons, but Novum Industria is incorporated in Bermuda. And according to this, she owns a private island here in the sound called Baker's Rock."

Kurt moved closer, looking over Priya's shoulder. "Show me Baker's Rock."

Pulling up the satellite map revealed Baker's Rock less than a mile from where the *Lucid Dream* was berthed.

"Zoom in."

Priya tapped the zoom key until the outline of Baker's Rock filled the monitor.

Kurt gazed at the setup. It showed a palatial estate built into the side of a hilly island with a semicircular bay surrounded in white marble like the seats of an amphitheater. The *Monarch* sat in the bay, its wings stretching from one side of the bay to the other, just barely fitting inside the confines of the curved space.

Up above it, a deck of travertine surrounded a large plantation-style house, fronted by an expansive pool, lit in purple and pink and shaped like a hibiscus flower.

"Nice digs," Priya said. "My apartment would fit into the shallow end of her pool."

"I know what you're planning," Joe said, "but she has another date coming, remember? Oliver Warren."

Kurt grinned. "Not once you two figure out how to intercept him."

25

KURT MADE HIS WAY to the top deck of the *Lucid Dream*, wearing swim trunks and carrying fins and a waterproof pack.

"Not exactly what I was expecting," Priya said.

She was a few feet away, sitting at a table overlooking the Great Sound. "Where's the face paint, commando gear and twelve-inch knife to fight off the sharks or the bad guys?"

"Hoping to avoid sharks and bad guys," Kurt said. "And if I'm right, the face paint is being applied in Tessa's luxurious bedroom suite. As for the rest of the gear, I have everything I need I here." He patted the waterproof pouch.

"I lifted that earlier," Priya said. "Surprisingly cold on such a warm night."

"As it should be," Kurt insisted.

Priya smiled. She had her own gear in front of her, including her ever-present laptop, a second computer that was connected to a portable satellite receiver, a handheld radio, a phone and an iPad.

"I'll keep an eye on you. And once you activate the listening device, I'll be able to hear what you say, so keep it PG-13."

"I'll try," Kurt said.

He raised a pair of binoculars and studied Baker's Rock in the distance. They'd moved the *Lucid Dream* to a new spot, gaining an unimpeded view. Kurt could see the entire side of the island and the half-circular bay that lay at its feet. The *Monarch* sat there, lit up on both sides by floodlights. A trophy on display.

Scanning the layers of stone behind the aircraft, Kurt saw two sets of stairs running up from the water and an arrangement of columns on the highest level that added to the sense that he was looking at a Greek or Roman palace.

As Kurt studied the island through the binoculars, Priya studied it on her computer, viewing the feed from one of the drones. Her view was far more detailed.

"There's a guard standing on the promontory on the right-hand side of the bay," she said. "Another one by the stairs and one patrolling the grounds. The one on patrol has a dog."

"I should have packed some treats," Kurt said.

He wasn't worried about the guards, but he did need to appear in the right place at the right time. He could be sure there were cameras situated at various points around the bay and possibly on the *Monarch*. He decided it would be best to emerge from the water where one of the guards might catch him.

Putting the binoculars down, he checked his watch. "Time to go. Stay in touch with Joe, he may need assistance . . . or bail money."

Priya held up the phone. "I've got him right here."

Shouldering his waterproof pack, Kurt took the stairs to the lowest deck, climbed down a ladder and dropped into the calm waters of Bermuda's Great Sound.

Once he was in the water, he pulled on a pair of compact fins, pushed away from the yacht and began his swim. He moved methodically, using a forward crawl, keeping up a brisk pace.

After five minutes, he was approaching the lighted bay. Here, he angled to one side, avoiding the aircraft. Once inside the bay, he went straight for the stairs, climbed out of the water and took a seat on the second step.

He sat there as if he hadn't a care in the world, calmly taking the fins off, removing a towel from the waterproof pack and drying his hair and face and body.

That done, he tossed the towel aside, shouldered the pack once more and began to climb the stairs.

If he wasn't on camera now, Tessa needed to fire her security team.

INSIDE THE COMPOUND, Tessa was exactly where Kurt predicted she'd be, sitting at a mirror, half dressed, applying makeup. A stunning evening gown waited for her a few feet away.

She had a mascara brush in her hand when the intercom buzzed and the voice of her security chief spoke. *"Sorry to interrupt you, Ms. Franco, but we have a breach."*

She finished her lashes and put the brush down. Pressing a button on the intercom beside her, she spoke aloud. "What kind of breach?"

"A swimmer just came out of the water. He's coming up the stairs toward the main house now."

"What do you mean, a swimmer?" she replied. "Are we being attacked?"

"Not exactly, ma'am." The chief seemed confused. *"Honestly, I'm not sure what to make of it. It's one man, on his own. He's*

made no effort to conceal himself. Maybe he thinks this is public property."

"Is he trying to get a look at the plane?" she asked. "We've had that before."

"No," the chief said. *"He's heading for the patio."*

"Put it on the screen," she said. "I want to see for myself."

A screen lit up inside the mirror in front of her. It was bright enough that she could see a figure walking calmly across her patio like he owned the place. He wore colorful swim trunks. He was admirably fit and carrying a pack, but there was no sense that he posed any danger. If anything, he seemed to be admiring the grounds or looking for a spot to relax.

As Tessa watched, one of the security guards rushed toward the new arrival, attempting to tackle the swimmer. The guard was immediately flipped and subdued on the ground.

"Zoom in," Tessa ordered.

As the camera closed in on the man in the swim trunks, a second guard arrived with his weapon drawn and Tessa exhaled in frustration.

"Order your men to back off," she said. "I'm coming down."

Tessa stood up, slipped into her dress and stopped to look in the full-length mirror. Satisfied, she glanced at the screen once more and then left the room.

26

CENTRAL BERMUDA

WHILE KURT was successfully getting captured at Tessa's compound, Joe was on the road, driving a small van toward a tricky intersection near the estate where Oliver Warren was staying.

"How do I let Kurt talk me into this stuff," he mumbled.

"What was that?" Priya replied over the phone.

Joe had almost forgotten they were on an open line. "Nothing, just wondering if my olfactory senses will ever recover."

He drove with the windows down, the fan on and the A/C running full blast, but nothing—and he meant nothing—seemed to reduce the smell of rotting fish coming from the rear of the van.

Piles of dead fish filled the back, packed with just enough ice to make it look like they were being shipped somewhere.

"Catch of the day," Joe said. "But which day?"

All he knew for sure was that the load of fish had been destined for a compost pile until Kurt's bright idea had put them in the back of Joe's rental van.

"You're coming up on the roundabout," Priya said. *"You sure you know how to handle that?"*

Joe was just fine remembering to stay on the left-hand side of the road. With a bit of traffic, all he had to do was follow the car in front of him. "I'll do my best," Joe said. "But what do the English have against traffic lights and cold beer?"

"Roundabouts are fun," Priya said, defending the country she'd grown up in. *"And you can't really taste ice-cold beer."*

She had a point. "Any sign of Warren?"

"I'm still tapped into the limo company's server," Priya said. *"The driver just reported picking him up. They're leaving the manor house now."*

"Thanks," Joe said. "I'll keep circling this roundabout like a vulture, just hope I can drive straight when I get back on the road."

"Don't get dizzy," she said. *"Also, the limo isn't a limousine, it's a silver Lincoln MKX. A big sport utility vehicle."*

"As long as it has tires," Joe said. "But thanks for the heads-up."

Joe could hear Priya tapping away at her keyboard.

"I'm going to program your map system with the GPS data from the limo company's internal tracking network," she said. *"That way, you'll be able to find Warren if you get separated."*

Joe had never worked directly with Priya before, but he was enjoying it. "Have to say you're a lot more organized and prepared than Kurt. Don't tell him I said that."

"Don't worry," she said. *"I would never violate hacker–client privilege."*

Joe looked down at the navigation display on his phone. He saw two moving dots on the street map, a blue one for him and a red one for the SUV that Warren was riding in.

"He's coming down the Middle Road as expected," Priya said.

Bermuda was long and thin. It had three main roads that ran the length of the island. North Shore Road on one coast, South Road on the other coast and the aptly named Middle Road running along the spine of the island.

"I see him," Joe said. "I'm going to make one more loop and then pull out in front of him."

Joe circled the roundabout once more, slowing so he could cut Warren off. Several passing cars honked their horns at him. Joe ignored them and continued to dawdle until he spotted the stark white headlights of the brand-new Lincoln coming his way.

He sped up, pulled hard to the left and then had to swerve at the last second to avoid a pair of tourists on mopeds. Horns blared again—and not in the friendly way that everyone on the island tended to honk at everyone they knew.

"*You all right?*" Priya asked.

"Barely," Joe said. "This is turning out to be more dangerous than I thought. I'm in front of the Lincoln now. Just need to get some open space before I stop him."

The problem Joe faced was stopping the SUV without causing a major accident. They had to inconvenience Warren, not injure him or anyone else on the road. At the moment, Joe could see additional mopeds in a loose line behind the Lincoln. He slowed down but made it impossible for the Lincoln to pass. This forced the mopeds to slow almost to a stop. Finally, the riders had had enough. They pulled wide, darting past the Lincoln, then Joe's van, all in one quick move.

With traffic gone, Joe accelerated, baiting the Lincoln into speeding up. Once Warren's driver began to close the gap, Joe put his hand on a hastily installed toggle switch that was taped to the console.

The switch was linked to a small set of explosives attached to the back doors of the van. When the explosives went off, the doors would blow open and allow the load of not-so-fresh fish to pour out the back, sliding down an angled ramp that Joe had wedged into place.

Hidden in the bed of ice beneath the fish was a tube of soft vinyl irrigation line. Inside that tube were additional explosive charges. Just enough to blow holes in the run-flat tires that any new SUV would be using.

It was a great plan, Joe thought. The explosives would blow the tires, the ice would smother the explosives and hide the residue. And the fish? . . . Well, that was just inspired window dressing.

With a final look, Joe flipped the switch and a bang reverberated through the van. Blue smoke swirled forward as the cargo surged out the back, spreading across the road behind him. The Lincoln ran over the mess, triggering three small flashes that took out the tires. It skidded forward another thirty feet before coming to a stop.

Joe slammed on his own brakes and brought the van to the side of the road. "Operation Fishmonger is under way. Getting out to make my apologies."

"*I'm here when you need me,*" Priya replied.

Putting one earbud in and placing the phone in his pocket, Joe put the emergency flashers on and stepped out of the van. By the time he reached the Lincoln, the driver was outside studying the mess.

"You idiot," the driver shouted.

"My load of fish," Joe said. "It's ruined."

"Who cares about your fish," the driver said. "Look what you've done. Look at my tires."

Joe looked at the Lincoln. Two of the tires were blown off their rims. A third had a gaping hole in the sidewall. The fourth was untouched but a single spare wasn't going to get the vehicle anywhere.

"Oh, man," Joe said. "That looks bad."

"Really bad," the driver said.

"I'm so sorry," Joe said. "I don't know what happened. Let me call my company. I'll get you the insurance information."

Joe pulled out the phone and pretended to dial. By now, the stench of the old fish was becoming more noticeable. It covered the lingering smell of the explosives and soon had the Lincoln driver putting a hand over his mouth.

Strangely, Joe could barely smell it anymore. He pretended to talk on the phone for a minute and then went silent. "I'm on hold," he said. "Typical . . . Absolutely typical . . ."

As Joe stood there, the back door of the SUV opened and a man got out. It wasn't Warren. Had to be a bodyguard. He walked carefully toward Joe and the Lincoln's driver, making sure not to step on any of the rotting fish.

Warren got out as well but stayed by the Lincoln. "What is this ridiculousness?"

"Just an accident," Joe said. "No big deal. We're going to fix everything. I'm calling my company now."

"I don't have time for this," Warren said, looking at his watch. "Let's get out of here."

The driver shook his head. "Sorry, Mr. Warren. I'll have to get you another car."

"Another car?"

The driver pointed to the ruined tires.

Warren looked down and then shook his head in disgust. "Make it quick," he snapped. "The stench is killing me."

With that, Warren got back in the SUV, slammed the door and

rolled the window up tight. Joe doubted that would protect him from the aroma. With all the rotting fish around, Warren might as well have been sitting in a bowl of day-old fish soup.

Joe continued to remain on hold. "High call volume," he said. "But my call is important to them."

The driver pulled out his own phone and called in for a replacement, but thanks to some highly inappropriate computer work, this call went not to the driver's office but to Priya. Listening to his own phone, Joe heard very word.

"Dispatch, this is Sherman in car six," the driver said. "Hate to report this, but I've had an accident. We're going to need a tow truck and a replacement car brought out for Mr. Warren as soon as possible. And I mean, as soon as humanly possible."

"I've got you at the intersection of Middle Road and Parson's Lane," Priya said, sounding authentically Bermudian with her British accent.

"We're a few hundred yards past that," the driver said.

"I'll call for a tow and send another car," she replied. *"Please tell Mr. Warren to remain in the vehicle for safety reasons."*

"Of course," the driver replied. "Just hurry. It stinks down here."

The phone call ended. Joe gave the driver a false set of insurance papers, made his apologies, taped the back doors shut and drove off.

Oliver Warren, his bodyguard and the Lincoln driver would wait a frustrating twenty minutes, call once more for another car and then wait further. After the second call—and realizing that the stench of fish had permeated his clothes—Warren contacted his secretary, had her reach out to Tessa Franco and cancel the date.

He offered his apologies and suggested they reschedule, indicating that dinner any of the next three nights would be fine—as long as it wasn't seafood.

27

KURT STOOD over the security guard whom he'd thrown to the ground while raising his hands, not wanting to be shot by the second guard.

"Sorry about that," he said to the first guard. "You surprised me and I reacted out of instinct." He offered a hand. "No hard feelings?"

While the officer on the ground looked wary and confused, the second man was downright hostile. "Stay where you are," he shouted, his weapon drawn and aimed at Kurt's chest.

"Relax," Kurt said. "I'm a lover, not a fighter."

"Just keep your hands where I can see them."

Kurt raised his hands and the man on the ground got up and backed away, grabbing Kurt's waterproof pack for good measure.

"Let's see what's inside."

"Be careful," Kurt said.

The man unzipped the bag, rummaged through one pocket and

then opened the main section of the pouch, pulling out a handful of melting ice. "What in the world?"

The sound of a sliding door opening violently stopped him from searching deeper. All eyes turned and Kurt saw his deliverance, Tessa Franco, stunning in a beaded evening gown, casting a reflection that danced in the soft evening light as she walked barefoot across the veranda. Her eyes were wide as she approached, her face slightly flushed. She was spellbinding.

"What, exactly, is going on out here?"

"We caught him before he could get to the house," the security guard said.

The question wasn't meant for him. Tessa was staring directly at Kurt. He shrugged. "I asked if you'd see me earlier tonight, you suggested perhaps another time. So here I am."

"I did suggest another time," Tessa replied, "but this is decidedly not another time. This is, in fact, the exact time I told you I wouldn't be available."

Kurt glanced at the security guards, who were rapidly getting the idea that he wasn't a burglar or an assassin. He lowered his hands and turned back to Tessa.

"True," Kurt said. "You were supposed to be otherwise engaged this evening. But plans have a way of changing and I was confident that yours would. After all, your last text referenced fate and I'm confident that fate meant for us to be together."

"You must be insane," she replied. "Did you swim out here from Hamilton?"

"No," Kurt said. "My yacht, the *Lucid Dream*, is anchored out in the sound."

"Well, you got all that exercise for nothing," she said. "There haven't been any changes to my plans. Now, if you'll kindly . . ."

As she was talking, her digital watch beeped, flashing brightly as it delivered a message. Tessa rotated her arm and read the words flowing across the small screen.

Kurt couldn't see them, but from the look on her face, he knew Joe had succeeded in diverting Oliver Warren and sending him home to regroup. He tried not to look too pleased.

Tessa read the message twice, tapped the screen to send off a preset reply and then paused. For several long seconds, she stared into the distance before slowly turning back to Kurt.

"I don't know whether to be aggravated, offended or flattered," she said. "I'm feeling a little bit of each, to be honest."

"Why don't we discuss your feelings over a drink?" he replied.

Careful not to startle the guards, he reached toward the waterproof pack and pulled a bottle of chilled champagne from inside.

Tessa took a good look at the bottle and then turned back to Kurt. The tension left her forehead and the corner of her lips turned up ever so slightly.

"The driven soul will always succeed," she said, quoting him from earlier in the evening. "Apparently, you're a very driven man, Mr. Hatcher. Just how did you persuade Oliver Warren to break his date with me? He was very keen on being the first to talk business."

"I had nothing to do with it," Kurt said. "Fate must have intervened. Now . . . shall we have a drink to fate . . . and anything else we can think of?"

He offered the bottle for her approval.

"Pol Roger," she said, studying the bottle.

"Favorite of Sir Winston Churchill," he added. "Another driven soul."

She studied the bottle and the label. "What year is this?"

"It was bottled for Churchill in 1940 as a celebration of his becoming Prime Minister of England," Kurt said. "I recovered it from a wreck off the coast of Ireland. The seal has never been broken."

"You recovered it?"

"Like you, I'm interested in history," Kurt said. "I've salvaged a few ships in my time. Like you, I'm interested in changing the world. Unlike you, I prefer to remain anonymous. I think we might make a very good team."

The smile grew, making her lips seemed fuller. She turned to her security team, who were standing there dumbfounded. "Gentlemen, you can leave us now."

The men nodded and walked off.

"You're not exactly dressed for dinner," she said.

"Drinks by the pool?"

"Which means, I'll have to change."

"Don't," Kurt said. "You look stunning."

"And if we go for a dip?"

"We can worry about that later."

An hour later, the twenty-thousand-dollar bottle of champagne was empty, replaced by a rare bottle from Tessa's own private collection in a silver bucket of ice. The new offering was almost as expensive, if not nearly as exotic, as the Pol Roger, 1940.

By now, talk of business and investments had given way to talk of changing the world.

"The difference between you and me is obvious," Kurt said. "You want to change the world for the sake of changing it. I'm only interested in change if it makes money. Lots and lots of money. You're not making money at this point or you wouldn't be looking for investors."

"We will be soon," she said. "Price of oil is climbing, supply is dropping, demand is increasing. All at the same time. That combination of factors will propel Novum Industria to become one of the largest corporations in the world. Invest a billion, you'll have ten more by the end of the decade."

Kurt poured more champagne. "That certainly qualifies as a lot of money. But every alternative energy company makes the same promise. Plenty of them have gone bankrupt doing so. I'm already wealthy, why risk it all on something so unproven?"

"Because that's how we keep score," she said.

"That's greed," Kurt said.

With that, Tessa pushed her chair back and stood. "I make no apologies," she said briskly.

"I mean that as a compliment," Kurt said. "Without a little greed, we'd still be living in the Dark Ages."

Kurt put his glass down, stood and stepped toward her. "Now tell me about your technology. Is it real or just pie in the sky?"

"I'm not sure you'd be able to understand the technical explanation," she said.

"Try me," he said, moving closer.

"I'm not that intoxicated," she replied. "You can see the designs after we have an agreement in place."

"Wise," he said, moving even closer. He put his hand softly on her cheek, brushed her hair back and kissed her. Her lips tasted of champagne. Her hair had the scent of jasmine "So, if you can't show me your technology, what can you show me?"

"Why don't we start with that swim?"

28

GREAT SOUND, BERMUDA

JOE MADE IT BACK to the *Lucid Dream*, took a hot shower and then made his way up to the top deck. He found Priya watching Kurt through the high-powered camera.

"How's he doing?"

"Not bad," she said, "if swimming with a beautiful woman fits that definition."

"You've got to be kidding me," Joe said. "I have cats following me around, looking for a free meal, and Kurt is making out with our prime suspect. There's no justice in this world."

"I only wish he'd activated the listening device," Priya said. "I wanted to hear them talking."

Joe laughed. "You don't strike me as the voyeuristic type."

"I'm not," Priya said, "but I haven't had a date in months."

Joe studied Priya. She was incredibly pretty and looking radiant in the moonlight. "If that's not by choice, then there's something with the men of Washington, D.C."

"Thank you," she replied. "I'll take that as a compliment."

Joe picked up the binoculars and trained them on the pool.

Kurt and Tessa had left the pool and toweled off. With Tessa in a robe and Kurt in his swim trunks, they walked toward the marble stairs that led down to the *Monarch*'s berth.

"They're heading down to the bay," Joe said.

"Maybe they're going skinny-dipping?"

"Let's hope not."

As Kurt and Tessa neared the water, she used a remote unit to extend a bridge toward the fuselage of the airplane. As soon as it bumped the side, she led Kurt across to it and opened the cargo door.

Tessa went inside, but Kurt paused by the entrance, visibly running his hand over the doorframe before disappearing into the lighted interior of the aircraft.

"Just when things were getting interesting," Priya said.

Joe lowered the binoculars. "For better or worse, Kurt's on his own now."

"THIS IS ONE impressive piece of machinery," Kurt said, admiring the *Monarch* as they went aboard. "Is it true you designed most of it yourself?"

"It is," Tessa said. "Does that surprise you?"

"Not at all."

"I had help, of course," she replied. "But I came up with the initial design, did most of the aerodynamic research on my own and then hired a small army of engineers to do the actual work. We built it in a shuttered factory in Poland that used to manufacture military transports."

Kurt knew all this already. "Why an amphibious plane? Just to be different?"

"Why did Hughes build the *Spruce Goose?*"

"He was trying to get a big contract to transport material across the Atlantic."

"I'm looking for the same thing," she said. "Three-quarters of the earth is covered in water. And many rural regions have no airports other than dirt strips, but they often have lakes to land on. The *Monarch* is eminently practical. One day, the world's leaders will see this."

They toured the aft section first, passing a boat and two automobiles protected beneath tarps. From the overall shapes and the low-profile tires sticking out, Kurt could tell they were performance cars.

"Bugatti?" Kurt asked.

"Ferrari, actually," she said, "though I have a Bugatti at my house in France and I once owned a Formula 1 racing team. How about you? Have you ever raced?"

"I wrecked an experimental Toyota in Japan once. Does that count?"

"Did you win?"

"Of course," Kurt said. "I cheated a little. But if you're not cheating, you're not trying."

She smiled with genuine glee. "I couldn't agree more."

The tour continued toward the tail end of the aircraft. A pair of Jet Skis and a powerboat were stored there. Beyond them sat a large cradle with hydraulic lifting arms. It didn't escape Kurt's attention that the cradle was circular in shape and, whatever it normally held, it was empty now.

He pretended not to notice, looked past it and studied the aft cargo door. The design of the door and placement of the hinges told him it could be lowered like a ramp. A conveyer belt system on the inside of the door could obviously be used to bring vehicles aboard and deposit them in the water.

"A rather ingenious setup," Kurt said. "And quiet. I don't hear an auxiliary power unit humming. How do you run all of this equipment?"

"I think you know the answer to that," Tessa said. "But, let me show you."

They went up to the middle deck, toward the nose. As the fuselage narrowed, they came upon an arrangement of gray metal boxes with orange stripes.

"These are the fuel cells," Tessa explained. "Most aircraft this size are forced to carry a dedicated APU to give them ground power for electrical, pneumatic and hydraulic controls. These are not small systems. On a typical 747, the APU puts out two thousand horsepower. The *Monarch* actually requires more power than a 747 due to our larger control surfaces and electrodes used to keep marine growth from forming on the bottom of the fuselage."

"And you get all that from these two small cells?" Kurt said.

She nodded. "All we need and then some. See for yourself."

Kurt studied a glass screen. According to the information on it, the fuel cells were running at sixty percent capacity and putting out enough electricity to light up a small town.

"This is a high-density unit," Tessa said. "It's being developed to replace diesel engines in semitrucks," she said. "A smaller version will be used for luxury cars. But, just making a dent in the trucking industry will turn us profitable. There are over fifteen million trucks in the U.S. alone, three million of which are tractor-trailers. Think of the fuel savings, the reduction in both air and sound pollution, when we've eliminated millions of noisy, smoke-belching trucks. And that's just one market. In twenty years, fuel cells will replace every coal-burning power plant, most of the gas-burning plants and every internal combustion engine in the industrial world."

She was back in sales pitch mode. Kurt acted as if he was considering the financial potential, but he was actually studying the schematic on the screen of the fuel cell. It looked a lot like a diagram Joe had drawn.

He turned to Tessa. "You should know I have nearly five hundred million dollars to invest—half my money, half from my partners. I won't say you're going to get it all, but if this all pans out, I'd be willing to offer a large portion of our funding in exchange for an exclusive deal."

Tessa looked confident now, radiant in the electronic glow of the small room. "I'm certain something can be worked out."

Tessa's phone buzzed. As she pulled it from the pocket of her robe, Kurt reached into the key pocket of his bathing suit and palmed a tiny, waterproof listening device. He would wait for the best moment to place it somewhere.

"*Sorry to bother you, Ms. Franco, but you have visitors coming in,*" the security guard said.

"If that's Oliver Warren, tell him he's too late."

"*It's Mr. Volke, Mr. Yates and Mr. Millard,*" the security leader said. "*They're on their way in by boat.*"

"Tell them I'm busy."

"*I told them as much already, ma'am. Mr. Volke insists on seeing you. He says the matter is urgent. Mr. Yates wants to speak with you as well.*"

Kurt let her off the hook. "Duty calls."

"So it would appear." Tessa sighed. "Send them down here when they arrive," she said to the guard. "I'll meet them on board the *Monarch*."

Kurt took her arm and she walked him back through the aircraft to the door on the lower deck. They paused in the doorway. Kurt drew her close and took one last look around as if admiring the plane. With his free hand, he placed the listening device behind a curved section of the fuselage.

"I hope I'll be hearing from you," he whispered as he stepped out through the door.

29

PAUL TROUT stood at the wheel of the *Raleigh*'s primary launch, which was basically a souped-up lifeboat without a top shell. Gamay was with him, heading north across the warm Gulf of Mexico waters.

"Didn't get much of a send-off," Paul said, glancing back at the distant lights of the *Raleigh*, almost ten miles behind them.

"That's what happens when you slip away in the middle of the night without telling anyone," Gamay replied.

That wasn't quite true. The captain and the executive officer knew, as did a few members of the third watch who saw them depart, but after Kurt and Joe had been ambushed in Florida, the Trouts had decided not to take any chances.

They'd loaded seven containers of the soil and bacteria onto the launch and pushed off, headed for New Orleans, where they would deliver the samples to a group of scientists handpicked by the President to study the bacteria and look for more efficient ways to kill, counteract or contain it.

"Do these scientists know we're coming?" Gamay asked.

"I figured we'd call them when we get into port," Paul said. "I didn't want anyone to know we were moving the samples."

Gamay nodded. "Speaking of that, I'd better check the containers. The bacteria are putting off more gas than we thought, and I don't want any explosions, which we might have if the pressure in those containers rises too high."

She left Paul's side and made her way to the short stairway that led to the boat's forward cabin. Stepping down to the bottom of the boat, she flicked the light on, lifted a tarp and then stepped back in shock.

"Derrick," Gamay said. "What are you doing here?"

He stood rapidly. "Quiet," he snapped, his voice a harsh whisper. He had a pistol in one hand and a radio in the other. The gun was pointed her way. There was no mistaking the message.

He put the radio to his mouth. "Prowler, this is Reynolds," he said. "You might as well move in. They've found me."

The response came through the radio just loud enough for Gamay to hear. "*You're still too far out. Keep them on their current heading, we'll intercept you in three miles.*"

"Who are you working for?" Gamay said.

"I told you to be quiet!" he snapped. "If Paul comes down here, I'll have to kill you both and I don't want to do that."

She knew Paul couldn't hear them. The wind of the open deck and the rumble of the engine drowned out any voice that wasn't shouted. "I don't know what you think you're doing, but you're making a big mistake."

"Thinking you could sneak away in the night was the mistake," Reynolds said. "Bringing all this with you . . ." He pulled the rest of the tarp back and tossed it aside, exposing the other containers.

"Those are soil samples from below the oil platforms," she said.

"I know what they are," Reynolds replied. "And I know you've been in the medical bay, adding chemicals and other things to the sediment. I've seen you in there. I heard the explosion when one of the experiments literally blew up in your face."

"What are you talking about?" she said. "We're not adding anything. We're simply studying the samples."

"You're altering them, so you can blame someone other than the oil company."

She looked Reynolds directly in the eye. There was a wild look about him. His face was red. She could see he was unstable and enraged by what he believed, but the voice on the radio had sounded far calmer. "Who were you speaking to?"

"Stop asking questions," he said.

"You're an environmentalist, right?"

"Of course I am," he said.

"I'm an environmentalist, too," she said. "I've testified before Congress for tougher laws on dumping waste in the seas and restricting drilling. I even chained myself to a few trees in my college days in the vain hope that they wouldn't be chopped down for a parking lot. I know what you're feeling, but—"

He cut her off again. "I'm not letting you blame radical environmental factions, or whatever else you might call them, for the negligence of the people who were operating that oil rig. I heard you talking to the captain about explosives. I know what your game plan is. We all know it. Big Oil and Big Government, can't tell where one starts and the other ends."

"We? Who are you working with?"

"A group who wants to do something about it," he told her.

At this moment, Paul shouted down the stairs. "Everything all right down there?"

The gun rose a fraction.

Gamay tilted her head toward the door and shouted back. "Just fine, honey. Be up in a few minutes."

Gamay could not remember ever calling Paul *honey*. She hoped the word would sound as strange to his ears as it felt coming from her lips.

"Just checking," Paul said calmly.

Reynolds grew more tense, gripping the gun, wiping some sweat from his face and splitting his attention between Gamay and the stairs, expecting Paul to come charging down to her rescue.

It didn't happen.

"So, what are you going to do here?" Gamay asked after another minute.

"Turn over the samples to friends of mine," Reynolds said.

"And then what?"

"They'll publish the truth."

"What are you going to do with us?" Gamay said.

He paused as if he hadn't thought it through. "They don't want you, they want the proof."

He was obviously being used by someone, but that didn't make him any less dangerous.

Paul shouted down to her again. "There's something up here you should see. Some weird lights on the horizon."

Gamay looked at Reynolds. "Sounds like your friends are here. Last chance to change your mind and do the right thing."

"I am doing the right thing," he said. "Let's go. Upstairs."

Gamay turned and pushed the door back.

"Slowly," Reynolds whispered.

She did as ordered, opening the door that led from the cabin to the stairs and climbing the flight slowly. Reynolds followed, gun in hand, eyes darting about, looking for trouble.

Paul wasn't waiting to ambush them. In fact, he was still at the helm. But the second Gamay reached the top step, he threw the wheel over and the boat swung wildly to port.

Gamay was knocked off balance. She landed on the deck and slid.

Reynolds—who was still halfway down the stairs—was thrown into the wall. He slammed against it, managed to hold on to the pistol and pushed off the wall, trying to stand up.

Immediately, Paul reversed his turn and the boat swung hard to starboard.

Reynolds fell the opposite way and slammed into the other wall. This second impact knocked the pistol from his grasp, causing it to discharge a single round into the wall.

Getting up, Reynolds lunged for the weapon, but Gamay's shoe caught him in the face and sent him flying backward into the cabin. Before he could get to his feet, Gamay had the gun and was holding it on him.

"Get on the floor," she shouted. "Hands as far forward as you can stretch them."

She watched him comply and then shouted up to Paul. "Nice work . . . *honey*. For a second, I thought you didn't hear me."

"We're not in the clear yet," Paul shouted down to her. "Those lights I told you about are for real. Two boats heading our way, one moving in behind us."

30

PAUL REMAINED at the wheel, while Gamay tied Reynolds up.

"I assume you secured our friend," he said when she appeared.

"Hog-tied and sheep-shanked him," Gamay said. "He's not going anywhere. But we should check on him in a little while."

"Assuming we survive that long," Paul said. "We're caught in the middle of a triangle. One boat off the port bow, another one off the starboard bow and one that crept in behind us."

Gamay looked aft, spotted the lights of the third boat and then turned back to Paul. "Have you tried calling for help?"

Paul turned up the volume on the marine radio. Every frequency hummed with a garbled electronic sound. "Jamming the entire spectrum."

"What other options do we have?"

"We're roughly halfway between the *Raleigh* and the coast," Paul told her, "but it's all open water back to the *Raleigh*. We disappear out there, no one will ever know what happened. But the closer

we get to the coast, the more likely we are to encounter other traffic. And within a few miles of shore, we should be able to use our
cell phone. They can't jam those. Then, there are the barrier islands
to think about."

He pointed to the chart. A long row of islands mirrored the
shape of the Gulf shoreline. The nearest was five miles away. "We
could hide in the shallows or even go ashore if we need to. At least
we'll have options."

"Let's go for the islands," she said.

Paul moved the throttle forward slowly and the launch surged
with surprising power. The crew of the *Raleigh* had tuned the engine, removed the governor and performed a few other tricks to
give their boat extra power.

It picked up speed easily and, before long, the lights ahead of
them began to widen out, not because they were moving away but
because the increased speed had changed the angle of approach.

It didn't last long. "Here they come," Gamay said.

Paul pushed the throttle to full and locked it there. The launch
picked up more speed and began to bounce on the chop. Each landing threw a sheet of spray over the top and, despite the windscreen,
Paul and Gamay were soon getting drenched.

The two boats turned hard, but the *Raleigh*'s launch was moving too quickly to be cut off. Before long, the three boats ended up
abreast of one another.

"Low-profile powerboats," Gamay said.

"They're small and fast, but we can pack a punch," Paul said.
"Hang on."

He cut the wheel to starboard and swerved toward the nearest of
the two boats, sideswiping it.

The boats rebounded off each other, but the smaller craft took the worst of it. Its bow was forced up and to the side, catching the air. It came down with the nose pointing sideways, flipped several times and vanished behind them in the dark.

"One down," Gamay said. "Great job."

Paul resisted the urge to smile and attempted the same tactic as the second boat swept in on them. The pilot of this boat was quicker. He pulled away and dropped back into a trailing position.

"They learn fast," Paul said.

With that boat dropping back, Paul could do nothing but concentrate on the course ahead. He took direct aim at the nearest barrier island and held the wheel, swerving only slightly here and there.

"We both know what's coming next," Gamay said. She ducked down, putting some amount of protection between her and the trailing speedboat.

Flashes from a firearm in the boat behind them were easy to see in the dark. The bullets were not. They whistled overhead and to the side. Invisible and deadly if they found their mark.

Paul crouched down, weaved a little more radically but kept the course changes to a minimum. Every turn cut down on their speed and added to the distance they had to travel.

With Paul handling the evasive maneuvers, Gamay began crawling toward the stern of the launch.

"Where are you going?" Paul asked.

"I have Derrick's gun," she said. "I want to test my marksmanship."

She reached the stern and took a position against the transom. Looking out over the stern, she zeroed in on the bow of the trailing speedboat. She tried to time the rise and fall of each boat, waiting as a large sheet of spray dropped behind them and then firing off several shots.

"Hit anything?" Paul shouted, turning the boat once more.

"Not that I can tell," she replied. "Between them moving and you swerving all over the place, it's impossible to aim."

"At least they're having the same problem."

"When I shout to you," Gamay said, "hold us steady. Just for two seconds."

"Will do," Paul said.

There was a reciprocal danger to that plan, underlined by the sudden shattering of the plastic windscreen as several bullets hit the boat, but Gamay trusted in her shooting skills.

She grabbed a life jacket, placed it on the transom and stretched her arms out over it.

"Are you ready?" Paul shouted.

"Almost," she said. She waited for the following boat to move in behind them. "Now!"

As Paul straightened the boat up, Gamay exhaled and pulled the trigger repeatedly. The automatic pistol recoiled, chambered a new round and fired it off in a rapid blur. In a few quick seconds, Gamay had sent eight shots out into the dark.

She ducked behind the transom and hoped to avoid return fire as Paul turned the boat again.

When she looked up, their pursuer was turning and heading off course. Whatever or whoever she'd hit, the boat continued out into the dark and vanished.

"Two down," she said.

Gamay checked the magazine as the third boat began to move in. There were only five shots left, a problem their new pursuer did not seem likely to have. "Looks like they're sending in big brother."

Though they couldn't see it, they could tell the third craft was more powerful by the sound of its engines. "Whatever it is, she's bigger and faster than us," Paul said.

They could never hope to outrun it, nor could they bully it like Paul had done to the first attacker. Making matters worse, the boat's pilot seemed to be an expert. Gamay could hear the throttle modulating precisely as it went over the waves. Because of that, its bow remained steady. And sitting up on that bow was a high-powered weapon on a tripod.

"Turn!" Gamay shouted.

Paul whipped the boat into a turn as a stream of red tracers flashed across the water. With five shells between each tracer round, that first burst would have been enough to shred the fiberglass launch.

"Sounds like fifty-caliber," Paul said. "Not that it matters."

"All that matters is, staying away from it," Gamay shouted.

Paul did his best, but the new attacker matched every twist and turn.

On the third change of direction, the .50 opened up and the launch took a barrage of hits. Chunks of fiberglass flew around them, one of the life rings was blasted off its hook and sent flying through the air. Gamay felt something tug on her windbreaker as if a bullet had clipped it, but fortunately neither she nor Paul nor the engine took any direct hits.

"We're coming up on the island," Paul said. "Maybe we can lose him in the shallows."

"I've got a better idea," Gamay replied. "Head for the rocks, if you can see any."

Continuing his evasive maneuvers, Paul did his best to be unpredictable. Two more bursts from the .50 lit up the night, but both were well wide of the mark.

Meanwhile, Gamay rushed down into the cabin and came out lugging two of the heavy steel containers containing the bacterial cultures.

Reaching the stern, she heaved the tanks up on the transom. "Head straight for the island!"

"We are!"

"Turn at the last second!"

"Got it," Paul said. "Ten seconds."

The speedboat was closing in again, lining up right behind them, setting up a kill shot for the man with the machine gun.

"Paul!"

"Wait," he said.

"I can't."

The machine gun began firing. Gamay ducked as more fiberglass was blasted from the transom. A sharp pain ran through her arm as a long splinter embedded itself in her skin. She winced and held on to the containers.

"Now!" Paul shouted.

Gamay opened the valves on the two tanks, shoving one off the transom to the left and one to the right. They hit the water just as Paul turned the wheel.

As the venting gas reacted, twin veils of fire spread out behind them. There was no explosion, no firestorm to cook the pursuing boat nor any thundering detonations to blow them off course, just two ballooning flashes of strangely colored fire, bright enough to blind.

The pilot of the following boat did the only rational thing. He avoided both fires by racing between them. He came out the other side with his night vision compromised. Even then, he saw the is-land, but it was far too late.

The boat hit the shore at forty miles an hour, tearing the bottom out, rupturing the tanks on the outboard engines and sending the remnants of the hull and the men flying onto the beach.

Paul and Gamay fared better in the *Raleigh*'s launch. They continued to turn, racing into the dark, scraping the bottom on some sand but otherwise emerging undamaged.

They left the barrier island behind and continued toward the mainland. After several minutes, without any sign of pursuit, they began to relax.

"I think we're in the clear," Paul said. Gamay pulled her cell phone out and began looking for a signal.

"I hope so," she replied. "Now, let's get in range and call the Coast Guard."

31

GREAT SOUND, BERMUDA

KURT WAS FERRIED back to the *Lucid Dream* in a 1963 Riva Tritone sportsboat. The perfectly restored craft was a work of art. Its polished wood gleamed beneath the moonlight. Leather seats dyed a powder-blue color were offset by chrome trim on the dash and around the windscreen.

Kurt sat back, enjoying the breeze and the rumble of the engine, while the flag of Bermuda fluttered on a short post behind him. Rarely had he considered the perks of wealth anything to aspire to—adventure was more his style—but he could have gotten used to owning a classic powerboat like the Riva.

Delivered to the yacht by the very security guard who'd attempted to tackle him, Kurt climbed aboard and saluted his nautical chauffeur. The gesture was not returned, but Kurt couldn't really blame the guy.

He made his way up the aft stairwell, finding Joe and Priya on the top deck, grinning like a pair of Cheshire Cats.

Joe tapped his watch. "You're well past curfew, young man."

"Ignore him," Priya said. "How was it? And don't spare the details."

"As missions go . . . it wasn't the worst."

Priya frowned. "Not the worst? How romantic. That's just the way every woman hopes to be described."

Kurt laughed. "Just trying to be a gentleman."

"Too late," Joe said, "we saw every move. You're far smoother than I'd have expected, but did you learn anything?"

"Tessa is a very determined woman," Kurt said, "with a plane full of dive gear, oxygen cylinders and a storage cradle the size and shape of our underwater flying object."

"Interesting," Joe said.

"Anything else?" Priya asked.

"Her corporate strategy seems heavily dependent on rising oil prices. And considering how aggressively she pushed me, they might not be rising fast enough."

"Sounds like she's our man," Joe said. "Our woman . . . Culprit, I mean . . . But, it's all circumstantial."

"I know," Kurt said. "Even if it wasn't, there's more here to figure out. There have to be other players. I want to know who they are and how they fit into this, starting with a trio of interlopers named Volke, Millard and Yates."

"Who are they?" Priya asked.

"No idea," Kurt said, "but they arrived just as I was leaving—ruining a perfectly good evening."

She began tapping away on her laptop. "We can cross-reference the names with all Tessa's known contacts. If anyone named Millard, Volke or Yates has been connected with Tessa or her company, we should be able to locate them."

It took less than a minute.

"No link to anyone named Volke," Priya said, "but Yates shows up. Brian Yates. He's an engineer. Head of her development team. Seems to be the lead designer on the fuel cell project."

Joe chimed in. "I saw his name on the letterhead at the conference. He was there, taking questions from a group of Tessa's investors. The ones you didn't interrupt."

"What about Millard?" Kurt asked.

Priya went back to searching. It took a little longer this time. "Pascal Millard," she said finally. "He's a French scientist. Genetic engineer. Primary field, bacterial crossbreeding."

Kurt's eyebrows went up. "What's his connection to Tessa?"

Priya read down further. "He worked for the French military and then for the civilian government in a scientific role. He was linked to a project that Tessa funded through charitable grants several years ago. Looks like he got into trouble shortly after that and was censured by the French Academy of Sciences. As a result, he was disciplined and then terminated from his government position."

"Does it say what he did?"

After scanning several articles, Priya shook her head. "No details. Only that he left France and moved to Martinique, then settled in Bermuda four years ago."

"What would a technology company need a genetic engineer for?" Joe asked.

"Nothing legitimate," Kurt said. "But according to Gamay's report, she and Paul found an unidentified strain of bacteria in the sediment beneath the Alpha Star. They suspect it's the source of the toxic and explosive gas."

"The trail is getting warmer," Priya said.

"Yes, it is."

Across the bay, the exterior lights surrounding Tessa's compound dimmed. Kurt picked up the binoculars and scanned the property. An open-topped fishing boat was heading out. It was the same one that had passed him as he'd left in the Riva. There were several men visible on deck. "Can you find a picture of Millard?"

Priya tapped a few more keys and then turned the computer toward Kurt and Joe. On-screen was the photo of an unassuming man in his late fifties. He had wispy gray hair and narrow shoulders. He wore rimless glasses.

Kurt felt certain it was the same man. He handed the binoculars to Joe. "What do you think?"

"Looks like Millard," Joe said. "A little thinner, but I'd say it's him. I don't see Yates down there, but I assume we're more interested in the genetic engineer at this point."

"You assume correctly," Kurt said. "Let's see where they're going."

32

KURT AND JOE went to the lower deck of the yacht and entered a compartment labeled *Boat Hangar.* Two Jet Skis were stored on one side while an aggressively designed powerboat was stored on the other side.

"Pavati 24," Joe said. "Normally, used for towing water-skiers or people on wakeboards. I've seen these in competition."

Kurt nodded his approval as he studied the craft. Its profile was jagged and angular instead of smooth and flowing. It had a wide, three-pointed bow, which the designers called a pickle fork. The hull was painted in a red and silver racing pattern, with the added touch of carbon fiber panels for looks and additional strength.

"Is our gear on board? If they go diving, we need to be able to follow."

"I loaded everything this morning," Joe said. "We've got all the new stuff."

"New stuff?"

"Advanced designs I've been working on," Joe said. "I think you'll like them."

Kurt wasn't sure what Joe had been up to, but he was looking forward to finding out. "You can tell me about them on the way."

They pushed the boat out into the water, climbed in and fired the engine up.

As they pulled away, a shout reached them from the top deck. "Don't mean to bother you gentlemen, but what should I do while you're gone?"

"Keep in touch with us by radio," Kurt said. "And see what else you can learn about Millard, Tessa and the *Monarch*. I'd like to know where that plane has been and compare its travels with the map of the dying oil wells."

"Sounds like a make-work job to me," Priya said, "but I'll do my best."

"I expect nothing less," Kurt said.

Joe pushed the throttle and the Pavati surged forward, accelerating away from the yacht. While Joe drove, Kurt moved to the bow and traded in the binoculars for a night vision scope. "They've got about a mile on us."

"Want me to close the gap?"

Kurt shook his head. "Save the power for later. They seem to be taking their time."

"You're no fun," Joe said as he eased off the throttle.

"Something tells me you'll get your chance to work that throttle before the night is over. For now, back us off and turn a little to the east, in case they're watching for a tail."

Joe angled slightly away from the fishing boat, which continued moving toward the mouth of the Great Sound. "Nothing but the Atlantic if they keep going that way."

The fishing boat held its course until it passed Spanish Point—the western end of the main body of land that made up Bermuda. From there, it turned northeast and ran parallel with Bermuda's north shore.

Joe followed suit.

"They're drifting wide," Kurt said. "Getting farther out."

"I'll keep us in the shallows," Joe said. "It'll make us harder to see."

Kurt nodded and sat back. For a moment, it seemed like a pleasure cruise. The island's long, low coastline, off to their right, was dotted with lights from homes, hotels and cars. Meanwhile, the fishing boat was easy to track against the pitch-darkness that loomed out to sea. At least until its lights suddenly went out.

"They've gone into stealth mode," Joe said.

Kurt sat up, put the scope to his eye and scanned for the telltale white foam at the aft end of the boat. He found it and followed it for a few seconds before it, too, vanished.

"That's odd."

"What happened?"

"The wake just ended," Kurt said. "It didn't peter out, it just stopped."

Widening the field of view, Kurt found the reason it had disappeared so abruptly. "They went behind a ship. A freighter, sitting out there, darkened to the world."

Putting the scope down, Kurt picked up the radio and called back to the yacht. "Priya, this is Kurt, do you read?"

"Go ahead, Kurt."

"I need you to pull up the AIS tracking service we use. Our friends have linked up with a midsized freighter anchored north of the island. I want to know what ship it is and who owns it."

"*Stand by,*" she said. "*Sorry, but there's no AIS signal in your area. Whoever they are, they're operating without broadcasting an ID.*"

"No surprise there," Joe said.

Kurt continued to study the freighter through the night vision scope. The fishing boat remained hidden behind it. "Find us a spot to anchor," he said. "Time to put these special dive suits of yours to the test."

33

WITH THE PAVATI anchored in the shallows, Joe opened the storage lockers and pulled out two wetsuits, a pair of rebreathers and two helmets.

"The new stuff," Kurt said. "You weren't kidding."

None of the equipment looked like standard gear. The wetsuits were ribbed, with pads in the thighs, hips and calf areas, and battery packs instead of weight belts.

The rebreathers were slim and compact, flat enough that one could wear a windbreaker over them and no one would notice. The helmets had strange protrusions sticking out either side that reminded Kurt of the mirrors on a small car.

Kurt picked up the wetsuit first. "It looks like superhero body armor."

"You'll swim like a superhero with this," Joe said. "The ribs and padded areas are power-assisted modules and artificial muscle."

"Artificial muscle?"

Joe nodded. "Those robotic assemblies we dealt with last year gave me the idea. I figured, instead of a bulky propulsion unit with a propeller, why not just enhance the diver's swimming motion? To make it work, I embedded a material in the neoprene that expands and contracts like muscle when an electrical current is applied. Once you turn it on, the suit will kick for itself, all you have to do is set the pace on the small touch screen on your forearm."

"How fast will this make us?"

"In this suit, you'll be twice as fast as the world record holder," Joe said. "It's strong, too. We tested it against a four-knot current and the diver made it two miles without even breaking a sweat."

"Two miles against a strong current," Kurt said. "Who was dumb enough to volunteer for that job?"

Joe pointed to himself. "That's the problem with being a visionary designer, no one believes in you till you prove it."

"You're starting to sound like Tessa," Kurt said, taking the dive helmet from Joe. "Now, what's the deal with these helmets? They look like a cross between Buck Rogers and a VW Bug."

Joe feigned distress at the comment. "Form follows function. With these helmets, you can see in the darkest, murkiest water like a dolphin."

Kurt studied the helmet a second time. He noticed the appendage on the right side was slightly different than the one on the left. "One for emitting the sound burst, the other for hearing what bounces back."

Joe nodded. "What's the one problem with a night dive? Aside from the creepy feeling that something might be sneaking up on you."

"Visibility."

"Exactly. Without powerful lights, you can't see much at all.

Even with them, you often attract sea creatures like moths to a campfire. And on a dive like tonight's, we're not going to be using lights at all unless we want to attract an entirely different kind of attention."

"Too true," Kurt said. "But I hope you don't expect me to interpret pings and clicking noises the way dolphins do."

"I'm aware of the limitations of your puny brain," Joe said. "The system uses a scanning sound beam to continuously paint the area in front of you. The emitter uses ten different frequencies simultaneously. The receiver picks up the reflected sound waves, runs them through a program Hiram and Priya developed and then projects a 3-D image against the glass of the helmet. It's monochrome for now, so it'll feel like you're swimming in a world of black and gray, but it's pretty amazing, if I do say so myself."

"Can't wait to try it," Kurt said. "And the rebreathers?"

"I simply miniaturized everything, added a powered filter and included a small reserve air tank in case the filters get corrupted or the pump breaks down."

Kurt began pulling on the gear. "You've outdone yourself this time. Let's give this stuff a try."

As soon as they entered the water, Kurt began playing around with the sonar system. He swam under the wake boat, flipping over onto his back and kicking deeper. The sonar buzzed softly in his ear, but was not obtrusive. The detail on the glass in front of him was incredible. He saw seams and welds, even a notch in the propeller where it had obviously hit something—all from twenty feet away.

The only real issues were shadows and loss of definition whenever something blocked the sonar wave, causing a delay in response and video projection.

With the human mind used to perceiving life in the all-but-instantaneous fashion of vision through light waves, the delay in response from the sonar system was obvious and mildly disorienting when one moved one's head from side to side. "That lag is going to take some getting used to."

Joe's voice responded over the intercom. "It's the one thing we can't engineer out. Best not to move your head too often or too suddenly. One of the test divers got really queasy doing that."

"Was that you?" Kurt asked.

"Like I said, it's hard to find good help. Ready?"

Kurt nodded.

"Use the internal navigation system and set your course zero-two-five. That will take us right toward the freighter."

Kurt looked at the forearm-mounted display, hit the navigation button and typed in 025 [SET]. A compass indicator appeared, projected on the glass of the helmet.

Submerging, Kurt turned until 025 was directly in front of him, then began the long swim, activating the power-assisted modules early in the journey.

The boost was sudden and unexpected, like stepping onto a moving walkway that was traveling faster than one realized. This sensation also took some getting used to. The wetsuit squeezed and released his legs rhythmically and, before too long, it felt natural, even soothing.

"This is like a compression massage," Kurt said. "I cannot believe someone didn't think of this before."

"Not everyone has the mind of a genius," Joe replied. "Keep an eye on your battery level. The power pack will give you an hour of full assist, with a reserve of ten minutes at half strength."

Kurt glanced at the arm-mounted display and saw that his power

level was ninety-seven percent. The rest of the journey was conducted in silence until the helmet-mounted GPS told them they
were nearing the freighter's location.

"Setting the sonar to maximum range," Kurt said. The change
brought the hull of a midsized freighter into view. "Let's go under
the ship and come up on the far side. Keep toward the bow in case
they start those props."

"Sounds like a reasonable plan," Joe said.

They kicked deeper, diving beneath the barnacle-covered hull
and turning toward the bow. Nearing it, they discovered that the
ship was tied off to a marine buoy and anchored.

As Kurt swam past the anchor line at a depth of thirty feet, a
thunderous crash sounded from directly above him.

He looked up to see a huge cylindrical object emerging from a
wall of bubbles and foam and plummeting toward him. He kicked
hard to get out of the way, but the object never reached his depth. It
slowed its descent and rose back up, bobbing to the surface, where
it floated half submerged like a log in the river.

As the foam and turbulence from the impact dispersed, Kurt
spotted eight tires in pairs at the back end of the cylinder. Large
valves, heavy coupling points and a stand on the other end of the
cylinder from the tires told him what he was looking at.

"Tanker truck," Kurt said.

Joe swam up beside him. "Only you could have a truck fall on
your head in the middle of the ocean."

"Notice anything strange?"

"Stranger than a truck in the ocean?" Joe said. "Not really."

"That's an eight-ton hunk of metal," Kurt said. "And it's
floating."

"It's empty."

Kurt nodded.

As they watched, additional splashes appeared in the water on the far side. These were smaller and more at home in the water.

"Divers," Joe said. "Our little corner of the Atlantic is getting crowded."

The warm glow of lights added some color to the scene that hadn't been there before as the divers clustered around the floating truck.

"I'm not interested in getting spotted down here," Kurt said. "Let's swim over to the buoy. We can hide behind it and enjoy a front-row seat to the goings-on."

34

VOLKE STOOD at the rail of the SS *Morgana*, shouting instructions to the men in the water. "Are you trying to get yourselves killed? Get back, you fools! Don't get between the truck and the hull."

It was no use. With the noise of the crane dipping down toward the tanker truck, the sound of the water slapping against the freighter's hull and the general pandemonium, no one heard him.

Volke turned to the crane operator. "I told you to lower the tanker, not drop it."

"Not my fault," the man said. "The cable snapped."

"Replace it," Volke said. "You have less than one hour."

Volke left the frustrated crane operator behind and went below, finding an open cargo door on the lower deck, closer to where the tanker floated.

"We need to get something between the ship and the truck," Volke shouted. He commandeered several crewmen and had them toss out anything that could be used as a bumper—life preservers, a raft and one of the ship's own bumpers.

While Volke worked, Pascal Millard arrived, clutching a folder and staring in disbelief at the chaos down on the water. "This is what I mean when I say we're running toward disaster."

"This," Volke said, "is a setback. *Disaster* is far too strong a term."

Volke expected Millard to back down, he was a quiet man in general, but the scolding brought a bold response.

"This," Millard replied, mirroring Volke's speech pattern, "is a sign of systemic problems. Too much, too fast, with too little thought as to what might happen if something goes wrong. Each little setback is going to compound the next and a disaster will ensue. Mark my words."

Volke laughed. Millard was probably right, but he wasn't about to let the little scientist know that. He grabbed Millard by the shirt, swung him toward the open hatch and pushed him toward the edge until only Millard's heels and the strength of Volke's arms were keeping him from falling. "Just do your job and keep your mouth shut or you might face a disaster of your own."

Grabbing for the edge of the door, Millard dropped the folder and his papers fluttered into the water. If he fell now, he would be another bumper, caught between the floating truck and the ship. "I'm just trying to help."

Volke held Millard hostage a moment longer, then pulled him back inside. Down below, an area of the seawater was brightening.

"The *Wasp* is here," he told Millard. "You're going down below to begin the transfer process. And don't plan on any delays, because I'm coming with you."

. . .

FROM BEHIND THE BUOY, Joe watched the action with a mixed sense of curiosity and wonder. When the damaged cable was cut from the crane and tossed into the water, it became clear that the splash-down was unintended.

"That free fall was a mistake," Joe said, "but they were still lowering the tanker when it fell."

"Why here?" Kurt said, still communicating over the helmet-mounted radios. "Bermuda has no oil."

"Getting rid of the evidence?" Joe suggested.

"Better off dumping it in the middle of the ocean," Kurt said. "The depth here can't be more than two hundred feet. I'd say they've chosen this spot for a reason."

"We can have Priya check to see if there's anything unusual around here," Joe said. "The comm system has a high-frequency link for use on the surface."

"Do the honors," Kurt said.

Joe pulled himself higher on the buoy and brought his arm out of the water. Tapping the control panel on his forearm, he switched his radio to the HF band. "Priya, this is Joe. Do you read?"

The reply came within seconds. *"Loud and clear. Are you on your way back?"*

"Not yet," Joe said. "We're watching the men on the freighter unload some very odd equipment. We're wondering why they chose this spot. Use the location info from the transponders in our helmets."

"I have you," Priya told them. *"Three miles west-northwest of Ferry Point."*

"Sounds right," Joe said. "Anything unusual about the area? Sinkhole or drop-off or anything like that?"

"Not that I can see. You're near the reef. Depth averaging one hundred and forty feet. You have to go out another mile before it truly falls off."

Joe looked back at the freighter and noticed a circle of light widening around the floating truck. Sliding back into the water, he stared through the gloom. The beams of a several spotlights were visible as a submersible ascended directly beneath the tanker.

Switching to the sonar system, Joe saw more detail. The submersible had a pinched waist and large claws that extended upward. As the claws wrapped around the body of the tanker, the divers swam about, checking the fit and inserting locking pins.

With the tanker locked in place, the submersible rose up a few feet, took on a couple of passengers and then vented a large volume of air, beginning a slow descent and dragging the tanker down with it.

"Volke and Millard just boarded that sub," Kurt said. "Tell Priya we're going to follow them down."

Joe relayed the information to Priya and then he and Kurt pushed off the buoy and slipped beneath the surface.

35

SITTING ON the *Lucid Dream*, Priya listened to Joe's call and was excited to be a member of the field team, yet slightly jealous that Kurt and Joe were having all the fun.

Diving had been a fascination of hers for years. The excitement to do more of that had been a big draw in joining NUMA, but the accident had taken most of that away.

She still dived on occasion, but it was only for leisure now and it was a complicated effort to set up those opportunities.

"*See what else you can find out about the* Monarch," Joe had suggested.

"Will do," she'd said dutifully. "Be careful down there."

"*You, too.*"

That was the last communication.

You, too? Priya thought. *What am I supposed to be careful about, not getting carpal tunnel syndrome from all this computer work?*

Self-pity was a trait she despised. She shrugged off the disappointment, got back to work and spent the next ten minutes searching fruitlessly for information on the *Monarch*.

She'd searched public sources, media references and even ran a query for sightings of the plane on Facebook and Twitter. She'd tapped into FAA and international air traffic control databases. Aside from a few air shows, boat shows and other carefully staged PR events, news of the *Monarch* appeared only on the rarest of occasions.

All of which suggested the plane rarely flew, but information she'd downloaded about its engine overhaul schedule told her the plane had logged nearly four thousand hours of flight time in the last two years. Enough to cover a million miles.

"You don't rack up all those frequent-flier miles going from Bermuda to Miami for boat shows," she said.

She looked across the water. Tessa's compound remained dimly lit, but a few security lights silhouetted the *Monarch*. It sat like a shadowy ghost. A ghost that went anywhere it wanted without the world knowing.

Frustrated by her inability to find anything of value and bored with sitting and watching, an idea occurred to her. It was an idea she should have pushed aside as soon as it came to mind, but instead she romanced the thought for a moment, considering the possibilities and potential drawbacks.

The more she thought about it, the stronger its pull became.

Staring across the water at the silent plane, she spoke as if addressing it personally. "If you won't be good enough to tell us where you've been, then perhaps we should stop asking and start tracking you."

The trip to Bermuda had been planned rapidly. Not wanting to get caught short, Kurt had ordered them to bring anything that might be helpful. In addition to Joe's powered diving gear, the high-tech cameras, listening devices and drones, they'd brought with them beacons the team called geotrackers.

With an incredible adhesive that bonded to everything it touched, the geotrackers could be attached to moving boats, floating garbage, even sharks, whales and other living things.

"Why not," she told herself. "If Kurt can swim across the bay for a date, why can't I do the same to advance our mission?"

She could accomplish the task using just her arms. But thanks to Joe, she didn't have to do it on her own.

She set the camera on record, wrote an entry into her computer log and wheeled herself toward the yacht's small elevator. A moment later, she was on the lower deck, retrieving one of the powered dive suits from the locker.

She disrobed and pulled the suit on, adjusting the fit until it was snug. That done, she pulled the top up over her shoulders, slid her arms in and zipped it up.

In comparison to getting the wetsuit situated, donning the rest of the gear was easy. She tested every item, double-checked the power pack and then pulled out one of the geotrackers.

With a rebreather in place, she scooted to the edge of the transom. With only the briefest of second thoughts, she pushed herself backward and plunged into the waters of Bermuda's Great Sound.

She swam with her arms for a minute, setting her buoyancy to a slightly negative level, while she submerged and activated the suit.

Her right leg kicked and then her left. The artificial muscle contractions happened slowly and awkwardly at first. Using the controller on her forearm, she increased the pace until it became a natural rhythm.

Over the past few years, she'd had many dreams in which she was running and climbing, but far more where she was swimming. And while she couldn't feel the squeezing sensation that Kurt and Joe felt, because the sensation could not pass the break in her spine, she felt the movement and the power in her hips and her lower back. The sensation of speed was incredible, euphoric. For just a moment, she felt as if she was flying.

36

WHILE PRIYA was swimming across the Great Sound, Kurt and Joe were descending through the open waters of the Atlantic.

Forced to avoid the divers who remained near the freighter, they'd swung wide around the ship's bow before descending in the direction of the tanker-laden submersible.

Kurt was a few yards ahead, kicking smoothly, allowing the power suit to do most of the work. The submarine was up ahead, running with its high beams on, but slowly getting dimmer with the growing distance.

"What's the max range on this sonar?" Kurt asked.

"About four hundred yards," Joe said, "depending on the water conditions."

Four hundred yards was much farther than one could see with even the brightest of lights.

Kurt switched the sonar system back on, dialing up the maximum range. The gray field of vision and the outline of the submersible appeared. It was leveling off and gliding across the top of a reef.

"Would you look at that," Joe said.

The sonar system gave a three-dimensional appearance to the view, and the ship on the bottom seemed to lengthen as they approached it.

The angled bow was pointed toward them. Behind it, three huge, dome-shaped structures protruded from the main deck. Each dome was actually the upper half of a spherical container, known as a Moss tank. They were designed to hold liquid natural gas under extreme pressure. The lower halves of the spheres were hidden below deck.

"That's a liquid natural gas carrier," Kurt said.

"Big one, too," Joe replied. "The question is, what's she doing down here?"

"Tessa has a foundation that sinks ships to encourage reef building," Kurt said. "Though, I have a feeling this vessel has a more sinister purpose."

"Mother ship," Joe suggested. "With this tanker coming in for a fill-up."

"Exactly," Kurt said. "I think we've found the source of infection."

They followed the submarine down, closing the gap as the ungainly vessel navigated cautiously between a field of coral and the side of the ship.

It slowed to a stop, pivoted and—after stirring up a cloud of sediment—disappeared into a gaping hole in the side of the ship's hull.

"That's a surprise," Joe said. "I figured they'd lock on, fill up and head back to the surface."

"As did I," Kurt said.

With the submarine gone, he could see a large section of hull plating moving back into position like a garage door closing.

"Let's get through the door before they shut us out."

Both men dived hard, swimming toward the rapidly shrinking gap and darting through the cloud of sediment and beneath the closing door.

They wound up inside the hull of the monstrous ship, listening to the audible clang of the hull plates shutting behind them.

The submersible floated ahead and above them, its lights illuminating the inner sanctum of the LNG carrier.

Kurt had been inside similar ships and one look told him the guts of the vessel had been torn out. Structural supports, machinery and entire portions of the inner hull had been cut away and removed. What remained was an open space, several hundred feet in length and a hundred and forty feet wide, with the lower halves of the spherical tanks hanging in place like the undersides of three great balloons.

The submersible with the tanker truck on top was inching upward into a gap cut in the first of the three spheres.

"Now what?" Joe asked.

"What else," Kurt replied. "We see what's inside the sphere."

37

VOLKE WAS at the helm of the submarine he and the crew called the *Wasp*. It had no official name, but it possessed a bulbous bow, pointed stern and a pinched waist like the insect.

Volke would have preferred they call it something more accurate—like the *Wallowing Hippo*. It was hard to maneuver, top-heavy, with the tanker mounted above it, and given to rolling badly on the surface, even in the slightest waves.

Thankfully, it was far more stable when the ballast tanks were full and it was operating beneath the water. Only, that made it slower than ever.

After they navigated into the hull, it took hours to line up with the gap in the docking sphere. When that was done, Volke grabbed the radio.

"Docking Sphere, this is Volke," he said into a microphone. "Anyone awake up there?"

A scratchy signal carried the response. *"We're ready for you,* Wasp. *Cleared to surface."*

Volke eased the *Wasp* upward until it cleared the waterline. "Shutting down," he called out. "Pull us to the dock."

Inside the sphere, a group of crewmen, walking on metal grates, jumped aboard the bow, tied the line off and pulled the submersible to the dock.

"Equalizing pressure," the copilot said.

Volke felt his ears popping.

"Pressure matched. Releasing the hatch."

A hatch opened directly above them. The copilot went out first, followed by Millard. Volke went through last and found the nearest crewman. "Is the next shipment ready?"

"You'll have to check with the foreman," the crewman said. "There was a problem with the new cultures."

Volke glared at Millard for a moment. He suspected the problem was the scientist's doing. "Come with me."

With Millard in tow, Volke walked along the metal grate, each footstep echoing off the curved steel walls around them. They made their way to the opening of a steel tube six feet in diameter. This was the conduit that had been welded into place between the docking sphere and the tank next to it, which they called the control sphere.

"After you," Volke said.

Millard disappeared into the tube and Volke followed just a few steps behind.

KURT AND JOE slipped through the gap in the bottom of the docking sphere far more easily than the bulky submarine.

Looking upward, Kurt noticed the same shimmer on the sonar

readout that he'd seen when looking to the surface before. There was air on the other side of that shimmering line. "They've turned this into an underwater habitat."

"We should examine their work," Joe said.

"I thought you'd never ask."

Kurt shut off the sonar system and studied the layout, using only the visible light. The submarine with the tanker was docked above them to the left. The illumination was brightest in that area. On the other side of the sphere was another submersible, the small, disk-shaped craft they'd battled in the Gulf of Mexico.

"Follow me," Kurt said.

He swam beneath the disk submersible and surfaced behind it. As expected, there were no crewmen in that area. Joe surfaced moments later and the two of them gazed across the water toward the larger submarine with the tanker on its back.

Three crewmen were working on it, blasting jets of hot air into the couplings of the tanker truck and then following that up with another gas.

"What do you think they're doing?" Kurt asked.

"Nitrogen," Joe said. "They're making sure there's no water or other impurities in the couplings that might contaminate what they're about to load. Assuming it's the bacteria Paul and Gamay discovered, I can't say I blame them."

With a second hose connected to the tanker, the men sat down on overturned buckets and waited while the entire truck was pumped full of inert gas.

"How long do you think that will take?"

"Depends on the pressure level," Joe said. "Speaking of which"— he looked at the screen on his arm—"we have eleven minutes down here before we're going to need to make a decompression stop.

Wouldn't want to have to tread water at sixty feet with this group chasing us."

Kurt nodded. "Eleven minutes should be plenty of time to throw a monkey wrench in their plans."

"What do you suggest?"

"This crew isn't exactly on high alert," Kurt said. "You go play Flipper and distract them from the water, I'll sneak around behind them and put them to sleep."

"And then?"

"We steal their overalls and walk around like we own the place. Possibly pressing a few buttons and throwing a few levers and doing whatever we can to put this place out of whack."

Joe slid back into the water while Kurt took off his fins, climbed carefully onto the decking and crept around the semidarkened sphere to a spot behind the three crewmen who were servicing the tanker.

As Kurt crouched there, waiting to attack, a large eruption of bubbles began to foam up on the surface directly in front of the crewmen. One of them stood, leaning forward for a better look. "It's coming from the *Wasp*."

As they looked on, Joe broke the surface, propelled upward by a combination of his own strength and the full energy of the powered dive suit. He surged toward the crewman like a crocodile at the edge of a muddy river.

Instead of a bite, Joe grabbed the man with both hands, yanking him forward and pulling him off the dock and into the water.

The other men stood and rushed forward in shock. They never saw Kurt coming.

Kurt clubbed one man in the back of the neck and he dropped straight down onto the metal grating without anything more than a grunt of pain.

The second man turned, took a punch to the gut, which doubled him over, and a knee to the face that finished him off.

By the time Joe surfaced with the third man—who was coughing and spitting out water and in no mood to fight—Kurt was tying the first two men up.

In a minute flat, all three were stripped of their coveralls, tied and stuffed into the passenger compartment of the strange submarine with the tanker on its hull.

"How many people do you have down here?" Kurt asked.

"Twelve," one of the crewmen said.

"Including the three of you?"

The man nodded.

"Where did Volke and Millard go?"

"The control sphere."

Kurt found some tape and slapped it over the mouths of the captives. Additional lengths of tape were wrapped around their ankles and wrists to ensure they wouldn't slip their bonds.

"You three, sit tight," Joe said.

With the men secured, Kurt and Joe took off their own helmets, stored them and pulled the crewmen's coveralls over their dive suits. The compact rebreathers were flat enough to be hidden, especially as the lines and regulators retracted into the unit itself. And while Kurt and Joe appeared slightly hunchbacked when studied in profile, the overalls were loose-fitting enough to disguise it.

Dressed appropriately, they climbed out of the submarine and made their way into the tunnel that Volke and Millard had taken.

"Brilliant idea to turn this into a habitat," Kurt said. "Spheres are naturally resistant to pressure. Like an archway, only in three dimensions."

"Normally, I'd agree with you," Joe said. "But they've cut a bunch of holes in them. This tunnel and the gap down below were definitely not part of the original design. From an engineering perspective, that weakens things considerably. I wouldn't want to live and work down here, and I wouldn't bet our lives on the structural integrity of this setup. Especially if anything goes wrong."

Kurt laughed lightly. "What," he asked, "could possibly go wrong?"

38

GREAT SOUND, BERMUDA

PRIYA SWAM toward the *Monarch*, aiming for a spot beneath the nose of the huge aircraft. If she was right, the security system would include cameras situated on either side of the bay and motion sensors protecting the grounds of the palatial estate, but nothing directly beneath the plane.

Swimming underneath the *Monarch*'s belly, she marveled at the size of it. The aircraft was nearly the length of a World War II destroyer. She noticed the details of the hull that weren't visible in photographs.

The front of the hull was thicker and covered with tiny lines and ridges like those used on America's Cup yachts. They would make the craft more slippery in the water.

Farther back, the underside of the plane took on a Coke bottle shape and, from that point on, was perforated with thousands of tiny holes that stretched from one side of the aircraft to the other.

They could only be high-pressure air valves, designed to pump millions of bubbles into the space between the fuselage and the water.

The process was called supercavitation. It temporarily and drastically reduced the drag on any object moving through a fluid. Using a similar method, marine engineers, including some in NUMA, were building torpedoes and specialized submarines that could do well over a hundred knots.

Priya marveled at the ingenuity and the extent to which it had been used. Without the system, she doubted the *Monarch* could ever leave the water.

Continuing toward the tail, Priya reached a spot where the hull began to curve upward. Shutting off the power assist of the dive suit and setting her buoyancy to neutral, she surfaced beneath the slope of the rising tail section. It stretched upward and back at an angle, keeping her in the shadows.

"Time for you to start giving up your secrets," she whispered to the plane.

She unzipped a small pouch and pulled out a device the size and shape of a smoke alarm. Next, twisting the top of the geotracker a quarter turn, she activated the device and then peeled a protective layer from the base, exposing the adhesive.

Reaching up, she stretched out of the water as far as possible and pressed the device against the flat skin of the aircraft's tail. It bonded instantly. In thirty seconds, it would be impossible to pry off without a crowbar.

Dropping back down into the water, Priya disappeared beneath the surface without a splash. She swam beneath the aircraft, using only her arms to pull her along, before reactivating the dive suit.

She swam past the nose, made a half turn and set course for

home. With a great sense of accomplishment, she left the amphibious aircraft behind.

AS PRIYA SWAM away from the *Monarch*, Tessa Franco was in her
office on the aircraft's upper deck, dealing with her chief engineer.

"I'm not talking to your investors again," Brian Yates informed
her. "Not if you're going to have me lie about the state of our technology."

Yates was a genius designer and brilliant chemist, he was also
stubborn and had very few interpersonal skills. If he hadn't been so
highly regarded by the tech community, Tessa wouldn't have trot-
ted him out in front of her possible benefactors.

"They're not my investors," she said. "They're our investors and
we won't have a company without them."

"We won't have a company with them," Yates countered. "Not
the way things are going."

"What are you saying?"

"Exactly what I've been saying for months," he snapped. "The
fuel cells don't work. Certainly not as well as you're representing.
And they never will, not without extensive design changes. They'll
also cost twice as much to manufacture as you're claiming. You
realize there will be no profit at all on the final product. And, I'm
not going to stand up in front of a bunch of investors who trust me
and tell them otherwise. I have a reputation to protect as well."

Tessa realized Yates had an overinflated view of his importance,
to the point where she'd caught him referring to the fuel cells and
the company as if he were the driving force.

"Listen to me, Yates, and listen to me carefully," she said. "It's
your job to fix that. I'm protecting you, not the other way around.

Everything you've worked for, everything you've been promised, it all goes away if the world suspects there might be a problem with what we're building. Do you understand?"

Yates was undeterred. "There's a difference between keeping it quiet and lying. I'm not going to lie anymore. You can find someone else to be your mouthpiece. The next time someone asks me about the system, I'm telling them the truth."

As Tessa stared, Yates took his conference ID badge and tossed it at her feet.

She ignored the tantrum, her blood running cold instead of hot.

Yates seemed disappointed. He turned his back on her and walked out. She allowed him to reach the hall before pulling out a snub-nosed Smith & Wesson .380 automatic.

"Mr. Yates," she said coldly. "I will not allow you to ruin me."

Yates turned, saw the pistol but never got the chance to retract his resignation.

Tessa fired repeatedly, hitting him four times squarely in the chest and sending him to the deck in a pool of spreading blood.

The gunshots echoed through the aircraft and the commotion brought Woods down the corridor.

He stopped and stared at Yates's body. "What . . . ?"

"Don't ask," she said. "Just get rid of him. Take him out to sea and dump him."

Woods looked at the body and shook his head. "Fine," he said. "But, we have another problem."

"Seems to be the night for them," Tessa said with a sigh. "What is it now?"

"A diver," Woods said. "A woman, by the looks of it. She swam underneath the plane and then back out into the harbor. We caught sight of her on one of the underwater cameras. She attached something to the fuselage near the tail. I have one of the men checking it out."

"Tell me you tracked her," Tessa said.

"We didn't have time to get a swimmer in the water, but I tracked her with one of the underwater drones. She swam back into Great Sound at a fairly rapid pace. We trailed her to a yacht named *Lucid Dream*."

"That's Hatcher's yacht," Tessa growled.

"The investor?"

Tessa shook her head. Things were going from bad to worse. "Something tells me he's not an investor. Get your men together. Get rid of Yates, then I want Hatcher and this woman brought back here."

"And if they don't want to come?"

Tessa glared at him. "I'm not sending you to deliver an invitation."

39

LNG CARRIER, AT A DEPTH OF ONE HUNDRED AND SIXTY FEET

KURT OPENED the watertight door to the control sphere with deliberate caution. There was no hiss of air, which told him the two spheres were kept at equal pressure and that there was also no one directly on the other side.

He stepped through onto the same type of metal grating that had been used in the docking sphere. Ahead of him stood racks of equipment and machinery, all connected by a maze of pipes that ran overhead. Pumps and cooling units could be heard humming, while a stack of the orange and gray fuel cells he'd seen on Tessa's plane ran along the left side of the sphere.

"No shortage of power," he whispered.

Near the fuel cells was a control area, with a wall of gauges and a computer screen displaying a diagram of the liquids and gas flowing through the pipes and the various valves.

On the far side, he saw a pair of large vats and several dozen tanks stacked up in racks. The tanks were long and cylindrical, like those used at gas stations to hold propane.

Because the space was a near-perfect sphere, sounds echoed at them from every direction. Footsteps, valves opening and closing, voices. Someone on the far side dropped a tool and the sound reverberated around the sphere multiple times.

Kurt took a path to the left, moved behind the nearest rack of equipment and continued forward, slowing to listen to an echoing voice.

"This . . . this . . . this . . ."

"Pressure at one-zero-five . . . zero-five . . . zero-five . . ."

"Primary vat ready for transfer . . . transfer . . . transfer . . ."

A loud bang sounded as a valve was thrown open and the echo circled them half a dozen times, drowning out the odd bits of conversation.

Kurt glanced through a gap in the machinery. Volke and Millard were at the console near the wall of gauges in the center of the room. They appeared to be having a heated discussion.

"Ever been to Statuary Hall?" Kurt whispered, leaning close to Joe's ear.

Joe grinned. "You're thinking of John Quincy Adams."

Kurt nodded. "Rumor had it, he would pretend to sleep at his desk while eavesdropping on his opponents as their voices echoed off the domed ceiling. If we can find the right spot, we might be able to overhear everything Volke and Millard are saying."

"Great idea," Joe said. "We'll cover more ground if we split up."

"You go that way," Kurt said, "I'll go this way. Keep an eye on the hatch. If anyone heads for the submarine, we need to beat them to it."

Joe nodded and walked off. Kurt went in the opposite direction, grabbing a clipboard from a hook and carrying it with him.

He wandered from one section of equipment to the next, passing the bank of fuel cells. The acoustics were such that he reached one spot where the machinery noise was amplified and painful to hear. A few feet away, it was almost completely silent.

He moved in closer to propane-style tanks. Each was labeled to hold five hundred gallons of liquefied gas. Oddly, the tanks were hot to the touch. Wandering among them, pretending to check the gauges, Kurt counted forty tanks in all, stacked two high on a scaffold and connected to one another by copper pipes, some of which led back to the large vats.

"We need more storage . . . storage . . . storage . . ."

The words came out of nowhere, but with a French accent. It had to be Millard.

"Pressure getting too high . . . high . . . high . . ."

Kurt moved to the right, heard less, and then moved back to the left.

"I don't have time to wait around . . . around . . . around . . ."

Kurt assumed the second voice was Volke's. He moved crouched down as if looking more closely at one of the gauges and found the sweet spot.

"That petrol truck was supposed to be used for siphoning off the gas," Millard said. "Nine thousand liquefied gallons of it. We're far beyond safe storage down here already. If you fill it with bacterial cultures instead, this whole production facility will be in danger of shutting down or, worse, blowing up."

"Relieve the pressure another way," Volke said. "Vent some of the gas into the sea, if you have to."

"It reacts with water," Millard reminded him. "You might as well send up a flare telling the whole world we're down here."

The argument ended and Kurt checked the orange-faced Doxa watch on his wrist. They'd spent six of the eleven minutes they had before needing a decompression stop on the way up.

Time to go.

Kurt moved back the way he'd come, but another crewman was heading his way. He veered off and took the stairs onto a catwalk that allowed for inspection of the second level of the stacked tanks.

The catwalk took him around the back half of the sphere, the long way around. He moved quickly, glancing at the gauges on the tanks as he went. Every pressure reading was in the red. The needles on some of the gauges had already crossed the max pressure line.

No wonder Millard was worried—he was working in a room with forty ticking bombs.

At the far end of the catwalk, Kurt reached a second stairway and made his way down. At almost the same moment, two men came past one of the large pumps and stepped onto the stairway, coming up toward him.

It was Kurt's intention to pass them with a polite nod, but the nearest of the two had his eyes locked onto Kurt.

"What are you doing up here?" he asked. "This area's off-limits to . . ."

"Checking the pressure," Kurt said, pointing to the clipboard.

Kurt saw the lack of recognition in his eyes. With a crew of only twelve, every face was familiar. "Who are you?"

Kurt acted instantly, jamming the clipboard into the man's chest, shoving him backward and down the stairs.

"Intruder!" the second crewman shouted. "We have an intruder!"

Kurt slugged him and sent him sprawling, but the alarm had been raised.

Volke and several others rushed toward them. Kurt couldn't punch his way through them all. He raced back up the stairs and along the catwalk, but two men appeared on the far end with over-sized wrenches in their hands.

Both groups closed in and Kurt leapt over the railing, jumping down between the cylindrical tanks and rushing for the exit.

It was not to be.

Volke jumped from the catwalk and tackled Kurt with a flying leap.

The two men rolled to the ground, got up simultaneously and charged at each other. Grasping Volke's arm with one hand, Kurt threw an uppercut toward Volke's jaw. The punch connected but only with a glancing blow as Volke turned his face away.

A brief separation allowed Volke to throw a counterpunch. Kurt ducked but was forced on the defensive as Volke pulled out a hunting knife.

He slashed at Kurt once, cutting through the overalls Kurt had stolen, then lunged forward with a much more dangerous stabbing motion.

Kurt caught Volke's arm and bent it back, but Volke spun free, turned and forced Kurt to retreat farther.

"Millard," Volke shouted, "get some more crewmen down here."

Kurt knew he was trapped, but he also knew that the more men who came to subdue him, the less remained out in the sphere to discover Joe. He planned on prolonging the fight for as long as his body could take it.

Another crewman moved into the maze of tanks. A third came in behind Volke.

Kurt feinted one way, got them moving to intercept him, then dove over a set of cross-feed pipes that led to the next tank. Hitting the ground, he rolled, sprang up and dashed forward, disappearing behind the next row.

Volke moved slowly. There was no need to rush. He had six men working with him surrounding the area.

"Spread out," Volke said. "Push him toward the back wall."

Kurt kept quiet, moving from one hiding place to the next. The acoustics of the sphere and the industrial lighting mixed with dark shadows made it easy to hide and change position. But he would run out of room in a moment.

In need of a weapon, he glanced around but saw nothing that could help him.

"Who are you?" Volke called out. "How did you get in here?"

Kurt said nothing.

"Don't be shy," Volke said. "Surely you want to boast about how you found us. If ever there's a time to brag, this is it. You won't be able to talk much after I've cut your throat."

Kurt moved again but was now coming up on the back end of the sphere, with only one more row of cylinders between him and the wall.

Instead of going back, he climbed up onto one of the tanks and lay flat, squeezing between the first layer of tanks and the second. He began to sweat instantly. Both tanks were hot to the touch, a sure sign that they were overpressurized. The heat wasn't scalding, but it was close enough to walking on blacktop in the Arizona sun that he didn't look forward to remaining longer than necessary.

One of Volke's men walked past him. Another passed by in the next row over. If they would just keep on moving . . .

The beam of a flashlight passed over Kurt. "Over there," someone shouted. "Between the tanks."

Kurt looked up to see a man on the catwalk. He'd been spotted from above.

Without delay, Kurt pushed out from between the tanks and dropped to the floor, where he was instantly surrounded.

One man swung a pipe wrench at Kurt's head, but Kurt ducked and it clanged noisily off the tank beside him. Kurt kneed the man in the stomach and then clubbed his wrist. The man cried out and dropped the wrench to the floor, pulling back and clutching his hand protectively.

Kurt grasped at the wrench, but someone grabbed him and pulled him back. A second man joined in and Kurt's arms were soon pinned.

With the two men restraining Kurt, a third crewman rushed forward. "Hold him up," the new arrival shouted. "I'll knock him out."

The captors hoisted Kurt to his feet and a mighty punch was thrown, but it missed Kurt completely and coldcocked one of the crew.

The man fell to the ground like a sack of rice while his partner looked on in shock. His expression changed as Kurt pulled loose, gut punched him and slammed him headfirst into one of the storage tanks.

"Thanks for the assist," Kurt said to Joe. "But I was keeping them busy so that you could escape."

"And swim back all on my own?" Joe said. "I prefer the buddy system."

"That's not going to help us much now," Kurt said.

He plucked the oversized pipe wrench off the floor, took a step forward and stopped. Two of the men who'd captured Kurt were out of the fight, but Volke and the rest of the crew had surrounded

them. It was now six against two, with Millard and another crewman watching from the catwalk.

"You'll never get out of here," Volke said.

"Neither will you," Kurt replied.

With a quick turn, he raised the heavy wrench and brought it
down on one of the cross-feed pipes. It hit with a thunderous stroke,
denting the pipe, bending it in the middle. Volke and his men froze
in their tracks.

"Don't!" Millard shouted, his shrill voice echoing around the
room. "You'll kill us all."

"That's the general idea," Kurt shouted, lifting the wrench above
his head. "I know what you've filled these tanks with. One more hit
and we'll all be out of our misery, so back off."

The rest of the crew moved backward, but Volke stepped forward with a smug grin on his face. "He's bluffing."

"Take one more step and you'll find out if that's true."

Even Volke stopped now. "You don't really want to die here."

"Who does?" Kurt replied. "But if it's between getting captured
and killed by you and your men or blowing this ship to kingdom
come and dying as a couple of heroes . . . well, then, I think you
know which one of those I'm going to pick."

Around Volke, the men started retreating. They were chemical
engineers, former roughnecks and people from other assorted back-
grounds. They wanted nothing to do with Kurt and the dented pipe.

Volke was different. He was a killer and he hadn't gotten where
he was by playing it safe. He regripped the knife and stepped forward. "And our options are life in prison or charge you and test
your mettle. I think you can imagine which one I'm going to pick."

Kurt saw instantly that Volke was ready to die rather than
give in.

"So be it," Kurt said. He brought his arm down, slamming the pipe once again. Sparks flew and everyone dove for cover, but there was no detonation, only a further bending of the pipe followed by a shrill whine as a tiny jet of high-pressure gas escaped from a pinprick-sized hole in middle of the dent.

Kurt didn't wait. He lunged in the other direction and dove for cover.

Volke wasn't as lucky. He turned and dove but was caught in the flash as the pipe blew itself apart and the escaping gas morphed into a twelve-foot jet of flame.

40

GREAT SOUND, BERMUDA

PRIYA WAS BACK on the top deck of the *Lucid Dream*, sitting at her computer console. She remained in the dive suit—in case she decided to go out again—but had wrapped herself up in a luxurious robe of Egyptian cotton.

Initiating the tracking program, she waited as the progress indicator crossed the screen from right to left. When it reached a hundred percent, a map of the world appeared, complete with a blinking dot in middle of the Atlantic.

At first, Bermuda remained invisible, but as she zoomed in, the island appeared and then the fishhook curve and finally the islands dotting the Great Sound including Baker's Rock.

The blinking dot was clearly visible in the water next to one of the small islands, flashing on and off, exactly where it should be.

Quite pleased with her work, Priya poured herself a glass of champagne. "Just try and hide from us now."

As she sat back, a chime sounded from inside the upper deck salon.

Priya recognized it as the alarm indicator. She pulled up an interface on her computer that showed a schematic of the yacht. The aft doors had been forced open.

It couldn't be Kurt or Joe, they would have radioed in and she would have heard the rumbling Pavati as they drew near.

A motion alarm on the lower deck sounded next. Onboard cameras showed a figure in the main passageway and another coming up the midship's stairwell.

Priya shut the laptop, put it on her legs and turned her wheelchair. With two quick thrusts of her arms, she propelled herself forward and into the salon, heading for the elevator.

She didn't make it.

A man rushed up the forward stairs and grabbed her chair, stopping it in its tracks, just as the elevator doors opened. He loomed over her, broad-shouldered, with a bushy beard.

"Where do you think you're going, little lady?"

He was leaning forward, his hands on the arms of the wheelchair. That put him in a vulnerable position. Priya made the most of it, grabbing the laptop and smashing him across the face with it.

He fell back in shock and Priya did a quick one-eighty, heading for the aft part of the yacht. The man she'd struck rushed after her, grabbing her chair from behind just as she made it to the aft stairwell.

Priya threw herself off the chair and down the stairs, crashing onto the landing and rolling. She crawled down the next flight, this time rolling on her shoulder and tumbling like a gymnast.

She was on the middle deck now. She heard the broad-shouldered, bearded man curse and throw her chair aside before lumbering down the stairs.

Her only hope was to get to the water. She pushed open the first door she came to and crawled into one of the cabins. Across the room was a balcony. Beyond that was the water.

She crawled to the door, slid it open and crawled through. She was two feet from the rail when the man rushed, grabbed her by the ankles and pulled her back. Her chin hit the floor and she lost her grip on the laptop.

"You squirm like a salamander," he said. "Do you really think you're going to get away?"

Escape was too much to hope for now. All she wanted to do was toss the laptop overboard so they couldn't hack into it.

As the broad-shouldered, bearded man stood over her, two other men arrived. "The other cabins are empty," one of them said. "There's no one else aboard."

"What happened to you?" the second man said, looking at the blood on the bearded man's lips.

"Never you mind," he snapped. "Check the engine room, check the galley, check every space on this boat. They wouldn't leave a cripple here alone."

Priya seethed at the word *cripple*. "You'll never find them. This yacht has a hidden panic room. By now, they're calling the Coast Guard or the harbor police. You and your friends are all going to prison."

The burly man stood over her, laughing. "Give me that computer."

He reached for it, but Priya had one last trick up her sleeve. Reaching under the arm of the robe, she tapped the screen on the forearm of the dive suit, pressing the swim mode button to full strength.

Her body flipped awkwardly as the artificial muscles in the suit squeezed. One leg went down, but the other flew upward, right into his crotch. The man dropped the computer and doubled over in excruciating pain.

Priya rolled onto her stomach, grabbed the laptop and pulled herself toward the balcony once more. To her surprise, the strange swimming motion of the legs helped her move more quickly.

She reached the railing, pulled herself up and was about to throw herself and the computer overboard when a hand grabbed her by the hair and yanked her back so forcefully that chunks of hair were ripped from her scalp.

She landed against the bulkhead. A pale hand with long, thin fingers reached forward and grabbed her arm. The power to the suit was shut off and Priya's legs stopped flailing. She looked up to see Tessa Franco standing over her. "What were you doing under my aircraft?"

Priya suddenly felt foolish. She'd brought this on herself. She should have stayed put as Kurt and Joe had directed her to.

She tried to play it off. "Hatcher wanted me to take pictures of the plane. He said no one knew how it got off the water so easily. You're using high-pressure air for cavitation."

"You're a very good liar," Tessa said. "Where are Hatcher and that weird friend of his?"

"Like I told the mountain man over there," she said, "you won't find them until the police get here."

Tessa didn't hesitate. She slapped Priya across the face once and then added a backhand slap for good measure.

Priya's face burned, but she said nothing more. Just then, one of the other men returned. "There's space for a powerboat on the lower deck, but the boat is gone."

As Tessa turned away, Priya took a chance. She threw her arm forward, punching the laptop. It skittered across the balcony, slid under the railing and dropped into the sea.

Tessa looked down at Priya. "There must have been something on that computer she wanted to hide. Look around," she said to her men. "Grab any other computers, phones or radios you can find. Anything that might be useful to us."

Priya wondered again if she'd done more harm than good.

"And pick her up," Tessa said to the broad-shouldered, bearded man. "She's coming with us."

41

LNG CARRIER, CONTROL SPHERE

KURT WAS in midair, diving away from the pipes, as the heat of ignition flashed across him, singeing the hair on the back of his neck. Bits of pipe flew in all directions, clanging off the other tanks, while the echo of the blast traveled around the sphere like rolling thunder.

Hitting the floor, Kurt rolled and popped up on one knee. Looking back, he saw a jet of flame pouring from the stub of the ruptured pipe. It shot outward and down, scorching the neighboring tank and rapidly beginning to melt the floor.

The fire scattered Volke and his men. They ran and stumbled in every direction.

"I didn't think you would really do it," Joe said, making his way to Kurt's side.

"He left me no choice," Kurt replied.

A secondary explosion knocked everyone to the ground and the floor tilted as one of the supports gave way.

Kurt and Joe rushed forward, jumping to the next section of flooring.

"Look," Joe said, pointing.

The catwalk had fallen. The crewman with the flashlight fell, dropping through the suddenly open section of deck and into the bottom half of the sphere. Another figure in white overalls clung to the railing.

"That's Millard," Joe said.

"Let's grab him and get out of here."

Working his way around, Kurt stretched out a hand, grabbed Millard by the back of his clothing and pulled him to safety.

"You're coming with us," he shouted.

The scientist did not protest. "The ship is going to explode, we have to get out of here."

The sphere shook with more tremors as a smaller tank exploded. They were all knocked off their feet.

The sound alone felt as if it would bust Kurt's eardrums, but it was the sudden pressure change that concerned him most. He turned back to see a rupture in the wall. Air and smoke were venting out and seawater was blasting in horizontally, crashing through the floor grating and swirling in the lower half of the sphere.

Kurt saw a churning vortex of foamy water rising. Storage tanks had been ripped from their moorings, barely hanging on the scaffolding. Like the pipe Kurt had damaged, many of them were spraying fire.

"I may have overplayed my hand," Kurt said.

"May have?" Joe replied.

Up ahead, several crewmen had reached the hatch that led to the docking sphere. They were frantically trying to pull it open.

"Stop!" Kurt shouted.

His voice was lost in the clamor. The men at the hatch raised the lever. The door flew open with such violence that they were thrown back across the floor.

With the control sphere losing pressure and the docking sphere at full pressure, that was the only possible outcome. That and the torrent of water that came blasting through the hatchway.

The control sphere was now being flooded from two directions. It was also burning and in danger of exploding—or, more likely, imploding. It all depended on whether the storage tanks blew up before the integrity of the sphere gave way completely.

Kurt began pulling off his overalls.

Joe did the same. "*What could go wrong?* you said. *Should be a piece of cake,* you said."

"Next time, I won't say a thing," Kurt promised.

"If we live to see next time."

"How can you two speak like this?!" Millard shouted.

"We still have hope," Kurt said.

"Not if we just stand here!"

Kurt tossed the overalls away. "Actually, that's the only thing we can do. At least until the pressure equalizes and the water stops pouring in."

Millard was too panicked to think. "What are you talking about?"

"You're a scientist," Kurt said. "What happens when the water rises above the gap in the sphere?"

Millard nodded as understanding came to him. "Equilibrium will be restored," he said. "The air will have nowhere left to go. The water will stop rushing in."

"And we can swim out of here once that happens," Kurt said.

"You two can," Millard said. "But what about me?"

"I'll drag you with me," Kurt said. He pulled out the backup regulator. "You hold on tight and breathe through this. Once we're out of the ship, we'll ascend slowly. If you panic or do anything foolish, I'll cut you free. Understand?"

Millard stared at the water flooding in around them. "Okay, I'm with you," he said. "All the way."

Spray began to rush up from beneath them, swirling up over the top of the grating at their feet. The flood churned in a circular motion and the gigantic whirlpool picked up everything it touched, including Kurt, Joe and Millard.

"Hold on," Kurt shouted.

Millard wrapped his arms around Kurt as water swept them away. Kurt held an arm across Millard's chest in a lifeguard's rescue hold.

They went with the current, which dragged them around the far side of the sphere, past the burning tanks and back toward the section where the hatch lay.

In the middle of their second lap, the water crested above the gap in the sphere. With nowhere for the air to escape, the pressure balance was restored.

"The bathtub's full," Kurt said. "Now, if the sphere will just hold together until we get out of here, all will be well."

Joe drifted ahead of Kurt and Millard as they neared the hatchway.

"I'll go first," Joe shouted.

He put the regulator in his mouth and dived without waiting for an answer. Kurt made sure that Millard had the backup regulator in his mouth, then clamped down on his own.

When he was sure the oxygen was flowing, he went under. The water was murky, lit only by the flickering of the fires. An ethereal light was coming through the hatchway. It was the spotlights from the submersible.

He followed Joe's blurry outline toward the hatch, kicking smoothly and holding on to Millard. They went lower, reached the open doorway and swam inside the pipe that connected the two spheres.

Joe was visible for an instant before he vanished through the far side of the tunnel.

Kurt kicked and stroked with his free hand. It was a tight fit with Millard attached to his side and they bumped the wall as soon as they went in. Halfway through, he felt the one sensation he'd been dreading.

The water surged, a brief push, like that of a passing wave, but it was followed by a sudden and violent undertow. Kurt knew instantly. The sphere behind them had cracked like an egg and the air was pouring out once again, drawing thousands of gallons of water a minute into the open space.

Kurt was sucked backward, Millard was ripped from his grasp and both were drawn through the tunnel and spat back out into the burning and flooding sphere they'd just left behind.

42

KURT BROKE the surface. In the light of the fire, he could see water pouring in from higher up. The gash in the wall had torn upward like a zipper and the sea was crashing down like a waterfall.

Kurt had no hope of swimming free. He was carried forward on the current to where the two streams met. There, he was pushed upward and then dragged under before being forced to the side and reaching the surface once again.

He bumped into a floating body. It was Millard. He was unresponsive and bleeding from a gash on the head. Kurt had no idea if the man was dead or alive, but he grabbed ahold of him as they were carried around the sphere and up toward the top of the dome.

Floating junk and debris gathered around them. Kurt protected his head as they banged the wall and he grasped at another body as it swept past. But it rolled and slipped from Kurt's hand, vanishing into the downwash from the incoming water.

Hoping to avoid the same fate, Kurt kicked hard and sped past the inflow point. On the next circuit, he grabbed onto a collection of pipes that spanned the dome's curved ceiling.

The current pulled hard, but he held fast, clutching Millard to him with his free arm. The current finally began to slow.

The water had climbed above the split in the wall once again and, for the moment, the remains of the structure held.

Kurt looked up, an eight-foot gap was all that remained between him and the very top and center of the sphere. A bubble of air and toxic gases were trapped in that gap and Kurt became thankful once again for his rebreather.

Drawing oxygen from the regulator was far preferable to searing his lungs on whatever was trapped around him.

There was a slight murmur from Millard and his eyes opened just a sliver. Kurt pressed the backup regulator into Millard's mouth. He immediately spat it out. "Where . . . Where are we?"

Kurt briefly pulled the regulator from his own mouth. "Back where we started," he said, "only higher up. The whole sphere is flooded. But we can still get out of here."

He took a breath from the regulator and forced Millard to do the same. Millard looked around groggily. "Where's your friend?"

"Hopefully, swimming free. We need to do the same."

Kurt looked at his watch. They'd been down there too long to get out without a decompression stop, but their position at the top of the sphere would work. They were only sixty feet below the surface.

He got Millard's attention, pointed to the crack in the wall of the sphere.

Millard nodded.

Kurt held up three fingers, then two, then one. Letting go of the pipe but holding on to Millard, he swam toward it, dragging

Millard with him. The swirling current had not completely disappeared, as the water continued to churn under its own momentum.
Intent not to miss the gap, Kurt bumped his way along the wall
until he found it.

The torn section of the sphere was too narrow to fit into at the
top, but a few feet down it was a gaping wound. Kurt dragged Millard downward, through the opening and out into the sea.

Without the helmet, Kurt had no hope of seeing anything. He
engaged the power assist and swam away from the ship as rapidly
as he could. Releasing a stream of bubbles now and then, Kurt kept
himself oriented. After a few minutes swimming at that depth, he
allowed himself and Millard to rise, ascending slowly and finally
breaking the surface.

Kurt spotted the lights of Bermuda, turned on his side and began
pulling Millard with him. The power assist was operating, but not
nearly as effective, without flippers. Kurt was glad for all the help
he could get.

A few minutes into their swim, he felt the rumble of several explosions through the water, which went off in series as one tank
after another ruptured down below. Seconds later, a single, much
larger detonation told him the rest of the tanks had gone up simultaneously.

A series of white water eruptions broke the surface and the re-
sulting waves pushed Kurt and Millard farther toward shore.

It would be another twenty minutes before Kurt spied the Pavati.

Arriving at the anchored boat, he pushed Millard up onto the dive
platform and climbed the ladder. The boat was dark and still. A quick
look confirmed that Joe was not aboard. Either he was out there in
the open ocean or he'd never escaped from the submerged ship.

43

BERMUDA'S NORTH SHORE

KURT'S PRIORITY was stabilizing Millard, who had fallen unconscious and was suffering from mild hypothermia and the head wound.

Kurt eased Millard onto the floor of the boat, dressed the head wound and strapped him down with a cargo net. He placed a life preserver under Millard's head as a pillow and covered him with a pair of thick towels.

"That's the best I can do for you right now," he said to the unconscious man.

Kurt went to the radio and dialed in the high-frequency band. "Joe, this is Kurt. Do you read?"

There was no response.

"Come in, amigo. Tell me where you're at and I'll come pick you up."

Nothing but silence. If Joe hadn't retrieved his helmet, communications would be impossible.

He switched tactics. "Priya, this is Kurt," he said, transmitting again. "I need you to ping Joe's transponder and give me a fix on him. He's in the water but not responding."

Waiting in painful silence, Kurt checked the transmitter to make sure it was operating correctly and then pressed transmit again. "Priya, come in, this is Kurt."

The sound of the sea breeze and the waves lapping against the side of the boat was all he heard.

"Forget this," Kurt said, hanging up the microphone.

He fired up the engine, pulled the anchor in and pushed the throttle forward. The Pavati began to move and Kurt steered to port, accelerating and heading back toward the waters above the sunken and obliterated LNG carrier.

Flicking through a battery of switches, he soon had every light in the boat shining. He grabbed the radio once again. "Joe, if you can hear this, I'm going to make a direct line between where we parked and the wreck. If you're in the water, wave me down."

With the boat at quarter speed, Kurt pulled out the night vision scope and scanned the area ahead. He was looking for Joe, but he noticed the freighter was no longer moored by the marine buoy. He looked to the horizon, but there were several ships to the north and he couldn't tell which, if any of them, was the freighter.

Kurt really didn't care, the only thing that mattered at this point was finding Joe. He slowed down as he moved into an area of floating wreckage. Despite a slow, careful search through every bit of floating debris he could find, there was no sign of his friend.

Circling around, he called for help once more. "Priya, this is Kurt, you're supposed to be on the radio. Joe is missing and probably injured. I need you to locate him for me."

At long last, the radio crackled to life with a response. A female voice came over the speaker. *"Your friend Joe is dead,"* the voice said coldly. *"You killed him by destroying my laboratory. I hope it was worth it to you."*

"Tessa," Kurt said in recognition.

"Yes," she said. *"That's my name. And I now know yours . . . Kurt . . . Austin."* She dragged the name out as she spoke it, but followed it up quickly. *"You can imagine who told me and what we had to do to her to get her to speak. This little helper of yours is tougher than she looks."*

Kurt's priorities changed instantly. Tessa had Priya. There was no point in asking how. He turned the wheel and gunned the throttle, setting a course back toward the Great Sound.

"So now you're adding kidnapping to your crimes," Kurt said. "That's not going to play well when they bring you in."

"You're laughable," she said. *"There's no one here to bring me in. Even if there was, it'll be too late by the time they act. I'll be off this island in five minutes. And you, Kurt Austin, will never see me again."*

Kurt knew Tessa wouldn't stay in Bermuda. Even if the Prime Minister of the island was in her pocket, he would rapidly switch sides with the full weight of the U.S. government and the world community coming down on him.

"It's over for you," Kurt said. "I'll have U.S. Navy divers on that site in the morning and an international warrant out for your arrest by lunchtime."

Her pitch went up. *"The only things coming to an end are the Oil Age . . . and this young woman's life . . . if you try to stop me."*

Kurt had every intention of stopping her. His boat was racing at full speed, flying across the waves. It would only take a small amount of damage to keep the *Monarch* on the water. He would come up with a way to cause that damage by the time he got to it.

"Think about it," Kurt said. "The world is not going to bow down to you or let you hold it hostage. Every country on earth needs oil. That makes you everyone's enemy."

The reply came with great confidence. *"I'm afraid you have it backward and upside down,"* she said. *"We've already infected half the world's major oil fields. Some of them are only now beginning to experience the slowdown, but, trust me, the progression is unstoppable and things will soon get rapidly worse. In a few months, most of the world's oil will be trapped and useless. It will be unreachable without causing disasters like what happened to the Alpha Star. And the bacteria will multiply and grow as long as there's oil in the ground to feed on. All of which means, I'm not the problem, I'm the solution. Trust me, the world will embrace me long after you've been swept aside."*

Kurt heard every word she said, along with a high-pitched whine in the background. The *Monarch*'s jet engines were spooling up. She would be gone in a matter of minutes.

He hung the microphone up and concentrated on his course. With his craft moving at breakneck speed, he'd almost reached the entrance to the Great Sound. Turning toward the shore, he angled across Spanish Point, cutting it so close that spray from the boat washed across the coastal road.

He was still several miles from Tessa's compound, but the aircraft would need a long stretch of water to take off. Instead of heading toward her island, he cut across the Great Sound, aiming for a spot where he could intercept her.

By the time he spotted the *Monarch*, it was already moving. He saw the uplit tails, the floodlights in the wings and the nose illuminating the water. The aircraft was out of the bay and taxiing into position for its takeoff run.

Kurt continued westward, crossing the bay, weaving around a sailboat and between several of the many yachts anchored there.

Beyond these vessels, he found himself in the channel reserved especially for the *Monarch* to take off from and land in.

He carved a white wake into the sea turning hard to the south. The *Monarch* was a mile away, picking up speed and heading north.

The radio crackled. *"You think we don't see you out there?"* Tessa's voice sounded both angry and uncomfortable. Clearly, when pressured, her choice was aggression. *"Get in our way and we'll run you down. I'll crush you like an insect!"*

Kurt grabbed the microphone once more. "Good luck flying with a giant hole in your bow. You won't even get off the water."

Kurt doubted Tessa would turn, but he gambled on the pilots' being more rational. He kept the throttle to the firewall and the nose of the boat pointed at the oncoming behemoth. It thundered toward him, the roar of its six monstrous engines growing louder by the second and soon drowning out even the rumble of the Pavati's V-8.

Kurt pressed forward, shielding his eyes as the plane's lights washed over him.

INSIDE the *Monarch*, the pilots were stricken with fear.

"He's not turning," one said.

"Neither can we," the other pilot answered. "I'm cutting the throttle."

"No," Tessa shouted. "Cavitation now!"

The copilot hit a switch and the vents beneath the aircraft opened. Huge volumes of compressed air flooded through the thousands of tiny holes on the bottom of the plane. In an instant, the water's grip was broken and the *Monarch* leapt into the air.

KURT NEVER SAW the plane leave the water, the light was too bright. But suddenly the glare tilted skyward and the *Monarch* was thundering overhead.

It cleared him by ten feet, though the jet blast swept in and hit him from the rear and the vortex behind the plane nearly threw the Pavati over.

The boat skipped twice. Kurt corrected for the turbulence and kept it from rolling. He backed the throttle down and sped onto the smooth water of the *Monarch*'s wake. There, the boat slowed and settled.

Kurt took it through a quarter turn and cut the throttle completely.

Glancing to the north, Kurt watched the *Monarch* climbing and turning. All at once, its lights went out and the great plane vanished into the night.

Joe was gone, Priya was gone and all Kurt had to show for it was an obliterated vessel at the bottom of the sea and an unconscious, possibly comatose scientist.

He picked up the microphone and held the talk switch down. "I know you can hear me, Tessa, so hear this. It doesn't matter how far you go, where you hide or who your friends are, I will find you and bring you down, even if I have to hunt you to the ends of the earth to do it."

44

KURT ARRIVED in Washington on one of NUMA's private jets. It pulled to a stop in front of a waiting ambulance and a gray SUV. With the help of the pilot, Kurt carried the stretcher down the stairs toward Rudi Gunn and a team of Navy paramedics.

They placed the stretcher on a mobile gurney and the paramedics took over from there. "I need a name for the record," the lead paramedic said.

"He's a John Doe," Kurt said, "but you can call him Jonah. He was spit out of the mouth of a whale."

The paramedic wrote both names down on the clipboard and rechecked the patient's vitals. After a few more questions, they loaded the gurney into a waiting ambulance, buttoned it up and drove off.

Rudi stepped forward. "That's not Joe," he said. "Word out of Bermuda was, you were bringing Joe home."

"I had to use Joe's name and ID to get that guy out of hospital."

"Who is he?"

"His name is Pascal Millard," Kurt said. "He's a genetic engineer who worked for Tessa. He was in charge of their bacteria production facility. He suffered a head wound during our escape."

"So, you kidnapped him?"

"I got him stabilized first," Kurt said. "But we wouldn't be able to question him if he remained on the island. And if Tessa knew we had him, he'd be in grave danger."

Rudi didn't bat an eye. "All right. What about Joe?"

At this Kurt paused. "The Bermudian Coast Guard is still searching for him. But it doesn't look good."

"How bad?"

"There's a thousand-foot hole in the reef where that ship was sitting," Kurt said. "If Joe was on or anywhere near it when it went up, then he's gone."

An outsider might have been shocked at Kurt's words, but Rudi understood his Special Operations leader's stoic demeanor better than anyone. There was a job at hand, emotions and mourning—if it came to that—would have to wait. "I'll make sure the authorities out there know this one is personal for us."

"That's the best we can do," Kurt replied. "What about the *Monarch*? We may have lost Joe. I'm not going to lose Priya, too."

"We're looking," Rudi said, gesturing toward his SUV and walking as he spoke. "But you might as well look for a ghost in the wind. That plane is covered with a stealth material and crossing an ocean with little to no radar coverage. It could be anywhere, from South America to Norway. It can land on any lake, river, bay or inlet, not to mention airports, abandoned runways, hard-packed dirt or fields of ice. Even with multiple satellites searching for it, our chances are slim. And that's only if it doesn't put into a hangar somewhere."

"Not a lot of hangars big enough to hide that monster," Kurt said. "As for all the places it can land, you're right, there's an awful lot of them, but it's still a finite number. That makes the plane something less than a ghost."

"And we'll keep looking until we find it," Rudi said. "But it's not going to be easy and it's not going to be quick."

"What about the freighter?" Kurt asked.

They'd reached the SUV by now. "Different problem, same result," Rudi explained. "Bermuda is on the path, or slightly off the path, of several major shipping lanes. There are hundreds of freighters and containerships within the radius that vessel could have covered since you and Joe saw it. Without any identification, there's no way to know which one it might be. And if the crew has even the slightest bit of sense, they've gotten rid of any evidence already."

"Which brings us back to Millard," Kurt said. "He's the only link we have left."

"He's in a coma," Rudi pointed out.

"Medically induced, at this point," Kurt said. "With the right drugs, we can wake him up and make him tell us everything, including where Tessa might be hiding."

Rudi unlocked the doors. "First, we go to the White House," he said. "The President would like to see you."

"I'm a little busy right now," Kurt replied.

"It wasn't exactly an optional invitation," Rudi replied. "With everything that's happened, our part in this mission is being reevaluated."

With that, Rudi climbed inside, with Kurt settling into the passenger seat.

"This is not the time to blink," Kurt said.

"Tell that to the President," Rudi said. "Better yet, make him believe it. Otherwise, we'll be searching for Priya on our time."

THE ARRIVAL at 1600 Pennsylvania Avenue was less than auspicious, entering via the back gate, a service door and then up through the kitchen. Instead of making their way to the Oval Office, Kurt and Rudi were shown to the lower level and the underground theater, where the President was rumored to watch classic movies from Hollywood's golden era.

At the moment, the theater was empty, but a black and white film was showing. With nothing else to do, Kurt and Rudi took a seat.

On the screen, Errol Flynn was getting ready to attack the Crimean artillery in *The Charge of the Light Brigade*, one of Flynn's biggest hits.

"Half a league, / half a league, / Half a league onward," a voice said from behind them. *"All in the valley of Death / Rode the six hundred."*

Kurt turned to see the President coming down the aisle. Both he and Rudi stood.

The President motioned for them to sit. "I hate to inform you gentlemen, but we're heading into an abyss of our own."

He handed each of them a newspaper and took a seat. Kurt received the *The Wall Street Journal*. On the front page was a bold headline declaring a new oil shortage.

OLD WELLS DRYING UP.
New Finds Disappoint. Demand Growing.

The paper in Rudi's hand was the pink, UK-published *Financial Times*. Its headline was more ominous.

Why Is the World's Oil Suddenly Vanishing?

"You can read them later," the President said. "For now, let's just say the cat's out of the bag."

"Intentionally?" Rudi asked.

"Of that, I have no doubt," the President said. "There are enough identical details in both articles to suggest the information was leaked from the same source."

Rudi put his paper down. "What's the reaction been like?"

"Oil prices opened thirty dollars a barrel higher this morning," the President said. "The front-end contracts have been riding higher ever since. The price could double by the end of the week. The shock is going to be sudden and severe. On top of what we've experienced since the Alpha Star catastrophe, and the slow rise before that, we're looking at prices three times what they were a year ago, with more to come."

"Not good," Rudi said.

"No," the President added. "All other stocks are tanking. The talking heads on TV are spouting off words like *correction*, *recession* and *depression*. If you look in the rearview mirror, you'll see that economic meltdown I told you about coming on fast. I was hoping NUMA would help us avoid that."

"We're making progress," Rudi said.

"Blowing up a sunken ship in Bermuda is not the kind of progress I'm interested in."

Kurt spoke up. "I took a chance and it went wrong. If that's indefensible, then the blame falls on me."

The President paused, surprised that Kurt would come right to the heart of the matter. Most men called on the carpet preferred to talk about other things as long as humanly possible.

"So, you prefer a quick death," the President said.

"I prefer not to die at all," Kurt said. "But we've lost too much time to talk around the issue."

The President crossed his long legs and nodded thoughtfully. "Rudi briefed me on your missing colleagues. You have my condolences. That's quite a blow. By the sound of it, you're not ready to get out of the fight. I admire that. Now, tell me how the next round is going to come out differently."

"Because we have a target now," Kurt said.

"We do?"

"Tessa Franco," Kurt said. "We get her, we get the truth."

A perplexed look swept onto the President's face. "Tessa Franco?"

"You've heard of her?"

"Everyone has heard of her," the President said. "She announced an IPO this morning and a plan to build fuel cell factories in seven different states. The senators and congressmen are falling all over themselves to praise her and vie for the business."

"Of course they are," Rudi said.

"You've picked an interesting target," the President added. "At this moment, she's as close to untouchable as any person on earth. For one, she's not an American. She has dual American and French citizenship. We can't simply go get her. Beyond that, she's the darling of the press. She's being treated like an international hero who's single-handedly going to save us from this oil crisis."

"She *is* the oil crisis," Kurt insisted. "Her people created this bacterium, snuck around the world pumping it into oil fields and then sat back waiting for the inevitable."

"Ah, yes, the bacteria," the President said, looking at Rudi. "I understand your people brought in samples of that last night."

"Not without trouble," Rudi said. "Paul and Gamay were attacked on their way in. They survived and made it to Biloxi by the skin of their teeth. A saboteur working on the FEMA staff was the initial problem. But they had to fight off some very determined hijackers along the way."

This was the first Kurt had heard of that. "What's happening with the samples now?"

"They've been divided up," the President said. "Half to a team from the CDC and the rest to the military germ warfare unit in Nevada. The two groups will be looking for methods to kill the bacteria. But even with a heap of good fortune, I'm told it might be a year or two before we create a method to attack the bacteria and deploy it on a worldwide scale. And that's if there is any weakness."

"There has to be a weakness," Kurt said. "Otherwise, Tessa wouldn't have risked trying to stop Paul and Gamay from delivering the samples."

"That may be so," the President said. "But time is still our enemy."

"I know someone who can speed that process up," Kurt said. "His name is Millard. He's a French scientist who was working with Tessa. If anyone knows how the bacteria was put together and what its weaknesses are, it would be him."

"And where do we find this Millard?"

"Bethesda Naval Hospital," Kurt said. "And before you ask, he's here because I abducted him from a hospital in Bermuda, used my possibly dead friend's name and ID to get him past security at the airport and then rushed him onto a NUMA plane before anyone learned the truth. Rudi knew nothing about it, not until I landed twenty minutes ago. That's why he never briefed you."

The President stared at Kurt, incredulous for a second.

"Millard was on the production ship," Rudi explained. "Kurt thought it wise to bring him back here, where we might learn what he knows."

"We have to wake him up," Kurt said.

"Wake him up?"

"He's in a medically induced coma."

The President paused, his expression opaque for the moment. "Going after Tessa directly would be fruitless at the moment even if this man implicates her. But that doesn't mean we're helpless. I'll try and put some pressure on the SEC to put a hold on her IPO paperwork and ask them to request all manner of documents and data above and beyond the usual. In the meantime, we could use Millard's help. You go wake him up."

45

BETHESDA NAVAL HOSPITAL

MILLARD WAS HELD in a private room with two stern-looking Marines at each end of the hallway and another pair guarding his door.

Kurt was glad to see the level of security.

After checking on Millard and finding his condition unchanged, Kurt began a conversation with Bethesda's Director of Medical Services and the hospital's chief doctor.

A discussion about the risks of waking Millard went several heated rounds. It ended when an Executive Order from the President arrived. The chief doctor, a resolute woman with short white hair, a stern demeanor and teal-rimmed glasses, chose to do the task herself rather than have any of her staff deal with potentially difficult decisions.

She worked on Millard with the help of a nurse and an anesthesiologist. Kurt took a seat, watching from afar.

Bringing Millard out of the coma was a slow, tedious process.

First, they had to undo the effect of the drugs Millard had been placed on, then they had to deal with his injuries.

As the effort progressed, the doctor spoke to Kurt. "You're a conundrum to me, Mr. Austin." She spoke while monitoring the patient and not bothering to look Kurt's way. "I'm told you risked your life to save this man. Pulled him off a burning ship. Is that true?"

"Something like that," Kurt admitted.

"That explains why you smell of diesel oil and why both of you are singed in places," she added. "It doesn't explain why you're willing to take a risk with his life this way. You do realize he has swelling in his brain? Trying to wake him up now is dangerous. You may end up killing him. Is that what you want?"

"Of course not," Kurt said. "This is not an easy decision, but we need to know what he knows. So please, just do the best you can."

The doctor said nothing more to Kurt and concentrated on Millard. She checked his vitals, as new drugs were added to the IV drip, and double-checked the contents of an injection that was being prepared.

Over the next twenty minutes, Millard moved closer to consciousness, his heart rate and respiration increasing, his blood pressure coming up.

"He's getting closer," the nurse said.

"The EEG shows no change," the chief doctor replied. "Brain activity is still in a vegetative state."

Another drug was administered and finally the brain waves began oscillating.

"He's coming around."

Kurt stood up and moved closer. Millard was waking up, but something was wrong. Tremors were running through the man's body. They began in his left hand, progressed up his arm into his shoulder and moved quickly to his head and neck.

Without warning, Millard kicked violently and then straightened.

"He's seizing," the doctor said. "More Epitol."

With the doctor and nurse holding Millard as still as possible, a second nurse pulled a small vial from the cart and prepared another injection. With the hypodermic filled, she held it up, flicked its side with her finger and pushed the plunger a fraction to get any bubbles out.

"Quickly."

She handed the hypodermic to the doctor, who injected it.

Millard's seizures faded almost instantly, though his hands continued to shake. After a minute of quiet, he began to stir again. This time, his movements were more conventional. Finally, he opened his eyes.

The doctor asked him several questions, which he responded to almost inaudibly. It was enough to satisfy her. She turned to Kurt. "You can speak with him now. I'm not sure you're going to learn much. This kind of head trauma normally leads to memory loss and incoherence."

Kurt placed a digital recorder beside Millard and switched it on. Leaning in, he got Millard's attention. "Can you hear me?"

The scientist didn't respond. His eyes were glassy and unfocused. Without warning, he began thrashing around again, not in a seizing motion but as if he were trying to climb free of the bed. "The ship is going to explode," he said. "We have to get out."

"We are out," Kurt said. "You're in a hospital. We swam free, remember?"

Millard relaxed for several seconds and then began thrashing around once more. This time, he spoke in French. Kurt didn't understand—and wasn't all that certain the words would have been comprehensible if he did—but at least they were on the tape.

"Look at me," Kurt said. "Do you recognize me?"

The French monologue ceased. As Millard focused on Kurt, he switched back to English. "Hold on . . . Breathe through this . . . Don't . . . Don't . . ."

Kurt recognized the words he'd spoken to Millard aboard the submerged ship. "That's right," he said. "Don't panic or I'll leave you here. That's what I told you when we swam out."

Millard jerked upward suddenly. "We have to get out. The ship is going to explode."

"We're already out," Kurt insisted. "You're safe."

"It's going to explode," Millard repeated. "It's going to explode."

Despite Kurt's efforts, Millard would come out of his panic only momentarily and then go right back into it. He responded to any question Kurt asked by repeating that they needed to get off the ship and then moving his arms as if he were trying to swim.

Kurt turned to the doctor. "What's happening to him?"

"The head trauma," the doctor said. "It often affects short-term memory. I've had patients from car crashes say the same thing over and over for hours. In the simplest terms, his brain isn't recording the fact that he got off the ship. You tell him that he's safe. He accepts that, relaxes and then instantly forgets. As soon as that happens, he reverts to the last thing he can recall and then he's right back on the ship. It's like a record with a scratch on it. His thoughts keep skipping back to the same groove."

"What about his long-term memory?"

The doctor adjusted her glasses. "I can't say it'll be sharp, but things that happened before the trauma are usually safe from this type of recall error. The further back they happened, the more likely they are to be unaffected."

Kurt leaned back down toward Millard and clutched him by the shoulders. "Hold on to me," he said. "I'll get you off the ship. But you need to stop thrashing around."

Millard held on to Kurt with a weak grip but this time remained calm. The doctor looked on.

"I need you to tell me about the bacteria," Kurt said.

"It devours the oil," Millard replied.

"I know that," Kurt said. "How do we stop it?"

"Stop it?"

"There has to be a weakness we can exploit. A way to counteract it."

Millard looked off into the distance. "It wasn't there . . . They must have . . . We didn't find it . . ." After this, Millard coughed, said something unintelligible and began to drift.

"Stay with me," Kurt said, "or I'll leave you here on the ship."

"No," Millard said, grasping onto Kurt with renewed energy. "The ship is going to explode. We have to get off."

The doctor put her hand on Kurt's shoulder. "Mr. Austin, you must finish quickly."

Kurt nodded. "I'll get you out. Tell me about the bacteria. Tell me how to destroy it."

Millard shook his head from side to side. "They knew how . . . but they're gone . . . poor souls . . . drowned . . . They never got out . . ."

More rambling followed. Kurt decided to ask something simpler. "Where can I find Tessa?"

"She never comes to see us anymore . . . not down here . . ."

"She left Bermuda in the *Monarch*," Kurt said. "Where does she go when she's not in Bermuda?"

"No one knows," Millard said. "She's always gone, these days. And we never see the daylight."

Millard's condition made it difficult to know what to ask. "Is there another lab? Another production facility? Someplace where we might find records of how you created the bacteria?"

"*Pas moi*," Millard whispered, gulping at the dry air and shaking his head. "*Le Dakar . . .*"

"Dakar?" Kurt replied.

Millard nodded weakly. "*Les Français*," he added. "They were there. They never got out . . . Pour souls, they all drowned." With that, he clutched at Kurt again. "We have to get off the ship . . . It's going to explode." The next words caught in his throat and Millard sank back into a coma.

The doctor turned on Kurt. "That's it," she said. "No more. He's staying under until the swelling in his brain has subsided."

Kurt picked up the recorder, switched it off and put it in his pocket.

"Who is he?" she asked.

"I can't tell you that," Kurt said. "But I can tell you he's partially responsible for dozens of fatalities and that he may have the knowledge we need to avert a worldwide crisis. So, treat him well, but don't forget whose side he's on."

The doctor said nothing in return and Kurt walked out, his mind already focused on finding a genetics lab in Dakar.

46

"THERE'S NO SIGN of a genetics lab in Dakar."

These were the first words Kurt heard upon waking up from several hours of desperately needed sleep.

After leaving Bethesda, he'd returned to his boathouse on the Potomac and fallen onto his couch. He'd closed his eyes, intending only to rest for a moment, but surrounded by the familiar scents and sounds of his own home—the aroma of varnish that wafted up from the workshop below, the hum of the oversized filter in the tropical fish tank—he was asleep before he knew it.

The phone call from Rudi had shocked him back to consciousness several hours later.

"Are you sure?" he asked. "Millard was pretty clear about the location."

Rudi didn't waver. "Both the CIA and NSA insist there is zero possibility of a genetics lab in Dakar. I had a search run for anything that would indicate Tessa's company or any subsidiaries acting in the region, but there's nothing to suggest she's ever been connected to that part of the world, let alone Dakar itself."

"What about Millard or any of his known associates?"

"Nothing there either," Rudi said.

Kurt could hardly believe what he was hearing. "What's the confidence level on this?"

"High," Rudi said. "There's a CIA unit specifically tasked with tracking genetic threats. Millard has been on their watch list for years. He's split his time between France, Bermuda and the UK. He's never set foot on African soil."

"What about other places named Dakar?" Kurt asked.

"Plenty of them," Rudi said. "One in Syria, three others in Africa, one in India. There's even a small city in the heart of Russia named Dakar. But there's nothing to indicate Tessa, or Millard, has ever been to any of them."

Kurt stared at the ceiling. There was no point arguing. "What about the French language portion of the recording? Have the interpreters come up with anything from it?"

"Most of it was unintelligible," Rudi said, "though Millard's voice was clear when insisting that he didn't create the bacteria and when he offered a statement near the end, stating, 'the French were there also.'"

"Is it possible to wake him up again?" Kurt asked.

"I checked on that," Rudi replied. "He's gone into a deeper coma. The doctors said trying to wake him now would probably kill him. And considering the head trauma, they're not sure what his cognitive state will be when he finally does wake up. It's a miracle you got from him what you did."

"Then, we'll just have to listen some more and figure out what he meant," Kurt said. "Not to change the subject, but what about the *Monarch*?"

"If we'd found it," Rudi said, "I'd have told you already."

"Sorry," Kurt said. "Keep me posted."

Rudi promised to do just that and hung up.

Kurt stood and walked to the kitchen. He switched the coffeepot on and left the lights off. Waiting for the coffee to brew, he went over Millard's words in his head.

Millard had been utterly clear about Dakar. He'd even mentioned that the French were there—and the French had controlled Dakar, and the region of Senegal where it is located, for centuries.

Picking up the recorder, he listened to Millard's words again, playing it section by section, stopping and rewinding repeatedly, until he'd gone through it several times.

Between the weakness of Millard's voice, his labored breathing and the background noise of the hospital room, it was hard to make out everything, but after listening to the same words over and over Kurt realized something small that he'd overlooked.

"Le Dakar," he said, speaking Millard's words. "The . . . Dakar."

Millard was referring not to a place but to a thing—and when he heard Millard mention that the poor souls had drowned, Kurt became certain just what that thing was.

He sat at his computer and checked the NUMA database, quickly finding what he was looking for. But the information was cursory, not much better than what was available publicly.

Rarely was that the case.

If he wanted anyone to take his theory seriously, he was going to need more. And if the information wasn't going to be found in the computers of the world, he'd have to seek out a different storehouse of knowledge. One made of flesh and blood.

Grabbing his keys, Kurt ran out the front door. He climbed into his Jeep and sped off toward Georgetown, heading for St. Julien's.

47

ST. JULIEN'S wasn't a church, a university or a hospital. It was St. Julien Perlmutter, an expert in all things nautical. A friend of NUMA, he'd spent decades collecting books, charts and other sources of information about the sea. If it was rare and unique, he searched it out and often paid top dollar to get it. In addition to auctions and private sales, Perlmutter had a network of contacts spread across the globe who would reach out to him if they found something of interest or if a rumor crossed their desk regarding any mysteries hidden in the oceans.

Kurt arrived at Perlmutter's home and pulled into the driveway, which ran between the ivy-covered walls of the neighboring houses that guarded the entrance to St. Julien's like the battlements of a walled city.

Beyond them lay a spacious carriage house with more land around it than any home in Georgetown had a right to. It even had a large courtyard that St. Julien had roofed over and later enclosed completely so he could store more of his treasures.

Kurt stepped from the Jeep and shut the door. It had been a while since he'd visited and he'd never arrived so late in the evening and unannounced. And yet before he could take a step toward the door, it swung open, spilling light onto the grounds.

Most of that light was immediately blocked by the imposing shape of a four-hundred-pound man in a silk robe.

"Kurt Austin darkening my door," a deep voice boomed. "What have I done to deserve this?"

Kurt grinned at the welcome, noticing that Perlmutter hadn't trimmed the long beard or changed the style of the mustache that covered his lip and twisted at the ends.

"St. Julien," Kurt said. "It's great to see you. But do you ever sleep?"

"Every chance I get."

"Then how is it you're always waiting at the door when I arrive? Cameras? Alarm system? Sixth sense you've never told us about?"

"Yes to all of the above," St. Julien replied. "And in your case, Fritz knows the sound of your Jeep. He wags his tail incessantly the moment you pull into the driveway."

Kurt laughed. Fritz was Perlmutter's dachshund. The moment his name was spoken, he appeared in the doorway. He'd been a puppy the first time Kurt met him, though he was fully grown now and becoming rotund like his master.

"You see?" Perlmutter said. "He's awfully fond of you, which doesn't say much for his breeding."

The joke didn't offend Kurt in the least. In fact, he laughed. This was how St. Julien greeted his true friends. If he'd been polite and proper, Kurt would have been worried.

"I'm sorry to bother you so late," Kurt said. "Can I bend your ear for a moment?"

"Certainly," Perlmutter said, waving Kurt in.

Kurt followed Perlmutter through the doorway and into the large but crowded house. They passed stacks of books five feet tall, tables covered with charts six inches deep and shelves filled with journals, logbooks, records and diaries from the owners, passengers and crew of long-defunct steamship lines.

Kurt marveled at it all. "How many books do you have now?"

"I stopped counting at ten thousand," Perlmutter said.

St. Julien had long ago filled his official library and since then had turned every room, closet and nook in the home into an extension of that library. The only space completely free of books was the expansive kitchen, where he spent his time creating sumptuous dishes that would have earned him a Michelin star or two had his home been a restaurant. Even now, the aroma was enticing.

"Cognac or port?" Perlmutter said, arriving at a bar that was stocked from his personal wine cellar.

"Don't waste the good stuff on me," Kurt said. "I'm only here for information."

"Nonsense," Perlmutter said. He filled two balloon snifters with golden brown cognac from an aged bottle and passed one to Kurt.

"Now," Perlmutter said, "what is it you're searching for?"

"Information on the INS *Dakar*."

Perlmutter's memory was as quick and accurate as any computer's. He rattled off the basic facts. "The *Dakar* was an Israeli vessel, purchased from the British. Lost with all hands in the Mediterranean, January of '68." Perlmutter raised an eyebrow. "A bad year for submarines, really. That same year, the French lost the *Minerve*, we lost the *Scorpion* and the Russians lost the K-129. Some people thought a secret war had broken out. As for the *Dakar*, its disappearance was considered mysterious due to conflicting time and position reports from the Israeli Navy and an emergency buoy that washed up near Gaza a year later. Repeated Israeli searches failed to locate wreckage and the ship's whereabouts remained unknown until '99, when a joint U.S.–Israeli team found the ship several hundred miles east of Crete. End of story."

"That's the public information," Kurt said. "I need the hidden truth. I have reason to believe that submarine was involved in something clandestine, but I've nothing to back that up."

Perlmutter's mustache twitched as he considered this. "Common sense would suggest that's highly unlikely."

"Why?"

"She was on a shakedown cruise when she vanished," Perlmutter said. "Her crew were mostly new recruits. They'd spent a month in England, training with the Brits. Nothing outlandish about that. Also, she was in the process of being delivered. Unlikely that she would be on a secret mission before she'd ever reached Israel to be fitted out."

"And yet the erroneous position reports suggest something was going on," Kurt said.

Perlmutter tugged thoughtfully on his beard. "I must admit there have always been rumors about that vessel. The sinking, the disappearance, even the search for it, were controversial. At one point, a high-ranking Israeli officer claimed the government had deliberately misled those who'd been looking for her because they didn't want the wreck to be found."

"But it was discovered," Kurt questioned. "And the Israelis had parts of the ship salvaged, including the bridge, right?"

Perlmutter nodded. "There was talk of bringing the whole ship up, but it was too costly and complicated an endeavor, especially as the wreck lies so deep."

Kurt said, "The question I have is, why consider it at all? We've salvaged a few ships in our time. No one goes to that expense unless there's an incredibly important—even singular—reason for doing so. Usually something on the sunken vessel that a government wants or something they don't want anyone else to have. Which makes me think the *Dakar* was carrying something the Israeli government wanted kept secret."

Perlmutter looked slightly out of sorts. He shifted in his chair and took another sip of the cognac and then placed the glass down slowly. "I have roughly thousands of volumes of various types here, Kurt, and I can assure you there's nothing in any of them to support your theory."

"I'll accept that," Kurt said. "But there are other forms of information, including word of mouth, and I know you speak with people who talk off the record. And honoring those commitments, I know you've never written a single word of it down. But you have it all stored"—Kurt tapped the side of his head—"up here."

Perlmutter's frame stiffened. "Talk and innuendo are dangerous things to trade in, especially when one is grasping at straws. You never know who will hand you a few, only to watch you fall. I imagine this has something to do with Joe and Ms. Priya disappearing?"

"It does," Kurt admitted. He brought St. Julien up to speed on everything that had happened, filling him in on the link to the oil crisis and to what Millard had told him. "Right now, I have nothing else to go on. I have no way to stop what we're dealing with, no way to track down the people who took Priya and no chance of bringing them to justice for what happened to Joe. If straws are all that are left, I'm reaching for them with both hands. So, if you have any information suggesting the *Dakar* was involved in a clandestine mission and carrying a secret cargo when she went down, I need to hear it."

"There have always been rumors about that vessel," Perlmutter admitted. "Most are frivolous, but there is one I've heard that may interest you. Several years ago—almost a decade now—I was in France having dinner at a wonderful gastropub with a colleague from the French Military Historical Society. We were on our second bottle of wine when the subject of missing vessels came up. I told him a few stories from NUMA's list of great discoveries—nothing classified, I assure you. Suitably impressed, he tried to match me, story for story. Eventually, he asked if I'd heard the true story of the *Dakar*.

"Naturally intrigued, I told him I had not. He agreed to enlighten me but spoke in the vaguest of terms. At any rate, his intimation was that the French Air Force had sent the *Dakar* to the bottom, not a malfunction or accident."

Kurt narrowed his gaze. "The French Air Force? Why would they sink an Israeli sub?"

Perlmutter stroked his beard. "My friend wouldn't say, but he offered a possible answer in the form of another rumor. This one suggested the French and Israelis had jointly developed a new weapon. Something to be used in the event of another Arab invasion. He told me others thought it might be a hydrogen bomb— which is logical, as the French were helpful in the creation of the Israeli nuclear program—but he personally thought it was something more sinister. He described it as being a doomsday weapon."

"Doomsday?"

"My friend is fond of dramatic terms," Perlmutter said. "Upon later explanation, I understood him to mean a weapon that couldn't be stopped once it was unleashed. Not even at the border."

"Biological," Kurt said.

Perlmutter nodded. "All too common today, but rare back then. According to my friend, the two nations had designed this weapon together before they began fighting over it. The French were afraid, insisting a countermeasure be developed. The Israelis were firmly against this but finally acquiesced. Once the weapon and its antidote had both been perfected, the Israelis stole the whole kit and caboodle, loaded it aboard the *Dakar* and sailed for Israel. Unwilling to lose what they believed to be their rightful creation, the French hunted the *Dakar* down and sank it."

Kurt knew he was onto the truth now. He took another sip of the cognac, reached down to scratch Fritz on the head and then stood.

"You're going?"

"You've given me what I need," Kurt replied.

"I've given you a rumor," Perlmutter corrected, "and only because you asked me to. You must know that particular friend has a fairly suspect record when it comes to veracity."

"I think your friend told you the truth," Kurt said. "What's more, he might have given us the key to prevent this oil shock from becoming a lasting crisis. I have to go. Keep well. I'll stay longer next time and we'll drink the rest of that bottle."

Kurt left Perlmutter's home with a wave of energy surging through his body. He dialed Rudi on his phone, using the Bluetooth connection in the Jeep to talk over the speakers.

"I'm headed to the airport," he told Rudi. "I need Paul, Gamay and all the deep-diving equipment you can pull together in an hour."

Rudi, who was rarely shocked, seemed at a loss. "Why?"

"Because I'm flying to Crete. And I'm diving on the INS *Dakar*."

"The *Dakar* . . . The submarine?"

"That's what Millard was trying to tell us," Kurt replied. "When

I asked him about the oil-destroying bacteria, he said *Le Dakar*—
the *Dakar*. The submarine. Not the city."

"Seems like a stretch," Rudi said.

"Not after what St. Julien just told me." Kurt went on to explain
the rumor Perlmutter had just relayed to him.

"He does have a spy network that would make the CIA proud,"
Rudi said, "but you're still making a giant leap of faith and landing
on a very shaky conclusion. How would Tessa even find out about
this weapon?"

"Pascal Millard," Kurt said. "He's the link. He spent years as the
Director of Biological Research for the French military and then
held the same role on the civilian side with the French Ministry of
Science. At that time, he was given the additional title Director of
Ethics Administration. He was in a position to know these secrets
and, once he was fired and censured, he would be in a position to
trade on them."

"I suppose the timing fits," Rudi said. "We've been piecing his
background together. He left France and started working for Tessa
before this oil crisis began."

"How they met, I don't know," Kurt admitted. "But at some point,
Millard told her about the oil destroyer and its resting place on the
Dakar. Tessa, being a risk taker whose alternative energy company
is floundering, comes up with the plan of the century. Destroy
the world's oil, tell yourself that you're saving the planet and make
billions on the back end."

"Audacious," Rudi replied. "Do you have anything beyond the
rumor St. Julien told you about and the circumstantial link you just
gave me? Like a method by which this oil destroyer gets from a submarine at the bottom of the sea and into Tessa's hands?"

"Tessa has a wealth of equipment at her disposal—submersibles, aircraft, ships. She also has a historical preservation society that's done work all around the globe. That LNG carrier in Bermuda was one of her presents to the world at large, but there have been others. Look up her efforts and I guarantee you'll find her historical preservation society operating near the *Dakar* between the time Millard began working for her and the start of this oil crisis."

"Stand by," Rudi said. "I'll check."

The wait was longer than Kurt expected, but he continued toward the airport without slowing down. "Anything?"

"You're dead-on," Rudi said finally. "Two years ago, Tessa's foundation spent three months and sixty million dollars on a deepwater archaeological expedition in the eastern Med. It was supposed to be cataloging and recovering Minoan artifacts, but despite the cost and time spent, there was very little to show for the effort."

"And the location?" Kurt asked.

"They did work over a small geographic area," Rudi said, "but never more than ten miles from where the *Dakar* went down."

"They weren't looking for amphoras and statues of Poseidon," Kurt said. "They were diving on the wreck, trying to find whatever type of sealed protective containers the oil-destroying cultures were stored in."

"You've convinced me," Rudi said. "But if she's already been there, what good is searching the *Dakar* going to do us?"

It was time to deliver the good news. "Perlmutter's friend said there was a countermeasure to the bioweapon. A counteragent, an antidote. The completion of which was the cause of the rift between the Israelis and the French in the first place. As it happens, I asked Millard how we could destroy the bacteria. His response was odd to me. He said they didn't find it, it wasn't there. At the time, I thought he was just confused, but now it makes perfect sense. Tessa's people found the oil destroyer but not the counteragent."

"Which means it might still be there."

"Exactly," Kurt said. "It's not easy to search every square inch of a sunken vessel. Especially at that depth. And especially when you're doing it in secret. For what they wanted to do, the oil destroyer was far more important than the counteragent. Once they had it, there was little incentive to keep looking for its antidote. But we have every incentive in the world."

"I assume you're still driving to the airport," Rudi said.

"Halfway there."

"Keep going," Rudi said.

"We should probably expect trouble," Kurt pointed out. "I think it's time we broke out more than the standard-issue equipment."

"I know what you'll need," Rudi said. "Don't worry. You'll have it. Just get to the airport and start loading. I'll make sure everything else is waiting for you in Crete."

48

ABOARD THE *MONARCH*

A DROP OF SWEAT meandered through follicles of thick, dark hair, trickling forward and down the side of a man's face. It reached his chin, mixed with a drop of fresh blood and fell to the deck below, splattering in a microscopic explosion like a Jackson Pollock canvas wrought on machined-aluminum plating.

Joe Zavala smiled at the thought. *Blood, Sweat and Tears*, he'd call it.

He was facing the deck, supporting himself on his hands as if he was doing a push-up. His jaw ached from the pistol-whipping that had drawn the blood, but he was a fighter by nature and going all the way to the floor was something he refused to do.

"Ready for more?" a brusque female voice asked.

"To be honest," Joe said, "I wasn't ready for that one."

Joe had endured a strange couple of days. At least he thought it was a couple of days. He couldn't really be certain.

One moment, he'd been on the verge of escaping from the docking sphere in Tessa's submerged production facility off Bermuda, the next instant the entire vessel shook and a wall of water had surged into the sphere and through the tunnel behind him.

Joe had pulled himself out of the water and onto the submersible, which was banging around inside the sphere. That kept him from being sucked back into the tunnel, but as he looked for Kurt and Millard, someone had clubbed him from behind.

By the time he'd returned to a conscious state, he was in the submersible, tied up and gagged like the men he and Kurt had left behind. The sub was descending into the outer hull and ramming its way out through the sliding door in the side of the ship.

When the submarine surfaced, Joe was hauled aboard the mystery freighter, which he learned was named the *Morgana*. He was kept in a dark hold, fed nothing and drugged when he started to complain about the accommodations.

Transfer to the *Monarch* happened the next night and, since then, his home had been a cargo compartment on the lowest deck of the plane. The compartment had been frigid when they were airborne, only to grow stifling and hot after they'd landed.

It was cramped, without any creature comforts or even a blanket, but it was better than the alternative.

"You're lucky to be alive," Tessa told him, raising the possibility of that alternative.

Joe looked up. Tessa stood there, flanked by several of her men. One was a big, bearded fellow who Joe had seen on the freighter after his capture. The others were smaller and seemed better at taking orders than anything else.

"Get up," Tessa demanded.

As Joe stood, Tessa snapped her fingers and another prisoner was dragged into view.

Joe recognized Priya instantly. "What are you doing here?"

Priya's eyes fell as she spotted him. She didn't say a word.

"She's here because she was foolish enough to place this on the hull of my aircraft," Tessa said. In her hand, Joe saw a geotracker. "We saw her, followed her back to the yacht and captured her. Just about the time you and Austin were blowing up my production facility. If you think you've stopped me, you're sadly mistaken. I have other facilities and the need for that place is just about at an end anyway."

"If we did you such a favor," Joe said, "how about just letting us go and calling it even?"

"Because things are never even," Tessa said. "You're either winning or you're losing and you and your friends in Washington are going to lose badly."

Joe had no desire for a long conversation. "Let's cut to the chase," he said. "What do you want from us?"

"You," Tessa said, "are here only as leverage." She turned to Priya. "This one, on the other hand, has useful skills. Convince her to hack into NUMA's computer system for me."

Joe saw where this was going.

So did Priya. "I won't do it."

"Of course you will," Tessa said. "The only question is whether your friend here will still be able to walk when you finally give in."

With that, Tessa turned to her men. "Stretch him out. If she fails us, begin showing Ms. Kashmir what leverage really looks like."

Joe's wrists were wrapped in electrical cables and pulled wide. As one of her men moved in to administer the same treatment to Joe's leg, Joe spun-kicked him in the face and then pulled his arm free.

The big fellow tackled him and put him in a headlock. Joe swung his head back, connecting with the man's chin, but the blow wasn't enough to set him free.

"Enough!" Tessa shouted. "One more act of resistance out of you and I'll cut her throat."

Joe looked over. Tessa had Priya by the hair with a knife against her throat.

"She's such a pretty thing," Tessa said, "but that can be changed." The knife left Priya's throat and migrated to her cheek, drawing a taste of blood.

Joe stopped struggling. Tessa had the upper hand. He could do nothing without them harming Priya. He wouldn't let that happen.

Tessa turned her attention back to Priya. "You friend has chosen you over his own pride. What will you choose?"

Priya stubbornly kept her mouth shut. And Tessa gave the order. "Break his back, turn him into an invalid like her!"

"No!" Priya shouted, tears welling up in her dark eyes.

"You want him to keep walking," Tessa said.

"Of course."

"Then get on that computer, log on to NUMA and tell me what they're up to."

Priya looked at Joe, tears running down her face, dropping to the floor to complete Joe's imaginary painting. Joe nodded softly to her. "It's okay," he said.

What he didn't say was obvious. If they were going to escape, they first had to survive.

49

PRIYA WAS LIFTED from her spot on the ground and placed in a chair in front of an industrial-looking work terminal.

While the computer booted up, Tessa pressed an intercom button. "Extend the communications array," she said. "Make sure to falsify our position and identity."

A voice responded momentarily, saying, *"Linkup complete. We're connected through a false data node in Mumbai. No one will be able to trace us back here."*

"You're now connected to the web," Tessa said. "Log on to NUMA's classified system, please."

Priya tapped away at the keys, speaking at the same time. "I'm not going to be able to get in," she insisted. "They know I'm missing. They probably know you have me. My clearance and access codes will already have been blocked."

"I don't expect you to log on like it's another day at the office," Tessa said, "I expect you to use your knowledge of NUMA's systems and hack them so I can watch their every move. And before you think of sending them a message or triggering some alarm, let me tell you that one of my experts is watching everything you do on a remote screen. If you try anything foolish, your friend Joe will never walk again."

Priya stared at Tessa. It was hard to believe she could be so brutal, but looking into the cold, malevolent eyes, Priya sensed her captor was capable of following through on every threat she'd uttered.

Turning back to the keyboard, Priya went to work, looking for ways to break into the NUMA defenses she'd helped Hiram Yaeger update over the last two years. The level of her own thoroughness now frustrated her. For half an hour, she tried without success, all the while the interior of the aircraft growing hotter.

"This is not going well," Tessa said, now sitting on a foldout chair on the far side of the fuselage.

Priya wiped the sweat from her face, scribbled notes on a pad and continued to search for a weak link. Finally, she was able to penetrate some of the less protected programs. "I've broken into the travel procurement office."

"What good will that do?" Tessa demanded.

"I'm not sure," Priya admitted, "but it's a start."

She studied the documents available to her. Most were as mundane as rental car receipts and meal vouchers. Then she came upon something that made her heart hurt.

"Joe, they're flying your parents to Washington. The tickets were coded under a bereavement program. They've listed you as missing and presumed dead."

Joe shrugged. "Mom and Dad will be awfully surprised when I show up and they have to give back all that life insurance money."

Priya almost laughed, almost.

"This is all very touching," Tessa snapped. "I need to know more than the travel plans of NUMA families. Where is Kurt Austin and what is he up to?"

"He went back to Washington," Priya said, finding another more pertinent record. "But he's not there now. He's in Crete."

While that information meant nothing to Priya, it struck Tessa hard. She stood up suddenly, her dark eyebrows knitting together. "Crete? Why? What's he doing there?"

"I have no idea," Priya said. "Paul and Gamay Trout are with him, and the quartermaster's office confirmed the requisition for a dive boat and several deep-sea vehicles, including an ROV, a three-man submersible and two deepwater atmospheric diving suits."

Tessa walked across the fuselage, leaned over Priya's shoulder and read the records for herself. The look on her face was malevolent. "Find me the reason for this trip. What are they looking for?"

"I can't access that information," Priya said. "All the operational reports are too well protected."

"Dig deeper," Tessa instructed.

"I can't get in any deeper!" Priya said. "They'll just detect the attempt and shut us down. Then you'll lose all access."

"If that happens," Tessa said, "your problems will be worse than mine."

"Use my codes," Joe said from behind them.

Priya turned his way.

"They're probably still active," Joe said. "No one rushes to clean out a dead man's office or shut down his email or access codes. At least give them a try."

"Do it," Tessa snapped.

Joe rattled off his codes and Priya entered them carefully. After a short delay, the codes were accepted, giving Priya—and Tessa—access to everything in the Special Projects database.

Priya found the information their captors wanted. She began reading the transcript to Tessa, slowing as she reached the crucial information. "Kurt's objective is coded as a deepwater wreck, identified as the INS *Dakar.*"

The name meant nothing to Priya, but Tessa froze at the sound of it. She read the rest of the information herself. By the time she finished, her previously smug face had been drained of color. Though it reddened quickly as anger replaced shock.

She turned to the broad-shouldered, bearded man. "Put them in the cargo compartment. Then find Volke and meet me up front. We cannot let Austin and his friends dive on that ship."

50

JOE AND PRIYA were taken to a compartment on the middle level of the aircraft and locked inside. Both of them had their hands zip-tied and Joe's legs were also bound, but he didn't think that would hold them long.

"I'm sorry," Priya said. "I shouldn't have left the yacht. I shouldn't have tried to place the geotracker on the plane. I was trying to help. Thought it'd be good to take some initiative." She paused. "And I was feeling left out."

"I wouldn't worry about it," Joe said. "Disobeying orders is kind of a thing at NUMA. You'll probably get a promotion out of it once we get back."

Priya smiled, but it quickly disappeared into a frown. "If we get back. This is a nightmare."

Joe pretended to be hurt. "That's the first time a woman has ever said that about spending time alone with me."

"You know what I mean," she said.

"Trust me, things are looking up," Joe said. "Tessa doesn't know it, but she gave up some vital information. To begin with, Kurt's alive. Something I've been wondering about since we were separated on that ship of hers. More importantly, Kurt is doing what he always does, making life miserable for his opponent. I have no idea what that submarine could possibly have to do with all of this, but Tessa's face went white when you said the name."

"But I feel like a traitor giving them that information."

"You give something to get something," Joe said. "You just logged in with my ID. Tessa seems like an obsessive-compulsive type. Now that she has access, she'll probably find it hard to resist using it again . . . and again. Eventually, someone will notice that a dead guy is checking his email. That will tell Kurt and Rudi that she has us. Just might lead to them sending help. Assuming they can find us."

"But if she has access, she doesn't need us anymore."

"She can't know when they're going to cut her off," Joe said. "That should keep us alive for a while. Long enough to get out of here. Trust me, this place won't hold us long."

"How can you be so confident?"

"Because Tessa isn't much of a warden," Joe said. "She's a businesswoman. Obviously, a brutal one at that, but she's not equipped to keep us here."

"We're tied up, in a locked compartment," Priya said.

"These zip ties won't hold us," Joe said, "not once I find something even moderately rough to use on them."

"And the door?"

"This is an airplane," Joe replied, "not Leavenworth. It's designed to be lightweight and flexible. The skin and the ribs of the plane are strong, everything else is paper-thin. We could break that door down with one strong charge, if we wanted to. The problem is, the armed guards on the other side."

"You're quite the optimist," she said. "Especially since it's me you're stuck with and not Kurt. I can't exactly make a run for it, you know. And I can't help you fight them unless you want me to trip someone or bite their ankles."

"Tripping works," Joe said. "Ankle biting, not so much. It'll probably just ruin that beautiful smile of yours."

The smile came out. "You should probably make a break for it on your own. I could at least distract them."

Joe shook his head. "There are no circumstances under which I leave you here, so you might as well let that thought go right now. As for escaping, we don't have to walk out of here. This plane is filled with submersibles, Jet Skis, boats. My plan has us riding to freedom in style."

"You already have a plan?"

Joe nodded. "Multistep, with different contingencies. Very organized, unlike that fly-by-night stuff Kurt comes up with."

Priya smiled. "Tell me more."

"It starts with the guards," Joe said. "We have to get rid of them." "How?"

"We use what we have around us," Joe said.

"We have nothing around us. This compartment is empty."

"We have light," Joe said. "Light means electricity. Electricity means wires. Would it surprise you to know that most aircraft have several miles of wiring running through the fuselage?"

"It wouldn't," she said. "I worked on a computer program for Airbus when I was in college. All powered systems were fly-by-wire. There were circuits running everywhere."

Joe nodded. "This plane also has cranes, ramps, powered flooring to move cargo pallets around. All of it powered electrically from the fuel cells."

Priya looked around. "I don't see any wires."

Joe reached over and rapped his knuckles on a sloped footer at the edge of the wall. The impact made a hollow sound. "It's because they're hidden. Though they need to be somewhere they can be easily accessed."

Priya was grinning now. She could see his plan.

"We have a few hours until dinner," Joe said. "I might as well get to work."

HAVING PLACED two men outside the compartment to guard her captives, Tessa met with her two trusted subordinates.

"Despite everything we've done, Austin and NUMA are rapidly putting the puzzle together. I want him eliminated."

Woods spoke up. "We could talk to—"

Tessa cut him off. "I'm not using any more of your local friends. Austin and his group are beyond their ability to deal with." She turned to Volke. "He almost killed you down on the LNG carrier. That should motivate you. Who can we reach out to? Who among your illegitimate friends can we use to get rid of Austin once and for all?"

"I have an old acquaintance who could do it for us," Volke said. "He and his people leave nothing but bodies behind when they act."

"Paramilitary?"

Volke nodded.

"Do they have the equipment necessary to get at Austin out in the middle of the Mediterranean?"

"His last operation was flying weapons from Albania to rebels across the mountains, in long-range ex–Russian helicopters."

Tessa didn't like the idea of involving more outsiders, but she was approaching a critical point. A meeting with Arat Buran and his Consortium was set for the next morning. She needed Volke and Woods with her when it happened.

"Hire them," she said. "Offer more than they ask for, but make it clear to them that half measures will not get them paid. I want Austin dead. I want his friends and colleagues dead. I want his ship at the bottom of the sea resting beside the *Dakar*."

Volke nodded. "I'll take care of it."

THE GUARDS placed outside of Joe and Priya's compartment grew bored and restless long before the dinner hour came. They'd sat and talked, made crude jokes, played cards and even taken turns napping. Eventually, they got hungry.

"Call Woods," one said to the other. "Tell him to relieve us or send down some food."

"If he hasn't eaten everything in the galley himself," the other guard joked.

A call was placed and a tray of sandwiches was sent down to them. "Two of those are for the prisoners," they were told.

The men considered eating the prisoners' food themselves, but the bread was coarse and dry and the meat gamey and possibly spoiled.

"I'm not eating garbage," the first man said.

"I'll give it to them," the second guard said. "Let's hope it doesn't make them sick."

He walked across the floor of the aircraft and banged on the door. "Step back," he ordered. "We have food for you."

Muffled noises that sounded like shuffling could be heard and the guard considered that to be compliance. He unlocked the door, put the key back in his pocket and grabbed the handle.

Sparks exploded from the aluminum handle the instant he touched it. The guard was thrown across the fuselage, hurling the tray up in the air as he went. He landed on his back with smoke wafting from his hand and the scent of burned skin filling the cabin.

The lights dimmed and the sandwich tray clattered to the floor.

The second guard was so surprised that he failed to see Joe charging through the now open door. By the time he looked up, Joe's fist was hurtling toward his face. The impact snapped his head to the side and put him out cold.

Joe enjoyed throwing a good punch and he felt that was one of his best. He dragged the guards back into the compartment, passing Priya, who remained crouched by the door with the leads of two long wires in her hands.

"That was shocking," she said, grinning and suspending the wires separately where they wouldn't touch the floor, the wall or each other.

Joe laughed. It was dark on the lower deck now, with only the emergency lighting coming on. "I think we tripped a breaker. That could be good or bad. Let's not wait around to find out."

He crouched down next to her. "Climb on. This is no time to be shy."

She wrapped her arms around his neck and pulled herself up. Standing, Joe grabbed her legs, held them tight and ducked out into the main section of the fuselage.

He moved toward the ladder, finding Priya easy to carry. Her arms were strong and she held on to Joe's neck and shoulders without any problem, even as he descended a ladder to the lowest deck on the aircraft.

"So far, so good," he said. "Now to get the aft door open."

Weaving around a Ferrari and Mercedes SUV, Joe accidentally bumped Priya's head on an overhanging section of the fuselage.

"Ouch."

"Sorry," Joe replied. "Took that turn a little wide. Been some time since I had anyone traveling piggyback."

"It's all right," she said. "Don't slow down. I want to get out of here."

Making their way to the tail, Joe bypassed the tarp-covered cars and stopped beside a fiberglass powerboat. It sat on a pallet connected to a conveyor belt system that allowed Tessa and her crew to move the vehicles and cargo around. Reaching down, he flicked a switch, brought the battery online and checked the fuel supply. "Three-quarters of a tank. That should get us away from here."

"What about the submersible?" Priya said. "They can't chase us if we're underwater."

The sub was up in its cradle. Joe shook his head. "The crane will be slow and noisy. We need to lower that door and use this conveyor belt to get ourselves out of here ASAP."

He gently lowered Priya into the boat and then moved to the controls. The setup was standard, although Joe noticed the writing on the pressure dials had been done in Cyrillic. Apparently, Tessa had built her plane from Russian parts.

He pressed a button to power up the system, turned the handle to unlock the door and waited for the light on the panel to go green. As soon as it did, he moved the door handle from up to down.

The hydraulic pumps kicked in and a crack of light appeared around the edge of the ramp.

As the ramp dropped, wind began whistling over the top, bringing a swirl of dust and an odd scent with it.

"Something's not right," Joe said.

The ramp was only a quarter of the way down when the power was cut from somewhere else in the plane.

"They're onto us," Priya said.

"No problem," Joe said. "I have a contingency for that."

He pulled the emergency release handle. The hydraulic pressure vanished and the ramp—which weighed several thousand pounds—fell hard and locked itself into a full-open position. Instead of a large splash, it hit with nothing but a solid thud, which raised an additional cloud of dust.

Joe stared out the back. He'd assumed they were on water. The *Monarch* was designed to operate on water, but all he could see behind them were acres of bone-white desert and a cloud of swirling dust.

51

"NOW I KNOW how Kurt feels," Joe said.

Out beyond the tail of the *Monarch*, swirling winds were lifting the bleached and dried soil and whipping it through the air, cutting the visibility to a few hundred feet. There wasn't a drop of water in sight, but even if the ocean lay beyond what Joe could see, there was no possible way to get a boat to it.

"Tell me you have a contingency plan for your contingency plan," Priya said.

"Of course," Joe said. "Who wouldn't?"

She gave him a look that suggested she'd like to hear it and quickly.

"If we can't float, we'll have to drive," he said.

He picked her up once again, carried her back toward the boxy Mercedes G 63 and put her down.

"This should be at home in whatever desert this happens to be," he said.

Before he could open the door, the sound of boots pounding on the deck came rushing toward them.

"Get down," Joe said.

Priya rolled under the Mercedes as Joe took cover by the cargo controls.

Two men raced by them without a glance, headed for the open ramp. Joe noticed they were running on the conveyor belt. He glanced at the controls. It still had power. He tapped the control for the aft belt, activated it and pushed the dial to full speed.

The belt engaged instantly and the men were thrown off balance, stumbled and landed on their hands and knees.

Joe stopped the belt, then turned it full speed in the other direction. This time, conveying the men forward, onto the ramp and into the dust bowl beyond.

Joe turned back toward the Mercedes and froze.

"Mighty clever of you," the big man named Woods said. He stood there with a pistol in his hand. "These are only rubber pellets, son. But I promise you, they'll dig into your skin something fierce."

Tessa had equipped her guards with something that wouldn't punch gaping holes in the one-of-a-kind aircraft. TSA agents carried similar cartridges.

Joe raised his hands in surrender, only to be surprised by the deafening echo of a car horn.

Woods flinched and turned instinctively to look behind, Joe was on him before he realized his mistake. Tackling the big man and snatching the gun out of his hand.

Woods threw Joe off like he was a small child, but Joe held on to the gun. He stood and fired. The first bullet hit Woods square in the chest, but the man only flinched and charged forward. Joe fired three more rounds, hitting Woods in the knee, shin and foot.

The bullet to the toes was what finally stopped the charge. Woods tumbled to the ground, rolling away and grabbing his foot.

Leaving him behind, Joe raced to the Mercedes, where he found Priya sitting in the driver's seat. She'd climbed up and gotten inside without a sound. How, Joe couldn't be sure, but he vowed not to put anything past her.

She held up a set of keys that she'd found above the visor. "How's this for a contingency plan?"

"It's fantastic."

Joe climbed in and pulled the door shut as gunfire erupted from the open ramp. The men he'd sent out the door had recovered from their unceremonious exit and were rejoining the fight.

The rubber bullets hit all around, ricocheting off the windshield and the walls around them with a strange sound.

"A little help," Priya said.

Joe stepped on the brake as she started the engine and put the car in gear. As soon as the motor fired up, he stomped on the gas. The big vehicle surged forward, slammed into the powerboat in front of them and promptly bulldozed it toward the opening.

Tessa's guards fired as they charged and then dove out of the way as the powerboat went tumbling toward them and the Mercedes rumbled down after it.

Priya turned the wheel to swerve around the wrecked speedboat and Joe kept his foot to the floor.

"Which way?"

"Take your pick."

Priya turned to get them out of the line of fire, drove a hundred yards or so, then turned again. They sped on into the swirling dust, until the wing, engine and tail of another huge aircraft appeared.

Priya swerved, drove under the wing and turned to avoid the dangling engine pod.

"Did we drive in a circle?" Priya said.

"No," Joe replied. "That's a different plane."

Roaring off in a new direction, they soon encountered another aircraft and then another. The aircraft were everywhere. Before they'd finished passing one, another wide-body would appear from the blinding dust. Some had missing engines, others had been stripped of their tails or wings or fuselage panels. Several of them sat on the ground like beached whales, their landing gear long removed.

"I've been wondering why we haven't been spotted," Joe said. "Now it makes sense. We're sitting in an airplane graveyard. I doubt anyone would ever look here. And if they did, it would only take the slightest bit of work to disguise the *Monarch* and make it look like another derelict."

The farther they drove, the more aircraft they encountered. Each time they passed one, they expected to find a gate or a fence, but, so far, an exit remained elusive.

"This place is huge," Priya said.

"It's probably an old air base," Joe said.

Smaller aircraft appeared. Older transports and Cold War–era fighter planes that Joe recognized as old MiGs.

Finally, a dilapidated fence appeared through the dust. Razor wire crested the top, dangling in places where the fence sagged. Priya took aim. "We should be able to crash through that."

"Do it," Joe said.

They sped toward the fence, hitting it between two loose poles and ripping the mesh from the nearest supports. It caught on the hood and they dragged it some distance before it finally scraped across the top of the SUV and fell off behind them.

A service road ran along the perimeter of the fence. It looked as forlorn as the rest of the complex. Priya turned onto it, but Joe let his foot off the gas.

"Turn us around," Joe said, looking back through the rear window.

"The other direction?"

"No," Joe said. "Back inside the fence. Hurry."

"But we just escaped from there," Priya said, turning the wheel as Joe pushed the gas pedal down once more.

"We escaped from the *Monarch*," Joe corrected. "If they find this section of the fence torn down, they will assume we smashed through it and took off. They'll think we're running for the hills— or whatever's out there on the other side of this dust storm—but the moment this weather clears, we'll be sitting ducks. They'll spot us with ease, but we can hide back there in the junk just as easily."

Priya was already turning the wheel as Joe pressed the gas pedal. They were soon back inside the fence, moving through a section filled with smaller aircraft. "We just need to find one of those big old transports and pull up inside it."

As Joe spoke, his eyes darted from side to side. He caught sight of headlights coming through the dust off to his left. He pointed to the right.

"Behind that one," he said, indicating a three-engine transport that had once served Aeroflot and sat on its side with one wing down like a wounded bird.

Priya drove with great precision, especially considering someone else was working the gas. They ducked behind the tail of the old plane, swerving and missing the aluminum skin by less than a foot.

Up ahead, Joe noticed a huge Russian helicopter sitting flat on the ground with its aft door missing.

"In there," Joe said. "That's our spot."

As Priya lined them up, Joe gave the vehicle a bump of gas and then took his foot off the pedal. They coasted forward, slowing as Joe reached over and put the transmission in low. They bumped up into the back end of the big military helicopter, still moving forward.

Joe couldn't hit the brake pedal without flashing a bright red beacon that might tell everyone where they were, but he pulled hard on the hand brake, which wasn't attached to the taillight sensor. It helped, but not enough.

They hit the wall separating the cockpit from the cargo bay with a solid thump. A blizzard of dust rained down upon them and the helicopter rocked back and forth several times. Priya turned off the engine and pulled out the key.

Turning around Joe looked for the other vehicles. "Hold your breath."

"Will that help?" Priya said.

"We're about to find out."

Gazing through the back window, Joe saw the lights of two cars pass by in the distance and vanish, heading toward the perimeter.

"Now what?"

"We find a way to call for help," Joe said.

52

KURT STOOD in the wheelhouse of the *Gryphon*, an all-metal, ninety-foot boat with a raked nose, wide stance and oversized air intakes for the gas turbine engine that powered it.

They'd picked up the *Gryphon* in Crete after the overnight flight to the island. Fueling and loading had taken them through lunch and a couple hours on the water had put them over the wreck of the *Dakar*.

They'd encountered nothing to suggest danger, but Kurt had a feeling that wouldn't last. And that's why he'd chosen the *Gryphon*. Not only was the boat armored, it carried hidden weapon systems, was capable of tremendous speed and could be operated remotely—or even autonomously, if necessary.

For now, it sufficed to hold station against a moderate current while the ROV was descending.

"Passing eight thousand feet," Paul said from beside Kurt, "fifteen hundred to go."

"Picking up something on sonar," Gamay said.

Kurt sat back, arms folded across his chest. "Make a high pass and then bring it around again, we need a full-scale picture."

Paul tapped away on the computer keyboard and ordered the ROV to begin a forward and back pattern.

"Setting sonar on virtual," Gamay said.

This would allow multiple sonar returns to be combined into one. A new image appeared on the right side of the monitor. It was soon filling with orange, gray and black details.

"Something isn't right," Gamay said. "Are we sure this is the right location?"

Kurt looked at the sonar image. He'd learned both how to interpret the images over the years and how to not overreact to their limitations. Sonar was a wonderful tool and it gave a picture of whatever it scanned, but it was easily obscured or distorted by changes in water temperature, salinity and even the angle at which the sonar beam hit the object in question.

That said, the image on the screen didn't look much like a submarine.

"We're in the right spot," he said, double-checking their position.

"Keep descending," Kurt said to Paul. "Let's see what the cameras show when we get in range."

It would be another five minutes before the lights from the ROV began picking up the bottom.

"Level off and maneuver east," Kurt said, tracking the ROV's location.

Paul used the computer to send the ROV on an easterly heading and the cameras began snapping high-definition photos of the seafloor and the scattered bits of wreckage.

There was little to see on the video feed.

"Lots of sediment floating by," Gamay said.

Kurt nodded. He was waiting for a different image, one formed by the computer as it took the photos from the high-definition cameras and merged them digitally with the data from the sonar system.

It took a few moments for the image to be processed, but eventually a three-dimensional image of the entire wreckage field appeared. The colors were false to show contrast, but the image itself was crystal clear.

The reasons for the skewed sonar readings became obvious. The submarine was no longer in one piece. It had been cut into three sections, one of which had been dragged away from the others.

"Someone took it apart," Gamay noted.

Detail on the largest section revealed scaffolding like a cage of metal bars. "They tried to raise it. Too heavy to do it in one piece, so they cut it into sections."

"Did the Israelis do this?" Gamay asked.

"No," Kurt said, "they took only the conning tower. This was Tessa's work." He glanced at Paul. "Make another pass, get in close to the scaffolding."

Paul guided the ROV back around and brought it in closer to the largest section of the wreck. At this closer range, the welded cradle that had been built around and under the submarine became easy to examine.

"Breaks there and there," Kurt said. "Stress fractures. They put enough lifting force into the effort, but they didn't build a strong enough cradle."

"Seems unlikely Tessa's people would get their math wrong," Gamay said.

"I'm sure they got it exactly right," Kurt answered. "But knowing how much each section of the ship weighed doesn't account for the inertia caused by the water-filled compartments or the force required to break it loose from the seabed. Nor is subsurface welding an easy art. Looks like the cradle broke at the welds."

"You seem excited by this," Gamay said.

"Absolutely," Kurt said. "Had they lifted this thing onto a barge and hauled it away, they would have had unlimited time to discover everything inside. A failure like this suggests a desperate second act to retrieve what they eventually found. It makes it more likely they left something behind."

Kurt stood. "Finish the survey. Find the best way in and out of each section and account for any danger you can spot. I'll be getting the Trench Crawlers ready. As soon as you're done, we're going down."

53

KURT AND GAMAY dropped silently toward the bottom of the Mediterranean in what looked like suits of body armor that had been crossed with robotic monsters from a comic book.

Seven feet tall and weighing nearly three hundred pounds, the Trench Crawler was the latest of NUMA's deep-diving creations.

Known as an ADS, or atmospheric diving suit, because it maintained a surface-level pressure of one atmosphere within its shell, the Trench Crawler allowed its occupant to dive deep and spend extended time on the bottom without the need for decompression stops or extended time in a decompression chamber upon surfacing.

It had a bulbous, rounded head, adorned with external cameras and lights, long mechanical arms that bent in directions no human arm could and legs that were bulky and articulated at the knees. Unlike other atmospheric diving suits, the Trench Crawler had fully robotic arms and a wider body, allowing the diver to keep his or her hands inside the shell, where they could manipulate the controls.

A pair of fully rotatable thrusters were attached to the sides, while a compartment on the back contained batteries, oxygen for eight hours, an emergency surfacing float and a pair of small submersible drones that could be deployed and controlled remotely from within the Trench Crawler's shell.

Sealed inside, Kurt's face was lit by the dim glow of small screens, two on the right and two on the left. They displayed the operating systems and the camera views, while a traditional curved helmet view gave an image of the outside world.

Descending beside him, Gamay Trout was in the Bravo model of the Trench Crawler.

"Now I know how a giant feels," she said over the hydrophone.

"I hope that's not a crack about my height," Paul said. He was on the surface, acting as mission control.

"Not at all," Gamay said. "Although, I wouldn't need four-inch heels if I wore this on our next date."

"Nor would you need a reservation, because the waiters would flee the restaurant in horror," Kurt added, interrupting the two of them. "Time to focus, we're nearing the bottom."

"Sonar has you just south of the wreck," Paul said. "With lights on, you should see it in thirty seconds or less."

Kurt switched the exterior lights on and the water around him lit up as tiny particles reflected it back in his direction. Kurt's left hand was on the thruster control. His right hand on a keypad.

"Angling lights downward," he said as he rotated the suit's exterior lights.

Above and to his right, a second set of lights appeared as Gamay switched hers on.

"Sixty feet," Kurt said.

For a moment, there was nothing to see but darkness, then, finally, a barren, grayish plain below.

Watching the depth control meter on one of the screens, Kurt saw the absolute depth at 9,758 feet. A second number underneath it read only 50 and was slowly clicking down toward zero. "Fifty feet," Kurt said. "Switch to neutral."

"Neutral buoyancy," Gamay said.

Kurt adjusted the ballast in his suit and his descent slowed and then stopped. Spread out on the plane were metal parts, junk and debris, but nothing more.

"Anyone see a submarine around here?"

"You've drifted a little farther south," Paul told them. "Head north. It's no more than five hundred feet from your present position."

Engaging the thrusters, Kurt and Gamay moved north, traveling in a slow formation.

The debris field thinned and then the curved hull of a submarine's central section came into view. Closer in, it was easy to see how the scaffolding around it had broken. Kurt said, "Where to, Paul?"

"You'll need to maneuver around the far edge for a safe entry. Too much damage to this side."

They'd planned the dive in advance, but to allow Kurt and Gamay to concentrate on their tasks, it had been decided that Paul would act as overall director.

Kurt and Gamay activated their thrusters again and moved past the near end of the hull. Impact damage, piping, wires and other encrusted debris made entry there impossible.

On the far side, they got a better view of the entire section. It was covered with marine snow and dripping with rust but in better shape than many wrecks Kurt had seen. Spread out in front of it was another debris field of equipment, machinery and assorted junk.

"Either everything fell out when they raised and dropped her," Gamay said, "or they just ripped everything out when they were looking for the cultures."

"Probably a little of both," Kurt said.

He slowed and held his position, studying the submarine. Looking at it was like studying the cross section of a model. The circular curve of the pressure hull was obvious even with the impact damage. The decks crossed at an angle because the hull did not sit perfectly flat on the bottom, but each deck was wide open to the sea.

"Looks like they cut the hull at the limits of the crew quarters and mess hall," Kurt said, gazing into the opening. "Obviously, they wanted to leave the heavy engine room at the stern and the dangerous forward torpedo room on the bottom. Have to give them some credit for thinking ahead."

"Should we go in?" Gamay asked.

Even though the hull was wide open, it was still no place for seven-foot-tall, man-shaped machines.

"No," Kurt said. "Release the drones."

As he gave the order, Kurt pressed two red buttons. "Releasing drones Alpha and Bravo."

A subtle vibration ran through the suit as the drones deployed.

"I'm releasing Charlie," Gamay replied.

The football-shaped drones would have a far easier time searching through the wreck. They could fit through gaps and hatches. They were smooth-sided, with nothing extending outside their shells that could snag on debris or cables. They could move and see in all directions.

"I have Alpha," Kurt said. "Paul, I'm releasing Bravo to your steady hand."

"Roger that," Paul said. "Telemetry is active. I have control of Bravo."

The drones entered the hull on a different deck, their lights illuminating the vacant spaces while their motors stirred up small amounts of sediment.

Gazing at the computer screen inside his helmet, Kurt watched the video from his drone as it navigated the wreck. The inspection was done at a painstakingly slow speed. Compartment by compartment, foot by foot.

The process would take hours. They didn't know exactly what they were looking for, but anything out of the ordinary, anything that could hold a dangerous bacterial culture and keep it secured against the sea for fifty years despite the pressure, depth and cold.

"Drone Bravo is searching the medical bay," Paul announced.

"Charlie entering the mess hall," Gamay said moments later.

In some ways, the work Tessa's people had done made the search easier.

"Looks like they used blowtorches to remove the hatches and watertight doors," Kurt said. "I've encountered nothing to slow our progress."

"There are several gaping holes in the upper deck," Gamay replied.

"They cut a hole in the side of the hull on deck two as well," Paul added. "Looks like they've looted the entire medical bay. There's nothing left in here."

"They've done the same thing to the mess hall," Gamay replied.

"No fryer, no refrigerators, no containers—they've left nothing behind."

Kurt was discovering the same thing. Not a footlocker remained in the crew quarters. Nothing that might be used to hide a sealed container.

"Finish the sweep and then search the aft section with the engine room," he said. "I'm recalling my drone and switching to the forward section of the submarine."

"That wasn't part of the plan," Paul reminded him.

"I'm calling an audible," Kurt said. "They've picked this segment clean. If the counteragent was here, they'd have found it."

"There are twelve unexploded torpedoes in there," Paul reminded him.

"Don't worry," Kurt said. "I left my sledgehammer on the *Gryphon* with you."

Using his thrusters, Kurt maneuvered toward the forward section of the wreck and then guided his drone in through a small gap.

This section didn't seem to have been ransacked. That gave Kurt some hope that they might find what they were looking for.

"Central hull cleared," Gamay said. "Heading for the engine room."

"I'm right behind you," Paul said.

Kurt heard the chatter but focused on his own task. The forward compartments were a jumble, skewed to the side and half filled with sediment. The torpedoes had come off their racks and lay about like fallen logs in a dark forest. That none of them had exploded upon impact was a testament to the design of their safeties. Still, Kurt avoided even bumping them. He didn't want to find out if those safeties were still working after fifty years.

Maneuvering past the last of the torpedoes, he found an area of smoothly deposited silt. As the drone's thrusters began to disturb it, the outline of a boot became visible. No foot. No bone. Just a boot.

Kurt knew from studying previous wrecks that marine life consumed almost everything organic within a few decades of a sinking. Still, the presence of the boot reminded him that this was a grave. He continued the quest soberly until he'd examined the entire forward section and come up against the damaged forward bulkhead. There was nothing beyond that except the sand and the sea.

He glanced at the chronometer. They'd been on the bottom nearly four hours. With the hour it had taken them to descend and the time required to surface, they were nearing a full day.

"Nothing in the forward section," he called out over the radio. "Any luck in the engine room or aft quarters?"

"We're finishing up now," Gamay said. "Nothing to report."

"Time to head up," he said. "Otherwise, Rudi will be screaming about the overtime. Recall your drone and get ready to surface."

As Paul and Gamay confirmed the order, Kurt maneuvered the drone back to where he'd found the boot. He allowed it to descend until it was almost touching the sand. As the sediment swirled, other parts of a uniform were exposed. This was someone's last resting place.

Opening a compartment in the nose, he extended a tiny arm from the drone. The arm held a small round stone that Kurt released, allowing it to fall onto the silt beside the uniform.

A small gesture of respect.

That done, Kurt retracted the arm. He was about to bring the drone out of the hull when he noticed a small metallic object sitting upright in the silt. It was a brass pin. A decoration given to sailors for completing a special type of mission.

As Kurt focused on the pin, he realized he'd seen that type of pin before, not on an Israeli sailor but on the uniform of a friend who was a longtime French submariner.

Without pause, Kurt plucked the decoration off the sediment and stowed it away. He then retrieved the drones and joined Gamay for the nearly hour-long trip to the surface.

All the way up, he mulled over a single question. *What was a French naval insignia doing in the wreck of an Israeli submarine that was supposedly sent to the bottom by the French Air Force?*

54

RUDI GUNN stood on the curb outside the main terminal at Ben Gurion International. Despite a lightweight linen jacket and a hat to keep the sun off his head, he was sweating in the August heat the moment he stepped out of the air-conditioned building.

Fortunately, a white Lincoln was already pulling up in front of him.

"Mr. Gunn?" the driver asked.

Rudi nodded and took off his jacket and climbed into the car. "How quickly can you get me downtown?"

"There should be no delays whatsoever," the driver insisted. "Traffic has been getting lighter every day. Where are you going? The message didn't say."

"The General Staff Building at the Kirya," Rudi replied.

The Kirya was an area in Tel Aviv where the Israeli Defense Force headquarters were located. In essence, it was the Israeli version of the Pentagon.

Rudi had been there several times, the trip from the airport usually started out smoothly and then got bogged down in traffic, but on this run the only traffic Rudi saw was a long collection of cars and trucks waiting to fuel up at a single gas station. "Have they started rationing gasoline?"

"Not officially," the driver said, "but many of the stations are closed. A large, new tax has been imposed on any vehicle that isn't a hybrid or electric. It's calculated based on mileage, so no one drives if they don't have to. It's my living, so I don't have a choice."

Rudi sat back. He'd seen lines at the gas stations in Washington before he left. The price of oil was going through the roof, just as the President said it would. Traders were riding the wave with glee, while regular people were acting the way they often did before a hurricane rolled through, filling up everything in sight in case there was no gas available next week.

Rumors of gas stations closing and oil companies withholding deliveries made it all worse.

Then, in an attempt to calm the public, the President had gone on television to assure everyone that there was enough oil in the strategic reserve and coming in from unaffected sources for the nation to function normally without grinding to a halt. The effect of that speech was panic.

Unfortunately, Rudi thought, a presidential denial of a problem served only to confirm in the minds of many that the problem was real. Silently, he wondered how far America was from mileage taxes, forced carpooling or people checking their license plates to see if they ended in odd or even numbers as they'd done during rationing in the seventies.

"Front gate of the Kirya coming up," the driver said.

He was soon passing through the outer gate. From there, he

quickly reached central reception, where Rudi's NUMA ID was enough to get him in front of a receptionist from the Office of Naval Records.

"I'm here to see Admiral Natal," he said, holding out his credentials yet again.

The uniformed aide checked his computer screen. "There's nothing on the Admiral's calendar about a visitor from NUMA."

"I'm an old friend," Rudi said. "Please, just give the Admiral my name."

"He's very busy."

"As he should be," Rudi said. "But tell him I'll wait. All day, if I have to."

Rudi's patience was not required. He would cool his heels for no more than five minutes before the aide returned and escorted him to Admiral Natal's office. There, the two men shook hands warmly and sized each other up after several years without face-to-face contact.

"Wait all day, would you?" the Admiral said. "You've used that trick on me before."

Admiral Natal was thirty years Rudi's senior, nearly the same height and pure gray on top. He'd spent two years as a visiting professor at Annapolis back when Rudi was a student at the Naval Academy. They'd seen each other occasionally at functions since then and had even worked together on a project several years back.

"You'd misgraded my test," Rudi reminded him.

"I misgraded everyone's exam," the Admiral said. "The true test was seeing who would come in and argue their score. You were the only one who waited for me to return. And all for a few meaningless extra points that wouldn't affect your A plus."

"I like getting things right," Rudi said. "Which is why I'm here. To make something right and to ask you several questions."

"Somehow, I didn't think it would be a personal visit. What's on your mind?"

"NUMA has a crew diving on the *Dakar*," Rudi said.

The Admiral's face tensed. "That boat is a tomb, Rudi. Of all people, I would expect you to understand that. What possible reason could you have for disturbing it?"

Rudi didn't offer any reasons just yet. "We've recovered personal artifacts that we'd like to return to the families of the men who were lost. I assume I can have them delivered here, to you?"

"Of course," Natal said, leaning back in his chair and staring at Rudi as if trying to gauge him. "But I'm sure you haven't come all this way just to ask me that."

"No, I didn't," Rudi said. "I came to ask you about the *Dakar*'s cargo. I need to know what she was carrying when she went down."

"Carrying?"

"I have good reason to believe there was a biological weapon on board," Rudi said. "A strain of bacteria that feasts on hydrocarbons, destroying the productive capacity of oil fields and creating dangerous toxic gases that cannot be safely handled."

The Admiral seemed unmoved. "Rudi, this sounds like fantasy."

Rudi had expected some pushback. "It cannot have escaped you what's going on around the world right now. It started right after someone else dived on the *Dakar* and cut that ship apart."

For the first time, Natal appeared unnerved. "Cut it apart?"

"It's sitting on the bottom in three sections," Rudi said. "It's been ransacked and cleaned out. We've found equipment and personal effects strewn all over the seafloor. We also found this."

Rudi reached into his pocket and pulled out the French naval pin that Kurt had recovered. He placed it on the Admiral's desk, pausing and then sliding it over to him.

The Admiral picked it up and looked it over, front and back.

Rudi gave him time to process what he was holding. "We've found the remnants of three separate uniforms belonging not to the INS sailors but to crewmen from *La Royale*."

La Royale was the nickname of the French Navy. He looked at the pin once more, shook his head softly and sighed.

"We know there was a weapon," Rudi said. "We know it was developed in conjunction with the French. We assume this pin came from a sailor working with your people before the weapon was stolen."

"It was stolen," Natal insisted, "but by the French, not by us."

"Then what was it doing on board the *Dakar*?" Rudi asked. "And why would the French Air Force sink a vessel partially crewed by their own personnel?"

The Admiral turned the pin over in his hand several more times. "I had a feeling someone would come to ask that question one day. I suppose I should be thankful it's you." He slid the pin back to Rudi. "This is not something my country can admit to. We have enough enemies in this world already. And, in all honesty, we assumed the weapon had been destroyed by the effects of time."

"I understand Israel's position in the world," Rudi said. "That's why I'm here in person. Nothing needs to be disclosed, but we need the antidote, the counteragent. Or at least the scientific data showing us how it was created."

"Don't you think we'd have already given it to you if we had it?"

"I would hope so."

"Of course we would have," the Admiral said. "Do you think we want our enemies earning three hundred dollars a barrel for their oil while our allies and our own economy suffer?"

"Then why can't you help?"

The Admiral stared off into the distance, contemplating a decision, then rose from his seat. "Come with me," he said. "I'll show you why."

55

A LONG HALLWAY led to an elevator with no interior controls. Once both men were inside, Admiral Natal gave a voice authorization that got the car moving. It descended to a floor several stories below ground level before stopping.

When the elevator doors opened, they entered a dimly lit hallway with stainless steel walls.

A checkpoint at the front of the hall was manned by two enlisted sailors and a lieutenant, all three of whom snapped to attention with the Admiral's appearance.

The Admiral looked the officer in the eye. "Take a break, Lieutenant. Take your men with you."

The order was so unorthodox that it took a moment before the lieutenant could process it. "Yes, sir," he said finally.

The men left their post and entered the elevator. Once the doors had shut, the Admiral moved behind their desk, where he began flicking through a series of switches. "Shutting off the cameras," he told Rudi. "Can't have a record of this remaining after we're gone."

With the surveillance system shut down, the Admiral took Rudi to another desk before disappearing into a labyrinth walled with numbered and locked cabinets. He returned with a metallic container, sealed with rubber around the edges.

"I've looked at this record several times myself over the last week. I should have destroyed it. But perhaps it's best someone like you sees it. You'll understand."

Rudi nodded.

"What I'm about to show you cannot be spoken about outside this room," the Admiral added. "Not without doing irreparable damage to my nation. I hope you understand that."

Rudi nodded. "You have my word that I'll keep the information to myself, and that anything we do use will not be sourced back to you or Israel."

The Admiral opened the container and pulled out several envelopes made of a fireproof material. "The program was known here as *Jericho*," he said, breaking the seal on the first envelope. "I'm not sure what the French called their portion, probably *Joan of Arc* or something. The idea was dreamt up in 1965 and launched early the next year. As you've already surmised, it was a biological weapon designed to eat oil and create dangerous waste products."

"Was the plan to use it as a deterrent?"

The Admiral nodded. "The Arab nations seemed willing to sacrifice untold numbers of lives to destroy Israel. By '68, they'd already attacked us three times. Despite heavy losses in each war, they simply retreated and rearmed, using oil money to rebuild their forces. Our leaders knew something had to be done or they'd overwhelm us. Some wanted nuclear weapons—which they eventually got—but others wanted a weapon that would render the threat moot without obliterating cities and killing millions. A panel of our scientists suggested genetically engineering a strain of bacteria that would take their wealth away from them before they ever pulled it out of the ground."

"They obviously succeeded."

"Not at first," Natal admitted. "Genetic engineering was in its infancy back then. What could and could not be done were complete unknowns. After a year with little progress, we were at an impasse. The problem was, expertise and equipment. The French had both and they had already helped us develop our nuclear reactors. Indeed, in the early days the French were one of our strongest allies."

"So, you made a deal."

Natal nodded. "The joint operation was undertaken. Two teams would work on the project, one from Israel and one from France. They were sent to the island of Jaros, in the Aegean."

"Why there?" Rudi said. "Jaros is neither Israeli nor French."

"You've answered your own question, my friend. It belonged to neither country, but is barren, uninhabited and not worth a visit from anyone. It served as a neutral spot, not quite halfway between our nations."

"Trust was already an issue," Rudi said.

"Isn't it always?" the Admiral said.

Rudi didn't respond, but said, "What happened?"

"The first year was uneventful but productive. The second year brought us stunning success, including several strains of bacteria that could live in the heat and pressure of the oil fields. We found the strongest and most voracious and crossed it with another strain of bacteria that consumes hydrocarbons—similar to the bacteria they use when trying to break down oil spills today. The results were spectacular. When the bacteria were exposed to crude oil, it grew at a phenomenal rate. It also produced a highly viscous sludge that acted to seal the wells, blocking them up like caulk. A final by-product was an explosive gas that, once released, would react instantly with air or water."

"My people have seen it in action."

"For that, you have my apologies," the Admiral said. "At any rate, with success comes greed. And the partner of greed is fear."

"From the French side," Rudi presumed.

Natal nodded. "By then, France was becoming dependent on Arab oil. And, as a result, becoming less and less interested in a friendship with Israel. After the early success, they demanded that we work on a method to kill the bacteria. The very antidote you've come to ask about."

"And?"

"It was developed," the Admiral insisted, "and its creation and successful testing brought a quick end to things on Jaros. As soon as the counteragent had been proven to work, a chill descended over the island. Our people realized that the weapon itself would be useless if the French could counteract it, while the French realized that we might wish to destroy the counteragent or to take complete control of it ourselves. Ultimately, they acted before we did, taking everything they could carry and destroying the rest."

"The facts don't support that," Rudi said. "If the French took everything, how did the oil destroyer and a group of French sailors end up on the *Dakar* at the bottom of the Mediterranean?"

"I said they took it. I didn't say they got it home. The French sent a submarine to Jaros with a squad of heavily armed commandos on board. They massacred most of our scientific staff and took every-thing they could carry. They destroyed what remained with explo-sives and kerosene. All the equipment, all the records. Everything."

The Admiral took a breath and continued. "We learned of the treachery within twelve hours, but it was too late to give chase. The French were out of range the moment they left the island. With sev-eral hundred miles between them and our nearest warship, we could neither stop them nor threaten them. They were home free . . . Or so they thought."

Rudi was starting to see the picture. "But the *Dakar* was coming in from the other direction. From the UK via Gibraltar. It was in position to cut them off."

"It was," Natal admitted. "We ordered it to intercept the French boat and spent the next several days broadcasting fake position re-ports while maneuvering the *Dakar* to a station between the French sub and their home port."

"How did you know where to wait?"

"We suspected their vessel would make for the submarine base at Toulon. It was a calculated risk, but it made the most sense. Now all we had to do was wait. For the next two days, a debate raged at the highest levels of government as to whether we should sink the French submarine or not. Some felt that that would be an act of war and that we should avoid antagonizing the French. Others pointed out that the murder of Israeli scientists and the theft of our labor was already an act of war.

"Finally, one voice clarified things for everyone, pointing out that while the French were unlikely to go to war with us over some-thing they would have a hard time explaining to the rest of the world, history suggested that the Arabs would most certainly at-tack us again in due time. That being the case, it meant that neither the submarine nor the scientists' lives nor relations with France were as relevant to Israel as the research material itself. The bacterial cultures and genetic codes were what mattered. Destroying the French submarine would be a wasteful act. Allowing it to reach France would be an act of cowardice. We needed to get the materials back and there was only one way to do that. The crew of the *Dakar* had to stop the French submarine without sinking it, boarding the vessel once it surfaced and taking it by force."

Rudi could scarcely believe what he was hearing. "Is that what happened?"

"That's how it began," the Admiral said, handing over the second of the sealed envelopes. "Read for yourself, you'll see how it ended."

Rudi opened the envelope and found that it contained dispatches from the INS *Dakar*.

27 January 1968, 0640 hours. Target located. Tracking. Expect target to surface prior to entering port.

27 January 1968, 0755 hours. Intercepted coded message. Decryption indicates target will not surface until it enters channel. By that point, we would be exposed to French radar and hostile vessels. Action would be impossible. Attempting to ram target vessel's snorkel and force them to the surface.

27 January 1968, 0819 hours. French vessel boarded and subdued. Three casualties. Due to mounting threat of detection by French Air Force and the nature of contraband cargo, we have only been able

```
to retrieve Objective Alpha. Objective Bravo remains
on the French submarine. Executive decision has been
made to divide the crew and sail captured vessel back
to Haifa. Releasing debris as countermeasure to con-
vince the French that she foundered. With luck, they
will conduct search-and-rescue operations for days
and never learn that we've taken her.
```

"They took the French sub as a prize," Rudi questioned. "Am I reading this right?"

"They couldn't leave her afloat to call for support," the Admiral said. "And considering the weather and time constraints, they couldn't transfer the entire crew or all the materials. The only other option would have been sending her to the bottom, but that would have been murder."

Rudi understood. There was a difference between acting in combat and killing prisoners. It was a line professional military men would not cross.

Rudi envisioned the situation. "Two submarines headed for Haifa," he said. "Each with a divided crew, each carrying some portion of the bacterial cultures on board. How could they not expect an uprising on one ship or both?"

"There were clashes," Natal admitted. "The captain's logbook, which we recovered from the *Dakar*, stated there were two attempts by French sailors to escape when the sub was surfaced briefly and one attempt to take the boat by force while running submerged. One Israeli sailor died. Three French sailors were wounded. But the voyage continued."

"Not long enough, apparently."

"No," the Admiral said. "And it did not end satisfactorily for anyone."

He gave Rudi the last envelope. Inside were scribbled notes. They were almost unreadable.

"Written in the dark," the Admiral explained, "after all power was lost. The words are in French. The next pages are a typewritten English translation."

Rudi switched from the scribbled writings to the orderly translation and went through it slowly, reading aloud as he went.

> "The engine room is flooded to the midpoint. We are dead in the water, bow pointed toward a surface we will never again reach. The Israeli captain has given us permission to write our families, to say our good-byes, but I wish only to commend him. He has treated us fairly. The governments of the world have their wars, but men of the sea are brothers and we are brothers who shall die together."

Rudi looked up at Natal and then turned the page. "This is from a French sailor."

The Admiral nodded.

> "The boat is sinking slowly, so slowly that we must be at almost neutral buoyancy. It has been hours. And will be hours more before we are crushed. And yet, still they circle above us, angry wasps waiting to land one more sting.
>
> "Occasionally, we hear another depth charge hit the water and then all we can do is wait. Most of us

would welcome a direct hit to end things quickly, but they must not know how far down we've drifted, the detonations are so far above us.

"Do they know they're killing their own? I wonder."

There was one more page, Rudi turned to it quickly.

"It has been eleven hours. We are past the boat's test depth and the hull is creaking. Each groan seems like the hand of death, stroking our vessel in search of a weak point to crush it.

"There is no light and nothing to breathe except poisoned air. It stinks of oil and sweat and filth. The carbon dioxide is so thick that many of the men have fallen asleep already. In a way, I envy them. Others have gone forward in hopes of getting out through the torpedo tubes. But their attempt is for naught. We are too deep. They will be crushed, if they succeed at all.

"At least they have their vain hope. I have none, except that perhaps those in the other boat will make it to port. That those members of my crew and the Israeli sailors who are with them will survive to see their families again."

The narrative ended there, followed by the name of the officer, which had been blacked out. The next lines of text told Rudi enough about the author to send a chill down his spine.

Honor, Homeland, Valor, Discipline.

Viva La France.

Viva La Minerve.

Rudi looked at the Admiral. "The captured French submarine was the *Minerve*?"

"You see why I can't help you?" the Admiral said. "The French took the research data, the genetic materials and the bacterial cultures from the island. Our people took half of it back and left the rest on the *Minerve*. Both sailed for Israel, but neither ship survived."

Rudi understood the task ahead instantly and clearly. "If the materials we're looking for weren't on the *Dakar*, they have to be on the *Minerve*."

"It would appear that way," the Admiral said, "but the French have been looking for that ship since the day she vanished. The search has gone on for two decades longer than our own search for the *Dakar*. I assure you, in all that time they haven't found a trace of it. Nor have we."

"That might play to our advantage," Rudi said. "If they haven't been able to find it, that means they didn't sink it. It means the material on board stands a decent chance of remaining intact."

"You're right, of course," the Admiral said. "But the Mediterranean is a big place. What makes you think you'll be able to find it when both we and the French have been unable to do so?"

"Because I have to."

56

NUMA VESSEL *GRYPHON*

"A STROKE of good luck," Kurt said upon hearing the news.

Gamay reacted differently. "Really? Some luck."

"It gives us a chance."

She folded her arms and narrowed her gaze. If she ever became a mother, that gaze would go a long way to keeping her kids on the straight and narrow. "You realize the chances of success are next to none."

"Better than no chance," Kurt said, "which is what we have now."

"Kurt's right," Rudi added from a video screen.

Everyone looked back at the screen, which had Rudi's image on the left and Hiram Yaeger's image on the right.

"And we need to do it quickly," Rudi added. *"This crisis is getting worse. This morning the Russians put out a statement saying they will no longer honor existing oil and gas contracts. All rates will be renegotiated to reflect spot prices as opposed to prices*

agreed upon months or years ago. OPEC is considering the same thing."

"We all sense the urgency," Paul said. "But if the French and Israelis haven't been able to find this submarine after fifty years of searching, how are we supposed to find it in the blink of an eye?"

"By looking where they haven't," Kurt said. "We can rule out everything west of Toulon because Israel lies in the other direction. We can also rule out everywhere the French and Israelis have dragged sonar sleds over the last fifty years." He turned to Rudi's image on the screen. "Can you get that information for us?"

"*I have the Israeli charts already,*" Rudi said. "*They spent a great deal of time searching for the* Dakar *publicly and privately. After the recovery of the logbooks, they spent two years in a clandestine search for the* Minerve. *They covered a large swath of the Med.*"

"Getting the French data will be a little more difficult," Paul said. "I'm sure they don't want to admit their part in this."

"*No doubt,*" Rudi said, "*but I briefed the President before contacting you and he's going to ratchet up the pressure to what he calls* an unbearable level. *I expect we'll have the French records by nightfall.*"

On the other half of the screen, Hiram spoke up. "*And if that doesn't work, we'll turn Max loose on their records and see what we can dig up.*"

Kurt broke out a chart of the Mediterranean and spread it across the table. He worked backward from their current position to Toulon. "Do we know the *Dakar*'s full route from the intercept point to the spot where the French caught and sank her?"

"*We do,*" Rudi said. "*Why?*"

"Because if the plan was to split up and double their chances of survival, we can rule out the *Minerve* taking the same course."

"*The* Dakar *took the straightest line possible,*" Rudi said. "*They were hoping speed would be their ally.*"

Paul looked over Kurt's shoulder. "If the *Dakar* kept to the northern Mediterranean, then perhaps the *Minerve* swung to the south, maybe even hugging the coast of Libya and Egypt."

"*You can rule Egypt out,*" Rudi said. "*The Israelis searched Egyptian waters, both in secret and in a rare moment of cooperation with the Egyptian government, in the eighties.*"

"That still leaves a hundred thousand square miles to look through," Gamay said. "I hate to be a pessimist, but we could have a fleet out here and not find anything for years."

"We have had a fleet out here," Kurt said. "For years."

The glare came back. "What are you talking about?"

"I've done at least twenty surveys covering various parts of the Mediterranean myself," Kurt said. "You and Paul have done similar work, three months off the coast of Italy last year. Two months around Elba the year before. Other NUMA teams have been doing similar work out here over the decades and NUMA isn't alone in that."

Gamay brightened and said, "I don't recall spotting anything that looked like a sunken submarine. But we did catalog a large number of sonar returns, including ten different aircraft, an Italian destroyer sunk by the British during World War Two and a containership that broke up in a storm off Tripoli."

"And even though that wasn't what you were looking for, the data was recorded," Kurt said. He turned to the screen again. "Hiram, ask Max how many surveys NUMA has done in the Mediterranean since 1968. Limit it to surveys that used equipment capable of detecting a sunken submarine."

Max answered momentarily. *"NUMA has conducted three hundred and seventy-one manned surveys of the area in question. An additional one hundred and fifty-eight surveys have been conducted using autonomous underwater drones. Three surveys are currently in progress."*

"That ought to cover a fair amount of the seafloor," Kurt said.

"Twenty-nine percent of the basin east of Toulon," Max replied.

"Not as much as I'd hoped," Kurt replied.

Rudi jumped in. *"Like you said, we're not the only ones who've been dragging sonar arrays around the Mediterranean. Hiram, have Max look over the old data for anything that might suggest a submarine resting on the bottom. I'm going to reach out to every country, aquatic organization and amateur wreck hunter I can find. You never know what information we might be able to beg, borrow or steal."*

Kurt took a quick look at the map. Their chances were rising. "In the meantime, we'll head west."

"Why west?" Paul asked.

"Because the *Minerve* won't be found between here and Israel," he said. "In fact, I'd suspect it's well to the west of our current position."

"And how do you know this?" Gamay asked.

"If the *Minerve* had reached this area, the French would have found it and sunk it, just as they sank the *Dakar*," he said. "And if it passed through these waters unscathed, getting any closer to Israel, the submarine's commander could have ordered the boat to the surface, radioed in to Haifa and called out a never-ending stream of IDF fighters to provide air cover and chase off the French antisubmarine patrols. Since neither of those things happened, we have to conclude that the *Minerve* never got this far."

"That covers the waters east of us," Paul said. "But what makes you think it will be found so far west? The two subs had similar capabilities, similar speeds. And they left the coast of France at the same time."

"But the *Minerve* was operating with a damaged snorkel," Kurt said. "Which means she couldn't run underwater for long periods of time or at a high rate of speed. If you were on the run in that condition, what would you do?"

A longtime Navy man, Rudi answered this one. *"Sit still and submerged during the day, conserving my batteries, and then run on the surface at night."*

"Which cuts her speed in half and limits how far she could have gotten."

"I'm sold," Rudi said. *"Head west. We'll contact you as soon as we have more to go on."*

Kurt took another look at the chart, picked a course that would take them south of Crete and toward Malta. He stepped to the helm, fired up the engines and got the *Gryphon* rolling. They'd covered ten miles when a radar contact appeared off the stern. It followed on an intercept course, closing in despite the *Gryphon* making thirty knots.

"What do you think?" Paul asked.

Kurt adjusted course to the south and the trailing contact followed suit. "I think someone out there wants to have a few words with us."

57

KURT PUT ON more speed and adjusted the *Gryphon*'s course to the north. The mysterious radar contact reacted predictably, mirroring Kurt's course change and continuing to close the distance.

Gamay came into the wheelhouse as Kurt straightened up. "What's with all the twists and turns?"

"We've picked up a tail," Kurt said.

"Faster than us?"

"Looks that way," Paul said.

Kurt pointed to the panel on Paul's left. "Check the cameras."

Paul switched on the camera system, slaving it to the radar contact. The natural light spectrum was useless, since night had fallen, but the night vision lens clarified what they were looking at.

"Helicopters," Paul said. "Two of them. Right on the deck. They look military to me."

Kurt looked. Gun blisters underneath the nose were obvious,

as were the lethal-looking missile pods on either side of the stubby wings.

"This is going to be rocky," Kurt said. "Time to break out our presents. Paul, you'd better man the surface-to-air launch panel. Gamay, you're the marksman of the group, you get on the CQW."

The two of them nodded, with Paul taking a seat behind and to the left, the controls for the missile panel in front of him, and Gamay right behind him, setting up behind another screen, with her hands on a joystick that would control the rapid-fire mini-gun NUMA labeled *Close-Quarters Weapon*.

"Range, four miles and closing," Paul said. "We can hit them in thirty seconds."

"We can't hit them until we know for sure they're not friendlies," Kurt said. "Aviators from plenty of different militaries sometimes practice mock attack runs on civilian vessels. I'd rather not blast them out of the sky or force them to practice evasive maneuvers they're not quite ready for."

"So, we can't fire until fired upon," Gamay said. "Not sure I like the rules of this game."

"Three miles," Paul said.

Suddenly the radarscope went white as if it were picking up ten thousand helicopters.

"They're jamming our radar," Paul said.

"Keep your eyes on the video display," Kurt said. "They can't jam that."

Paul glanced at the monitor. The camera system had the ability to track ranges. "Two miles, according to the camera. Speed one hundred and forty knots, heading right for us."

Kurt let go of the throttle for a moment and pressed two buttons on the panel in front of him. The first was labeled *Foils*, the second was labeled *Armor*.

From the wide aft section of the *Gryphon*, a series of heavy plates moved forward, covering the windows and the vulnerable areas around the fuel tank. Meanwhile, beneath the vessel, a pair of wings deployed on thick hydraulic struts.

"One mile," Paul said.

The armor clinked into place as a flash on the screen told everyone they were under attack.

"Rockets," Paul said. "Unguided."

Kurt turned the wheel hard and shoved the throttle forward. The *Gryphon* heaved over to starboard, picking up speed in the turn.

The first wave of rockets hit behind and to port. A second wave was so far off that the explosions sounded only like distant thunder.

With the hydrofoils fully extended, the turbine engine howling in full voice, the *Gryphon* was passing seventy knots and hitting eighty before the helicopters reacted.

"They're turning and following," Paul said. "More rockets inbound."

This time, the spread of rockets hit much closer. The first four up ahead and the second wave were straddling the *Gryphon*. One hit the water to the left, two to the right, a fourth slamming into the armor on the aft deck.

The *Gryphon* shuddered and surged from the impact but emerged from the firestorm mostly unscathed.

ON BOARD the lead helicopter, Alexander Vastoga couldn't believe what he was seeing.

"Direct hit," the gunner said.

"No effect," Vastoga said.

By now, the helicopters had overshot the speeding boat. Vastoga looked out the window as it vanished behind them. "Turn back and make another pass. We get nothing if that boat doesn't go down."

"*It's heading north*," the pilot of the second helicopter radioed. "*Speed, ninety knots.*"

Vastoga shook his head. The boat was almost as fast as his helicopters.

"Close within five hundred yards before you open fire," he ordered.

"Rockets or guns?"

"Both!"

THE *Gryphon* was flying across the sea, but it could not escape the helicopters.

"They're coming in again," Paul said. "Staggered formation. One at our six o'clock, one farther off the port beam."

"You have my permission to fire," Kurt said.

"About time," Gamay replied.

She'd already switched her scope to infrared, now she activated a targeting laser. The range, speed and distance of the helicopter moving in from the port side were quickly logged and computed.

"Just out of range," she said.

"Paul?"

"Radar is still jammed. There's no way for me to get a lock on them."

The helicopter trailing them launched another spread of unguided rockets. Kurt weaved to starboard, but that set them on a direct line for the second helicopter and it unleashed all eight of its remaining rockets.

One hit the forward deck, sending a shock wave through the *Gryphon*. A second hit low on the side of the hull, but the explosion was a glancing blow and the hull maintained its integrity. The same could not be said for the ribbed Zodiac attached to the back deck. It was blasted to confetti when a third rocket hit.

"I've had enough of this," Kurt said.

He cut the wheel again, this time turning hard directly toward the nearest helicopter.

As the range closed, the lights on Gamay's screen flashed green and she opened fire.

Near the bow, lethal fire spat from an innocent-looking dome. Inside, a six-barreled Gatling gun unleashed a hundred and fifty shells in three seconds. Half of these found their mark and the helicopter was perforated from front to back. Both the pilot and the gunner were killed instantly, saving them from suffering in the explosion that followed.

"One down," Kurt said. "One to go."

The surviving helicopter crossed overhead, its own nose-mounted cannon rattling as it went.

The *Gryphon* took several hits, noted by bowl-shaped dents in the armored roof and wall. Hairline cracks that spread from each one told Kurt all he needed to know about the shape of the armor.

"We can't take much more of this," he said. "Paul?"

"Radar is still jammed. I can't get a lock."

"Just aim and fire," Kurt said. "Maybe we can scare him off."

Paul checked the helicopter's position on the camera system. "Target is to the south of us. Here goes nothing."

He selected a section of the sky, set an arbitrary target point as near to the helicopter as possible and launched a missile. It streaked from what looked like a supply locker on the side of the top deck.

Kurt turned as soon as the missile fired. If the pilot took evasive maneuvers, he might get within Gamay's range.

Watching the video screen, he saw the missile racing into the dark. It went nowhere near the attacking copter, but, as Kurt had expected, the helicopter took an evasive course anyway. It turned to the right, setting itself up broadside to the *Gryphon*. Gamay opened fire, holding the trigger button down and filling the sky.

The *Gryphon* raced under the helicopter, which continued past and then turned to come back once more.

"What do we have to do to get rid of this guy?" Kurt said.

"Radar is up," Paul said. "You must have hit something."

On-screen, the helicopter's nose turret began flashing. More dents appeared and the panel guarding the left window was torn away. Glass blew into the wheelhouse. Kurt and Gamay ducked, but Paul was locked in and so was the radar.

He fired a second missile as the helicopter flew past, this one tracked it, turned and scored a direct hit on the engine compartment. The helicopter burst into flames and spiraled into the sea.

"Nice work!" Kurt said.

"Are we clear?" Gamay asked.

Paul looked at the radarscope. "Clear," he said, turning toward them.

He had blood coming down the side of his face where shattered glass had hit him and his hair was whipping in the breeze.

Kurt backed off the throttle, let the *Gryphon* level off. A search for survivors proved fruitless. And with the distinct possibility that they might be attacked again foremost in everyone's mind, Kurt powered up and took the *Gryphon* west with the night.

58

CENTRAL KAZAKHSTAN

TESSA LOOKED OUT through the dusty, pitted window, nine stories up in the old air traffic control tower. The windstorm had passed and, with the air now clear, the entire base stretched out before her. The view was a sea of derelict planes, discarded machinery and junked vehicles, including tanks and trucks and armored personnel carriers, all stripped of their guns, tracks and wheels. At the far end, a giant smelter worked twenty-four hours a day melting down the scrap, which was shipped out and sold as recycled steel.

She turned to Volke, who stood off to one side. "During the Cold War, this base was home to hundreds of frontline Russian aircraft and two Special Forces brigades. Now it's a boneyard."

He nodded slightly. "Your point?"

"Things are discarded when they're no longer needed. A situation we seem to be falling into."

"I thought this was our moment of triumph," Volke said. "The price of oil is going through the roof, the news media are reporting on the crisis twenty-four/seven. Buran is finally coming to pay us. Not to mention the IPO."

It was true. When viewed from the outside, everything Tessa had promised seemed to be coming true in spectacular fashion. But up close, each glittering reality faded like a mirage.

"The American government is holding up the IPO," she said. "They haven't blocked it outright. But until it's approved, the private investors will never bite. Even if the American SEC relents, the longer it takes, the more difficult it will be to get the money we hoped for."

He grew agitated. "Why is that?"

"Because the fuel cells don't work," she said. "More accurately, they don't work for long. They're fragile, easily overloaded and twice as costly to manufacture as our worst-case estimates."

"Aren't Yates and his design team working on that?" Volke said.

"Yates is dead," she told him.

"What?"

"He was going to quit and tell the world what I just told you," Tessa explained. "I had no choice."

Volke put the dominoes in order. "Without the fuel cells, no one is going to invest. Without Yates, there won't be any redesigned, operative fuel cells. Any more good news?"

"That's it."

"That's enough. We're dead in the water."

She nodded. He stared. The silence lingered.

"Now I see why this meeting is so important to you," he said. The edge grew sharper in his voice as he spoke. "Except Buran is the one element in this equation that we've never been able to control. Now you're telling me he's our only hope of getting anything."

"It would seem that way."

Volke shook his head in disgust. "And just how do you propose to force a man who's already gotten what he wants to give us anything at all?"

"I'm not sure. Yet," she said. "But I will. Your job is to be ready when he resists, as he most certainly will."

Silence followed. She knew what she had in Volke. He was easy to motivate. He would do anything to get the payout he'd been waiting for two years. Her other problem would be Woods. He would have to be dealt with, too.

"I'll be ready," Volke said. "But you should know Buran is not our only problem. Austin and his crew have survived."

"How could they?"

"I have no idea," Volke said. "But according to an update in the NUMA location system, they're heading west at high speed."

"I'd have preferred to hear that they were dead, but if they're running for cover, at least that's something."

"They're not running for cover," Volke said. "They're looking for the *Minerve*."

She tilted her head as if she hadn't heard correctly. "The *Minerve*? Are you telling me they've learned in three days what took us three years to put together?"

"They live up to their reputation," he said. "Regrettably."

"They cannot be allowed to find that submarine," she said. "If they pull the antidote off that ship, it will destroy everything we've done."

"I'm not sure we can stop them," Volke said. "All the more reason we need to close this deal and get out of here."

"I'm not settling for a pittance," she said.

"Better than nothing."

Tessa had a feeling it wouldn't be quite that easy.

She looked out the window as the sound of helicopters approaching reached them. Shading her eyes against the sun, she looked across the base. From out of the northwest, a pair of helicopters came in low, crossing slowly above the rusted-metal bones of their ancestors.

"We'll have to worry about Austin later," she said. "Buran and his people are here."

She and Volke left the high ground and descended the tower. By the time they reached the ground floor, the helicopters had landed in a swirl of dust. As the dust dissipated, Arat Buran and his honor guard stepped from the lead helicopter and strode toward the base of the tower.

Tessa studied Buran as he approached. Muscular and strong beneath his dark blue overcoat, he appeared much as he had when Tessa had first met him years before. The same eyes that drooped slightly at the corners, giving him a serious, glum look that she had found so appealing. His thick, dark mustache brought Stalin to mind, but Buran was no communist. In the years since Kazakhstan had gained its independence, he'd gone from a roughneck working on a leaking oil rig to one of the richest men in Central Asia.

Using a combination of guile, brute force and military contacts, he'd slowly cornered the market on Kazakhstan's oil, before branching out into other countries. He now controlled seventy percent of everything produced in the region. His friends, members of a group he called the Consortium, controlled the West.

That kind of power didn't remain confined to the business world, it extended to the political realm. At Buran's urging, ties with the West had soured, foreign diplomats and military personnel had been sent packing and Kazakhstan had turned inward, with Buran and a few of his allies living in the shadows and controlling the government.

They were profiting now, but when all the infected fields stopped producing, these men would control half of the world's remaining untouched oil.

Another woman might have looked upon a wealthy, handsome ex-lover like Buran and wondered what could have been. Tessa felt nothing of the sort. Buran had been an interesting plaything and an avenue of assistance, nothing more.

Buran stepped toward her and kissed her hand. "My Tessa," he said in broken English. "You have exceeded even my expectations."

"I've exceeded everyone's expectations," she replied. "And yet the funds I was promised have not been released."

"Always straight to business," he said. "You miss out on the beauty of life."

From the pocket of his overcoat Buran produced a small box and opened the lid. Inside lay a walnut-sized emerald set in a ring of sapphires and held by a delicately wrought gold chain.

"Twenty carats," he said. "Worth a million dollars. It is a thing of beauty like you."

Tessa smiled politely, closed the box and pushed it back toward him. "Thank you, I'm flattered, but you know I don't get out of bed for anything less than a billion these days. Now I would like my money. I've done my part."

Buran's eyes smoldered with a hint of indignation, but he placed the box back in his pocket and shrugged. "Let's go inside, shall we?"

The meeting moved into the bottom level of the air traffic control tower. They were joined by several of Tessa's men, who stood there beside a multitude of computers. The machines were networked, powered by one of her fuel cells and linked to a satellite dish.

Before Tessa could speak, Woods unexpectedly walked in. But before he could speak, Volke quickly moved next to him and drew a gun, placing it in the small of Woods's back.

"These computers are encrypted with the latest technology," Tessa said, "and connected to banks around the world. The financial transfer can be made swiftly and cleanly via this system. Your people are free to examine them, if you like."

"You are prepared," Buran said.

"As always," she replied. "I want what you promised me."

"Ten billion dollars is a lot of money."

"You and the Consortium will make more than that every six months, thanks to what I've done."

"True," he said. "But there are expenses to consider and there are reasons for renegotiation."

"Renegotiation?"

"I'm afraid so," he said. "But, you had to know this was coming."

"Fine," she said. "Twenty billion. All cash and cryptocurrency."

This time, Buran laughed—nothing loud or haughty, just a deep, heavy laugh like a father amused by a small child. It was all Tessa could do to keep her anger in check.

"Ah, Tessa," he said smugly. "My beautiful, arrogant Tessa. You have done what the Consortium thought impossible. But you've made one tremendous mistake. Small, but fatal. In your desire to prove yourself, you've allowed your leverage to evaporate. The Consortium has its high oil prices already. There is no going back—thanks to you. But that being the case, they see no reason to pay you what they formerly considered paying. They will not be extorted for billions of dollars when there is no need to pay it now."

Tessa's demeanor remained icy. She'd expected some treachery, but nothing so blatant. The very lesson she'd just reminded herself of came to mind. *Things were discarded when they were no longer needed.*

"The Consortium offer is nothing? Is that what you're telling me?"

"The Consortium appreciates your services and they may be convinced to give you something," he said, "but it will not approach what you think you deserve. Perhaps fifty million. And for that, they want everything—including all stocks of the oil destroyer itself."

"Fifty million won't pay my interest," she said.

"Your problem, not ours."

The sense of entrapment was palpable. Fate and her enemies had encircled her now. She needed some way to reverse the situation, to turn everything back in her favor.

She thought briefly of threatening Buran's wells with the oil destroyer, but it would be a futile gesture. He knew enough about how the destroyer worked to protect his fields. Her operatives would never be able to get near the injection equipment. And his response would be violent and inescapable.

The bitterness of the moment prompted waves of emotion. For just an instant, she hated Buran more than Austin. She almost hoped Austin would find the counteragent and cut the legs out from under Buran. Its discovery and announcement alone would send oil prices crashing even faster than they'd gone up.

The racing thoughts stopped.

The counteragent . . .

Its very existence had troubled her from the moment she'd begun the effort. She'd looked for it as desperately as she'd sought the oil destroyer, intending to find it, eradicate it and erase its presence from the face of the earth.

Failure to do that had been the one great disappointment. But suddenly the counteragent could be her salvation. It could restore her leverage and put Buran and his Consortium at her feet.

"I'll take your fifty million," she said, "as an apology for the insults you've delivered. But if your friends want to continue enjoying the windfall they've come into, they will pay fifty billion, in gold certificates and cryptocurrencies. They will also agree to pay a billion dollars in royalties per year, ad infinitum, and they will apologize for insulting me the way you have today."

Buran clenched his jaw, the broom-like mustache settling deeper over his lips. "You have an acid tongue, despite your beauty. More than that, you are a fool, Tessa. This is not a boardroom on Wall Street. You're a guest here, but you could quickly become a prisoner. Even if I forgive your rebuke, the others will not. They will not take your offer, but they'll take your life for speaking to them this way."

"They won't raise a finger against me," she said. "Not once did you explain the danger to them."

"And what danger would that be?"

"I got rid of the oil," she told him. "But if I'm not paid, I'll bring it back."

Buran's expression froze. His eyes widened in reaction. He hadn't expected this. "What are you talking about?"

"I have the antidote," she said. "The counteragent that will feed on the bacteria, just as the bacteria feeds on the oil. Someone will compensate me for it. Either you and your friends or the Americans and the Chinese. Sky-high oil prices will cost them a trillion dollars each over the next decade. They will pay anything to prevent that. You know that."

"They will take what you give them and copy it," Buran said.

"Perhaps, but at a very high price," she said. "Which is why I'd rather be paid by you not to release the counteragent. That would make this a win-win situation. But if I can't win, no one will. Mark my words on that. If I'm not compensated fairly, you and your Consortium will suffer right along with me."

Buran lost it. He reached into his coat, pulled out an ornate but deadly knife and stepped toward her. "I'll kill you myself for such insolence."

Tessa stepped back, but Buran froze as Volke's men produced weapons far deadlier than a knife. Across from her, Buran's honor guard raised their own guns. For a second, it appeared they all might die in a hail of bullets fired at close range.

"Everyone needs to calm down," Tessa said. "We can all die here or we can all get rich. You and the Consortium are set to prosper for decades to come. The higher price of oil has already increased the value of your reserves by hundreds of billions of dollars. You don't need to pay me out of pocket. You can borrow the money and transfer it. You won't even feel a pinprick of pain."

Buran glared at her. "You'll never get out of Kazakhstan alive."

"Not only will I leave here in perfect health," she corrected, "you, Arat Buran, will ensure that I do so. Otherwise, the counteragent—which I have duplicated and stored in various locations around the world—will be delivered to specific government agencies along with detailed instructions explaining what it is, how to grow it and the quickest methods by which to benefit from it. Kill me, if you like, but all you'll have done is triggered the collapse of your own—suddenly quite prosperous—empire."

Buran's face was purple-red. A vein throbbed like a lightning bolt in his forehead. "Where did this counteragent come from?"

"The French created it," she said. "To protect themselves from the oil destroyer. It now protects me. I'll send you the reports Millard smuggled out of France. That should be all the proof you need to motivate your associates."

"Even if that's true, even if we agree to pay, how are we supposed to justify transferring fifty billion dollars to you? In return for what?"

"You don't have to justify it to anyone," she said. "But if you must have something in return, you can buy my company. As you may have heard, it's for sale."

Buran stared at her.

"Consider it a double victory," she said. "The counteragent remains under wraps and the fuel cells my people have designed never go to market."

He continued to stare, but the intensity had diminished. He lowered the knife slowly. "You're cunning."

She met his gaze every step of the way. "Did you really think I would give away all my leverage, my dear Buran?"

The decision came to him quickly after that. The tension and fury left his face. He stepped back and put the knife away. At the wave of his hand, Buran's men lowered their guns.

"I'll take your offer to the Consortium," he said. "Let's hope the banks are as free with money as you believe."

"With the economies of the world suddenly begging for oil, they'll be shoveling cash into your hands."

Buran turned on his heel and left without further comment. His men followed behind him, swept out of the room like leaves by a strong breeze.

Tessa stood in place, left behind with her people, her computers and her mounting list of problems. They were on a razor's edge now. And she wasn't the only one who knew it. She could feel Volke and Woods staring at her.

She knew what they were thinking because she was thinking the same thing. They had to go back to sea. They had to find the counteragent before Austin and NUMA or their lives would be worth even less than the failed fuel cell design.

59

JOE LISTENED as the departing helicopters traveled overhead and the staccato song of the rotor blades echoed through the shell of the old craft he and Priya were hiding in. They'd heard drones earlier, and trucks and other vehicles had come and gone with some regularity.

"Are they looking for us?" Priya asked. There was a raspy quality to her words, brought on by the dust and a lack of water.

"I don't think so," Joe said. Making his way to the cockpit, he put his face to the dusty glass, gazing through a tiny section he'd cleared during the night. "The helicopters are heading toward the mountains."

"Maybe she was meeting with her broker," Priya said. "Some of her gray money came from this region."

"Gray money?"

"Of suspicious origin."

Joe nodded. "She took more than money. By the look of things, she patched that plane together with parts from this place."

"Which suggests a long history here and powerful friends. That doesn't bode well for our efforts to escape."

Joe knew that. Scrapped Russian aircraft, hot days and frigid nights told him they were somewhere in the high deserts of Central Asia. Most likely in one of the *Stans*—Kazakhstan, Uzbekistan or Turkmenistan. All former Soviet Republics with barren areas and plenty of leftover, cast-off Red Army equipment.

It made sitting still their best bet, but remaining in place didn't mean inaction.

Joe watched Tessa and her people until they disappeared behind another aircraft. With nothing more to see, he returned to the cargo bay. "How's it coming?"

Priya was sitting on the floor, surrounded by electronic parts. Some of the parts had come from the helicopter's old avionics system, others had been taken from the Mercedes. She made a soldering iron from a copper wire, powered it with electricity from the SUV's battery and began building a receiver and transmitter from scratch.

"I still have work to do on the transmitter," she said, "but the receiver is ready to test. Care to do the honors?"

Joe disconnected power from the soldering iron and rerouted it to the radio receiver.

Using a dial taken from the helicopter's audio system, Priya applied power slowly. Too much, too quickly, could melt down some of the connections.

Joe sat down beside her and placed two leads on a small speaker they'd lifted from the Mercedes. As Priya adjusted the frequency, they heard static, silence and then finally a station playing Arabic music.

"Not exactly the Top 40 countdown," Priya said.

Joe smiled. "Still a beautiful sound. What else can you pick up?"

"We should be able to pick up anything that's transmitting," she said. "We can go all over the dial."

With precise movements, she tuned the radio to lower and lower bands. The static returned in various forms and intensities. "We might need a better antenna."

"Wait," Joe said, holding up his hand. "Go back . . . Right there . . . Stop."

"What is it?"

Joe had his ear next to the speaker. "English."

The reception was so weak and the volume so low that Joe couldn't make out what was being said.

"Can you fine-tune it?"

Priya put her fingers on another dial, making tiny adjustments. The voices vanished completely for a second and then came back, slightly louder and significantly less garbled.

Joe listened closely. He could barely believe what he was hearing.

Priya heard it, too. "It's Tessa."

"And one of her men," Joe said as another voice chimed in. "But how?"

"We've locked onto the bug Kurt placed. It's still transmitting," Priya said. "It's sound-activated, so it stays in battery-saving mode until it picks something up."

Joe held his ear closer to the speaker, struggling to make out the words. "They just stepped inside the plane," he said. "They're standing next to the doorway."

"Let me boost the power," Priya said.

She adjusted another dial and the audio came through with more clarity.

"*Have you lost your mind?*" the man was shouting. "*If Buran and his people call your bluff, we're all dead.*"

Tessa replied just as sharply. "*Without something to hold over them, we're dead anyway.*"

Muffled sounds that were indistinguishable came next. Followed by more from Tessa.

"*Buran and his friends are making unspendable fortunes. I promise you, they will do anything—absolutely anything—to keep the price of oil up in the stratosphere. They've spent billions cornering their own particular markets and they've been waiting decades for this opportunity. They're not going to go back.*"

"*And what happens when they ask for a little proof?*" the male voice demanded. "*Surely you don't expect them to hand over all that money without a demonstration? If we can't show them the countermeasure and prove that it works, we're right back where we started—dead all over again.*"

"*You think I don't know that?*" she said. "*That's why we have to find the counteragent.*"

"*We spent plenty of time looking three years ago. What makes you think we're going to get lucky this time?*"

"*Because we're going to let the experts do it for us,*" Tessa said. "*Austin and his friends.*"

For a moment, everything went quiet. Then Tessa's voice returned. "*As you pointed out, they're looking for the* Minerve *already. And since finding sunken wrecks is something of a specialty for them, I imagine they will discover it quite soon.*"

"*And how exactly does that help us?*" the man asked. "*Even if they find it, they'll put a wall of ships around it. We'd need an armada to get through."*

"*They will,*" Tessa acknowledged. "*But not instantaneously. There will be a brief window of time, a gap, in between the moment of discovery and the arrival of any support ships. We'll make our move while that window is open, descending upon them from the heavens like an angry angel and taking what's rightfully ours.*"

The words lingered in the air. When the man spoke again, his tone had changed.

"*They do the work, we take the prize,*" he said. "*It's not as crazy as it sounds. Good thing you didn't manage to kill Austin since he's suddenly our only hope.*"

"*We'll kill him once he's found what we're after,*" she said. "*For now, we need to move closer to where they're searching. That way we'll be able to react the instant they find something.*"

"*It wouldn't hurt to put some distance between us and Buran either.*"

"*No, it wouldn't.*"

"*I'll get the plane fueled and bring the drones and the men back,*" he said. "*But what about Zavala and the Kashmir woman?*"

"*I'll tell Buran there are a couple of traitors running loose who might upset the table for all of us. He'll send people out with orders to kill them on sight. He might even enjoy taking his anger out on them, but they'll die here in Kazakhstan, one way or another. Now, let's move.*"

Nothing else was said and the transmitter shut down after recording footsteps moving away.

Joe and Priya exchanged glances.

"I've put Kurt, Paul and Gamay in terrible danger," she said. "I should have never given in, no matter what they threatened."

"They would have tortured us until you gave in," Joe said. "By letting them win up front, we kept ourselves from being broken. And put ourselves in a position where we can still be of use."

"How?" she asked.

"By warning them," Joe said. "Can you redesign it to broadcast in a shortwave band?"

"It'll add some time to the project," she said.

"We don't have much choice," Joe said. "We're not going to get any help around here."

Priya nodded. "I better get to work. Shortwaves propagate in the deep of night."

"Good," Joe said. "And I'll help however I can until dark. After that, I'm sneaking back onto the *Monarch*, where I can sabotage it. With a little hard work, I can keep it on the ground for days."

60

NUMA VESSEL *GRYPHON*

KURT WAS ALONE at the helm, lit up by the glow of computer controls, as he piloted the craft westward through the night. A makeshift panel covered the shattered window and the remaining armor had been slid back into position.

It was past midnight when the radar display indicated another helicopter coming in. This time, it was expected. Kurt picked up the microphone, dialed up the NUMA frequency and spoke. "That you, Rudi? Or should I call Paul and Gamay to battle stations?"

"I'd rather not get shot down tonight," Rudi said. *"Permission to come aboard?"*

"Permission granted," Kurt said. "Let me find a spot to park."

"No need," Rudi said. *"I'm still young enough to slide down a cable."*

Kurt turned the exterior lights on and set the *Gryphon*'s automatic controls to match the helicopter's course. That done, he pressed the intercom. "The boss has arrived. Better get topside and keep him from going overboard."

Paul and Gamay heard the call and went to the aft deck to help with Rudi's arrival. The helicopter was approaching from directly astern, a pair of floodlights on its lower side illuminating the water.

It closed the gap slowly and matched the *Gryphon*'s speed once it was overhead. A side door came open and Rudi could be seen in the doorway wearing a life preserver and a suit of all-weather gear.

With the two craft traveling in unison, Rudi descended on a cable. The wind and the downwash from the helicopter pushed him backward as he dropped, but the pilot compensated nicely. As he came into range, Paul reached up, grabbed his feet and helped him to the deck.

Rudi unhooked himself and waved to the pilot, who flashed the lights, pulled up and flew off to the north.

"Welcome to the party," Paul said.

"Looks like I've missed it," Rudi replied, noting the burn marks, dented armor and missing equipment.

"Be glad about that," Gamay said.

"Let's go inside," Rudi said. "I was just on the line with Hiram. He and Max have something to tell us."

Back inside the *Gryphon*, Rudi took off the life jacket and the rain gear and found a seat. "The ride on the hydrofoils was incredibly smooth. You'd never know we were cruising at fifty knots."

Kurt turned. "She runs like a Thoroughbred," he said. "Even after all we put her through."

With the four of them crowded into the wheelhouse, Kurt switched the communications system on and accepted an incoming transmission from Washington, D.C. As soon as the link was established, Hiram Yaeger's face appeared on the screen.

"I see you survived your journey," Hiram said.

"Are you talking to Rudi or to us?" Gamay asked.

"All of you."

"We're just getting started," Kurt said. "What's the word?"

"Our search has been successful," Yaeger announced. *"Too successful, I'm afraid."*

"Didn't think that was possible," Rudi said. "What gives?"

"We found a possible submarine on one of the old surveys," Hiram explained. *"Then we found another. And, later, we found yet another. We've now located six possible sonar contacts that might be the* Minerve.*"*

"Six," Kurt said sarcastically. "Is that all?"

"Still, better than none," Hiram said.

"You're right about that," Rudi replied. "Send the data through. We'll take a look."

"Sending it now," Yaeger said.

The information streamed in from Washington and a map of the central Mediterranean appeared on the screen. The boot of Italy occupied the middle, with Libya and Tunisia at the bottom, the Greek peninsula on the far right and Corsica and Sardinia and the southern coast of France in the upper left.

One by one, blinking dots popped up on the map. The first was just eighty miles south of Toulon, the second appeared in shallow waters near Sardinia. The next two dots appeared in deep water between Italy and Greece. A fifth just off the coast of Libya. A sixth near Malta.

The sonar pictures came in next. Kurt, Paul, Gamay and Rudi took their turns and examined the raw images.

"The older images are awfully blurry," Rudi noted.

"Systems have progressed since you were a lad," Kurt said.

"Very funny," Rudi said. "I'm not much older than you."

By the time all the data had come in, talk turned to narrowing down the list.

"I've ordered additional teams to be set up," Rudi explained. "But it'll be a couple of days before anyone else is ready, so we'll get first crack at this. Which door do you want to look behind?"

"We can rule out the wreck near Toulon," Kurt said.

On-screen, Yaeger disagreed. *"Max has that listed as the highest physical match to the* Minerve's *profile."*

"It's definitely a submarine," Kurt said. "But there's no chance the French could have missed that."

Yaeger didn't argue.

"What about the deepwater wrecks?" Paul suggested. "They're relatively close to our current position and checking them first would speed up the timetable."

"You're not taking into account the descent and surfacing time," Kurt said. "Besides, I don't think either of those are the *Minerve*."

"What makes you say that?"

"Because they're on a direct line toward Israel," Kurt said. "Would you take the straightest route to your destination if you knew you were being hunted?"

"The *Dakar* did," Paul pointed out.

"Another reason to rule those locations out," Kurt said. "We know the intention was to take different routes home. The course lines leading to the deepwater locations are too similar to the *Dakar*'s."

Rudi spoke up. "Rule them out for now. Same with Malta. That leaves the Sardinia wreck and the target off the coast of Libya."

Kurt stared at the map, running courses and headings through each of the possible locations, making calculations of the time, distance and danger.

"It comes back to the damaged snorkel," Kurt said. "Assuming the *Minerve*'s temporary commander did what Rudi suggested— sitting still and submerged during the day and traveling on the surface at night—he would still have to worry about French radar. How does he do that?"

"Two options I can think of," Rudi suggested. "Travel where French radar won't find you—in the territorial waters of other nations—or line yourself up in the shipping lanes and appear—on radar at least—like just another vessel."

Gamay spoke next. "The shipping lanes get crowded around Sicily with all the traffic rounding Isola delle Correnti at the southern tip. A missing submarine might easily be spotted, even at night. A chance our friend can't take."

A good point. With the French telling the world they'd lost a submarine, the *Minerve* would have to stay out of sight. "That leaves one option," Kurt said. "Get as far away from France as quickly as possible and then turn east and hug the African coast."

"The French were primarily searching with aircraft," Paul noted. "And every mile away from France means longer transit times out and back and less time on station."

Kurt nodded. "Going south also puts a larger gap between the *Minerve* and the *Dakar*, making it less likely that the French would find both."

"And if the French are steadily shifting their search grid to the east to account for the known speed of the submarines, they would soon be searching an area out in front of the *Minerve* while it crept along behind," Rudi said. "That might explain why they never found it."

All eyes focused on the target off the Libyan coast. It lay seventy miles offshore in shallow waters of the Gulf of Sidra.

"That sonar image is one of the oldest," Hiram said. *"It's not very clear."*

"All the same, that's our target," Kurt said. "At top speed, we can be there by morning."

61

CENTRAL KAZAKHSTAN

JOE LAY ON his stomach in the dirt and dust. After leaving the helicopter, he'd made his way past two abandoned airliners and into a weed-strewn section populated by old trucks sitting up on blocks. He'd moved through the collection of vehicles relatively unhindered and had crawled under the last truck in the long line. On the far side, he was less than a hundred feet from the *Monarch*.

There was now nothing but open ground between him and the aircraft. Open ground and a hive of activity. While Joe watched, a small fleet of vehicles streamed in. None of them went aboard the *Monarch*. Instead, they parked nearby, dropping off equipment and armed men.

As the men climbed the ramp into the *Monarch*, a larger vehicle pulled up. From this truck, long crates were removed. They were heavy enough that four men struggled to carry them.

"Missiles," Joe said to himself. "Meant for Kurt, Paul and Gamay."

As the missiles were loaded aboard, the drones Joe had heard earlier began returning. They landed, one by one, in a clearing beside the plane, where they were collected by Tessa's people. All the while, a pair of tanker trucks pumped fuel into the great plane's wings.

"Pulling up stakes and heading west," Joe said to himself. "Not if I can help it."

The activity was a double-edged sword. On the one hand, it put a lot of boots on the ground and that made it much more likely he would be spotted as soon as he left his hiding spot.

On the other hand, with all the people milling around, Joe might be able to walk right up to the plane without raising anyone's suspicions. There were too many people around each truck to sabotage the fueling procedure.

He needed to do something mechanical, preferably something that would be difficult to fix quickly. His eyes were drawn to the nose gear of the aircraft.

When the plane landed on the water, its hull remained sealed and it steered itself like a boat. But on land, of course, it used wheels and the stubby nose gear was crucial to maneuvering the behemoth around.

If Joe could damage or disable the nose gear, the pilots wouldn't be able to navigate the other derelicts and get the *Monarch* onto the runway to take off. Tessa and her crew would be as trapped as he and Priya were.

Easing his way back under the truck, Joe crawled to the front end of a third truck. He came to a spot across from the nose gear.

A swath of light surrounded the nose of the aircraft, spilling out from inside the fuselage. Standing in that light was a lone guard with a metal thermos cup in his hand.

Shouting from the crew beneath the wing told Joe the fueling was done. The tanker trucks rumbled to life and pulled away and moments later the first of the six engines began to turn, starting with an electric whine, becoming a howl as the engine fired and then settling into a whistling hum.

A second engine fired up. Still, the guard remained at his post.

Joe backtracked, found a broken camshaft that he could use as a weapon and crawled back to the edge of the truck.

With the last of the equipment loaded, the aft door began to rise. Someone shouted to the guard near the nose and he tossed the contents of his cup onto the ground and left his post, rushing to the tail section to climb aboard.

Joe sprinted from his hiding spot toward the front of the plane. He had to worry about the same cameras that had spotted Priya during her attempt to place the geotracker on the aircraft, but the entire fuselage of the *Monarch* was coated with a layer of gray dust and he hoped it left the camera lenses smeared-over and useless.

Joe reached the nose gear. It was a simple, rugged design. Two large-diameter wheels attached to a thick central strut. To Joe's misfortune, the important parts were hidden beneath steel plates and rock deflectors—typical of aircraft designed to take off from and land on unimproved fields.

Joe had to look higher for a weak spot. He ducked down, moved under the plane and then climbed up inside the landing gear bay, standing on the top of the wheels. There, he found the unprotected hydraulic lines.

He attempted to dig his hand between the first line and the metal wall of the bay, but the fit was too tight. He placed the rod against the line and punched the end of it, pushing the line sideways.

The line bent out and then up as Joe slipped the camshaft beneath it and pulled like he was using a hammer to remove a nail.

It was a partial success, but there was enough play in the line that it didn't pull loose from the connector or split open. Before Joe could try again, the brakes released and the aircraft lurched forward.

Standing on the wheels, Joe was thrown off balance as the plane began to move. Joe dropped the camshaft, leapt forward and grasped a ledge inside the landing gear bay. His feet dangled beneath him, swaying back and forth, as the ground rolled by.

Stretching, Joe reached for the hydraulic lines he'd been trying to dislodge moments before. He grabbed them, pulled himself up and spread his feet wide on the inner ledge of the landing gear door.

The plane was rolling now, rumbling over the dusty ground at a fast walking pace. He went back to work, pulling at the lines with his bare hands.

Beneath him, the wheels turned. For a second, he thought he'd been the cause, but when the aircraft had come around, the wheels straightened and the engines roared.

"Not good," Joe said.

They'd turned onto the runway and were picking up speed.

Joe stopped watching the ground and turned back to the hydraulic lines, grabbing and pulling unmercifully at a second line. Each hard pull caused the line to cut into his fingers and Joe was soon bleeding, but he didn't relent.

When the line had been stretched to its limit, Joe reared back and pulled it hard one more time. The seal ruptured and red hydraulic fluid sprayed all over interior of the bay. It lasted only a few seconds before an emergency shutoff closed the line.

Joe looked down. It was too late now. The nose wheel had straightened and was now locked into place for takeoff. The otherworldly howl from the engines was growing and the ground beneath him was passing by ever more quickly.

It was too late to jump. They were already doing forty miles an hour. If the fall didn't kill him, the sixteen wheels of the main landing gear would crush him and finish the job. With no way to go down, Joe looked upward. He and Kurt had once climbed into a Russian bomber through a door in the landing gear bay. Maybe he could do the same here.

As the plane picked up speed, the nose gear started vibrating. Tiny rocks and swirling wind were kicked up into the compartment. Joe hung on and climbed higher. A small hatch, probably nothing more than an inspection bay, but at this point anything was better than remaining where he was. Joe grabbed the handle, wrenched it down and pulled the hatch open. There was enough space for him to fit.

He pulled himself up, drawing his legs in and turning around, just as the plane rotated and the front of the aircraft left the ground. As soon as they were airborne, the nose gear began to retract.

There was no escape now. Joe pulled the hatch closed and sealed it tight.

He had no idea where he was in the plane. And no idea where the plane was going. But he was going along for the ride.

ON THE GROUND, still hiding in the old Russian helicopter, Priya heard the *Monarch* take off, noting its departure with mixed feelings. Tessa and her crew being gone meant she was less likely to be discovered, but the aircraft's successful takeoff also meant Joe had failed. He might even have been captured or killed. And if the *Monarch* was departing on a mission to obliterate Kurt, Paul and Gamay, then Priya had run out of time to finish the shortwave transmitter.

She looked back at her contraption. She had no plans. No paper and pen to make notes with, she'd built everything from memory and theory. Working in the dark was impossible, so she'd ripped out and rigged up one of the Mercedes's dome lights to help her see. But every minute she used it drained more power from the battery and that was power she'd need to transmit the signal.

She got back to work and rushed to finish the job.

An hour after the *Monarch*'s departure, tired and cold and fighting a throat that had grown as dry as the dust around them, she was ready to attempt her first transmission.

She added power carefully. With her ear next to the speaker, she searched for any sign of a signal. Finally, she heard something. More English, this time—*British* English.

"This is Edward Bannister with the day's Premier League action . . ."

The BBC World Service coming in exactly where it was supposed to be! Never had she heard a more beautiful sound.

The next task was to change frequencies to one she could broadcast on, one NUMA was likely to hear her message on. She adjusted her frequency to 12.290 kHz. The marine shortwave emergency band. Most groups no longer used it. But NUMA still monitored it. That meant it would be free of other traffic and easier for her signal to stand out and be picked up.

Engaging her transmitter, she began to speak. "Mayday! Mayday! Mayday!" she said. "This is Priya Kashmir transmitting on 12.290. This is an emergency message. Can anyone hear me?"

She released the transmitter and waited for a response. Thirty seconds went by. And then a full minute.

"Too far away," she whispered to herself. Even with the antenna Joe had built and extended out above the cockpit of the helicopter.

Cautiously, she upped the power level. "Mayday! Mayday! Mayday! If anyone can hear me, please respond?"

Still, there was nothing.

She raised the power one more time.

The result was disastrous as one of the circuits flared and sizzled.

"No!" she said, cutting the power even as the compartment filled with the acrid smell of an electrical fire.

It was too late. The transmitter was dead.

Priya began to cough. The smoke brought it on, but the dryness and dust made it worse. After twenty-four hours without any real water, she'd become very dehydrated. Her lips had cracked, her eyes burned incessantly and her mind felt sluggish and slow. All she wanted to do was lie down and go to sleep.

She pushed the feeling aside and felt around for the power cord, disconnecting it from the transmitter and reconnecting it to the dome light. Even with that light, the damage was easy to see. Several of the circuits had burned. Other spots she soldered had melted. Hours of work had been destroyed.

She looked at the mess and then at the pile of spare parts on the floor. There was no other choice. She slid herself over, picked through what she had and began the painstaking process of rebuilding.

62

MORNING SPREAD across the Mediterranean, revealing pristine waters, a cloudless day and the *Gryphon* on station seventy miles off the coast of Libya.

Kurt and Rudi remained on the bridge, watching the video relay as the Trouts made the first dive.

The waters off the Libyan coast were shallow, warm and clear. Even here, seventy miles from the coast, the depth never exceeded two hundred feet. The bottom was sandy and flat, a combination that made for excellent diving.

"Wreck in site," Paul said. "It's definitely a submarine."

Kurt and Rudi saw the wreck on the video screen. Even though the vessel was lying on its side, covered in marine life and partially buried in the sediment, its shape was unmistakable.

While Paul dropped toward the stern, where the sub's rudder and one of its twin propellers could be easily seen, Gamay swam along the length of the hull.

"I'm not seeing any damage," she said. "In fact, I'm not seeing anything to indicate a traumatic impact. More like it settled gently into the silt and then rolled over on its side."

"That's good," Paul suggested. "Should make it easier to search."

"Assuming this is the right submarine," Kurt said. "Let's make sure it is what we think it is. Head around to the bow."

The *Minerve* had a distinctive bell-shaped housing jutting upward near the bow. It allowed a powerful sonar system to be installed without forcing the relocation of the torpedo tubes, of which the *Minerve* had twelve, eight in the front and four in the stern.

Engaging his thrusters, Paul traveled the length of the hull, passing the conning tower and maneuvering toward the front of the ship. He paused over a mound of silt that had covered the bow like a sand dune. Using his thrusters, Paul scoured away the sediment.

Kurt and Rudi watched the results. The distinctive sonar housing and the opened outer door of the number one torpedo tube were plainly visible. "That's her, all right," Rudi said. "Your skills of divination have few equals."

"Thanks," Kurt said. "I'll take the pat on the back later. Let's get that sub open and find what we came here for."

AS KURT, PAUL AND GAMAY began working on the French submarine, Hiram Yaeger sat at his desk five thousand miles and seven time zones away watching the progress remotely.

It was just past midnight in Washington, D.C.

"Does it look like they're cutting in the right place?" Hiram asked Max.

Max replied with typical precision. "Based on the camera angle and the orientation of the submarine's centerline, Paul and Gamay appear to be cutting within six inches of the optimal location. A perfectly adequate level of precision for human work."

"What are the chances that submarine is filled with explosive gas?" Hiram asked.

"Unknown," Max said, "though unlikely, in general."

"That's one less thing to worry about." Hiram leaned back, put his feet up on the desk and kept his eyes focused on the monitor. Using the Trench Crawler's welding tools, Paul had just finished removing a section of the outer hull. He and Gamay were now going to work on the submarine's inner pressure hull.

The process was slow and Hiram began to feel drowsy as he watched. He was just starting to nod off to sleep when his desk phone rang in a particularly shrill tone. Jerking upright, he pulled his feet off the desk. "Max, if this is you, I'm disconnecting your power supply."

"The incoming call is not my doing," Max said. "It's the communications office."

"At this hour?" Hiram picked up the phone. "This is Yaeger."

"Mr. Yaeger, this is Ellie Ramos in communications."

"What can I do for you, Ms. Ramos?"

"I have something you need to hear. It's coming in on the 12.290 kHz band."

"The old shortwave emergency band?"

"Yes," Ms. Ramos said. "It's the marine band. Even though it's not officially in use anymore, we still monitor it."

"If someone is declaring an emergency, you need to put it through to the Coast Guard or—"

"It's not a marine emergency," she replied. "It may even be a joke, I'm not really sure. But, please, could you just listen."

"Put it through."

A brief click tied the transmission into Hiram's phone and Hiram put the phone on speaker. At first, all he heard was static, then a low squeal that faded, leaving only a continuous background buzz. Finally, words emerged.

"... *unsure of our exact location, somewhere in Kazakhstan between* ... *and forty-seven degrees north latitude* ... *one hundred and fifty miles east of the Caspian Sea* ..."

A chill ran down Hiram's spine as he recognized the voice. "Priya?" he said. "Priya, can you hear me?"

Ellie Ramos replied. "We tried to speak to her already. Either it's a one-way broadcast or she's simply unable to pick up our response. Either way, she has been speaking continuously since the transmission started, repeating some of what she's already said."

"Because she has no idea how much is getting through," Hiram said. "Tell me you're recording this."

"We're following standard emergency broadcast protocol."

NUMA recorded all emergency radio calls, storing important ones in a computer archive indefinitely.

Priya's voice returned and Hiram fell silent.

"... *Joe assisted my escape* ... *now missing* ... *Had been attempting to sabotage the* Monarch ..."

"Did she say Joe?"

"Affirmative," Max said.

"... *Tessa Franco working with members of regional oil Consortium* ... *ecological intentions fraudulent* ... *Goal is permanent worldwide oil shortage* ..."

Another squeal interrupted the broadcast.

"Max, triangulate the signal. We need to know where she's broadcasting from."

"Triangulation impossible," Max said. "None of our other

shortwave receivers are picking up the signal. Perhaps due to the transmitter location, atmospheric effects or the quality of receiving equipment."

The antennas built into the NUMA HQ were among the most sensitive in the world, designed to pick up even the faintest radio calls from around the globe. The only equipment matching what they had in D.C. was at another NUMA facility in Hawaii, five thousand miles farther away, too far to pick up Priya's broadcast.

The signal cleared and Priya's voice returned once again, this time it was so faint that Hiram could hardly hear it.

"... *have been forced to hack* ... *NUMA system compromised* ... *Kurt's location known and being tracked* ... *In danger* ... *Will be attacked upon discovery of French submarine* ... *Tessa desperate to possess antidote* ... *Claiming possession of guided antiship missiles* ... *Please warn before* ..."

A long squeal interrupted the broadcast and, when it faded, there was no sound whatsoever.

"Ellie, what happened?"

"We've lost the signal," she replied. "Transmission has ceased. I'm sorry. I'll have the recording logged and labeled appropriately."

"No," Hiram said. "Make no record of it."

"But—"

"Store the recording under a miscellaneous file, label it something innocuous like *Sunspot Interference* and speak to no one about this."

"But, Mr. Yaeger, that's not our standard protocol."

"Do it," Hiram said. "I'll explain later."

"Yes, sir," she said.

Hiram put the phone down, breaking the contact. "Max," he said. "Have we been hacked?"

"My systems are secure," Max said. "But NUMA has other servers and stand-alone systems."

"Please check them thoroughly," Hiram ordered.

It took a few minutes, but Max answered exactly as Hiram expected him to. "Ninety-two percent chance that supply and logistics module has been compromised. Other applications show similar intrusions."

"That explains how they found Kurt in the Mediterranean," Hiram said.

"Would you like me to secure the system with revised procedures?"

Hiram debated for a second. "No," he said. "Leave it alone for the moment."

"Allowing a known security breach to remain open is inadvisable," Max said. "It will only invite further intrusions."

"I know," Hiram said. "But I'd rather they not know we're onto them."

"A reasonable gambit."

"A gambit is right," Hiram said. "I need to speak with Kurt and Rudi. But not via the satellite network, in case that has been compromised as well."

"The *Gryphon* is equipped with encrypted radio receivers," Max said. "Impossible for a third party to listen in."

63

KURT WAS GETTING READY to join the dive when the blue radio squawked. The call struck Kurt oddly. Blue—or encrypted radio—was an older system. It was rarely used anymore, as NUMA relied almost exclusively on satellite links for communications these days.

The radio alert repeated and this time it was followed by a voice transmission. *"Kurt, this is Hiram, do you read? Over."*

Kurt picked up the microphone, held it near his mouth and pressed the talk switch. "Coming in loud and clear," he said. "What's with the old-fashioned radio call?"

"We have reason to believe satellite communications have been compromised."

"Roger that," Kurt said. "We'll keep off the satellite network."

"I have some good news," Hiram added. *"We've heard from Priya. Both she and Joe are alive."*

Kurt clenched his hand. "I knew Joe would find a way off that ship. Where are they?"

"Priya's somewhere in Kazakhstan, exact location is unclear. Joe's whereabouts are even more of a mystery. They appear to have escaped together but have since become separated. According to the message, Joe was attempting some act of sabotage when he vanished."

"That sounds like Joe," Rudi said.

"There's more," Hiram said. *"Tessa hacked our data network and has been watching your every move. She knows you're diving on a wreck believed to be the* Minerve *and she knows what you're looking for. She intends to stop you and take it for herself."*

"How?"

"The Monarch *is now armed with air-to-sea missiles and heading your way."*

Kurt envisioned the strategy. "She won't risk getting close to us. Not after what we did to those helicopters. She'll hit us from long range and then drop off her hired hands to clean up whatever's left."

"How much time do we have?" Rudi asked.

"We've been using long-exposure satellite images in hopes of catching a blur that could be Tessa's plane," Hiram said. *"We've spotted one that doesn't correspond with any listed airline or military flight plan. It puts her a hundred miles east of your position and closing fast. It would probably be wise for you vacate the area until we can provide defensive units and reestablish control."*

Kurt glanced at Rudi. "We just cut that sub open," he said. "The entire vessel is sitting down there in one piece, completely intact, ready to be searched. If we leave now, they'll land the *Monarch,* dive on the wreck and be gone with the countermeasure before anyone can even put up a speed trap."

Hiram interjected, *"But if you remain where you are, you'll be destroyed and she'll still get what she's after."*

Rudi looked Kurt's way. "I came here to help," he said. "But if we can't run and we can't fight, then what are we going to do?"

An icy calm settled on Kurt. "We get the countermeasure out of that submarine and away from here, then leave her to pick over the bones."

64

THIRTY MILES EAST of the *Gryphon*, a brightly painted fishing boat rolled on the gentle swells as the crewmen hauled in the nets they'd cast during the night.

It was hard labor and these men had come out much farther than their fellow fishermen to do it, but it was worth the effort because the catch was larger.

With the lead lines pulled in and attached, the captain threw the switch on an old winch, allowing it to do the rest of the job. It clanked to life, drawing the net upward. As it reached the surface, his men spoke excitedly in Arabic, marveling at the number of fish they'd caught.

The captain grinned, shut the winch off and stepped forward. He stopped in his tracks when he heard a strange whistling sound. It grew louder and closer on the far side of the boat, building to a crescendo and then crashing down on him as a huge winged shape thundered overhead.

It passed no more than a hundred feet above them, crossing the fishing boat from one side to the other. A maelstrom of wind followed it, tilting the boat, whipping the captain's hat into the air and tossing one of the men into the sea.

FROM THE COCKPIT of the *Monarch*, Tessa watched the small boat pass beneath them. She grinned at the thought of little men in the boat nearly being capsized by her passing.

"Austin won't be so easy to impress," Volke warned.

"He won't have time to be impressed," she said. "In fact, he'll never know what hit him. Do we have satellite confirmation?"

"Patching it through now."

A screen to her left flickered to life, revealing a detailed image from a commercial satellite service. The shot wasn't quite military grade in terms of clarity, but it was close enough. It revealed the lethal little vessel NUMA called the *Gryphon*, sitting off the Libyan coast.

"They're directly above a wreck," Volke said.

"Can we zoom in?"

"Stand by."

Volke tapped a few keys and the image pixelated and then refocused, much closer this time. A crane at the rear of the boat had been swung out over the transom, an arrowhead-shaped vehicle dangled beneath it.

"They're deploying a submersible or ROV," Tessa said. "It must be the *Minerve*."

"They're just getting started," Volke replied. "We've caught them at the perfect time. They're preoccupied and there isn't another ship within thirty miles."

Tessa turned to the pilot. "How soon can we get a missile lock?"

"We need them on radar," the pilot said. "From this distance, we would have to climb to five thousand feet."

"Any risks in doing that?"

"No," the pilot said. "We're invisible at this point."

"Climb to five thousand feet, lock onto that boat and launch three missiles with staggered timing."

"One missile will do the job," Volke said. "Using three is—"

"Overkill," Tessa said. "Which is exactly what I intend."

65

NUMA VESSEL *GRYPHON*

KURT'S EYES were glued to a monitor every bit as intently as Tessa's had been. One part of the screen showed the camera view around the *Gryphon*, another section showed the status of the boat itself, engines idling, foils waiting to be deployed. "Anything on radar?"

Sitting beside Kurt, Rudi was studying another screen. This one displayed a circular red image with a sweeping white line that moved around it in a clockwise direction.

"Nothing," Rudi said. "But, then, that's why she paid extra for a stealth aircraft."

Kurt set the cameras on Autopano and they scanned back and forth, looking for movement. "In theory, a giant plane should be easy to spot in broad daylight," Kurt said. "But with the sun behind her, it's going to be that much harder."

"The Red Baron used that tactic, too," Rudi said. "Very effective."

"Don't remind me," Kurt said.

Finally, one of the cameras locked onto something and zoomed in. The image on the screen blurred and then refocused. At first, it looked like a bird. "That's the *Monarch*, all right. Range, twenty miles and closing fast."

"Don't mean to be a backseat driver," Rudi said, "but I'd deploy the foils and get moving."

Kurt used a touch screen to control the vessel. He nudged a virtual throttle lever forward and watched the rpm gauge jump, but, for now, most of the power was held in reserve.

Switching to an underwater transmitter, Kurt called out to Paul and Gamay. "The guests have arrived. What's your status?"

"We're almost through the pressure hull," Paul said.

"We're only going to be able to entertain for so long," Kurt said. "Don't dawdle."

The display in front of Rudi began flashing. "Radar contact," he said. "Two contacts . . . Make that three. Moving faster than the *Monarch*. Must be missiles. I'd say we're out of time."

"I'll see if I can buy us some more." Touching the screen again, Kurt extended the hydrofoils and set the gas turbine to full power. The *Gryphon* began to move, accelerating like a normal boat, while the foil indicator went from red to yellow and then green.

As the boat began to pick up speed, the cameras left the *Monarch* and locked onto the incoming missiles. The projectiles themselves were impossible to see, but the white vapor trails were obvious.

"Missiles are supersonic," Rudi said. "Range, fifteen miles and closing."

The *Gryphon* was rising up on its legs and accelerating. With the hull out of the water, the drag vanished and the speed increased suddenly, feeling like a turbocharger kicking in.

Kurt felt the g-forces pinning him to his seat and then pushing him forward. Rudi gripped the arms of his own chair, as they swayed back and forth.

"This ride is going to be wilder than I expected," Rudi said.

"It might be shorter than expected, too," Kurt said. "How much time do we have?"

"The lead missile is nine miles out," Rudi said. "Less than one minute. The others are trailing it by two miles each."

Kurt kept the throttle open and the *Gryphon* reached its top speed of ninety knots. It might as well have been crawling in comparison to the missiles.

"Eight miles," Rudi said calmly. "Seven . . . Six-point-five . . ."

"I don't need the entire countdown," Kurt said. "Just tell me when to turn."

"Turning isn't going to help," Rudi said. "Even if we avoid the first one, the second will hit us for sure. We should think about jumping ship."

"Too late," Kurt said. "At eighty knots, we'd break every bone in our bodies."

"Might be better than the alternative."

"It might at that."

"Three miles," Rudi said. "Two . . ."

Kurt nudged the rudder control to the starboard and the *Gryphon* carved a tight line on the high-speed turn. Both Kurt and Rudi struggled to stay in their seats, but the missiles continued to track them.

"One mile . . ." Rudi said.

Kurt chopped the throttle a bit and deflected the rudder hard in the other direction. The *Gryphon* reacted instantly, cutting back tightly to port side.

The first missile shot past, wide by a hundred feet or more.

"That was close," Rudi said.

"The next one's going to be closer."

Kurt punched the throttle back up and turned the *Gryphon* to starboard once again. The second missile shot by as well, but it came close enough that its proximity sensor detonated the warhead. A billowing explosion caved in the armor and windows on the *Gryphon*'s left side while superheated shrapnel tore through the hull and the shock wave collapsed the forward hydrofoil.

The *Gryphon* dove nose-first into the water, rose up and crashed back down, still moving at relatively high speed. Kurt and Rudi were thrown from side to side.

"Now," Kurt said to Rudi.

Rudi pressed a switch and Kurt threw the rudder hard in the other direction one more time.

It was not enough. The third missile hit the craft amidships, penetrating the hull and exploding out the far side, sending a fireball upward through the middle deck and blowing the craft apart.

TESSA WATCHED the explosion from her position in the *Monarch*. As the glare of the fireball diminished, she saw that the *Gryphon* had been split in two. What remained of the aft section went down quickly while the bow section burned and smoked and slowly foundered.

"Those missiles were worth every penny," Woods said to her.

Volke was even more ecstatic. "May you burn worse than I did, Austin."

"So ends the contest," she whispered. "And so begins a new one." She turned to Volke and Woods. "Our clock is ticking. Get your men and equipment ready. I want you ready to deploy the minute we hit the water."

66

GAMAY SWAM into the *Minerve* through the opening Paul had cut. She was still getting her bearings when the tremor of the *Gryphon's* explosion reached her. "Is that what I think it was?"

The rumbling came in two waves, with the second vibration much larger.

"Sounds like the fireworks have begun up on the surface," Paul replied. *"It won't be long now."*

"Any word from Kurt or Rudi?"

"Nothing. First things first. Find that container."

Gamay looked around. She'd entered the submarine on the side of the control room and began moving aft.

Unlike the *Dakar*, the *Minerve* had been sealed against the outside world for fifty years. Saltwater had come in, but sea life had been kept at bay. She found three bodies partially preserved in the control room. Another two in the next compartment.

The third compartment should have been closed off by a watertight door, but Gamay found a chain wrapped around the hatch wheel.

"Whether this sub was scuttled or sabotaged, it was definitely sent to the bottom on purpose," she said. "Someone chained these doors open."

"*Wouldn't surprise me if the French members of the crew realized they were in shallow waters and decided to act,*" Paul said. "*They might have thought they were closer to shore than they actually were.*"

Gamay found another body just beyond the purposely opened hatch. "Doesn't look like many of them escaped."

"*We need to hurry if we're going to escape,*" Paul said.

Swimming through the hatch, Gamay shined her light around, looking for the container. They'd been briefed by the Israelis to look for a three-foot-long, stainless steel cylinder with a diameter of twenty inches. It had bands at each end and held two smaller containers inside.

The plan was simple. Find the counteragent and get far enough away from the *Minerve* that Tessa's men would never spot them. Even in clear water, visibility was no more than a few hundred yards. Beyond that, they'd vanish in the scattered blue light.

Without an acquisition and targeting sonar, it would be nearly impossible for Tessa to find them. That would force her to choose between hanging around and prolonging the search or heading for the hills with all possible speed.

Every minute the *Monarch* spent on the water increased the risk of detection and retaliatory action. None of them expected Tessa to give up without a fight, but she couldn't risk staying too long.

It was a good plan, Gamay told herself, but not without problems.

The entire plan depended on finding the container holding the countermeasure and getting out of there before Tessa and her crew made visual contact. And they'd been planning to use the *Gryphon*'s high-speed submersible to tow them into the endless blue.

If that submersible had been destroyed or damaged beyond repair in the attack, the only real method of putting distance between themselves and the *Minerve* was to use the thrusters in the Trench Crawler. And that would be a much slower method of escaping. After clearing the compartment she was in, Gamay moved aft yet again.

PAUL FLOATED outside the submarine, near the opening he'd cut, and was taking advantage of the Trench Crawler's automatic station keeping feature to remain in place.

He continued turning from quarter to quarter, scanning the sea around him for any sign of Kurt and Rudi but saw nothing but blue water.

The only company he had was a curious barracuda that swam up over the top of the submarine and hovered there, eyeballing him for a moment. It held itself in place as easily as Paul did, then turned slightly and darted away at incredible speed.

The next sign of movement came from directly above. Paul looked up as a line of foam and bubbles streaked across the surface as the keel of the *Monarch* touched down, carving a straight line to the west.

"The *Monarch* has landed."

67

THE *Monarch* landed with an incredible amount of grace, considering that she had the length and beam of a World War II destroyer.

She'd come in slowly, extending large flaps and dropping to a position just above the water, where the high-pressure cavitation system was engaged.

With a cushion of air to break up the surface tension, the plane had landed smoothly, the central spine of its keel cleaving the water in two. Only when the speed dropped below forty knots was the cavitation system shut down. By then, the entire lower fuselage of the aircraft had been cradled by the sea and the *Monarch* was settling gently.

It eased to a crawl and stopped near where the *Gryphon* had been destroyed, but nearly a mile from the wreck site.

Tessa left the cockpit. "I'll be on the lower deck," she said. "Keep the engines turning. I want to be able to leave here at a moment's notice."

The pilots responded in unison and Tessa left them behind,

racing to the bottom deck and heading aft. She arrived to find the tail ramp already lowered and Volke and Woods working together to get the recovery teams into the water.

The disk-shaped submersible was lowered first, followed by a slower, bulkier sub, which her people called the *Bus*.

Volke was in the *Discus*. Woods drove the *Bus*.

Behind them, two high-speed boats were launched, each with four divers aboard. The group in the first boat were commercial divers Woods had rounded up. The group in the second boat were the remnants of the mercenaries Volke had hired. He called them the predator team.

Tessa intended to keep in contact with all of them. She put on a headset with noise-dampening earcups so she could hear over the continued whistle of the engines. After plugging the jack into the transmitter, she moved the microphone in front of her mouth. "How long will this take?"

"No time at all," Volke insisted. "The depth is a hundred and twenty feet. The vessel seems to be intact. And this time we know what we're looking for."

"Get it and get back here," she said. "Austin may have called for help, we might not have a lot of time."

VOLKE GRIPPED the controls of his submersible. It felt good to be back in control again. "Woods, are your men ready?"

Volke didn't trust Woods. Even with the threat of death, the man was a fanatic. When told they'd be recovering the antidote, Woods had been furious. He wanted it destroyed, claiming it could only lead the world back to the Oil Age. Tessa had had to explain again that their lives were worthless without the antidote, then Woods had finally come around. Still, Volke and Tessa had agreed to keep a close eye on him and use him only when absolutely necessary.

"They're ready," Woods said.

"Tell them to follow me down. We don't have time to wait for you."

Volke engaged his propulsion jets and the *Discus* began crossing the water toward the wreck site. The powerboats passed him, one to either side, while the *Bus* trailed well behind.

Reaching the dive coordinates, Volke tuned a valve and flooded his ballast tank. The *Discus* submerged and began dropping toward the bottom. The commercial divers went in the water, swimming beside him in a steady descent.

Volke spotted the *Minerve* and approached it from the broadside, noticing the opening that had been cut in it.

"NUMA's already been down here," he reported. "I only hope the counteragent wasn't on board their vessel when we blew it apart."

"They wouldn't have been sitting around if they had it," Tessa insisted. *"It's down there."*

Volke looked around. It dawned on him that some of the NUMA personnel might have been in the water when they attacked the *Gryphon*. He doubted a lone diver or even a group of them would be brazen enough to attack his men, not when it would be far wiser to swim away and call for help, but he put nothing past these men and women from NUMA.

"Group one, take up positions on the hull where you can watch for trouble. Group two, get inside and see what you can find."

As the divers swam to their new positions, Volke backed away from the submarine, giving himself a wider view. He watched as the two men swam up to the opening and shined their lights inside.

"Looks like the control room," one of them reported.

"A hundred thousand euros to whoever finds the canister," Volke said.

THE FIRST DIVER went in, disconnecting the small air tank from his dive harness and pushing it in front of him. *"I'm going aft."*

He knew he had the best chance of finding the canister. He'd been part of the team that found the oil destroyer in the *Dakar* and he would know the canisters by sight.

The Israelis had stored them in a refrigerated compartment meant for food. Why, he didn't know, but he expected the French would do the same. He went aft, heading for the galley, came to a bulkhead door and found it chained in the open position.

He grabbed the door and shook it, interested in whether it would even move at this point. As he did so, his light illuminated the skeletal remains of a crewman, stuck behind the door.

He pulled back instantly, exhaling a cloud of bubbles. It wasn't fear, just shock, made worse by the adrenaline and the high level of oxygen running through his body.

Waiting for his heart rate to slow, he drifted backward and bumped into something. Spinning around, he saw a metallic monster, bulbous and grotesque, with copper-colored skin. He saw his own reflection in the curved glass of the huge head. Far too late, he noticed a weighty arm crashing down toward him.

The metal fist slammed into his skull and knocked him out cold.

THE SECOND DIVER had entered the open space of the submarine's control room, saw the lead diver going aft and turned toward the forward part of the sub. He swam past the periscope housing and through the forward hatchway door. Like the other doors, this one was chained in the open position.

Confidently, he kicked smoothly and entered the compartment, moving methodically and removing his tank as the first diver had. He went one compartment at a time, shining his light in every nook.

He'd reached the forward torpedo room when a strange sound reached his ears. *Sizzling, bubbling, burning,* is how he would have described it. He looked around for the source of that noise, noticed a glow coming from far behind him and turned, swimming back toward the control room.

He kicked harder and faster as he neared the hatch, a supernatural sense of danger driving him forward. Getting closer, he saw a jet of fire lighting up the hatchway. He quickly realized it was a cutting torch.

He swam for the gap, caught sight of a diver in a bulky ADS on the far side and then realized what was happening. The armored diver was cutting the chain that held the hatch open.

The links were severed, the chain dropped to the deck and the hatch began to swing closed.

The diver shoved his air tank forward and wedged it in the gap, momentarily preventing the closure. The hatch rebounded open and he tried to swim through.

It was not to be.

The diver in the ADS blocked him and grabbed at his face with the metallic arms. The diver pulled back, only to have his helmet ripped off his head.

Bubbles exploded in all directions and the world was instantly blurred. All he could see were indistinct shapes and shadows moving around as his dive light bounced loose.

He grabbed for his backup regulator, got it into his mouth and took a desperate breath. Before he could do anything more, a re-sounding metallic clang told him his fate had been sealed.

The hatch door had been slammed shut. The wheel turned and locked.

He grabbed the handle and tried to twist it. His only hope lay with the other divers still outside of the submarine. But without his helmet, he couldn't even call for help.

PAUL STOOD BESIDE the sealed hatchway. He'd knocked one foe into unconsciousness with a single blow and sealed the second one in the forward part of the hull—after removing his helmet with its communication system.

He moved back in the other direction, spotting Gamay as she emerged from the aft section of the submarine, dragging the banded steel cylinder behind her. It was partially encrusted with salts and rust but identifiable as the canister they were after. "You found it."

"I did," Gamay said. "Now we have to get out of here."

"That's going to be a challenge," he said, pointing at the man he'd knocked out. "This guy wanted to join you in the mess hall."

"How did they not see you?"

"I hid on the ceiling," Paul said. "They swam right under-neath me."

"What happened to the other diver?"

"He went forward. I locked him in. But I'm pretty sure they're not alone."

Gamay twisted, exhaling a stream of bubbles. "We're trapped."

Paul nodded inside the suit. "Unless we get some assistance to break the blockade, this submarine is going to be our Alamo."

.   .   .

WAITING OUTSIDE the *Minerve*, Volke drummed his fingers on the control panel. The delay soon became too much for him. "Divers, report. What's going on in there?"

Wreck diving was dangerous business, but the *Minerve* was in such good condition it was doubtful his people faced the kind of dangers usually associated with sunken ships.

With no response forthcoming, Volke's frustration grew. Underwater radios were not that reliable, it was possible the hull of the submarine was blocking the signal.

"Team two, get in there and find out what's going on," he said. "Stick together."

The second pair of divers moved toward the hull, reaching the opening and entering more cautiously.

Almost immediately, Volke knew something had gone wrong. A wave of bubbles exploded through the gap in the hull and the beams from divers' hand lights could be seen dancing around chaotically.

"They're in here!" a shout came over the radio.

"Get out!" the other diver shouted. *"Get out!"*

One of the men burst from the opening, swimming hard. The second diver was halfway out when he was grabbed by a large metallic arm, which clamped down on his leg, raking his calf and drawing blood.

He squirmed and twisted, shouting as his ankle snapped and the fin was ripped from his foot. With another kick, he pulled free and went right for the surface.

"Two members of the NUMA team are in there," the first diver reported. *"One in regular gear and one in a hard suit."*

A moment later, the diver in the hard suit emerged from the opening, the suit's huge shoulders barely fitting through.

Volke instinctively attacked, pushing the throttle of his vessel to full.

As the *Discus* sped forward, the pincers at the front opened wide, targeting the diver's helmeted head, but the armored figure dropped back into the *Minerve* and hid before Volke could hit him.

Volke pulled up, crossed over the top of the submarine and spun his vessel around. This time, he set up closer to the opening, ready to hammer anything that emerged.

BACK ON THE SURFACE, Tessa heard the radio chatter. Through a set of binoculars, she saw one of her scuba divers popping to the surface. He was bleeding and swimming for one of the dive boats.

A radio call from Volke arrived next. *"They're down here. At least two of them. We have them trapped in the* Minerve, *but we can't get inside."*

She pressed the transmitter. "Don't let them escape."

"That's not what they're trying to do," Volke replied. *"This is obviously a delaying tactic. The longer we stay, the more likely help is to arrive."*

"Help is coming," she insisted. "But not for them."

She contacted the second team of divers, the predator team who were used to fighting and killing. "You're needed," she said. "Go."

They went in the water one after another, four men carrying spearguns with explosives-tipped heads.

68

TWO MILES from the *Minerve*, another submersible drifted slowly downward. It was scorched and silent.

"Would it help if I got out and pushed?" Rudi asked.

"It might," Kurt said.

Kurt and Rudi had been controlling the *Gryphon* remotely from the submersible while it hung from the crane over the transom of the boat. They'd held on until just before the final missile impact, when Rudi had pressed the button to release them from the crane.

They'd dropped free just before the explosion, but the fire had toasted the exterior, coating the submersible in burns. While the shock wave battered the sub, no mortal damage had been done, but the submersible had been shaken so severely that the computer-based systems had shut down.

Going through the restart procedure for the third time, Kurt finally got the power restored and the systems up and running. Lights on the control panel came to life, followed by the subsurface comm system.

". . . *We're completely surrounded. If you're out there, now would be a good time to show up and render assistance.*"

"Your plan seems to be working perfectly," Rudi said from the copilot's seat, "if it includes us nearly getting incinerated and the Trouts coming under attack with only the creaky hull of an old submarine between them and certain death."

"The plan was to buy Paul and Gamay some time while lulling Tessa into thinking she'd killed us," Kurt replied. "I never intended our deception to come that close to reality."

"She has to have counted us out by now," Rudi said. "So that part is a success."

"I'm sure she has," Kurt said, pushing the throttle forward. He got his bearings and turned toward the *Minerve*'s position. "Time for us to surprise her by returning from the dead."

VOLKE WATCHED the new team of men descending toward him. The grenade-tipped spears they carried wouldn't be enough to destroy the submarine, but they would be more than enough to put the last of the NUMA operatives out of their misery.

"Predator team," he called out. "Stop your descent seventy feet above the *Minerve*'s hull. Be ready to unleash a barrage directly into the opening."

The divers did as ordered, forming up high above the hull of the old submarine. As they got into position, Volke cycled through various channels on the aquatic communications system. There were only so many frequencies used for underwater radio. The NUMA divers would be using one of them.

"NUMA personnel hiding in the *Minerve*," he announced. "My name is Volke. I wish to discuss terms of your surrender."

He repeated this greeting on a dozen different channels before finally getting a response.

"You'll be the one begging for a chance to surrender when the U.S. Navy arrives," a woman's voice said.

"We'll be long gone by then," Volke assured her. "As for you, they can either arrive to rescue a couple of forlorn survivors or to pick up your broken and battered bodies. The choice is yours."

"I'd tell you what you can do with that offer," the woman said. *"But my parents taught me to act like a lady, even when I didn't want to."*

Volke almost laughed. "Let me demonstrate what's about to happen here," he said, before switching channels. "Predator leader, fire a single charge, target the hull beside the opening."

Up above the *Minerve*, one of the divers shouldered his speargun, tilted his body to aim and pulled the trigger. The thick elastic cords released instantly, propelling the iron spike with its explosive tip downward. It traveled sixty feet on its momentum and then continued forward assisted by a burst of gas from a small canister in the tail.

The rounded tip of the spear hit the *Minerve*, detonating in an orange flash and sending a reverberation through the submarine's hull and the waters around it.

Had they been asked, the divers would have said seventy feet of clearance was not enough, as the shock wave hit them with the strength of a solid punch. Inside the *Minerve*, the impact was louder and more painful, even with the hull to deflect most of the blast.

Volke allowed the water to clear before he switched back to the NUMA radio channel. "That was a demonstration. Assuming you can still hear me, I renew my offer to let you simply swim away. Otherwise, the next grenade comes through the opening, and it won't be the only one we fire."

"*Go pound sand,*" the woman said.

"Show her we mean business," Volke ordered.

The other three men on the predator team moved into position, a little higher and a little farther away. They raised spearguns and took aim.

"*Look out,*" one of them shouted.

From out of nowhere, several high-speed projectiles the size and shape of American footballs came rushing toward them. Two men were hit. One firing his spear as he tensed, the other taking a head-shot that cracked the glass of his helmet.

The man with the shattered helmet began swimming upward, the others turned to track the danger only to see the small objects coming back their way for another ramming attempt.

"They're just sea drones," Volke said. "Ignore them."

Barely had the words left Volke's mouth when the *Discus* jerked violently forward. The impact was sudden, forceful and unstoppable. He knew in an instant it wasn't caused by a sea drone.

He snapped his head around. Another submersible—one of the NUMA designs—had rammed him and locked onto his stern, using its front claws. It was pushing the *Discus* forward, driving it away from the *Minerve* and down.

Volke's reactions were quick. He pushed the throttle to full and grabbed the control stick. The *Discus* was larger and more powerful. Once he got free of the grasp, he would punish the fools who'd attacked him. With the throttle at the firewall, the engine revved quickly and the intake at the nose began gulping seawater.

Volke pushed the stick to the side, but the attacking submersible refused to let go and it continued to shove Volke deeper and deeper. Only at the last second did Volke realize the danger.

He yanked the controls in the other direction, trying to twist free, but it was too late. The NUMA vessel drove him into the sandy bottom and kept pushing. The water intakes for his propulsion system gulped huge helpings of silt and the turbine cried out with a painful screech before shutting down.

He was trapped, with the nose of his sub buried and the engine drowned in sediment.

"Woods," he called out on the radio. "Where are you? We're under attack. I need help . . . Woods!"

The NUMA submersible gave him one last shove, pushing the front end of the *Discus* even farther down before releasing its grip and speeding away.

"A little late to call Triple A," a voice told him over the radio.

Volke could hardly believe what he was hearing, but as the NUMA submersible raced by, his eyes confirmed it. Kurt Austin was alive and well and manning the controls of the submarine that had just bested him.

A FEW HUNDRED YARDS from where the *Discus* lay stranded on the bottom, a different type of battle was being fought. It was more ballet than brute force.

The divers with the explosives-tipped spears were spinning and turning and kicking furiously. The drones, controlled by Paul from within his suit, were buzzing around them like humming birds, too fast and too small to grab and way too close to hit with an explosives-tipped spear.

One of the divers found himself getting dizzy. Another took a direct hit to the stomach, doubling him over, knocking the wind out of him.

"*Smash them when they come in,*" the team leader said, demonstrating with the butt of his weapon.

This method proved effective at deflecting the drones, but they were hardy little machines and they kept coming back for more.

Finally, the lead diver had had enough. He stopped fighting and dived back toward the *Minerve*. As soon as he had clear shot, he leveled the speargun and fired.

The explosives-tipped spear tracked downward and just off target, hitting several feet behind the conning tower and blasting a cloud of silt through the water. Though he'd missed, the explosion was effective. The drones stopped their maddening attacks and buzzed off in opposite directions.

"Hit the submarine," he ordered. "Hit it hard."

As he loaded a second spear into his gun, his men launched their attack. One spear hit near the stern of the *Minerve* while the second exploded only inches from the opening. The rolling shock waves rattled the divers and had to be absolutely debilitating to the people inside the *Minerve*.

Proof came as a wave of bubbles erupted from the opening, followed by a yellow lifting bag that squeezed through the gap, expanded and then floated toward the surface. Dangling beneath that bag was a three-foot-long metal cylinder, with bands around each end.

"*That's the canister,*" the lead diver shouted. "*Grab it.*"

Breaking into a furious swim, the diver led his comrades toward the slowly rising bag.

Before he could reach it, the NUMA submersible that had forced the *Discus* into the bottom emerged from the opaque blue background.

It raced toward the lifting bag, grasped the lines stretching between it and the canister and continued forward. The bag folded over the top of the submersible while the forward motion caused the canister to be pulled up beneath it.

The lead diver reacted on instinct, firing his speargun and being blown backward as the explosives-tipped shaft hit the NUMA sub and detonated.

69

JOE ZAVALA had spent hours crawling around the hold of the *Monarch* as it flew from Kazakhstan to wherever they were now. He'd explored the maintenance conduits and found they ran the entire length of the plane.

As the aircraft climbed into the cold layers of the upper atmosphere, he'd found a warm spot to hide. As it descended toward the water, he'd resumed his mission, probing for a weakness he could exploit.

The truth was, there were several ways he could damage the plane, hydraulic lines, electrical systems, fuel systems. The problem was redundancy. The *Monarch* had it. All those systems had backups. And backups to the backups.

Ruining any one of them would be no more than a minor inconvenience. But there was one system on Tessa's plane that no other aircraft possessed. And while it wasn't critical for flying, it was absolutely necessary for getting off the ground—or, more accurately, the water.

Working his way along the inspection conduit, Joe had come across the high-pressure lines that fed air from the engines into the cavitation system. Without the cushion of air to separate it from the water, the giant aircraft could never overcome the drag, suction and surface tension of the sea.

Tracking the main high-pressure line to a splitter, Joe began to do his worst, disconnecting fittings, ripping trunk lines from the feeder valves, smashing pressure release valves so that they would vent any air that came through them.

By the time he was done, Joe had crawled half the length of the plane and back. He was dirty, grimy, bleeding from several cuts and grinning from ear to ear. A true gremlin.

Now all he needed to do was find a way off the plane before it attempted to fly again.

TESSA STOOD AT the aft end of the *Monarch*, watching for any signs of success. One after another, her men surfaced, bleeding, unconscious or in obvious pain. This was not the type of progress she'd hoped for.

She held the radio up to her mouth. "Volke," she called. "What's going on down there?"

The response was almost inaudible, but it made perfect sense. *"Austin,"* Volke said. *"He's alive."*

"We blew his ship up," she said. "It has to be someone else."

"It's him," Volke said. *"He must have been in the water when we attacked. He's operating a submersible. He's taken the counter-agent."*

Tessa grew angry at herself for underestimating Austin yet again. *What lengths did she have to go to to rid herself of this man?*

She held the transmit switch down once again. "Woods, where are you? Volke needs help. NUMA has the counteragent."

"*Forget Volke*," Woods replied. "*I'm going after the canister. Stand by.*"

AS THE CONVERSATION between Tessa, Volke and Woods played out, Kurt found himself trying to clear his head and wondering exactly where he was.

The truth was disturbing. He was upside down in a submersible that was filling with water and sinking. Rudi was beside him.

"One of these days, I'm going to wake up to a beautiful blonde, brunette or redhead," he mused.

"Don't I count?" Rudi asked.

"Not by a mile."

Kurt could see from the damage that there was no hope in restarting the submersible. "Time for us to exit the vehicle."

The two of them had prepared for this and were already wearing the power-assisted wetsuits. They pulled dive helmets on and attached small oxygen bottles.

Rudi offered the thumbs-up, Kurt pulled the release handle. It opened a series of valves, allowing the cockpit to fill rapidly with water and also disconnecting the canopy.

When the pressure equalized, Kurt gave the glass a powerful shove. It tilted upward and floated away.

Rudi went out first, pulling himself forward and swimming free. Kurt followed, careful to avoid the yellow bag and the lines connecting it to the canister. He pulled out a diving knife and went to cut it free.

"*Look out!*" Rudi shouted.

Kurt glanced up. At first, all he saw was the yellow plastic wafting in the current. But as it swept to the side, a blunt gray shape came into view. From this angle, it resembled the square snout of a sperm whale, but made of metal.

Kurt dived out of the way and the bulky vehicle swept in above him. It grabbed the canister with a robotic arm and continued on its way without ever slowing down.

70

AS PLANNED, Kurt swam after the submersible. But even with the power assist from the suit, he was losing the race. The ungainly sub was still faster than the fastest swimmer. It pulled away on a direct line to the *Monarch*.

Kurt realized he could never catch it. He turned and swam the other way, heading for one of the powerboats still bobbing on the swells above the *Minerve*.

He reached it, found it empty and climbed in. By the time he started the engine, the submersible had reached the *Monarch*. He saw the crewmen gather around, pull the canister free and discard the submersible as if it was nothing.

They didn't bother trying to haul the sub aboard. They hadn't sent any help for the injured divers and they'd abandoned Volke at the bottom of the sea. They were about to hightail it out of there.

Kurt gunned the engine and turned the wheel. His last chance to stop the *Monarch* and grab the canister was fading fast.

. . .

TESSA WATCHED as Woods brought the canister on board.

"Is that it?"

"Looks like the one we found on the *Dakar*," Woods said.

Tessa used a crowbar to knock the accumulated salts and rust from the latches. "Open it," she ordered.

Woods dropped down and pried the canister open, revealing two smaller, hermetically sealed containers. They were untouched by corrosion. "The seals are good," he announced. "The cultures should be intact."

"Great work," Tessa said. She immediately contacted the pilots. "Power up. Get us into takeoff position."

Woods looked out the back. "What about the rest of the men?"

"We don't have time to wait," she said. "Austin may have called for help. We don't want to be here if any arrives."

Woods hesitated for a second and then nodded. "So long, Volke. Looks like you're the one being left behind."

Tessa thought about rescuing Volke, but even that effort would have been too time-consuming. "Secure the canister," she ordered. "I'm going to the cockpit."

She rushed forward and up the ladder, never looking down. Had she even glanced below, she would have seen a figure emerging from the hatch that led to the maintenance tunnel beneath the bottom deck. She might even have recognized him as one of her former captives.

JOE HAD ALREADY OPENED the hatch when he heard Tessa running his way. Pulling it down, he waited for her to pass by and go up the ladder. He could feel the plane moving and picking up speed and had no desire to be on it when it tried to get airborne again.

Glancing along the bottom deck, he was surprised to see it completely empty. No cars, no boats, no submersibles, just a vast, cavernous space and the bearded man named Woods working to secure a metal cylinder.

Joe stepped onto the deck, began moving aft and then rushed at Woods.

Woods looked up from the cylinder at the last moment just as Joe swung his leg. The blow caught Woods on the side of the face and sent him tumbling. Before the big man could get to his feet, Joe dropped down on him and threw a knockout punch. "That's for Priya."

The punch left Woods unconscious and sprawled on the deck. Now he needed to get off the plane. Joe rushed to the back of the aircraft, rolling the container along with him.

It banged against the upraised tail ramp and stopped. Joe didn't bother with the regular controls. He went right for the emergency release, pulled it down and watched the ramp fall.

This time, it hit with the splash he'd been expecting before. It locked into place, creating an instant wake and pulling water back up onto itself in two swirling eddies.

KURT HAD THE SPEEDBOAT running flat out, but with the *Monarch*'s engines spooling up to full thrust, he couldn't close in. He ducked behind the tail, to avoid the jet blast and bring the boat up onto the *Monarch*'s wake.

With the smooth wake of the aircraft to travel on and the suction effect caused by the *Monarch*'s forward progress, Kurt picked up more speed, drafting the big plane and nearing the tail.

Now he needed some way to stop the plane. Looking around, he spotted one of the grenade-tipped spearguns. He reached down, grabbed it and brought it up to his shoulder.

He was about to fire when the tail ramp dropped and a long-lost friend appeared.

Dropping the speargun, Kurt nursed every last ounce of speed from the boat, closed in on the ramp and bumped up onto it.

Joe shouted to him, "And they say there's never a cab when you need one."

"Get in," Kurt shouted back. "This ride's on me."

Joe heaved the banded cylinder in the boat. "Have a feeling people might be looking for this."

"Only for the last fifty years."

Joe gave the boat a shove and jumped in the moment it began to move. As soon as they reached the water, Kurt turned away from the plane.

"It's too bad she's going to get away," Kurt said. "But we have what we need."

"I don't think she's going very far," Joe said.

SITTING IN THE COCKPIT, Tessa shouted at the pilots, who were slowing the plane after a warning light alerted them to the tail ramp's position.

"Override the emergency release," she said. "Raise the aft door and get us out of here."

The copilot did as ordered, while the captain put the thrust levers back to full. The plane accelerated, but only to a point. "Fifty knots," the pilot said. "Activate cavitation."

The correct switches were thrown, but the high-pressure air bleeding off the engines never reached the lower part of the hull.

"We have multiple failures on the high-pressure air system," the copilot said. "Low-pressure lines failing also."

As Tessa struggled to believe what was happening, a transmission came over the radio. In a reversal of the incident in Bermuda, Austin was talking to her on a captured transmitter.

"*It's over, Tessa,*" Kurt said. "*We have military aircraft inbound and you'll never get off the water.*"

The captain confirmed the last statement. "We can't take off without the cavitation system. The drag is too high."

"*You might as well stand down,*" Austin said.

His voice infuriated her. "Full power," she demanded. "Turn into the swells. As we begin to pitch, we'll break free of the water."

"But Tessa—"

"Do as I say!"

The pilots followed her commands and the *Monarch* turned slightly and began to accelerate once again.

As it picked up speed, the plane rose and fell. It began to bounce across the swells, skipping and grasping at the air. Each new wave bumped them higher, each return to the sea brought a more painful impact than the last.

"The vibration is too much," the captain said. "The airframe is going to buckle."

"I built this plane," Tessa shouted. "I know what it's capable of."

The pilot shook his head and went to retard the throttles, but Tessa reached forward and leaned on them, keeping the power at full.

The aircraft leapt again. Seventy knots . . . Eighty . . . With each jump, the plane picked up more speed and remained airborne a little longer.

One more bounce, she thought. One more leap . . .

The next impact was sudden and jarring, with the nose crashing through the top of the wave and the wing pylon bending.

The pylon twisted and tore free. The plane tilted to the right, the wingtip hit the sea and the entire structure buckled as it was torn away. The *Monarch* slewed to the side traveling at a hundred knots and billowing fuel from its ruptured tanks. The heat of the engines ignited the cloud of vapor, causing a chain reaction of explosions that blew the plane apart.

KURT AND JOE watched the failed takeoff from well behind the aircraft. Reaching the crash zone, they found only wreckage, floating debris and a swath of burning kerosene that stretched for several hundred feet.

They circled the inferno several times, but upon finding no survivors, they returned to the waters above the *Minerve* to pick up their own people.

Rudi came aboard first, with Gamay next and—once he'd exited the ADS suit—Paul.

The injured divers on the surface were kept at arm's length, while the two divers trapped in the submarine below were released and allowed to surface. They were also forced to remain in the water until help arrived in the form of three Marine helicopters dispatched from Sicily.

With two dozen Marines deployed in several inflatable boats and the helicopters circling, the situation was well in hand. Kurt and a pair of Marine divers swam down and released Volke from his half-buried submersible and brought him to the surface. He and the other survivors from Tessa's crew were placed into custody and taken to a military base on Sicily.

The NUMA crew flew to Malta, where a Gulfstream aircraft waited to take Rudi, the Trouts and the bacterial cultures of the counteragent back to the United States.

Kurt and Joe had one more task to accomplish before they could rest. They took a different aircraft and flew eastward, landing at the abandoned air base in Kazakhstan and searching for Priya.

Joe found the section of the base where the *Monarch* had been parked and from there made his way to the helicopter that he and Priya had been hiding in. He stepped inside.

The Mercedes was there, still parked in the back, but there was no sign of Priya. He walked through to the cockpit, where Priya was sleeping in one of the pilots' chairs.

Joe touched her face and Priya woke up. She was disoriented and looked at him as if she might be dreaming. "Joe?"

Her voice was hoarse, her lips cracked and her face dirty, but at least she was alive.

"Are you really here?" she asked.

"I am," Joe said. He leaned down, scooped her up and carried her out through the back of the helicopter. "And I've come to take you home."

71

KURT AUSTIN arrived at the Four Seasons in Georgetown to have dinner with Rudi, Joe and St. Julien Perlmutter. He found them standing in the softly lit cocktail lounge, gazing at a pair of TVs behind the bar.

"Did I miss something?" Kurt asked, walking up behind them.

Rudi explained. "The President just made the announcement about the countermeasure. It's been successfully tested and we're making it available to every country and corporation that wants it. It'll take a while before oil production gets back to where it was, but the crisis is over. Oil is expected to drop thirty to forty percent in the morning, with the price at the pump coming down sharply in the next few days."

"Someone might have told me," Kurt said. "I just filled up on the way over here. Two hundred bucks for a tank of gas. Which means someone here will have to buy me dinner."

Joe shook his head. "Sorry, amigo, I have someone far prettier and more interesting to spend my money on tonight."

As Joe spoke, Priya came around the corner—walking. She wore a beautiful black cocktail dress, a sparkling necklace and was supporting herself partially on a pair of crutches that were strapped to her arms. She also wore a pair of thick, sturdy boots.

"Surprised?" she said.

"Completely," Kurt said.

"Joe and I spent the last three weeks building a version of the dive suit that uses carbon fiber braces and allows me to walk . . . with a little bit of help. The crutches are necessary right now. And these boots, which go halfway up my thigh, are not exactly fashionable, but it's a start. I'm applying for a grant to build on what he and I have done. It may be possible to help thousands of people walk again. The only downside is, I'd have to go back to MIT and leave NUMA if I get it."

"You'll get it," Kurt said. "And we'll miss you. But Boston isn't that far away."

"In the meantime," Joe said, "we're going to celebrate. Starting with a walk around town."

Kurt leaned in, gave Priya a kiss on the cheek and then straightened Joe's tie. "Don't worry," he said. "I won't tell Misty you've strayed."

Joe gave him a threatening look but said nothing and carried Priya's purse as the two went out the door.

Kurt turned to Rudi and St. Julien. "Looks like it's just the bachelors tonight."

"Sorry, my boy," St. Julien said. "I have a flight to catch. Heading back to Paris to meet with that friend of mine I told you about. He wants to bask in the glory of how *his rumor* helped avert this crisis. I'll be only too happy to indulge him if he follows through on his promised invitation to Dulcinéa."

"Dulcinéa?"

"The most exclusive restaurant in all of Paris," St. Julien explained. "You almost have to be royalty to get a table. I'd regale you with details of the menu, but"—he tapped his watch—"have to go. When I get back, there's a bottle of cognac for us to finish."

As St. Julien made his way to the door, Kurt turned to Rudi. *"Et tu, Rudi?"*

"Sorry, Kurt. I have to meet with the President as soon as he's finished accepting kudos for his speech. He wants to discuss additional missions for NUMA and a large increase in our budget. In cases like this, it's best to strike while the iron's hot—and before you and Joe blow anything else up. Do you have any idea how much the *Gryphon* cost?"

"Do I want to know?"

"Not really." Rudi smiled.

"This is a first," Kurt said. "Even St. Julien has a date."

Rudi laughed. "Being a hero is a thankless job sometimes." He patted Kurt on the shoulder. "Rain check. How about next week?"

"Anytime," Kurt said.

Rudi left, the President finished his speech and Kurt found himself almost completely alone. Because of the continuing gas shortage and the President's speech, few people were out and about.

He took a seat and smiled as the bartender came over. She had a pretty face, bright blue eyes and long blond hair, which was currently tied back for work.

"You seem to have lost all your friends," she said, wiping down the bar and placing a coaster in front of him.

"They have better things to do," he said.

She paused, studying him. "You look familiar," she said. "Do I know you from somewhere?"

To Kurt's chagrin, the President had shown a photo of him and Rudi when referring to the "unnamed heroes" who'd brought about the end to the fabricated crisis. Kurt had looked like five days of bad road in the image, but his rugged features were not easy to hide.

"Would you believe I'm the guy who ended the oil crisis?"

The corners of her mouth turned upward in a warm smile. "Not for a second," she said. "But my shift ends in twenty minutes. If you're still around, I wouldn't mind finding out what you really do."

Kurt laughed. "In that case, I'll take a Don Julio Silver on the rocks with salt on the rim and spend the next twenty minutes trying to come up with something interesting to tell you."

She delivered the drink with a mischievous grin and then made her way to the far end of the bar. Kurt watched as she checked her makeup, let her hair down and shook it out.

He took a sip of the tequila. *Perhaps being a hero had a few advantages after all.*